A SIXPENNY CHRISTMAS

As the worst storm of the century sweeps through the mountains of Snowdonia and across the Mersey, two women, Molly and Ellen, give birth to girls in a Liverpool Maternity Hospital. Molly and Rhys Roberts farm sheep in Snowdonia and Ellen is married to a docker, Sam O'Mara, but despite their different backgrounds the two young women become firm friends, though Molly has a secret she can share with no one.

A SIXPENNY CHRISTMAS

A SIXPENNY CHRISTMAS

by

Katie Flynn

Magna Large Print Books
Long Preston, North Yorkshire,
BD23 4ND, England.

British Library Cataloguing in Publication Data.

Flynn, Katie
A sixpenny Christmas.

A catalogue record of this book is available from the British Library

ISBN 978-0-7505-4011-7

First published in Great Britain by Arrow Books in 2012

Published in Large Print 2014 by arrangement with Random House Group Ltd.

Magna Large Print is an imprint of Library Magna Books Ltd.

Printed and bound in Great Britain by
T.J. (International) Ltd., Cornwall, PL28 8RW

For Jean and Sam Flavell, good friends
whose holiday home enjoys a
wonderful view of Snowdonia.

Acknowledgements

I am most grateful to Wyn Williams of Penrhyn Farm on Anglesey for checking, and in some cases unscrambling, information about sheep farming both in mountain and lowland country. I've tried very hard to follow his advice and get it right but when I have failed to do so, it is my fault and not Wyn's.

For anyone who is interested in the joys and sorrows of life in the mountains of Snowdonia, Thomas Firbank's brilliant book, *I Bought a Mountain*, is a must and I am most grateful for the information I found in it.

Dear Reader,

How does one choose a title? I thought it might interest you to know how I arrived at *A Sixpenny Christmas*.

Many years ago I was the youngest typist in a large typing pool attached to a drawing office in the Highways Department. I loved the work and my colleagues, but became rather anxious as Christmas approached since I was paid a salary so tiny that it barely covered my bus fare, lunches and other small expenses; how was I to buy presents not only for my family but also for my many friends in the department?

Then I was told about the sixpenny Christmas tub, and in later years, as I went from job to job, I realised that most of the big companies for whom I worked had one thing in common (apart from me that is!); they all ran a Christmas tub, which enabled everyone to receive a present without breaking the bank.

The system was simple; all us girls bought one present which, in the old days, was not supposed to exceed sixpence, though by the time I started work the sum had risen to half a crown. These were then wrapped and popped into the Christmas tub, and on Christmas Eve each girl rummaged around in the sixpenny tub, as we still called it in the Highways Department, and fished out a gift.

Of course there were snags. Some gifts appeared year after year, only in different wrapping paper, but mostly we girls stuck to the rules. Scented soap, small manicure sets, a tiny bottle of nail polish, even a new paperback book were all put in the Christmas tub, so when I was searching for a title for this book, and realised that Molly, before her marriage, had worked in a big typing pool, I remembered the sixpenny Christmas, because such a title tells the reader a lot in three words. In those days salaries for young girls were barely above subsistence level; for most of us it was a constant battle to keep our heads above water. A dinner in the canteen cost one and six; we were paid monthly so we had one dinner at the end of each month, otherwise it was four pennorth of chips, or one of the huge Jaffa oranges, which a market trader would sell you for sixpence. So the Christmas presents which we fished out of the tub were needed as well as eagerly anticipated.

Even when Molly and Rhys are living on their farm in the heart of Snowdonia, Christmas presents, though gratefully received, tended to be small and inexpensive. The bicycle for which Molly's son longs was just an impossible dream.

So that's how I got the title for this book!

All best wishes.

Katie Flynn

Chapter One

Rhys Roberts, lying in his lonely bed, heard the storm approaching, but thought little of it; storms in Snowdonia at this time of year were not uncommon, especially amidst the high peaks. They had enjoyed a mild but windy autumn at Cefn Farm, a cold but snow-free November, and now, with December well advanced and Christmas only a matter of days away, the muttering of distant thunder, and the snow – or hail – which he could hear tapping against the window pane, should have been expected.

Looking at the sky as he made his way up the stairs, Rhys had decided to put extra blankets on the bed, and now he reminded himself how much warmer he would have been had his dear Molly been beside him. She had been away for only three days but already the time seemed endless. He knew that as soon as the hospital had something to report they would notify him by telephoning the village post office; so far he had visited the post office three times every day, but without success. The maternity hospital was always busy but the staff were kind and realised that he was worried, and with good reason. Molly had had a bad time with their first child, little Chris, who lay in his bed in the slip of a room close by, slumbering peacefully, Rhys hoped. When Molly had felt her first pains she had been at Cefn Farm, assuring Rhys that he was not to worry, that she and the nurse would soon have the child born. However, on that first occasion she had been in labour for three days and nights, for Chris's had been what they called a cross-birth, and when it was discovered that she was expecting again Dr Llewellyn had advised that she should go to a proper maternity unit, with staff who could call on all the most modern equipment should Molly need help with the birthing of her second child.

Rhys put out a strong brown hand and felt under Molly's pillow for the little wisp of nylon which had been her trousseau nightie. The touch of it comforted him, made him remember their first meeting. He had been a sergeant in the RAF, she a Waaf, secretary to a wing commander on a bomber station not far from Lincoln. They had met at a dance, fallen in love at first sight, and married a month later. Their wedding had been typical of the times; austerity and all that, Rhys thought now, cuddling the nightie. No wonderful white dress, no piles of presents, no honeymoon in Paris, or anywhere else; just two days in a bed and breakfast in the city and then back to work. They had managed to rent two rooms above a cycle shop near the Saracen's Head, the public house most popular with the air crew stationed nearby, where they were idyllically happy until the war ended.

When Rhys and Molly were demobbed, things had moved fast. Rhys's parents had both died a few years previously, leaving everything they possessed to their only son, and Molly had inherited her grandparents' small flat and all their worldly goods, which was not saying a lot. But when they combined their assets they found they had sufficient capital to take out a mortgage on a hill farm, which was the desire of Rhys's heart, and after very little searching they had chanced upon Cefn Farm. It was not large, but it was not expensive, either, and the land was in good heart, the sheep fat with the good mountain grass, and the owners, both in their eighties, eager to give the young couple all the help and advice possible.

It was summer when they took possession and very soon they realised that a baby was on the way, so that their cup of happiness seemed full to overflowing. Rhys once remarked that Molly never stopped smiling, and this, they both knew, was because they were so happy. Hard work, small returns and the fear that they might make mistakes were all offset by the clean mountain air, the sweet silence after years of noise, and their very real affection for their livestock, their horses and their prick-eared, tongue-lolling Border collies, without whom they would, Rhys knew, have made many bad mistakes.

But it had been a hard labour, and this time Rhys had agreed with the doctor that his wife would be better in a proper maternity hospital, so a couple of days before the expected birth Molly had gone off to Liverpool, promising Rhys that she would ring the post office as soon as she had news to impart. She had taken with her a couple of sensible cotton nightgowns, some of Chris's old baby clothes and a couple of farming magazines, and when Rhys had found her flimsy honeymoon nightie when tidying their room he had taken it to bed with him, enjoying the faint flowery smell of the talcum and soap she used, finding it a comfort.

The storm was getting closer, and a good deal louder. Rhys half sat up, wondering whether he should go to Chris, tell him that the thunder posed no threat. But before he had done more than swing his legs out of bed there was a crack of thunder so intense that it sounded like a bomb exploding, and his little son appeared in the doorway, crying for his mummy.

Immediately, Rhys held out his arms and the little boy struggled into them, his own small arms curling round his father's neck, his curly head butting Rhys beneath the chin. 'I'm frighted; I shake,' he muttered. 'Where's Mummy? I want Mummy!'

You aren't the only one, Rhys thought, cuddling his son's small body and dropping a kiss on the child's damp curls. 'Don't you remember, old lad? Mummy's gone to Liverpool to bring you home a little brother ... or sister,' he said, aware that Molly wanted a daughter though he would have preferred another son. Farmers need sons as fish need water and Rhys was no exception. However, Chris was only a baby still, probably didn't know what a sister was, for the farm was remote and though Molly took him into the village a couple of times a month he was too young to play with other children or indeed to pay them any attention. He likes animals better than people, same as I did when I was a kid, Rhys told himself. The way he behaves when Molly is busy, staggering round after the sheepdogs as though he were a small pup himself, is enough to make a cat laugh. He reminds me of Mowgli, Rhys thought, remembering the boy who was brought up by wolves in Kipling's Jungle Book.

Another tremendous crash of thunder brought with it a gust of wind so strong that the curtains were dashed to one side. As the vivid lightning flashes lit up the room Rhys clutched the baby involuntarily, expecting that Chris would begin to cry once more, but this time Chris seemed rather more interested than afraid. He wriggled out of his father's arms and ran over to the window. 'Where doggies?' he asked anxiously. 'What made the big bang? Train? Car? Tractor?'

Rhys hurried across to draw back the curtains so that he could see what was happening in the yard outside, and saw with real dismay that the corrugated iron roof on the pigsty was flapping up and down in a manner that boded ill for the occupants. Rhys hesitated. He dared not leave the baby whilst he ran into the yard and tried to secure the roof, but he could not take the child out with him, for the storm, far from easing, seemed to get wilder with every moment and the sleet and the cold were intense. He was fond of the pigs but they would simply have to take their chance, along with the rest of the stock, most of which was out on the hillside. He and Chris had better simply sit in the kitchen and wait for the storm to pass over.

He scooped up his son and went down to the kitchen, sat in one of the well-cushioned and comfortable basket chairs and watched quite enviously as Chris's thumb slid into his mouth and his eyelids drooped. Wish I could sleep, he thought, but the noise of the storm alone would have kept him awake even had he not been worrying over Molly.

The roof of the pigsty, which had been crashing at regular intervals, was suddenly silent. Rhys heard what he thought was a frightened grunt, but then the thunder roared again and through the closed window he could see the lightning, bright as day as it stabbed to earth. In the lull which followed the last crash, Rhys heard Feather, the mother of his two other sheepdogs, barking outside. He got carefully to his feet, still holding Chris in the crook of his arm, and opened the back door. The dogs tumbled in, wide-eyed, ears a-prick, seeming to say that it was about time someone remembered them. They crowded round Rhys as though anxious for an explanation, but he could only ruffle their heads and soothe them with promises that it would soon be over and everyone would be able to sleep.

But the storm raged on and Rhys began to fear for the trees which protected the cottage and for the hay in its ancient Dutch barn. Then there were the horses in the stable, for though a good deal of his work on the farm involved the ancient tractor, on the steep hillsides horses were essential. They had two, Guinness and Porter, as well as Cherry the pony, and all three were as liable as any other of their kind to take fright at loud unexpected noises or movements. Rhys thanked his stars that he had decided to bring them in tonight, for the stable building was old and solid, built of stone and roofed with shingles.

Thinking of the work he would have to do to repair the storm damage brought Rhys's mind full circle, back to Molly, who would normally have helped him but now was fighting her own battle – one in which he could no more help her than she could help him in his.

Rhys sighed and looked longingly at the kettle. The fire in the range had been out for days and rather than relighting it he had been heating water, Chris's food and anything else which needed cooking on their small Primus stove. Molly, good little wife that she was, had cooked soups, pies and loaves of bread before she had left for the city; Rhys just hoped these would last until she came home again, for his own abilities as a cook were small: he could boil an egg and heat some milk and that was about it. Now he was old enough Molly fed Chris on what they ate themselves. When he was a baby she had pressed his food through a fine wire sieve; Rhys had once eaten a crafty teaspoonful of the mixture and had nearly thrown up. How could good food, when you ate it from your plate, become disgusting pap when pressed through a wire sieve? But Chris had appeared to notice nothing amiss. He was a bright little boy who had walked before he was a year old and now, at two and a half, chattered away to anyone who would listen. Rhys looked fondly down on his sleeping son and wondered whether he should try to put him back in his own small bed, but the warm little body was a comfort and anyway should the child wake again he might feel himself abandoned and begin to wail once more.

Rhys got stealthily to his feet, but did not return to the bedroom. He would lie down on the comfy old-fashioned sofa in the parlour and try to snatch an hour or so of sleep before it was time to get up and begin his daily tasks. Most parlours were rarely used but Molly had furnished theirs with care, saying that she wanted comfort more than a lot of fancy furniture. She liked them to use the parlour on weekday evenings as well as Sundays, and when she was pregnant she had her midday rest on the comfortable sofa. Settling himself with the sleeping child still in his arms, Rhys jumped and swore softly beneath his breath when lightning lit up the room again and a gust of wind blew into the room, presumably from under the kitchen door, wrenching the parlour curtains apart. But by now Rhys was truly sleepy and settled down with his head on one of the beautiful cushions which Molly had made and stuffed with their own goose feathers.

Lying curled round the baby, he remembered suddenly how Molly hated storms, reminding her as they did of the May blitz which had destroyed half her home town of Liverpool. He told himself that the storm was a local one, caused by the great mountains of Snowdonia, and would not affect his wife in her comfortable bed at the maternity hospital. Smiling, he thought it fortunate that she was not here to be cast into misery and fear by the cracks of thunder and the lightning which either lit up the whole sky or stabbed to earth, causing damage to both buildings and animals. He must remember to tell her about the dreadful storm she had missed, the fearful wind which was even now blowing snow under the kitchen door, and Chris's bravery in the face of all the noise and confusion.

He lay quietly for a little while, telling himself that he should get up off the sofa and pull the curtains closed again, but sleep was too urgent now and soon the storm raged unheard as Rhys and his little son slumbered.

Molly lay on the delivery couch, feeling the beautiful peace that comes after the struggle to give birth. The nurse who had held her hand and encouraged her throughout the whole business came over to her, a green-wrapped bundle in the crook of her arm. 'There you are, Mrs Roberts, your beautiful little girl; want to hold her?'

'Oh, yes please,' Molly said eagerly, holding out her arms, but though the nurse smiled she shook her head.

'She's a fine healthy girl, my dear; she weighed in at eight pounds four ounces, so just you lie back and I'll put her against your shoulder...'

Molly was preparing to curl an arm round the baby when there was a tremendous crash, which made both the new mother and the nurse jump convulsively and caused the baby to give an indignant hiccup. The nurse laughed and began to speak but she had scarcely got more than a couple of words out when the thunder roared again and the night, which had seemed calm, was suddenly calm no longer. Outside, the wind howled and shrieked, the thunder rumbled and cracked and lightning lit up the long windows of the delivery room. Molly was about to say that she would take the baby now when, abruptly, the room was plunged into inky blackness. Molly and the nurse shrieked again and through the long window Molly saw only Stygian blackness: the lightning had caused a massive power cut.

Someone came hurrying across the delivery

room, a dark figure which could have been a man or a woman, until more lightning shivered across the sky – sheet lightning this time – and lit the scene with an unearthly violet glow long enough for Molly to see it was a woman; a sister. The newcomer tapped the nurse on the shoulder. 'Mrs Roberts and Baby had best get back to the ward now. A porter is outside with a wheelchair for the mother, who is to go to room eight. You take the baby straight to nursery eight and make sure she's labelled.' She patted Molly's shoulder and probably smiled, though Molly could not see her face. 'The nursery is adjacent to your ward, and for the first couple of days the baby will be brought to you at feeding times.' She addressed the nurse once more. 'See if you can rustle up a cup of ... oh my God!' The nurse gave a nervous laugh but Molly, who was terrified of lightning, found nothing amusing in Sister's squeak of fright. She could not remember a worse storm, and as another nurse helped her off the delivery couch and into the waiting wheelchair she had hard work to suppress her own fear. She had only caught one glimpse of her baby's small crumpled face, still red with the strain of birth and wet from its recent cleansing, but she thought that the infant was bound to be pretty, for was she not Chris's sister? He had been a delightful baby, despite her protracted labour, and this little one had popped into the world after only half a dozen hours. It had taken baby Chris a whole week to recover from his experience; this child should be pink and white and beautiful in no time.

Whatever the lightning had done to the electricity supply, it seemed it could not easily be undone. The porter produced a torch, and as he pushed her wheelchair along the corridors he told her that she was fortunate indeed to have given birth before what he guessed was half the city had lost all their electric power. 'It'll be chaos tomorrer; perishin' chaos,' he said with a sort of ghoulish cheerfulness. 'As bad as the bleedin' blitz in '41, blinkin' near. Someone's in the operating theatre right now havin' what they calls a caesar-een and all the instruments and stuff is down. The lifts is out too, but you're one of the lucky ones, 'cos rooms seven and eight are on this floor so I shan't have to try and carry you up the stairs in me strong and manly arms.'

'Oh, good,' Molly said faintly. If it isn't just my luck to get a porter who fancies himself as a comedian, she thought. I know for a fact that this is a single-storey hospital and the upstairs is just administrative offices. But it would not do to say so, of course; the man was only trying to amuse her, and to take her mind off the uncanny darkness through which he was wheeling her and the occasional stabs of brilliant lightning, to say nothing of the thunder which, though it occasionally seemed more distant, only redoubled its force on its return.

The porter swung her through a pair of doors and into a ward, shining his torch ahead of him, and in its light Molly saw another mum, probably just as tired – and as pleased – as she was herself. Then the wheelchair stopped and the porter shouted to the nurse to come over and give a hand, and very soon Molly found herself between the sheets. She realised as she turned her head into the pillow how very tired she was, and would have slept instantly had a voice not addressed her from the adjacent bed.

'Hey, missus! Did you have a gal or a boy?' The woman giggled. 'Wharra Christmas present, eh? Bet your ole feller's over the perishin' moon!'

Molly smiled at all she could see of the other woman, which was the pale disc of her face. 'You're right there! A sixpenny Christmas we told each other this one 'ud be, 'cos money's scarce. But my little girl is worth a lot more than that to me!'

Her companion looked puzzled. 'A sixpenny Christmas? I ain't never heard of that before,' she remarked. 'What does it mean, eh?'

Molly laughed. 'It's plain you never served in the forces,' she said. 'I was in the WAAF and there were more than a dozen girls in my hut. If we'd had to exchange gifts with all our friends we'd have been broke for a twelvemonth. Instead, each girl bought something worth no more than sixpence, wrapped it, and put it in a big box, and on Christmas morning everyone took a parcel from the box. They were only little things, but somehow just getting a present started the day off well, even if it was only sixpennyworth of chewing gum, or a length of hair ribbon. See?'

The other woman nodded vigorously. 'Wharra grand idea. Well, it looks like you won't be the only one havin' a sixpenny Christmas this year. But what does that matter? We've both got daughters. I allus wanted a daughter; eh, come to that I allus wanted a baby so I s'pose it didn't much matter if it were a boy or a girl. I'm gonna call mine suffin' real fancy – what's you gonna call yours? Who's you, by the way? I'm Ellen O'Mara.'

'I'm Molly Roberts,' Molly said wearily. Trust me to get landed with someone who wants to talk when I'm so dreadfully tired, she thought. But she could hear the excitement in the other woman's voice and answered patiently. 'I'll – I'll think about a name tomorrow.' And with that, despite the dark, and the noise of the storm, she fell at last into a deep sleep.

Ellen had been prepared for a long and arduous labour, for it is no small thing to have your first child when you are past the age of forty. Her mother had warned her that she would likely have a hard time, and so had various aunts and cousins, but Ellen had just smiled happily and told them that to have a baby of her own would be worth a bit of pain.

And then what had happened? She had been wheeled into one of the delivery rooms at just about the moment when the storm had come roaring down from the mountains of Wales, charged across the Mersey, and descended upon Liverpool. Ellen was not afraid of much, but she had never come to terms with thunderstorms. Her grandmother had once scared the life out of her with a story about her own father, who had been a farm labourer and had been struck by lightning as he ran for shelter from the heavy rain. 'It did suffin' to his poor brain,' her grandmother had said impressively. 'He were never the same again, weren't my poor old dad.'

So naturally enough as soon as the thunder began to rumble Ellen's thoughts, which had been upon the task in hand – delivery of her first child – wandered out of the hospital and into the outside world. She saw in her mind's eye lightning zigzagging across the river and down onto the docks where her husband worked, though obviously he wouldn't be there at this time of night. He ought to be longing for news, striding up and down the waiting room like any other expectant father, but knowing him as she did Ellen suspected that he would be in a pub somewhere, never giving her a thought.

Sam was not a good husband. He was a docker and quicker with a punch than a kiss; in fact Ellen could not remember him showing her a single mark of affection in all their married life. Of course it was her own fault in a way; she should have left him years ago, when he first took a liking to using his fists on her, but he earned a good wage and handed over the housekeeping each week, and though he would occasionally take her small earnings to fund his insatiable thirst she could not accuse him of meanness. The fact was, Ellen was lazy, and though she knew Sam had no affection for her she also knew that if she left him he would pay her back for her desertion. Her mother thought her a fool to put up with such treatment, but Ellen and Sam had stayed together – so far.

And now, as the thunder rolled overhead, and lightning lit up the delivery room as brightly as though it were day, Ellen obeyed the nurse's instructions to 'Bear down!' by giving a tremendous push, and to her delighted astonishment the next words she heard were: 'Well done, Mrs O'Mara; you've got a dear little baby girl. My goodness, and you've barely been in here ten minutes! When I've settled you back on the ward I'll go straight to the waiting room and tell your husband that he may visit you for five minutes.'

Ellen reared up on one elbow to gaze at the tiny crumpled red face and dark wet hair of her very own baby. She could feel an enormous smile spreading across her face, but when she spoke her tone was rueful.

'I don't think he'll be in the waiting room, chuck; he's workin', and since he don't know I were took to the delivery room he won't be expectin' the news yet for a while,' she said. 'Oh, nurse, ain't she just perfect?'

The nurse agreed, then called a porter to wheel Ellen back to the ward and carried the baby off to the nursery.

Ellen was back on the ward, far too excited to sleep as the nurse had advised, when the lights went out. But she, who had been terrified of thunderstorms, was too happy to worry about this one. She just wished that someone else on the ward was awake, so that she could tell them all about her beautiful baby girl. But she knew there had been another mother in the delivery suite; perhaps she would be along presently, having had her baby, and they could compare notes. Ellen lay back on her pillows and snoozed.

Sam emerged from the dockside pub he favoured in a murderous rage and almost indifferent to the storm, although he pulled his coat around him against the driving rain. He had been made a fool of, and if there was one thing he hated it was being made to look a fool. And of all people the one who had turned against him had been Billy Bates, a feller he had thought of as a friend. Sam considered going on to another of the many pubs down by the docks, but his money was running low and his belly felt full to bursting. Besides, after a bout of drinking the previous week he'd been pretty ill and seen strange things, and he had no desire to repeat the experience. Billy Bates had warned him that it might well be the start of something called the DTs and he didn't want none of that. On the other hand he wanted to smash Billy until the grin disappeared from his one-time friend's face. He had been so happy until Billy had opened his big mouth. He had been boasting that he'd got a kid of his own now, someone to look after him in his old age, someone to listen to his tall stories. He had even bought a round of drinks, which had cost a good deal, but he knew that the men would buy him drinks in return; it was the done thing, after all, when the man became a father, to treat him to a glass of whisky or rum. He was preening himself, enjoying the unusual popularity – for his temper and his willingness to use his fists had made most other men wary of him – when bloody Billy Bates had burst the bubble. Billy was a big man, bigger than Sam and a great deal stronger, which was probably why they got on. But now Billy raised gingery eyebrows. 'You've not said, me ol' pal, so before I wet this baby's head, wharrisit?'

Sam had not understood at first. 'Wharrisit?

It's a perishin' baby, din't you hear wharr I said?' he demanded truculently. 'Me and the missus, old Ellen O'Mara, have done the trick at last and we gorra baby.' He looked defiantly around the bar and saw that a great many people were grinning, though when their eyes met his the grins were wiped off their faces and they turned away.

If only bloody Billy Bates had kept his big mouth shut all might yet have been well, especially as Billy was now the only one still grinning, but Billy was three parts drunk and clearly could not resist. He slung a heavy arm around Sam's shoulders and shook him. 'Is it a boy or a girl, you great fool?' he said. 'Is it a Sammy or a Sally? I don't go wettin' no baby's head till I know what's what.'

Irritated, Sam shook himself free of his pal's grip. 'How the devil do I know?' he enquired irritably. 'It'll be one or t'other; what's it matter?'

Billy started it, the swine. A slow grin spread across his ugly face and then a chuckle escaped from his lips, and in half a minute or less the whole pub was convulsed with mirth. Billy turned to the barman, who was chortling even though he probably had no idea what was funny. 'Sam's wife is in 'ospital, havin' a baby, and he wants us to wet the kid's head before he even knows if it's a boy or a girl,' he said. 'Come to that, with a dad like Sam it might turn out to be a perishin' donkey!'

Sam looked around the pub and there wasn't a single man without a grin on his face. Men who usually agreed with everything Sam said, laughed at his jokes, never contradicted him, were laughing like hyenas, and Billy Bates who was supposed to be his pal, his bezzie in fact, was laughing loudest of all. He balled his left hand into a fist and smacked it into the palm of his right. If Billy Bates hadn't been so bloody enormous he would have lain in wait for him, and used his docker's hook or a cudgel or some other weapon to teach him not to have such a smart mouth, but Billy was quite capable of holding his own against Sam. There were other men in the pub, of course, smaller men, but they would make their way home in groups, knowing how Sam always took his anger out on someone smaller than himself, and bloody Ellen was tucked away in the maternity hospital with nurses and doctors on every side. Now that he came to think of it, it was all Ellen's fault really. He hadn't wanted a baby – more expense, more irritation – but Ellen had simply told him that the kid was on the way, so what choice did he have? He played with the idea of going up to the hospital; if she'd not had the kid by now he'd teach the perishin' lot of them a thing or two. But then he remembered that Ellen had bought a bottle of rum, his favourite tipple, so that they could drink the child's health; she had dared him to so much as touch it until the baby was born.

Making his way back towards Dryden Street, Sam decided that by now he must be a father. He would go home, take a glass of rum mixed with hot water, get out of his soaking clothes and go to bed. Time enough to visit the hospital the following day. He quickened his pace.

Florence Lana Manners heard the storm coming as she was finishing an eight-hour shift as ward maid at the maternity hospital. Despite her rather imposing name, – Flossy was skinny and underfed, the youngest of three children and the only girl. Though it seemed strange to Flossy, both her parents favoured the boys and regarded her as someone else to wait upon their strong, healthy and exceedingly selfish sons.

Flossy, just fifteen, was in her first job and absolutely adored it. Miss Raines, whose job it was to supervise all the cleaning staff, porters and ambulance attendants – in fact everyone bar the actual medical staff – was delighted with Flossy's work, although she probably never noticed that Flossy came in early and left late in order to ensure that ward eight and the adjacent nursery, which were her special preserves, were almost unnaturally clean and tidy. The girl was popular with the mothers because she was always ready to run an errand or fetch a baby for a woman too tired – or too lazy – to get out of bed, and executed many small commissions for both patients and staff. When a mother was ready to leave the ward Flossy would trot down the road to the nearest shop and buy a little box of chocolates, if the mother in question still had any sweet coupons, or a box of biscuits or some other little luxury such as scented soap if coupons were not forthcoming. The gift would then be handed graciously to a favourite nurse, or 'to Sister, for the staff'.

But Flossy didn't mind. She adored the babies and, even though she knew she should not do so, hurried to the nursery as soon as she heard a baby wail, whipping it out of its cot, cradling it in her arms and kissing the petal-soft cheek until, soothed, it slept once more.

If it had been possible, Flossy would have remained at the hospital for twenty-four hours at a stretch, for here she knew she was appreciated, regarded as a worthwhile member of the nursing team, though of course she had no qualifications. Her brothers, Hubert and Horace, sneered at her, called her a skivvy, but objected when she was not there to dance attendance upon them. Both boys followed the example set by their parents. They were always quicker with a cuff than a word of encouragement, so Flossy could not love either of them, and the more she was appreciated at the hospital the more she resented the treatment which was meted out to her at home. Tonight she had signed off and gone to the cloakroom to get her coat when she heard the first rumblings of thunder. She paused, a hand reaching up to the peg. Her coat was thin and much patched, and she doubted it would afford much protection in such rough weather. Nevertheless, she took the garment off its peg and went reluctantly towards the exit, where she stepped through the revolving doors and was decanted on to the pavement just as a terrible crack of thunder and a stab of lightning pinned her to the spot, too shocked and terrified to move. A passer-by told her to get back into the hospital unless she wanted to risk being lightning-struck, and Flossy grinned at the man, only too glad to obey, and bolted back into the hospital almost happily. The nurse on the big reception desk smiled at her.

'You go back into the staffroom, Flossy, and wait for the storm to ease,' she advised kindly. 'Did you count the seconds between the thunder and the lightning? I reckon the storm's pretty well overhead now and will move off any minute.'

Flossy muttered something and fled to the staff-room, but it was just her luck that the probationer nurse who most disliked her was ensconced in the only comfortable chair. She stared accusingly at Flossy and dropped a hand negligently over the arm of the chair. Flossy knew the older girl had been smoking, knew that it was forbidden to do so in any part of the hospital, but would not have dreamed of telling tales, not even on someone whom she knew to be her enemy. Instead, she backed out, closing the door softly, just as another tremendous crash was closely followed by a sort of sizzling sound and every light went out.

Flossy found herself running towards ward eight and its adjacent nursery without any real intention of going there. She had always hated storms, feared both thunder and lightning, for when she had been quite a little girl, no more than four or five, her brother Horace had brought a young lady into their house, announcing that he was giving her shelter from the storm which was raging outside, and had thrust his little sister out into the yard, telling her to take shelter in the privy if it came on to rain. Ever since then Flossy had been terrified of storms, and now in the pitch blackness she fairly flew along to ward eight. Other people were also hurrying along the corridors. Some had torches, while those who had not relied on what little light came through the windows between the flashes of lightning that lit up everything. Flossy reached ward eight without difficulty and stopped outside the swing doors, then went through the ones which led to the nursery. Her poor heart was fluttering in her breast like a terrified butterfly, but as soon as she entered the nursery with its dozen small cots and its long windows she began to feel calmer. It seemed strange that no one was in here with the babies, but then she realised that they were not crying, did not seem at all ruffled by the noise, the darkness, or the sudden stabs of brilliance which lit up the room as though it were midday.

Flossy was bending over the nearest cot when she heard footsteps approaching down the corridor and the swish as the swing doors began to open. Her heart, which had started to beat at its normal rate, speeded up again. If it were that wretched probationer she would be in trouble, because once her shift was over she should not really have been in here in the pitch dark. Hastily she dropped to all fours and squiggled beneath the nearest cot. Odd how safe she felt, not only from the storm but also from the spite of the cigarette-smoking probationer. God, she thought, would take special care of twelve brand new babies, would not let lightning enter a room containing so many tiny new souls. And with the thought she heard the doors swish again. Whoever had come in had gone out, having reassured themselves that everything was all right.

With a satisfied sigh, Flossy made herself comfortable. Because of the cold, extra blankets had been hung on the foot of each cot, and she reached up, pulled a couple down, rolled them into a ball and laid her head on the resultant cushion. She realised suddenly that she was very tired indeed.

She had had a long and exhausting morning at the beck and call of both her mother and her brother Horace. Then she had come in to the hospital for what they called the afternoon shift, two till ten, and now that fright had eased exhaustion took over. Curling up, she began to enjoy one of her favourite daydreams. One day, when she was old enough, she meant to apply to the hospital to be taken on as a probationer. Then she would work very hard, pass examinations and become a proper nurse. She would have a room in the nurses' home and a real salary, for even though she knew the nurses were miserably underpaid they got more than a ward maid did. She dreamed of wearing the lovely blue and white striped dress of a qualified nurse, dreamed of never having to go home again to the ramshackle little house in Dryden Street. She dreamed ... she dreamed...

She was almost asleep when she realised two things. The first was that the thunder was rumbling off into the distance, to be replaced by rainfall so heavy that it streamed down the windows like a river, and the second was that someone was entering the nursery; a mother no doubt, come to check on her baby. Or perhaps one of the nursing staff. Flossy's heart began to beat uneasily once more; she knew very well she should not be here at all, let alone curled up under the babies' cots with the babies' blankets as a pillow. She thanked God that the lights had not yet come back on and shrank even further against the wall as the woman – it was definitely one of the mothers, for though there was very little light coming in through the rain-drenched panes Flossy could see a regulation dressing gown as well as a pair of slippers, far too large for the wearer – passed very quietly along the row of cots.

Flossy thought hard. Before she had gone off duty there had been two mothers in the delivery room; doubtless it was one of them, anxious about her new baby. Well I just hope she doesn't go picking it up and setting it wailing, Flossy thought apprehensively. If she does, she'll set the whole lot off and one of the nurses will come in and find me, and if that happens Matron will sack me ... oh please, please God, don't let the stupid woman wake the dear little babies!

Anxious to see what was happening, she craned her neck and looked sideways. The woman was lifting a baby out of its cot and cradling it in one arm; she was actually singing a calming tune beneath her breath. Then she bent over another cot, murmuring words Flossy could not quite make out, and plucked up another child, cradling it in her other arm, and with a sudden stab of real fear Flossy remembered the gypsy woman who had come into the ward the previous day and given birth to a puny little thing, all straggly black hair and sticky, half shut eyes. Was the visitor the gypsy? Had she come to look at her odd little baby, to make sure that it was still alive? Flossy remembered that the doctors had had real worries over the state of its health. The mother was old; she had had a great many children before this one and had not taken care of herself ... the woman turned unexpectedly and Flossy banged her head against the bottom of the cot in her anxiety to get back out of sight. There was not sufficient light to identify the woman, but it might be the gypsy; the thick grey clouds from which the rain was pelting obscured so much light that it was impossible to tell for sure. And even as Flossy withdrew once more, like a snail into its shell, the intruder replaced the babies in their cots and hurried out of the nursery, pushing the swing door so cautiously that it made scarcely a sound.

Flossy waited for what seemed like an age but was probably only a few minutes, then crawled out of her hiding place, put the blankets back where they belonged and stole over to the babies the woman had picked up. Had she put them back in the right cots? Not that it should matter, because as a rule all the babies were labelled. But on this occasion the newborns who had arrived during the power cut had been placed in their cots without ceremony. Suppose, just suppose, that it was the gypsy who had lifted the babies from their cots, meaning to change her sickly baby for a healthy one? Flossy was telling herself that she should go to someone in authority and explain what she had seen when she realised that if she did so she would be in deep trouble. She had no right to enter the nursery when she was not on duty and in any case what could she say? She had not seen anyone remove a child from the nursery, merely lift a couple up. The visit might have been completely innocent, and anyway from what she could, remember the gypsy's baby had been very different from the others on the ward, brown and wrinkly rather than pink and white. If the woman had indeed changed the babies it would not need Flossy to inform the nurses; they would know at once and take the appropriate steps.

Reassured, Flossy went over to the swing doors and listened. Then she slipped out and unobtrusively joined the staff making their way towards the foyer. She would go home now and not worry herself about people changing babies; it was not her affair. Folk were always telling her to mind her own business and on this occasion at least she would obey them. She pushed out through the revolving doors and turned in the direction of home. It was awfully late, but because of the storm and the power cut it was very unlikely that she would be able to catch a tram. At least the rain, which had poured down so hard, was beginning to ease. Flossy started to walk

Police Constable Alex Jamieson had continued solidly to pound his beat throughout the storm and was actually approaching the maternity hospital when the rain started. He was wearing his thick overcoat but had not thought to bring his cape, and he sprinted towards the windows nearest him hoping to take cover whilst the rain lasted, for there was an overhang along here which he had used on previous occasions. He reached the shelter, which was in fact a sort of alcove, and backed into it; from here he could see what was going on, paying particular notice to the doings of his sergeant, who checked on his men at regular intervals. Alex would telephone in to his police station every hour or so, but that didn't stop Sergeant Crawley from making spot checks, and though in his heart he might applaud

Alex's seeking shelter from the downpour, for he was a kindly man, it might still put a black mark against the young constable's name, which was the last thing Alex wanted.

If he had had his waterproof cape, he told himself, he would have slogged on, but what was the point in getting his heavy serge uniform soaking wet? Surely any sergeant, even the most critical, would understand his decision to take shelter for a few moments, until the cloudburst – for it was no less – had passed over. The rain was pelting down, hitting the pavement with such force that each heavy drop made its own fountain of spray, when a movement in one of the long windows against which he was pressed caught his eye. He looked in and saw a row of what looked like cots, and a woman – he assumed it was a woman, this being the maternity hospital – hurrying towards the end of the room furthest from him. He saw her bending over the cots and was wondering how these young women knew one baby from another when his tall helmet funnelled what felt like a river of icy water straight down the neck of his uniform tunic. Alex was unable to prevent a squawk of surprise from escaping his lips, and by the time he looked again the woman had gone. He was about to turn away when he saw another movement in the room to his right. The rain was beginning to ease and as the small figure crawled out from beneath its sheltering cot he had no difficulty in recognising young Flossy Manners.

Alex grinned to himself. He had known Flossy since she was a toddler and though as a boy he had joined in the jeers caused by her name – the other kids had called her brothers Bad Manners and Flossy's nickname for years had been Goody Manners, so meek and eager to please had the little girl been – he had always been carelessly fond of her. But even as he raised a hand to knock on the glass and ask young Manners just what she was doing, crawling about the floor, all the lights went on. Light streamed out from every window of the hospital, street lamps blazed, house lights shone once more and Alex, realising that he could have been taken for a peeping Tom, moved hastily away from the ward windows and headed for the wide entrance. As he approached the glass revolving doors he could see that the hospital, at least, was very much alive. Nurses, who he knew, were not allowed to run, were gliding to and fro with the rapid walk they had learned to use. Doctors with case notes under their arms hurried about and Alex realised that all this activity was due to the power cut and the subsequent restoration of electricity. Normally at this hour, as he well knew, the hospital was a hushed place, for patients slept, as did their babies, and the staff appreciated the quiet night-time hours.

There was little activity on the pavement, however, and Alex was just falling into the long slow strides he had perfected over the months of patrolling his beat when he heard, from behind him, pattering footsteps and a hushed but persistent voice calling: 'Constable, do you know if the trams is still running? Only I'm awful tired and me home's a good way off.'

Alex sighed. The telephone box was only another quarter of a mile or so. He had the necessary pennies in his tunic pocket, and if no one was already occupying the box he had planned to ring his sergeant and then turn for the police station to complete the last section of his beat. But duty was duty; he was here to give aid and succour to anyone who needed it, so he stopped to let the caller catch up. As he turned he could not prevent a slow smile from spreading over his face. He should have guessed who it would be: little Goody Manners herself, fair, stringy hair plastered to her small round skull, eyes wide with appeal and her thin coat clinging to her skinny person, making her look more like a child of ten than a girl of fourteen or so, which he supposed she must be since he knew she had left school. Now that he came to consider, though, he had no idea what she had been doing in the hospital. Visiting? But not between ten o'clock and midnight, surely? Come to think of it, what the devil had she been up to, crawling under babies' cots during a power cut? But she was tugging at his wet sleeve, beginning to repeat her question, and then as he pushed his helmet to the back of his head a smile of recognition dawned. 'Oh, Alex, I didn't know it were you! Well, of course, I knew you were in the police force, but you look different in uniform; I expect I do as well.' She looked up at him, her face proud, and pulled open the top of her coat to show him that she was wearing, beneath the soaked and ragged coat, a uniform of some sort. Green cotton? It was difficult to tell since street lamps changed everything, but Alex knew enough to realise she couldn't possibly be a nurse. He raised his brows enquiringly. 'I'm a ward maid,' Flossy said proudly. 'I look after ward eight. Mothers and babies, you know. Only today, because of the storm, I missed me tram and now I've got to walk home, unless they're running a special because of the power cut.'

Alex grinned. 'You aren't telling me a little pigmy of a thing like you is actually working?' he asked with feigned astonishment. 'Why, you can't be more than twelve or thirteen at the most, Goody!'

Flossy stiffened. 'I'm fifteen. Only just, mind, but I am fifteen,' she insisted. 'And don't you go calling me names, Alex Jamieson, 'cos I can remember things an' all. They used to call you Pally Ally, as I recall. And anyway, I asked you a civil question – as a police constable not as a person – so you should give me a civil answer.'

Alex looked down at the small figure by his side, and his heart smote him. 'I've got to make a telephone call to my police station when we reach the box on the next corner,' he told her. 'I'll explain to my sergeant that because of the power cut you missed your tram, and ask his permission to let me see you home. Only you'll have to wait while I make the telephone call, that suit you?'

Flossy took a deep shuddering breath and clutched Alex's arm, gazing so worshipfully up into his face that he felt quite guilty. He was only doing his duty, after all. But clearly, his company meant a lot to the little waif by his side. So he set off with Flossy trotting beside him, and once the call was made and permission given he slowed his pace to match hers, and the two of them talked comfortably as they walked.

Alex noticed, however, that every now and then his companion started a sentence but did not finish it, and in the end he confronted her. 'Whatever is it you want to say, young Flossy?' he enquired rather crossly. 'It's pretty clear you've got something on your mind.'

Faced with a direct question Flossy, apparently, felt she had to answer with equal directness. 'I saw you sheltering in that little alcove on the corner just before the light came back on – at least, I didn't know it were you then, of course, but you were wearin' that uniform – so I reckon you might have seen me crawling out from under the cots,' she said. She looked shamefaced. 'I – I shouldn't have been there, so when one of the mums came in to tek a look at her baby, and lifted it out of its cot, I didn't say nuffin'. Well, how could I? She had a perfect right to be there, which was more than I had.'

There was a long pause, which Alex broke. 'So what?' he said a trifle impatiently. 'I saw the woman myself; of course I didn't know her but she was definitely a patient. She was wearing a hospital dressing gown.'

'You must have noticed if she was young, blonde, dark. Oh, Alex, you must have noticed something!'

Alex shook his head. 'I didn't, but what does it matter? As you say, she had a perfect right to be there; a perfect right to pick up her baby as well.' He added, with more than a trace of sarcasm, 'I believe it's customary for mothers to pick up their babies when the little blighters scream for food or need their nappies changing.'

'Oh, Alex, will you be serious?' Flossy begged. 'She didn't just pick up one baby, she picked up two, and I have a feeling that she might have put them back in the wrong cots. Of course, it shouldn't make any difference because babies are labelled before they leave the delivery room, but tonight people were running around in the dark like chickens with their heads cut off. And there was this gypsy...'

'A gypsy?' Alex asked, surprised. 'I thought they never entered hospitals, unless they were dying, of course, and couldn't help it. So if what you're asking me is whether the woman I saw was a gypsy, I'm afraid I simply can't tell you. For a start she had her back to me and then the rain was streaming down the window panes, distorting everything inside. But I'm sure mothers know their own babies, so if I were you I'd forget it. It's none of your business, after all, especially if you shouldn't have been in there anyway. When you go to work tomorrow you'll soon find out whether there's a big ruckus going on over babies in the wrong cots.'

At this point they reached Dryden Street and Alex slowed beside the house which he remembered was home to the Manners family. He looked doubtfully at the house, which was in total darkness, then gave his companion a little push. 'Stop worrying and get yourself to bed,' he ordered. 'I'll wait until you're safe indoors.'

'Thanks, Alex, you are kind,' Flossy said, heading for the door. 'I'll let you know what happens next time we meet. Good night!'

Alex raised a hand, then turned smartly and set off to return to his beat and then to the police station. When he got there he would have to write a report before he could seek his own bed, and he thought almost enviously of funny, scrawny little Flossy, probably already crawling between the sheets. But then he remembered her bullying, impatient father, her sharp-tongued, ungrateful mother, and horrible Horace and hateful Hubert; no, she was not to be envied, but rather pitied. Still, she had talked happily of her work in the hospital, her ambition to become a probationer as soon as she was old enough and the fact that, hard though it must be for her, she was already borrowing books from the hospital library and studying anatomy and simple medicine. He decided that all things being equal, Flossy would go far. Only when he had almost reached the police station did he allow his thoughts to return to another of the nurses, whose corn-coloured hair and bright blue eyes had caught his attention when the pair of them had met at the Grafton Ballroom a couple of weeks earlier. Her name was Annabelle, and they had spent most of that evening together and had made a date to go to the cinema the following week. Ah, but she was beautiful! He knew that many girls were attracted by policemen and hoped that she would prove to be one of them. Certainly she was not indifferent. Thinking about her made the walk seem short, and by the time he was reporting to his sergeant, and hanging his wet garments over the clothes horse in the back room, he had forgotten Flossy and her peculiar problem and had allowed dreams of the beautiful Annabelle to oust everything else from his mind.

Chapter Two

Molly awoke, and wondered for a moment where on earth she was. The ceiling was far too high; the one in the cottage was so low that if you jumped out of bed carelessly you might easily bang your head on a beam. Momentarily disorientated and frightened, Molly stretched out a hand, groping for Rhys's broad and comfortable back, but all her fingers met was a starched, chilly white sheet, and with the touch she remembered. She was in hospital, in bed on one of the wards, and it was all over! Her baby had been born the previous night in the middle of the most fearsome thunderstorm she could ever remember, but despite the conditions everything about the birth had been fine, or as fine as such an experience could be, at any rate. Molly sat up on her elbow and gazed around the room. There was a clock at one end of the ward and in the moonlight that shone through the windows she saw it was still only five thirty. Remembering that hospitals always roused one early, Molly sighed. Because of the power cut she had only had the briefest glimpse of her new little daughter before she was taken off to the nursery adjoining the ward, and now she wondered whether she had time to visit her baby before that wretched strident bell began to ring, announcing that the staff were about to come round to their still sleepy patients, since the day, in the hospital's opinion at any rate, had begun.

She was sitting on the edge of her bed, reaching for her slippers, when a voice spoke near her ear, causing her to jump quite six inches. 'Mornin'! Is you goin' along to the nursery? I'll come wi' you.'

Molly swung round. She was being addressed by a large fat woman who must be in her forties; surely too old to have had a baby? But then Molly remembered the woman who had greeted her the previous evening as the nurse helped her into bed. She remembered, too, that the woman had said she had had a girl but would have been glad of any baby, so now she greeted the older woman pleasantly, adding: 'I remember you now! We must have been in the delivery suite at about the same time and we both had little girls. You were saying you were going to give yours a fancy name, but I feel I have to consult my husband.'

The woman snorted. 'My feller's a docker; he wouldn't care if I called the baby Barnacle Bill,' she said. 'He'll come a-visitin' tonight, of course, same as your feller will no doubt, but I'm tellin' you, this 'un's my baby and I'll give her any name I want. If it had been a boy, Sam might ha' felt differently, but he's got no time for girls.'

'Oh,' Molly said rather feebly. She took the dressing gown from its peg at the end of her bed and began to put it on just as a nurse, wheeling a trolley, pushed through the swing doors at the end of the ward. 'Tea, ladies,' the girl shouted. 'Come along now, rise and shine! I'll give you ten minutes to drink your tea and then we'll bring the babies through and you can feed them.'

She began to distribute cups of tea from a large

urn, and as she came level with Molly she gave her a friendly smile. 'Well, Mrs Roberts, you're an example to all these mothers,' she said cheerfully. 'The staff in the delivery room said you didn't give so much as a squeak. Baby won't be hungry, because a full milk supply doesn't come in until the third day after the birth, but she'll still need a cuddle, so she'll be brought in with the rest.'

'Wharrabout mine, nurse?' Molly's new friend asked plaintively. 'She's me first; will she need to be fed?'

The nurse gave the other woman a reproving look. 'Didn't you listen to what I was telling Mrs Roberts here? Baby O'Mara will need exactly the same treatment from you as that which we advocate for all babies, regardless of the mother's age or previous experience. Now drink your tea, because we nurses have a great deal to do today, thanks to the storm and the power cut last night.'

As soon as the nurse had gone further down the ward, Mrs O'Mara picked up her cup of tea and carried it round so that she might sit on Molly's bed and talk as they drank. 'I've decided I'm a-goin' to can me baby Lana after Lana Turner, what's me favourite film star,' she announced in a breathy whisper. 'What's more, no one can't shorten Lana. I hates being called Ellie instead of Ellen, so she'll be spared that. What'll you call yours then?'

'I told you; I can't decide until I've spoken to my husband,' Molly said, trying not to sound impatient. Was the woman deaf, or merely so bound up in her own affairs that she did not bother to listen to what was being said? 'I chose our little son's name – he's called Chris – so I think it's only fair that Rhys should have the final word on what we call our little girl. I rather like Sally-Anne, or Laura-Jane, but as I said, I mean to let Rhys choose.'

The older woman drained her teacup noisily, then turned back to Molly. 'Do you like, your feller? I mean really like him?' she asked incredulously. 'I don't like my old man; can't imagine why I ever wed him ... well, I can, actually. I were in the family way and he were the father all right.' Her mouth drooped and Molly saw with some distress that the older woman's eyes had filled with tears. 'But the baby never come to nothin' and though we stayed together I never quickened again until now. So you see, I reckon I've earned the right to name the baby and to say she's mine.'

'I see,' Molly said slowly. 'Do you blame your husband for losing that first baby, then?'

'Yes I does, 'cos he wouldn't never leave me alone, too handy with his fists when I were upright and his boots when I were down,' Ellen said, causing Molly to gasp with shock. Ellen, however, gave her a grin, and patted her shoulder. ''Sawright, chuck, now I've got the baby I'm goin' to kick him out, big though he is,' she said breezily. 'I won't have him ill-treating my little Lana, and these days the scuffers can put some sort of order on a feller what stops him from approachin' your house or even speakin' to you in the street. Besides, I hit him with the coal scuttle last time he tried it on, and he's never been the same since. Still an' all, I won't take no chances in future. My

Lana will need me and she won't never need Sam ... eh up, here come the nurses with our babies. Ain't they the prettiest things?'

Molly had explained to Sister that the farm was so remote that Rhys might arrive late that evening, but despite her fears, when visiting time arrived and a stream of men, all looking self-conscious and smart, came on to the ward, Rhys was among them. Alerted by the interested postmistress, he had left Chris with their nearest neighbour, promising to return just as soon as possible, and now he told Molly regretfully that he doubted he would be able to visit her again whilst she remained on the ward. 'But I'll come and pick you up when they discharge you and baby Rhiannon,' he assured her, for they had agreed that the baby should be named after Rhys's much loved mother, and Molly thought it was a pretty name and went well with Roberts. 'After that storm last night – only I don't suppose you got it here – I've a heap of things to do on the farm and can't simply go off and leave the stock to manage for itself. What's more, I've left Chris with the Pritchards, and though Mrs Pritchard is very good, they've got their hands full running their own place. Chris thinks Rhodri is wonderful, follows him round everywhere, which means the poor lad has to keep an eye on Chris all the while, and he's only ten himself.'

'I know, or I can imagine,' Molly said rather wearily. 'I'm sure they took Chris in willingly, but they're both old, and Mrs P doesn't speak much English, which must make things harder for them.'

Rhys laughed. 'Chris was chattering away in Welsh when I left him; it's amazing how quickly children pick up a language if they don't realise they're learning,' he said. 'Believe me, sweetheart, our children will be bilingual before they start school.'

Molly laughed with him, but inside she was dismayed. She had lived in the valley for a while now, loved every stick and stone of it, yet still could not speak the language herself, though she tried diligently to learn. She was grateful to the neighbouring farmers' wives, who gave her every assistance though they themselves spoke little English. Their husbands, too, might have little in common with Rhys, but their helpfulness in times of trouble could not have been bested.

When the fathers had seen their babies, talked to their wives and taken their leave, she turned to Ellen, who had been visited by an even fatter version of herself and no one else. A nurse told Ellen and Molly later that Mr O'Mara had tried to gain admittance to the ward after visiting time was over. It had taken four brawny porters to eject him but he had left at last, screaming threats of what he would do to his blankety blank of a wife when he got her home again.

'I suppose your visitor was your mother; she is very like you to look at,' Molly said as the two women sat on their beds drinking the hot milk which was supposed to help them to sleep. 'She was thrilled with the baby, wasn't she? Is it her only grandchild?'

Ellen laughed scornfully. 'Nah! I've got three sisters and a brother, though none of them live local, 'cept for me brother. Between them they must have a dozen kids, but me mum and meself have allus been close. She's been on at me for a while to kick Sam out and she's rare glad I'm going to do it at last. She don't hold with violence, so I never told her I'd crowned him with the coal scuttle, and near on cracked his head open when I locked him out and he came yellin' at me winder.' She chuckled. 'I meant to empty the chamber pot over his head but it slipped out of me hand and landed right on his noggin. Laid him out flat and cold it did, and left him with a scar slanting right across his forehead and chopping his eyebrow in two. He thinks he's such a handsome feller but really he's ugly as a pan of worms, with or without the scar.'

'Goodness! Did you call an ambulance?' Molly asked, but was not really surprised when her new friend shook her head.

'Did I hell! I just slammed the winder shut and got back into bed. When he come round, I told him the pal he'd brought home with him from the pub had whacked him on the head with a bottle of porter. I'd already cleared up the broken china, but I reckon he were suspicious so I cleared out. I'd already quickened with Lana, you see, so I didn't mean to give him no chance to hurt the babby. To be fair, once I told him I were in the family way again, after more'n twenty years, he give me a wide berth, knowin' the neighbours would call the scuffers if he attacked a woman in my condition, but as I said, from the moment I go home, I'll have one of them police orders placed on him, so he can't come near nor by.'

'Gosh,' Molly said faintly, 'and I thought I had problems! Only they aren't in the least like yours because Rhys is a wonderful husband. Why, he's taking care of Chris whilst I'm in hospital, making their meals, running the farm and doing the jobs of two people. We'd like to employ a farm labourer but to be honest we can't afford it yet. You see, it's like this...' and for the first time she confided, in someone other than Rhys, how hard it was to make ends meet. She had been ashamed to mention it, but Ellen's problems cast her own into the shade, and made it easier to tell her that life on their little farm, though it might sound idyllic, had its drawbacks. 'But at least we're making enough money to cover our expenses,' she concluded. 'If you throw Sam out, though, Ellen, what will you live on? Will he pay you maintenance, or whatever it's called?'

'I'll work,' Ellen said briefly, 'I've always worked. Don't you worry about me, queen, I'll be a deal better off without that bugger stealin' every penny I earn.'

'Yes of course,' Molly said feebly. A Liverpool girl herself, but living in one of the suburbs outside the city and attending a convent school, she knew very little of the life of the enormous number of impoverished people who lived in the tiny courts and alleys in the centre of the city. She knew she had been lucky, for despite the fact that both her parents had died before she was five years old she had never really suffered as a result and now could not even remember them. She had been brought up by maternal grandparents who had given her love in abundance. They had enrolled her as a pupil in the nearby convent school, then had sent her to a secretarial college, actually selling their house and moving into a flat when their money began to run out.

They had not been young before the war, but now, thinking back, Molly realised how the conflict had aged them. Queuing, traipsing around the city in search of the necessities of life which they had once taken for granted, patching their own once good clothes in order to save their coupons for their adored granddaughter, even the terrifying raids, though the docks were several miles away from their suburban home, had affected them deeply.

Molly had worked hard at secretarial college, wanting to reward her grandparents in some way for the many sacrifices they had made for her, and in a way she had managed to do so, for she had come out head of her year, knowing that she was in line for a first rate job with excellent prospects of promotion after the war.

Then she had met Rhys. They had had a whirlwind courtship, and had married with her grandparents' blessing, though Molly had reflected later that had they lived long enough to see Cefn Farm they might not have been so delighted.

In the event, they had both died before Rhys was demobbed, which was probably as well, Molly thought now. Rhys, a dozen years older than herself, had tried to describe the kind of farm for which he yearned, but his deep and abiding love of his homeland must have made him see it through rose-coloured spectacles. Molly could still remember the shock she had felt when the ancient baby

Morris had turned in to the first of the rocky, un-made-up drives on their list and Rhys had pointed proudly at what at first glance she had taken to be a cattle shed. 'That's the sort of farm I want. Take a good look, because something like this will be your future home, my darling,' he had said proudly. 'I know you'll love Snowdonia as I do.'

Molly was just thinking that Rhys had been right, though he had not realised, any more than she had, how very hard was the life of a hill farmer in the Welsh mountains, when her thoughts were interrupted.

'Here we are, Mrs Roberts; Baby Roberts has come for a bit of mothering and a nice drink of milk.' The nurse thrust the shawl-wrapped infant into Molly's arms and the second one she was holding she handed to Ellen. 'There you are, Mrs O'Mara...' She heaved a deep sigh. How many times have I told you ladies not to sit on the beds? There's a perfectly good padded bench which you can pull out if you must sit and gossip, though during feeding you should be in your beds because the pillows give your back something to rest on, and we don't want mothers complaining that their bad backs are our fault.'

'Sorry, nurse,' Molly said humbly. 'I forgot.'

Ellen, however, though she waited until the nurse had disappeared, gave a scornful sniff. 'They oughter provide us wi' nursin' chairs; they'd be a deal better for us than sittin' up in bed,' she told Molly. 'I'm a-goin' to buy one with me allowance, just as soon as I'm out of here.' She unbuttoned her nightgown and the baby, feeling her mother's flesh against her soft cheek, began to weave her head, plainly searching for the nipple.

Molly smothered a chuckle. 'It's a miracle to me how babies know what to look for,' she confided. 'Chris was just the same, so I s'pose they all know instinctively that they need to suck. They'll suck your little finger, if there's nothing else available.'

'Mmm hmm, I guess you're right,' Ellen droned, sounding like a contented bee which has just entered a flower and begun to enjoy the honey. 'They say the milk don't come in until the third day but this little 'un of mine thinks otherwise.'

Molly smiled. It was odd that she was more experienced than Ellen, who, she guessed, was so much older than herself, but rather pleasant, too. It was also pleasant to have found a friend after so long alone on the farm. Ellen might not be the sort of person she would have chosen to pal up with once, but now she knew better. She looked approvingly at the other woman. Ellen's dark hair, a mass of curls, was tied back from her face with what looked suspiciously like a piece of hairy parcel string, and her nightgown had several cobbled tears. But Ellen's skin was creamy, her cheeks pink, and her large dark brown eyes full of humour and intelligence. Earlier, a glance around the ward had shown Molly that most of the occupants of the beds were young girls, who were unlikely to have much in common with herself. Ellen, on the other hand, was bright and intelligent, and though they came from very different backgrounds and had led very different lives, Molly realised that they could become good friends, though the distance between the farm and the city might make such a friendship difficult.

She was still wishing that Ellen lived nearer her when both babies stopped sucking simultaneously and the nurse came round, reminding the mothers to lay the babies across their shoulders and rub their firm little backs in a circular movement to bring up the wind. When they had done that they could try the babies on the other breast. As Molly obediently draped Baby Roberts across her shoulder, Ellen leaned forward and stared at the child's pink face, then at her own little one. 'Gawd almighty, ain't they alike, though? They could be perishin' twins,' she said. 'Still an' all, I reckon babies do look alike – remember what Churchill said? "I look like all babies, and all babies look like me."' She chuckled. 'And weren't he just right? I reckon most of the babies on ward eight look the same.' She lowered her voice. 'Oh, not that gypsy's brat. I never see'd a kid so hairy. If I'd not known I'd ha' thought it were a young cat.'

Molly glanced cautiously around the ward to make sure that the gypsy woman could not possibly overhear them, and Ellen gave a throaty gasp. 'I don't s'pose you know, queen, but the gypsy lit out after that terrible storm was over last night. I heard two of the nurses talkin' about it; they said it weren't just her baby she took either, but two good blankets, a couple of feedin' bottles, a quarter-pound of tea from the kitchen and one of the nurses' cloaks. I reckon we're lucky she didn't fancy a proper baby instead of that hairy little bugger. Mind, I've always reckoned it's lies that gyppos steal kids; judgin' from what I've seen they've gorr enough of their own.'

Later in the morning, Molly tried to find out

just what had happened to the gypsy woman and her baby, for the thought of anyone's voluntarily leaving the dry and well-heated hospital for the cold, wild night appalled her. But Nurse Middleton, when questioned, could only shrug. 'I wasn't on nights, chuck; better ask Nurse Reid when she comes on duty,' she advised. 'But all gyppos is alike in hating roofs over their heads. I know she had a hard labour – it was a cross-birth – but once she'd got her child safe, I reckon all she wanted was to go back to her camp, wherever that may be.'

A passing nurse stopped to give a derisive laugh. 'All she wanted was to go back to her camp with an armful of stolen property,' she said. 'Ah well, you live and learn. Next time a gypsy comes in they'll put her into the private room at the end of the ward and lock the door on her.' She smiled and patted Molly's arm. 'Just be thankful she's gone, 'cos they ain't just brown from the sun, you know, and Sister likes ward eight to shine like a star.'

The rest of the day passed uneventfully. The bed which had contained the gypsy woman – and several other unwanted visitors – was stripped and the mattress taken to be fumigated, and the new mothers bathed their babies, Ellen almost drowning poor little Lana when she seized her by one soapy arm, which promptly slid through her fingers. Molly showed Ellen the safest way to bath her child, soaping Rhiannon's tiny limbs one at a time in order to have a firm purchase and thus prevent the child from slipping too low in the water, but once the babies were towel-wrapped, both Lana and Rhiannon giving every appearance of having enjoyed their first bath, Molly could not resist glancing at the empty bed and wondering who would occupy it next. Because she had it on her mind she was less surprised than she might have been, when she was in the ablutions later, to find herself addressed by the ward maid, who, when she entered, had been industriously polishing the taps.

'Hey, missus, is – is your baby right well? Only thing is, there was some muddling over labels. Course, I know nothing about it official-like, but the word's gone round as two of the little 'uns might have gorrin the wrong cots. It were the last two to be born – well, the only two – in that perishin' dreadful thunderstorm.'

Molly was amused rather than worried by the strange little person's warning, but she said soothingly, 'It's all right, honest to God it is. The other mother concerned was Mrs O'Mara, and I'm sure if there had been a mistake someone would have noticed; we might even have noticed ourselves! You needn't worry; I'm certain Rhiannon is my own dear little baby.' She smiled kindly at the ward maid, dug a hand into the pocket of her hospital dressing gown and produced a small bar of Fry's chocolate. Rhys had bought her three such bars the night before, and she thought this one might be put to good use if it enabled her to extract a promise from the ward maid not to make any more fuss. 'What's your name, queen?'

'Florence Lana Manners, only they calls me Flossy,' the girl said. Her eyes glistened as they spotted the chocolate.

'Listen, Flossy; Mrs O'Mara and myself have become good friends and we hope to continue our friendship after we leave the hospital. Mrs O'Mara's life is hard – her husband is not supportive – and if there were any doubt as to the parentage of their little girl a great deal of harm might come of it. Will you promise me that you will say nothing of this to anyone? I suppose you might mention it to a member of staff...'

'No, no, I couldn't,' Flossy broke in, her pale little face flushing. 'You see, I'm skeered of thunderstorms and though I were off duty and should have gone home, I – I hid and saw what I shouldn't have seen. Honest to God, missus, I thought someone switched two of the babies, only it was so dark and the thunder roared so loud...'

'Very understandable,' Molly said. The poor kid must have fallen asleep and dreamed the whole thing, she told herself. 'But put it right out of your mind, Flossy, because only harm can come of planting such thoughts in people's heads. Shall we shake hands on it?'

Flossy agreed and accepted the chocolate bar with real gratitude. 'Well, I've telled you wharr I saw,' she said happily, making for the door into the corridor. 'And I won't say a word to anyone else, I promise on me mother's grave.'

'Is your mother dead?' Molly asked; the child looked young to be orphaned, but...'

Flossie looked puzzled. 'Dead? I sometimes wish she were, but ... oh, I *see!'* She chuckled. 'I promise I'll never say a word to a soul.' She drew a hand across her throat. 'See this wet? See this dry? Cut me throat if I dare to lie!' She smiled seraphically at Molly. 'That do?'

Molly chuckled. 'That'll do,' she confirmed. 'And now I'd best do what I came in here for, or the staff will think I need nappies as well as Rhiannon!'

Molly and Ellen were ready well before the appointed hour of their discharge from the hospital. Since Ellen admitted she still had some sweet coupons and Molly had money, they had decided to share their gift for the nurses, which was to be a box of Black Magic chocolates and a packet of Player's. Most of the nurses smoked, and though Sister disapproved Ellen and Molly knew how eagerly the cigarettes would be shared out amongst the staff and were glad to give pleasure, for though the chocolates would be welcomed they were not forbidden fruit, like cigarettes. Rhys had visited the previous evening, to make sure that he would arrive at the right time, for there were formalities – form-fillings and such – to be attended to before Molly would be allowed to leave. He had asked idly, as he sat on the padded bench drawn up close to Molly's bed, who was calling for his wife's new friend, and upon hearing that she did not know offered to give her and her baby a lift. Ellen, however, though she thanked him politely, refused the offer. 'Me mum would be right put out if she came all the way to the hospital, thinkin' to give me a hand with Lana here, and found us gone,' she explained. 'If she don't come, Sister says the hospital will give us me taxi fare, so I'll be just fine and dandy, wharrever way the cookie crumbles.'

So when Rhys drew up outside the revolving doors his wife was ready and waiting, the baby in the crook of her arm, her friend by her side and her small suitcase at her feet. She waved joyfully as soon as she saw the baby Morris approaching and her waving redoubled when she saw Chris bouncing up and down on the back seat. Ellen, who was standing beside her with her own baby in her arms, grinned at the little boy. 'I guess that's your Chris; ain't he a grand kid?' As she stopped speaking a tram drew to a halt and she gave a squeak of excitement. 'Here comes me mum; can you see her, Moll? Ain't that just the luckiest thing? We had our babbies on the same day and now we're leaving hospital on the same day as well.'

Rhys jumped out of the car and came round to take Molly's suitcase and help her into the front passenger seat, whereupon Chris flung his arms round her neck, squeaking with excitement and chattering away nineteen to the dozen, whilst Molly and Mrs Meakin exchanged polite conversation through the open window and Ellen informed her friend, with some pride, that her mother had arranged for a feller who drove a taxi cab to pick them up. 'He'll be around in five minutes or so,' she said happily, as Rhys slid back behind the wheel. 'Goodbye, Molly, and don't forget to write. You'll have more to say than me, I guess, but I'll do me best to tell you all our doings.'

'I won't forget,' Molly said happily. It was another cold day and babies are delicate creatures, in their mothers' eyes at least, so she cranked the window up and they set off. Rhys, not used to city traffic, proceeded with caution, particularly when they reached the tunnel beneath the Mersey, but once well clear of both Liverpool and Birkenhead he speeded up a trifle, every now and then casting a loving glance at Molly and the child in her arms.

'I know I'm prejudiced, but I do think that our little Rhiannon was the prettiest baby in ward eight,' he said as the little car trundled along. Chris, squeezing between the two front seats, extended a small and rather grubby hand and touched his sister's cheek.

'Nonny,' he announced. 'Her Nonny.'

Both his parents laughed but Molly corrected him at once. 'It's not Nonny, sweetheart, it's Rhiannon,' she said, speaking slowly and clearly and turning to give Chris's cheek a kiss. 'Can you say Rhiannon? Baby Rhiannon?'

'Yes; Nonny. Baby Nonny,' Chris said definitely, and though Molly laughed she guessed that it would be some considerable while before Chris could get his tongue round his sister's proper name. In the meanwhile she would be known as Nonny, by the family at least.

The journey was a long one and Chris used his little blue plastic chamber pot twice before they had even stopped to eat the sandwiches and drink the flask of tea which Rhys had lovingly prepared. They sat in a lay-by beside a tinkling stream to enjoy their picnic and then Rhys took Chris for a wander whilst Molly fed Rhiannon, decorously draped in a muslin nappy for fear a passer-by might be offended at the sight of a woman breastfeeding her child.

Not that there were any passers-by, Molly told herself, bringing up the baby's wind and deciding not to change her damp nappy until they reached the farm. Then she signalled to Rhys that she was ready to leave and cuddled the baby back into her shawl whilst Chris, full of excitement over the little fishes he claimed to have seen in the stream, fell asleep in mid-sentence on the spare blanket which Rhys had put on the back seat of the car.

When at last they reached the potholed driveway which led to Cefn Farm, Molly felt a surge of excitement and pleasure. This was her home and she loved it! The car drew up outside the back door and to Molly's surprise it opened and a face appeared in the aperture, a wrinkled little face, shyly smiling. Mrs Pritchard, their nearest neighbour. She and her husband and ten-year-old son lived five miles further on along the rough little lane and were always eager to help the Robertses in any way they could. Molly turned round, bewildered eyes on her husband. She had assumed he had brought Chris to the hospital so that he would not have to ask another favour of their neighbours, who had had their only child late in their forties and seemed permanently exhausted by the demands of the hard life they led, yet here was Mrs Pritchard walking towards them, smiling her sweet, anxious smile.

'I asked her to come to feed the hens and the pigs because I didn't know what time we'd be home,' Rhys said rather guiltily. 'But I didn't mean her to hang around until we got back. However, it was good of her, so give her a nice big smile.' Molly did her best to comply and Chris, bouncing out of the car, ran over to their neighbour and began to tell her that his mummy was home with the new baby. He spoke in Welsh, but when Molly began to thank Mrs Pritchard for feeding the stock the other woman answered so haltingly in an accent so strong that Rhys, carting the suitcase and the baby bag, broke into hasty speech. 'It's good of you to stay, Mrs Pritchard; I'm sure Molly will put the kettle on, so we can all share a cup of tea before you go back home.'

As they entered the kitchen Molly said, 'Thank you very much, Mrs Pritchard; you are good! If you would like to sit down and wait for a moment, I will make the tea, but I must put Rhiannon in her cot before I do anything else. As you can see, she's fast asleep, and I don't want to wake her.'

Mrs Pritchard smiled again, then held out her arms and said slowly: 'She iss beautiful ... may I...?'

Molly did not hesitate but willingly laid the baby in her neighbour's arms.

Mrs Pritchard began to say something in Welsh and Rhys translated quickly, speaking directly to Molly. 'Mrs Pritchard says she would like to hold the baby whilst you make us all a cup of tea. She says any time we need a babysitter she will be delighted to give a hand.'

When the tea was brewed, Molly put Rhiannon into the old Moses basket, settled Chris on the hearthrug with a jigsaw and a piece of cake and turned to her neighbour. 'I will really try to learn to speak Welsh, Mrs Pritchard, but I'm afraid I was never much good at languages at school,' she said apologetically. 'Do you think your Rhodri might pop into Cefn Farm on his way home from school a couple of times a week? If he could teach me some useful words and sentences I'd be so grateful.'

Mrs Pritchard agreed at once and sat smiling contentedly whilst Chris chattered to her about his new little sister. Rhys insisted on giving Mrs Pritchard a lift home in the baby Morris and later that evening Molly asked him if he too might begin to speak to her in Welsh, for surely if Chris could learn she should be able to do likewise.

'I hope so,' Rhys said, but he spoke rather doubtfully. 'Our language means a lot to us all; did you know that during the war the men who sent the radio messages from ship to ship in the Navy and from one division to another in the army were nearly always Welsh? The enemy could not understand a word. So you see, Welsh really isn't a dead language and we don't want it to become one. If you're sure it's what you want, I'll speak Welsh to Chris, and I expect you'll soon find you begin to understand everything we say.'

Molly was anxious to do as Rhys suggested and produced an exercise book which she had bought in the hospital shop, announcing that it should become her Welsh dictionary. 'By the time it's full I'll hardly ever need to use it,' she promised Rhys. 'In fact by the time Chris's old enough to go to the village school we'll both be chattering away in English and Welsh. And by the time Rhiannon's in school...'

'Oh, by the time Rhiannon's in school you'll be a positive professor,' Rhys said, laughing. He glanced at the clock above the mantel. 'Do you want me to fetch Nonny through? It's twenty past ten; she's already late for her next feed.'

Ellen and her mother climbed aboard the tram with the baby in Ellen's arms. Mrs Meakin hustled her daughter into a seat, ordering the conductor, in a very peremptory fashion, to 'let the gel sit down. That baby's a new 'un, and don't want no more jiggling about than she can help.'

The conductor grinned. 'Right you are, missus,' he said breezily. 'We don't want to turn the milk sour, do we?'

'Cheeky bugger,' Mrs Meakin said disapprovingly, but Ellen could not forbear to smile. She was so happy with her beautiful baby that she did not care whether she was jiggled or not. All she cared about was getting back to 21 Dryden Street so that she could settle the baby into the Moses basket her mother had given her, and start her new life as the mother of the beautiful little girl who slumbered now in the crook of her arm.

The tram decanted them at the appropriate stop, the conductor shouting to the driver to give these ladies plenty of time to alight. 'They got on at the hospital so the baby's only a few days old,' he assured his colleague, jumping off the tram as soon as it stopped and tenderly assisting Ellen to get down. Then she and her mother waved him a cheery goodbye and set off to walk the short distance between the tram stop and Dryden Street. Ellen had thought the baby a light little burden when they left the ward and was astonished and even a little dismayed to find how heavy the child became as she walked. She said as much to her mother, making Mrs Meakin give a snort of amusement.

'I'd take over, 'cept this here suitcase weighs four times what your babby does,' she assured her daughter. 'What have you got in it, anyway? Bricks?'

Ellen laughed, 'Nah, just me night things and baby stuff,' she said. 'I've never thought of meself as superstitious, but oh, Mum, I wanted this baby so bad and I were so scared something awful might happen that I wouldn't go buyin' anything more than the hospital needed. But I got money hid away so's I can buy her an old pram. Whilst she's little she'll sleep in one of the drawers of the big dressing table, but later on I mean to see she has a proper cot wi' bars an' that; you know, the sort with the side that lets down.'

'Aye, I know what you mean; your sister Myrtle had one when her kids were small. I reckon young Toby is only just out of it so if you can arrange for someone to pick it up I'm sure she'll be glad to give it you.'

'To lend it maybe,' Ellen said cautiously. 'You never know, Myrtle might have half a dozen more kids. She's got five already.'

Mrs Meakin sighed. 'She's a good girl our Myrtle, but she can't say no, nor ever did, and of course Jimmy's a strong Catholic and comes from a big family hisself. He's one of eleven, ain't he? So you're probably right and the cot'll be a loan rather than a gift.'

Ellen thought of her sister Myrtle's three-storey house in Blackpool. It was a happy house. Myrtle's kids shared the big attic rooms on the top floor and her sister and Jimmy took in paying guests in the summer. Jimmy ran a pleasure boat which he was buying on the never-never, and a happier family you would have to go a long way to find. If only Sam were like Jimmy, Ellen found herself thinking. If only he didn't drink; that'd be something. I dare say Jimmy has the odd bevvy from time to time – well, I know he does – but he'd no more dream of being nasty to our Myrtle than he'd fly to the perishin' moon. Still, I s'pose it's just possible my darlin' Lana will make Sam a changed man. Mebbe I shan't have to get one of them court orders to keep him out of the house. Wouldn't it be just grand if he turned into another Jimmy?

She was saying as much to her mother as they reached Dryden Street and her own small terraced house. They approached the front door and Mrs Meakin hauled the key up through the letterbox, fitted it into the keyhole and swung the door wide. 'In you go, chuck,' she said breezily, dumping the suitcase at the foot of the stairs and heading for the kitchen. 'I'll put the kettle on; after carting that big fat babby of yours all the way from the hospital I reckon what you need most will be a nice cuppa.'

Ellen, agreeing with her, followed her into the kitchen and was surprised, even a trifle alarmed, to see that the kettle was already on the stove and hissing gently. She looked round wildly, expecting to see Sam looming up, but instead her neighbours, Mrs Rathbone and Mrs Durrant, stood by the kitchen table beaming at her. 'Welcome home, Mrs O'Mara,' they said, beaming,

Mrs Durrant adding: 'How do, Mrs Meakin? Me and me pal here is longin' to see the little 'un!' Both visitors clucked over the baby, then Mrs Rathbone pointed to the kitchen table. 'I made a cake and there's some biscuits what Mrs Durrant here brought round earlier. We knew you was coming out today but we didn't know what time you'd arrive.'

Ellen licked her lips at the sight of the big soggy fruit cake and the plate of mixed biscuits standing in the middle of the table. The neighbours on either side of her had both moved out since her pregnancy, going to live with married daughters some way off, and their houses had been taken by the two women smiling across at her. So despite having lived in Dryden Street all her married life, Ellen hardly knew them. She supposed that the furious fights between herself and Sam had kept folk at a distance, but Mrs Rathbone and Mrs Durrant were clearly offering friendship and she appreciated what a difference good neighbours could make. They would not interfere between a married couple, but she was sure, now, that these women would give her what support they could.

Mrs Meakin, having seen her daughter and granddaughter safely home, left to catch her tram, and Ellen thanked her new friends profusely, saying that she was just going to put Lana down but would be very glad of a cuppa and a bite when she returned. 'And you must call me Ellen,' she instructed. 'And I'll call you...?'

'I'm Hannah,' Mrs Durrant said, 'and this here...' she pointed to Mrs Rathbone, 'is Janet. If there's anything you want, 'cos you won't be up to gettin' your own messages for a while, I reckon, just give us a knock and let us know.'

Ellen felt tears rise to her eyes. When she had lived with her parents she had taken good neighbours and friends for granted, but now she realised how Sam's attitude had alienated people. She looked hopefully from one face to another. 'You're new to Dryden Street, ain't you? I just hope my husband hasn't disturbed you when he comes in late. He's – he's a docker, you know, and it just so happens that there's a deal of work down on the docks at the moment which means he's got money in his pocket when it comes to finishin' time. I'm – I'm afraid he's fond of a bevvy and sometimes he gets a trifle rowdy. I hope as how he's not disturbed you...'

The two women laughed and began to disclaim and Ellen, taking a good look at them, decided that they were much of an age, probably in their mid-thirties. Since they were both married and since no man was perfect she supposed that from time to time they must have problems of their own. Husbands who drank a little too much, sons who kicked footballs through other people's windows, possibly even daughters who got in the family way and couldn't name the father. But of course at this stage in their relationship it was unlikely that they would divulge any of their own problems to someone they had just met.

In a way, however, Ellen decided that this was all to the good since she had told her friend Molly that she was starting a new life, a life without Sam. Well, time alone would tell whether she had spoken the truth or whether it had been mere wishful thinking. She realised that if Sam had to force his way into the house, kicking doors down or smashing windows, he would be in no very pleasant state of mind when he did gain admittance. She would simply have to let him in, turning him out only if he tried to use his fists and boots on her or the baby. Once he had done that she could go to the scuffers and get one of the court order things which would mean he would not dare to come near her.

But her two new friends were pouring fresh tea, cutting the cake once more and pointing out the pie they had bought so that she might have a meal ready for her husband when he returned home.

''Cos like all fellers, he'll be all the sweeter if there's food on the table,' Hannah remarked. 'My Fred's like a bear wi' a sore head if he comes back to a cold kitchen and the kids hollerin' that they ain't ate nothin' since school dinner.'

'Mine an' all,' Janet Rathbone admitted. 'I've only the one child – Cyril – but he can make as much noise as his da if he ain't fed regular.'

Ellen hesitated; should she say what was on her mind, which was the recollection of the last meal she had made for Sam before going into hospital? She had baked a meat pie, saving up for the ingredients over several weeks, for the austerity which had gripped the land ever since the war ended was still very much in force. A lot of food had been taken off ration but seemed to have completely disappeared and everyone was horribly aware that the lease-lend arrangement with America had ceased as soon as the war was over. This meant, so far as Ellen could make out, that the country had to tighten its belt and pay back as soon as possible every penny that the Americans had poured into the war. So shortages had remained a way of life, but even so Ellen had managed to make a large and delicious beef, onion and carrot pie and had presented it to Sam with more than a touch of pride, but not without a flicker of fear, for he had come into the kitchen as surly as a bear and obviously looking for a fight.

He had found one in the unlikely shape of the pie. He had flicked its glorious golden crust with a disdainful forefinger before announcing belligerently that pie and mash was only good for kids; he was a man he was, and after a hard day's work on the docks he fancied steak and chips.

The sheer idea of laying her hands on a steak was so absurd that Ellen had laughed and that, it seemed, had really put the cat among the pigeons. Since her pregnancy, the threats she had made to kill him as he slept if harm came to her or her child had kept him at bay until the beef pie incident. Then he had forgotten caution, picked up the delicious pie and hurled it through the open kitchen door into the yard. Ellen's cry of distress as she ran outside had only served to increase his rage. He had come at her like an enormous bull charging a very small matador, but Ellen did not think he had actually touched her because she had skidded on the gravy from the pie and ended up on all fours. Sam had tripped over her and gone head first into the privy door, knocking himself out cold. Scrambling to her feet, Ellen had returned to the house for just long enough to pick up the Gladstone bag she had already packed in readiness for her time in hospital. She had cast one disgusted glance at her husband and another sad one at her lovely pie. Then she had lit out for the nearest tram stop, arriving at the hospital just as her pains had started and the first faint rumblings of thunder could be heard on the icy air.

So now, she looked curiously at her neighbours. She could not for the life of her remember whether they had been around at the time when the pie – and Sam – had bitten the dust, but remembering that her husband had just returned from work she supposed that their men, too, had probably just arrived in their kitchens, where the women would be far too busy with the preparation of the evening meal to take notice of the angry mutterings from next door. After all, why should they? On that particular occasion at least Sam had not reached the noisy stage, so that the only unusual sounds the neighbours would have heard would have been the pie crashing to earth in the yard, her own muffled grunt of pain as she fell and the thump of Sam's head as it hit the privy door.

Reassured, Ellen was able to thank both women most sincerely for the shop pie and the jacket potatoes they had baked in her oven so that she could feed Sam when he came in without effort. She was equally grateful for the fact that they jumped to their feet the moment the hooter went, indicating that it was leaving-off time, exclaiming that they would be round first thing in the morning to give a hand both with the new baby and with any messages she might need.

'You are good, both of you,' Ellen said gratefully. 'When I come home first I were a bit scared 'cos I don't know much about new babies, but now you may be sure I'll come runnin' if things get on top of me.'

Both women laughed and Mrs Rathbone went over to where the baby lay and spoke admiringly. 'Ain't she sweet? I well remember how scared I was when I brung my Cyril home, and I'd no need to be afraid 'cos me mum lived with us in them days and knew everything there was to know about babies. So if you need a hand just stick your head out the back door and holler.'

Ellen promised to do so and bade her new friends goodbye. Then she set the table, put the pie in the oven to warm and awaited Sam's arrival, determined to greet him with a cheerful smile and tell him how good their neighbours were. By the time she heard his step in the yard she was ready; the baby, having been fed, slept soundly, and all was in readiness for her husband's return.

Sam came in and crossed the kitchen in a couple of strides. 'Good to have you back, you and the little 'un,' he said gruffly. He thrust a newspaper-wrapped parcel into her hands. 'Brung you a bit of a present,' he muttered. 'I meant to give it to you t'other night when I come hospital visiting only I were late and the bastards wouldn't let me in. So you might as well have it now.' He hesitated for a moment, then spoke so low that she had to bend forward to catch the words. 'I bin talkin' to the fellers at work and they say a kid makes all the difference. They say a feller what falls out wi' the mother of his child has to bite on the bullet and stay away from the house till he's conquered his temper. That's wharr I mean to do now I'm a dad.'

'If you mean it then I'll do everything I can to help you,' Ellen said. She indicated the parcel between her hands. 'Can I – can I open it now?' She took Sam's grunt for agreement and unwrapped the newspaper slowly, half expecting to find something horrid inside. She remembered being told by one of the men on Sam's shift that he had found a bird-eating spider, its body six inches long and its legs twice that length, still alive and kicking after its journey in a crate of bananas. There had been other incidents as well, but common sense told her that Sam was just as frightened of snakes, alligators and other such creatures as she was herself, so she tried to look excited and not apprehensive. Inside the newspaper was a white leather case and when she opened it she saw a truly beautiful necklace made up of crystal drops. She guessed that it had once been part of a cargo intended for a jeweller's shop, possibly in Liverpool, but more probably further away. Sam's nickname on the docks was 'Snatch' and often he would return from work with goods which he had managed to get past the dock police. But right now his eyes were upon her so she gasped with real delight, picked the necklace out of its white satin bed and tried it on, then gave Sam a chaste kiss upon the cheek. 'It's beautiful; thank you so much,' she breathed, carefully replacing the necklace in its case. 'And now, if you'd like to have a wash, we can start our meal.'

As he ate, Ellen told Sam about their neighbours, stressing the fact that both women had offered help. She thought that if Sam knew she had support, he might think twice about coming home drunk and attacking her. He had looked at the baby as she lay cuddled in her blankets and Ellen thought she had detected a slight softening of his grim and deeply seamed face. She thought she could put up with any amount of bad treatment herself – she had grown good at dodging drunken blows – but knew she must make it clear that Lana must never so much as hear Sam's voice raised in anger, far less feel the touch of his huge fists.

But judging by the present he had given her and his whole attitude, perhaps he really was going to change, to become a husband who supported his wife and did not merely take it out on her whenever he was in a bad mood. Crossing her fingers that this would prove to be so, Ellen began to eat.

Chapter Three

Molly woke early because her feet were cold, and her feet were cold because Rhys, sliding silently out of bed in an endeavour not to wake her, had not tucked the blankets at the bottom in properly, leaving a small gap through which an icy draught whistled.

Molly curled into a tight little ball and began trying to rub some warmth back into her cold feet, but after ten fruitless minutes she sighed and gave up. She might just as well get up; heaven knew, with Christmas only days away, she had plenty to do. Now that the children were older – Chris was seven and Rhiannon just five – she and Rhys had saved every penny they could so that the children might have a really good Christmas. Last year both Chris and Rhiannon had had the measles and Molly still remembered that Christmas Day if not with revulsion, at least without much pleasure. Scarlet-faced and feverish, Chris had been cross and aggressive and Nonny had cried every time things did not go her way, which was often. Toys which had been urgently desired were greeted with lethargy, and the thing Chris wanted most – a bicycle – had been sought for all over the house, for Chris still believed in Father Christmas and was sure that his careful note, written some days before, had sailed up the chimney on its way to the land of snow and reindeer, so there was no possible excuse for the absence of his present.

Even this year, the bicycle would not materialise on Christmas Day. For one thing, the Robertses could not afford it – even second-hand bikes were beyond them – and for another thing the country in which they lived, as they had frequently explained to Chris, was not really suitable for cycling. Their lane was a morass when it rained, and carved into ridges of iron-hard mud when it was dry. The farmyard was cobbled and though Chris had pointed out that Daddy could drive the tractor down to the village with the bicycle in the trailer, even he realised that this would be a tedious business.

Rhiannon wanted a doll's pram and they had found one advertised in the village shop for a small sum. Rhys had painted and polished, mended the hood and replaced the brakes whilst Molly had cut an old sheet and blanket to fit and stuffed a neat little pillow with feathers collected from the hen house. They had bought Chris a scooter and would try to explain on Christmas morning that Santa brought bicycles when children got into double figures.

For a moment she clung to the warm bed and then, with the air of a Channel swimmer plunging into the briny on Christmas Day, she threw back the blankets and slid on to the floor. Her feet met one of the three sheepskin rugs that meant she could undertake the journey from bed to washstand without stepping on the lino. Today, however, she bounded briskly past the washstand, grabbed her clothes and stole quietly out of the room. She knew from bitter experience that the water in the ewer would be frozen solid so she had best descend to the kitchen. Rhys would have boiled the kettle, so she could use some of that to wash herself and the rest to make them both a good strong cup of tea. She hurried down the stairs which led straight into the kitchen, but hesitated and turned back when she heard her son's voice. 'Mummy! Wait for us; we're awake so we are!'

Molly laughed and began to retrace her steps, but there was no need; Chris and Nonny, hand in hand, were descending at a good rate, so that they entered the lamplit kitchen together. The previous evening Molly had draped the children's garments on the clothes horse before the range, and now they struggled into them whilst Molly washed at the sink. Then she padded across to the pantry, cut two slices of bread, smeared them thickly with honey and handed them to her offspring. By now she was beginning to shiver and hastily dressed, glad of her thick woollies and the old tweed skirt which still fitted her despite the fact that it had been bought when she was still a bride.

She refilled the kettle and stood it over the flames. Then she began to prepare breakfast, for any minute now Rhys would be coming in and the porridge could simmer while she laid the table. She was cutting and buttering the loaf when Nonny swallowed the last of her bread and honey and jerked at Molly's arm with sticky fingers.

'Mummy, is it Christmas?' she asked eagerly. 'Has Father Christmas been? It was so cold that I didn't even stop to see if there was a stocking on the end of my bed.'

Chris, who had been staring at the flames as though mesmerised, spun round, his eyes bright with excitement. 'Of course it's not Christmas Day, you little silly,' he said scornfully. 'Don't you remember? We went out with Daddy yesterday to cut holly, and we're still making a paper chain long enough to go right the way round the kitchen. Besides, if it was Christmas Day my bicycle would have arrived.'

Molly sighed. She thought that in his heart her son had no expectation whatsoever of receiving a bicycle, but she supposed that hope springs eternal in the human breast and Chris could not help hoping. Perhaps there was also a degree of cunning in the way he harped on about his bicycle. He probably thought that if he nagged hard enough his parents would redouble their efforts to procure for him the present he wanted more than anything else in the world. So Molly smiled at him, for of course he was absolutely right. One of these days, when money was a little easier or a bicycle was advertised for sale at a sum they could afford, then it would be the very first thing they would buy. Smiling to herself, Molly tipped oats and milk into the big porridge pan and set it on the back of the range, glancing up at the clock as she did so.

Rhys would be checking on the sheep – his big flashlight was missing from its hook by the door – though heaven knew they did not want the ewes to lamb in the depths of winter. But with hill sheep it was impossible to say for certain that one or two of them might not have jumped the gun. Every lamb was precious and the sheep tended to return to the flock when the first pangs of birth made themselves felt, so Rhys would do his rounds as a careful shepherd should. And when he had satisfied himself that all was well, he would go into the cowshed and milk their two house cows, and bring the bucket into the kitchen for Molly to use.

Rhys had not drawn the curtains back when he had entered the kitchen but now Molly did so and thought she could discern a faint greying of the light, for though frost flowers made it impossible to look through the glass her glance at the clock had told her morning was coming. Any minute now Rhys would be in for his breakfast, eager to get out of the cold, though even with the fire in the range alight one's breath emerged from one's mouth in puffs of mist.

'Mummy, I don't need porridge now that I've had bread and honey. Can I go and help Daddy with the milking?'

That was Chris, always eager to be with his father, helping to the best of his ability with any farm work of which he was capable.

'No indeed. Porridge lines your stomach...' Molly was beginning as the back door opened, letting in an icy blast before Rhys came in and slammed the door behind him.

He patted Chris's head, then grinned at Molly. 'It's perishin' brass monkey weather out there,' he said. 'But earlier on there must have been a mist; have you taken a peep?'

Molly shook her head. 'Not yet; I've only just dressed and made the porridge,' she told him. Then, eyes widening with dismay: 'Oh, Rhys, don't say it's snowing! A white Christmas is all very well – there has been snow on the tops for days and days – but what with coal being rationed still and the wood pile getting low...'

Rhys went over to the back door and opened it a crack, then changed his mind as the icy wind screamed through the gap and slammed it shut once more. He went over to the window shedding coat, scarf and mittens and placed a hand firmly on the frost flowers, holding it there until the glass had a clear porthole. Then he took his hand away and gestured to Molly to look out of the little window he had made for her.

Molly looked, and gasped. Every tree, every branch, indeed every twig and blade of grass, was dusted with frost. All the buildings were rimed with it, as were the cobbles of the yard, and icicles hung from the cowshed roof like the Christmas decorations she had once helped to put up back home in Liverpool, only those icicles did not sparkle and gleam like the ones she was looking at now.

She turned from the window, almost speechless with the beauty of it, and Rhys, looking at her face, was clearly satisfied with her reaction. 'Isn't that the most beautiful thing you've ever seen, Molly?' he said. 'You won't see nothin' like that in the big cities. Here, Nonny, let Daddy lift you up to look through the window...'

Nonny squeaked with excitement. 'Pretty, pretty!' she said, her button nose pressed to the pane. 'Mummy, can I go out after breakfast?' She wriggled out of her father's arms and ran over to Molly, who was ladling porridge into four dishes.

'It's like the three bears, isn't it, Mummy? Daddy gets the fullest bowl, you get the next and poor Chris gets a tiny one, and I'm Goldilocks and don't get nuffin'.'

Both adults laughed. 'So far as I remember, Goldilocks ended up by gobbling all Baby Bear's porridge,' Molly said. 'I can just imagine the uproar if anyone tried to do you out of your grub, young lady.' She turned to her husband. 'I'm going into the village later to buy a few little extras; is there anything you want?'

Rhys waited until both children's heads were bent over their porridge, then mouthed, 'Sweeties?' which made Molly giggle, though she nodded vigorously. She had saved her coupons and though the toe of each child's stocking would have the traditional orange – or possibly tangerine – the next thing would be a bag of brightly coloured sweets, then a little book and sundry other tiny gifts to swell the stocking into something magical.

Later that morning when Rhys had gone back to his work, taking his son with him, Molly was just thinking that she ought to walk into the village with Nonny when someone banged on the back door and, without waiting for her to cross the room, shot it open and came into the kitchen bringing a breath of icy air with him. Molly, who had been washing up, turned from the sink, dried her hands on the roller towel and jerked a thumb at the kettle. Mr Jones the post, she knew, would be glad of a hot drink. 'Tea or coffee, Mr Jones?' she asked and was not surprised when he gave her a toothy grin and said: 'Oh, a cup of tea, please, missus, strong enough for the spoon to stand up in.'

'Right,' Molly said briskly, whilst Nonny, who had been doing a jigsaw on a tray set out on the hearthrug, jumped to her feet and clutched the postman's trousered knees.

'Jones, Jones, have you seen Father Christmas?' she asked anxiously. 'He's bringing me a doll's pram. I need it, really I do, Jones.'

Mr Jones laughed. He often stopped at the farm for a cuppa and a chat, even unbending enough to pass on bits of gossip; the other day he had related how a child had made a slide in the school playground and the teacher had not seen it until too late. 'Ten feet on his bum, he must have travelled,' Mr Jones had told her. 'And him a man who guards his dignity!'

Molly had laughed. 'Is he that funny little man with very thick black hair which touches his collar?' she asked. 'I suppose I'll get to know all the teachers in time, but though I've lived here for years I still get confused.'

Right now, Mr Jones was assuring Nonny that Sion Corn – 'Welsh that is for Father Christmas,' he added – was having a hard time making Christmas presents for all the children. 'Too little you are to remember the war, but what with rationing and shortages poor old Santa has his work cut out just to fill the children's stockings,' he explained. He took the cup of dark brown tea which Molly was offering and sat down at the table, then clapped a hand to his head. 'Forget my own head next I will! There's a letter for you and a couple of Christmas cards. Open them you can, while I drink this good strong brew.'

Molly took the three envelopes, recognising the writing on each. The Christmas cards came from an aunt and a former neighbour, both in Liverpool, but the letter, she saw with delight, was from Ellen and must be the reply to a missive she had sent her friend the previous week. She picked it up eagerly, slit open the envelope and pulled out three wonderful pages. It was odd, she thought, how close the two of them had grown despite not having met since their daughters were born. But Mr Jones was looking at her bright-eyed, and she smiled at him, realising that she did not want to read the letter with his eyes upon her. He was extremely curious – Rhys said all the Welsh were – and no matter what the letter might say she did not want Mr Jones guessing at the contents from her expression as she read.

She tucked the letter into her skirt pocket. At the kitchen table Nonny and Mr Jones were discussing Christmas. Unfamiliar words such as mince pies and roast chicken were being translated from the English into the Welsh so that Nonny could add them to her already extensive vocabulary, and Mr Jones was telling his small friend of the skating which would take place on the nearby lake when the ice was strong enough, and of the parties and fun which would follow the breaking up of school which would happen the very next day.

Molly half listened, but as so often happened she was actually scanning Nonny's small face, bright with laughter, looking for a likeness ... but to whom? Hard though she had tried, Molly had never managed to completely forget Flossy's words. 'I thought someone switched two of the babies ... the last two to be born,' the girl had said. Molly was almost sure the girl must have been dreaming, or misinterpreted something half seen and not truly understood – it had to be nonsense, after all – but she had not quite managed to convince herself. She thought it was odd that Chris resembled his father so closely that folk remarked on it, whereas Nonny did not seem to take after anyone in particular. Sometimes Molly looked at her and just for a second thought she caught a fleeting likeness to her friend Ellen; at other times she thought that Nonny resembled her own mother. But children change with every passing day, she told herself...

But now Mr Jones had finished his tea and was getting to his feet and Nonny, as she always did, was clutching her friend's trousers and trying to stop him from leaving. 'Please, Jones, stay with me and Mummy. We get lonely when you're gone,' she said. 'Wish I was in school, like Chris. Wish I had a little sister as well as a big brother. I want someone to play with.'

The postman gently detached the child's hands from his navy serge trousers. 'When you get to school...' he began, but was swiftly interrupted.

'I can't go to school for ages and ages and ages,' Nonny wailed. 'I wanted to ask Father Christmas for a brother or even a sister but Mummy says whichever you have it'll come as a baby first, and she can't be doing with another baby anyhow. Oh, it's not fair!'

Molly picked Nonny up and squiggled a kiss into her soft little neck. 'Never mind, Nonny darling, never mind,' she soothed. 'Shall we wrap up warm after we've had our dinner and go into the village for some shopping? We might find something nice for you to have for your tea. But we can't go buying toys or Father Christmas might think we were a greedy family and decide not to come calling.'

Nonny saw the sense in this, and when her father came in for elevenses she urged her mother to get dinner at once, so they could collect Egg and go down to the village to meet Chris out of school. If it would not displease Father Christmas, they might buy a tiny tiny bar of chocolate for her and another for Chris. So as soon as dinner was over, Molly, Nonny and Egg set off.

Egg was five months old, and was already showing signs of being as good with the sheep as his mother, Feather. Chris had had the naming of the pup, the one they had picked from Feather's last litter, and though everyone had laughed when Chris had christened the little dog Egg he had stuck to his guns and the name had stuck to the puppy. Feather's previous litter had produced Caspar and Herbie, each excellent at his work but without that special something which might one day make him into a champion; for Rhys took his dogs to the trials even when they were held at a considerable distance from Cefn Farm and came home with a good few prizes.

As she walked slowly along, picking her way through the deep ridges and hollows, Molly's mind went back to a visit to the nearest town which had been Rhys's surprise present for her. She had revelled in the brightly lit shop windows, the clean pavements and the friendly faces of both shop assistants and other shoppers. They had taken the children to see Father Christmas, and though Chris had thought the water pistol he was given a rather silly present, Nonny had loved every moment and her parents had enjoyed the wonder on her small fair face. Father Christmas had promised that he would bring Chris a bicycle, which had made Molly truly cross. Silly old fool, she thought, where the devil did he expect a hill farmer to find money for a bicycle, let alone somewhere for the child to ride it? Molly had asked herself the same question a hundred times since that day, but now, as she made her way along the track admiring the beauty of the frosted trees, it no longer seemed important. Chris might be disappointed when no bicycle arrived down the chimney on Christmas morning, but she and Rhys had done their very best to fill his stocking with small objects which they thought he would like. All would be well, Molly was sure of it, as she slogged along with Nonny's warm little hand in hers.

Thinking about Ellen, she realised how very lucky she was. To be sure, Ellen and Lana had friendly and helpful neighbours, lots of wonderful shops and the market stalls which had once entranced Molly herself, but they did not have her darling Rhys, who was such a wonderful support, or the beauty of Snowdonia which surrounded Cefn Farm. She decided she would reply to Ellen's letter that very evening. She longed to ask her friend to pop over for a couple of days, but the distance was too great for casual visiting and anyway Ellen's mother had already invited the O'Mara family for Christmas dinner. Ellen had written exuberantly that there was always a neighbourhood party on the afternoon of the twenty-fourth, ending in a wonderful high tea and many silly but exciting games. And what do I have to offer, Molly asked herself ruefully. The farm is too remote for parties, and when we meet at the gatherings, either to dip the sheep or to tag the lambs, everyone is far too busy to sit down and chat or play games. It wouldn't be fair to expect Ellen and little Lana to come to stay when they'd be alone at Cefn Farm with only Molly and the children for company. To be sure, Chris had lots of friends in his class and Molly was sure that Nonny, when she started school the following autumn, would also make friends easily. She was a pretty little girl with light brown curls, round blue eyes and a scattering of freckles, and like her brother she was friendly and easy-going.

Thinking of the entertainment she could offer her friend, Molly had to smile, though as her own grasp of the language improved, so did her social life. She had joined the Women's Institute and made a point of attending the monthly meetings. Rhys drove her down in the little car, often giving Mrs Pritchard a lift as well, for the older woman was plagued by arthritis and would not otherwise have been able to attend, since the long walk into the village was out of the question, especially in inclement weather. Also, when she could be spared, Molly went to the monthly whist drives. These were a bone of contention amongst the villagers, some of whom still clung to the belief that playing cards was somehow sinful, but all the younger women and quite a few of the men enjoyed the evenings in the small community hall attached to the chapel, and Molly knew that mixing with people who spoke Welsh and rarely broke into English was a tremendous help.

Nonny had been gambolling ahead of her, but slowed as the school gates came into view. Already the children were emerging from the small stone building and Chris, spotting them, shouted and waved, then raced up to them and skidded to a halt inches away, rosy-cheeked and breathless. Molly saw that he was only wearing one mitten and that the muffler which should have been wound carefully about his neck had somehow slid off and was hanging off the shoulder of his duffel coat. Molly rewound the muffler, reflecting that children simply did not seem to feel the cold. Her own hands were not only gloved but had been plunged into her pockets for extra warmth, yet here was Chris, losing a mitten and not even appearing to notice.

'Mummy, can I ask Owen to come back to the farm for tea?' Chris said eagerly. 'We could ask his sister as well so Nonny would have someone to play with.' He put his head on one side and smiled beguilingly. 'It would be nice for her to have a friend when she starts school, don't you think?'

Molly smiled and rumpled her son's thick black curls. He and his father were so alike! Nonny had her own colouring, and Molly's hair had darkened as she got older and was now what Rhys told her could be described as chestnut. But Chris was staring up at her, waiting for her answer. 'That's a very good idea, Chris. But what's happened to your mitten? If you've lost it I'll be really cross.

I'm not the world's best knitter but I was rather proud of those mittens. Isn't your hand freezing cold?'

For answer, Chris plunged his hand into his duffel coat pocket and produced the mitten. 'I took it off so's not to get it wet when I picked up some ice off the puddle to suck,' he told her. 'But my hand's not cold, truly it's not.' He looked accusingly at his mother. 'You shouldn't dawdle; if you ran about like me and Nonny you'd soon be toasty-warm.' He seized Molly's hand in his own and even through the wool she could feel his warmth. 'Can we have Owen to tea, Mummy? And his little sister?'

'I just said it was a good idea, which means "yes" if their mummy will let them,' Molly said. 'Now sober down, both of you. If Mrs Enfys the shop has some of those candy walking sticks, I mean to get some to hang on the Christmas tree. We've still got a few baubles left over from last year, but the walking sticks are pretty and taste good as well.'

Ellen was making a cake when the postman rattled on the front door, pushed it open and shouted through the gap. 'Letter for you, missus! There's a couple of cards as well. Want me to bring 'em through?'

Ellen smiled to herself. What the postie meant was did she have the kettle on, but he was far too polite to put his request so frankly. So she just shouted: 'Yes please, Freddie. D'you fancy a cuppa? And there's some biscuits in the tin; just rich tea or digestive, but they fill a gap.'

Freddie, entering the kitchen, slung his mailbag

on the floor and then frowned at his hostess. 'Cup of tea would be grand, and I'm rare fond of digestive biscuits,' he said. 'But it's perishin' cold in here, girl. Where's that sausage thing what you made to keep the draught out?'

Ellen sighed and touched her eye, which was still sore, with a fingertip. 'Sam chucked it on the perishin' fire, and blacked my eye when I tried to hook it out with the poker,' she said glumly. 'But it won't happen again, 'cos I've got one of them court injunctions agin him. I were determined he shouldn't ruin another Christmas for me and Lana so I went and saw a solicitor. I wish I'd done it long ago, but like a fool I believed him every time he vowed he were a changed man. Still an' all, me and Lana are rid of him at last. He knows he'll go to prison if he sets foot inside this house and the bobby on the beat – Constable Jamieson – has promised to keep an eye on us. You know what Sam's like: drinks like a fish and then fights like a wounded rhinoceros, especially at Christmas.' She poured the strong brew of tea into two cups, handed one to Freddie and pulled the other towards herself, sitting down in the creaking wicker chair with a sigh of satisfaction. 'He come down the jigger, screamed abuse at Lana and her friends who were playin' at shop there, and then sloped off, muttering threats that he'd not be turned out of his own home by no bleedin' woman. I tell you, Freddie, getting that injunction was the best thing I ever did in my whole life.'

Freddie sipped his tea and helped himself to another biscuit. 'I'll be bound it was,' he said rather thickly. 'But why did he burn that sausage thing, what I seen you making only three or four weeks back? You said it kept the draughts out lovely. I don't see no point in chuckin' it on the fire 'cos all it would do was douse the flames and make a heap of smoke.'

Ellen chuckled. 'He didn't do it to make up the fire, he did it out of spite,' she explained. 'He said it was because he'd come in and not found his dinner on the table, but it weren't that at all really. I've been hiding a bit of money away towards Christmas out of my wages and when I came down to the kitchen, having settled the child for the night, I found him going through the dresser drawers. I'm not such a fool as to keep cash there, but like an idiot I laughed and asked him what he were looking for. He gave a sort of growl and demanded any money I'd got, 'cos he was skint. I was in the middle of telling him I were skint meself and bending over to lift the casserole out of the oven – it were his meal – when he suddenly gave a sort of roar, grabbed up me lovely draught excluder – that's the real name for the sausage – and poked it into the fire. Then he punched me in the face and crashed out again. By the time poor little Lana came down to see what the noise was about I were picking meself up off the floor and deciding that Sam had belted me for the last time. Me mum cleans for a solicitor, so she took me to see him the next day and the rest you know.'

Freddie was a tall thin man whose drooping moustache was yellowed by nicotine, but he was well known for his willingness to give a hand to anyone in trouble. So it was no surprise to Ellen when he nodded approvingly, unfolded his long legs from the wicker chair and offered to fill the battered hod with fuel for her. Ellen thanked him but said she could manage, and felt excitement warm her face because this would be the first Christmas which would not be ruined by Sam's greedy and spiteful presence.

She had done her best to protect Lana from Sam and had managed pretty well, she thought now, mainly because Sam spent the time when he was not in work drinking, carousing and fighting, and by the time he came home in the evening the little girl was usually in bed. Because Mrs Meakin always invited her family for Christmas Day itself and Sam was always keen to have a free meal, he behaved pretty well over what might be called the three days of Christmas, Christmas Eve, Christmas Day and Boxing Day. He bought small presents for his wife, daughter and mother-in-law, and congratulated Mrs Meakin on the spread which she put before them, and though he did not join in the games with which the rest of the family passed away the rest of the afternoon, he either snoozed in a chair or watched the youngsters playing and gave no one any trouble.

Boxing Day was spent at home, but towards, evening Sam usually grew both restless and bad-tempered. He would take a few mouthfuls of his meal, complaining that it was poor stuff, and then disappear, coming back at closing time roaring drunk and usually failing to negotiate the stairs, so that he spent the night on a chair in the kitchen, always waking in a foul mood for which he blamed his wife. But most of this was already known to Freddie, so Ellen did not labour the point but merely said that though she knew the life of a docker to be a hard one, she was sure that not all the men so employed were as bad as Sam.

'You're right on all counts, queen,' Freddie said. He picked up his mailbag and settled it on his shoulder, then clapped a hand to his head. 'Well, I'll go to the foot of our stairs! I swear I'd forget me own head if it weren't sewed on.' He opened his bag and produced several envelopes, which he handed to Ellen. 'There you are, old love. See you tomorrer. I won't say happy Christmas 'cos the post goes on coming right up till the last minute.' He was heading for the hallway which led to the front door when a shrill little voice caused him to stop in his tracks. Lana came scampering down the stairs, still clad in her nightie but with slippers on her feet, and grabbed the postman's arm.

'Mr Elnett, is it Christmas Day yet? You should know, 'cos you took my message to Santa, the one I threw in the fire like they said you had to. I watched it float up the chimney and Mummy said you'd take it to the North Pole.'

Ellen smiled to herself at the hunted expression on the postman's face. 'Oh aye, I deliver everyone's mail, even Santa's,' he said uneasily. 'But of course I don't have no hand in what Father Christmas gives you. Things is short and lots of stuff is still rationed so poor Santa has a deal to do just to fill your stocking...'

'Oh, but Mr Elnett, I want a doll's pram, I want one more than anything in the world,' Lana said, her voice trembling a little with the strength of her desire. 'It needn't be a big one – there are quite small ones on Paddy's market – but my baby doll what I got last Christmas needs a pram and once I start school I'll be too busy to play with her much.'

The postman gently detached himself from the child's clinging fingers and spoke over his shoulder as he headed for the front door. 'I'm sure Santa will do his best, queen,' he said rather evasively. He cocked an eyebrow at Ellen who gave a little nod; a very small pram was hidden away in the attic at that very moment. Freddie obviously read the meaning of the nod right, for he paused as he pulled open the door. 'But I dare say, if you could make do with a small pram, kind old Father Christmas will pull out all the stops,' he said, then stepped out, closing the door firmly behind him, for the wind was bitter. Lana, having got the answer she wanted, danced back to the kitchen. Her mother smiled lovingly at her, thinking her daughter quite the prettiest child in the whole of Liverpool. Her soft golden-brown hair was cut short and curled round her head and her big blue eyes were always full of laughter and the innocence of childhood. Impulsively, Ellen pulled her thin coat off its hook, wrapped it round the child and sat her down on one of the hard kitchen chairs.

'Porridge for two first, then a nice round of bread and honey, and then I'll give you a hand to dress,' she said.

'Can I bring my clothes down here, Mummy?' Lana asked. 'It's awful cold in the bedroom, though it isn't very warm in here either. Why is the wind coming under the back door?'

Ellen sighed. 'Because the lovely sausage I made to lie along the bottom of the door to stop the wind getting in got itself too near the fire and was burnt up,' she said tactfully. But Lana gave her a knowing look and shook her head till her curls bounced.

'It never got on to the fire by itself; Daddy Sam chucked it there,' she said. 'I heard you telling Granny Meakin how it happened. He did it outer spite, you said.'

Ellen giggled; she could not help herself. She had always tried to play fair by Sam, making excuses for him to the child because she knew how easily, if Lana were to say a word that Sam took amiss, he could do the small girl a real injury. But now of course, with the injunction in force, she would not have to lie. In fact she guessed that it would be a case of out of sight out of mind, because children forget easily and the best thing that Lana could do was to forget her father and everything that had happened in the past. The solicitor had told Ellen that sometimes a man, denied access to his own home, would begin to reform his ways. He admitted that this was rare, but it had happened, and Ellen, remembering the early days of their marriage, could not help feeling wistfully that the Sam who had courted her had been not such a bad sort after all. If only this particular leopard could change his spots, how pleasant life would be! But somehow she doubted that Sam had sufficient strength of character to become once more the eager young man he had been, fun to be with, and a help as well as a companion.

Porridge and bread and honey disposed of, Lana scampered upstairs for her clothes, and Ellen helped her to dress in front of the range, the little girl chattering all the while. 'Mummy? Do you want any messages? Can Janet Cobbler and Phil come with us? Phil's me bezzie, though Janet thinks he's hers. But you can't have two bezzies, can you, Mummy, 'cept when one's a boy and one's a girl; then it's all right, ain't it?'

Ellen smiled at her daughter. 'There's no messages that I can think of, queen. In fact I've so much work in the house – getting ready for Christmas, you know – that I'd like to give shopping a miss. So why don't you, Phil and Janet Cobbler play out? Only don't go catchin' cold, 'cos it's an icy day.' She rummaged in the dresser drawer and produced some small change. 'Here, take that and buy yourselves some roast chestnuts from the feller what stands outside the market. There's enough for the three of you.'

Janet was one of the huge family of Joneses living in the area, singled out by her father's profession as a shoemaker. She was a quiet, neat little girl, like Phil Hodges, a couple of years older than Lana and already in school, so when her daughter was with Janet or Phil Ellen felt she would come to no harm.

Ellen took Lana's old coat from its hook by the kitchen door and helped her daughter into it. Then she wrapped her in a bright red scarf and matching mittens, made sure the pennies were safely tucked into her pocket and saw her off into the icy morning. 'Be back when the clock says half past twelve or you'll go hungry,' she called as Lana crossed the back yard. 'Don't wander too far from home and do as Janet tells you. See you later, queen.'

Janet only lived three doors away so Ellen watched until both small girls emerged into the jigger once more. Then she went back into the kitchen, refreshed her cup of tea and sat down to read her letter. She was thrilled to see that it was from Molly, for Molly's letters were, Ellen thought, like reading a serial story in a magazine. She told of the doings of herself and Rhys and also, of course, of the children. Ellen now understood a great deal about sheep and the life of a hill farmer in Snowdonia; she could even visualise the beauty which was commonplace to her friend but which, nevertheless, she always described in detail. Molly had explained that as well as a good amount of flat land in the valley they owned grazing rights on the nearby mountainside where grass grew wherever it could, even amongst the rocks and the steep screes. The sure-footed sheep grazed on the very narrowest of ledges, but it was rare indeed for a ewe or her lamb to come to grief by a fall. They had a small orchard and a large vegetable garden, both of which were the prerogative of the farmer's wife, and judging from her letters Molly loved the life and would not for the world return to the city, although it was in its way a life as hard as that lived by Ellen herself. However, Rhys was a constant help in every way. If Molly wanted an outing to the village Rhys would take the children round with him, and when next autumn came and both children were in school things would be easier. Molly was talking about getting work, though she was rather vague about what sort, since not only was the farm a long way away from the nearest village, but what little work was available went to

Welsh-speaking people. Molly's grasp of the language improved daily, she told her friend, but she could not claim to be as fluent as someone whose first language was Welsh. However, there were things called 'correspondence courses' which apparently could lead to work even in an area as remote as Snowdonia.

Ellen scanned the pages feeling a little stab of envy. Molly's children never had to worry about traffic or getting involved with drunks from the docks. Lana had had her Saturday sixpence stolen from her by a gang of older children, and had lost a beautiful scarlet woolly cap and matching mittens to a bigger and nastier child. Ellen had had to knit her another pair, but when she had suggested changing the colour to something less attractive her daughter had insisted that red was her favourite. 'Phil and Janet say they'll stick with me and won't let anyone rob me again,' she told her mother. 'Red's a real Christmassy colour, Mummy; holly berries are red and so is Santa's coat and cap. I'll stand up for meself like Phil's always telling me to.'

But Chris and Nonny could play in the surrounding countryside, secure as though they were in their own back yard, and of course Rhys was never far away and was as good a parent as one could desire. Ellen sighed and sipped her tea. Sam was the worst, and lately he'd been downright unbearable, which was another reason why she had applied for the injunction. He had what he called a 'bad belly' and though he ate his food he always grumbled that whatever she put on the table upset his digestion. At first Ellen had felt sorry for him when he'd groaned and griped and sat over the fire drinking hot water and burping like a volcano, but since these attacks simply made him more evil-tempered and violent she soon learned to simply keep out of his way as much as possible.

After the police had served the injunction on him he had come to the front door, trying to persuade her to let him spend Christmas Day at least with his family, but Ellen, usually the most soft-hearted of women, had been warned by her solicitor that this would just be the thin end of the wedge. If she let him break the injunction it would no longer be effective and he could simply come back into her life, probably treating her and Lana even worse than he had before.

Ellen picked up Molly's letter again and read with real pleasure of her friend's most recent doings. She and the two children had taken an old meal sack, a pair of shears and some stout leather gloves, and walked to the woods on a holly-cutting expedition. It had been extremely cold – Molly described how the icicles had tinkled as they cut the scarlet-berried branches – and when Rhys had taken the holly, a great mass of it, into town and sold it, some sprigs of mistletoe and some of the baby clothes his wife had made, they had quite a nice little nest egg to spend on the children. They were having a chicken for Christmas dinner and a pudding in which Molly had buried the traditional silver threepenny bits, and Chris and Nonny were already getting so excited that Molly thought they would probably scarcely eat more than two mouthfuls of the wonderful feast she intended to prepare. Rhys had cut a Christmas tree from the woods, and Molly had made their own mincemeat using fruit jealously saved in the apple loft from their three small wind-bent trees, so they would have the traditional mince pies.

Ellen, reading all this, felt her mouth begin to water, but she told herself firmly that simply because of Sam's absence she and Lana would have a wonderful Christmas. Lana would open her stocking as soon as she awoke, then there would be a cooked breakfast and they would be off to Granny Meakin's for the rest of the day. Of course it would have been lovely, to have the help and companionship of a proper husband but it was not to be. I was a bad chooser, Ellen told herself mournfully as she folded Molly's letter and put it right at the back of the dresser drawer. Even before I took up with Sam I'd gone with big brawny fellers who lost interest if you refused to play when they tried it on. Ah well, that was all in the past. She did not think Sam would approach Lana when she was with her friends, and Ellen herself, with a black headscarf borrowed from her mother, would surely be safe from his attentions. Certainly he would not attack her in the open street or anywhere where there were people who would most certainly interfere. She was sure he would not risk breaking the injunction, so it looked as if she was rid of him at last. Ellen found she could not stop smiling. They would have a *real* Christmas at last!

Chapter Four

Sam awoke on Christmas Day feeling the first rumblings of pain in his stomach and similar rumblings in his mind. He had managed to get a bed in a dirty, dingy lodging house down by the docks. The landlord reminded him irresistibly of Popeye, for he had a chin which stuck out four inches further than his nose, and his teeth were permanently clenched round an empty pipe. He seldom shaved and was covered in fat, or muscles, Sam was not sure which.

Sam had woken chiefly because he was so cold, but also because his head was whirling like a gramophone record on a turntable, and he knew with horrid suddenness that he was about to throw up. Groaning, he lurched out of bed, his feet cringing away from the icy boards. For a moment he was so disorientated that he thought himself at home, and wondered what had happened to the nice soft rug Ellen had placed on his side of the bed. Then his situation came back to him in a rush; she had kicked him out of his own home, the ungrateful bitch. He had paid the rent – not always but sometimes – kept the yard neat, filled the coal scuttle…

A tremendous heave from his inside reminded him of the pints, quarts, or possibly even gallons he had drunk the night before which were now fighting to get out. The room was a dormitory with five beds beside his own, all occupied by sailors who had not managed to get a bed in the seamen's home. They, lucky beggars, snored and slumbered still, but he, who had been a respectable homeowner until he had been ejected by his evil bitch of a wife, was awake and unwell. The room was long and narrow and Sam was scarcely halfway towards the door when the rumblings within became the rumblings without and he vomited all over the floor. The stench was awful, even Sam would have admitted that, had he been able to admit anything. As it was he lurched over to the row of pegs where the men's clothing hung, took down trousers and a thick sweater, neither of which were his, opened the door and stumbled dizzily down the steep stairs. He was muttering: 'Christmas bloody morning and I'm stuck in this horrible hole, debarred from me rightful place by the wickedest woman on God's earth. Well, we'll see how she likes it when I turns up, blacks both her eyes and knocks her bleedin' teeth down her throat. We'll see what she'll do then.'

It was still dark, however, and halfway down the stairs his feet got tangled up and he fell the last half dozen steps and crashed into the newel post. Blackness descended and when he came round he could not imagine where he was or, for that matter, what he was doing there. Where was his cosy bedroom, his plump but comfortable wife and the blankets which he was sure must have been cuddled round his ears only seconds before? He pushed at a door and tumbled into the dirty greasy kitchen of some lodging house – he imagined it was a lodging house – without another soul awake. There was barely any heat left in the stove but there was the odd glowing coal or two and Sam knew that if he used some of the wood chips standing by the hearth and added coal, using the bellows of course, he could soon have a bit of a fire. He was dry as a desert and terribly thirsty and considered a cup of tea, but the way his stomach reacted to the mere thought was sufficient to knock that idea on the head. No, he couldn't face up to tea; what he needed was a hair of the dog that bit him. His eye brightened at the thought of a double gin; now that would warm him all through in the way a glass of water wouldn't. He picked up a pile of wood chips and thrust them through the hole in the top of the stove, added some bits of coal, picked up the bellows and began to work them. Immediately, ash flew everywhere, making Sam stagger back flailing the air and trying to breathe through the whirling cloud, but as soon as he stopped wielding the bellows the dust began to settle and he was able to crouch close to the stove and struggle into the thick serge trousers and seaman's jersey he had nicked out of the bedroom. The fire started to blaze and Sam began to feel warmer at last.

He looked around the room, thinking disapprovingly that it could do with a damned good clean, not connecting the thick layer of dust over every surface with his own recent activities. He was beginning to remember what he was doing in this place, why he was no longer in his comfortable home. He still had his socks on – nobody in the long bedroom had undressed completely, just removed their outer clothing – but he could not remember what he had done with his boots. He slumped into an armchair and looked round blearily. He saw another row of pegs holding donkey jackets and duffel coats and beneath it a line of boots.

Sam had big feet – he took a size twelve – so he would have to be careful when selecting footwear. He could see his donkey jacket on the very end of the row, with its leather patches on shoulders and elbows. He checked the buttons with his eye, because when he was drunk he frequently ripped his coat off without bothering to undo them – pop, pop, pop – and he did not want a coat that did not fasten in this cold. But at least no one had nicked it and probably his boots would not fit anyone but himself. He found them after a short search and was forcing his feet into them when he heard an indignant shout from the upper floor, followed by a crash. Sam grinned to himself. One of those lazy layabouts must have slipped in something; serve 'em right! Still, since it was he who had been sick all over the dormitory floor perhaps he'd better get a move on, be well out of the way before anyone else came down. Hastily, Sam grabbed a handsome fawn-coloured muffler from its peg, then with the speed which only fear could bring went through the pockets of every coat but his own, reaping a better haul than he might have expected: half a crown in one, a pile of coins, too many to count, in another, a couple of empty ones and then – oh joy! – a ten shilling note.

Despite his queasy stomach and the hangover

that was making his head spin, Sam was out of there and legging it up the road within seconds of hearing the first footfall on the steep wooden stair. When he reached the main road he stopped for a moment, shaking his head slowly from side to side. What the devil was happening? He remembered it had been dark when he first woke, but now it was light, light with the pearly grey of early morning, and far away to the east he could just make out the pink and gold of winter sunrise. He also remembered falling on the stairs and giving his noggin one hell of a bump. He believed he'd actually lost consciousness for a few minutes. Sam scowled; what the devil was going on? This road should have been crammed with vehicles and people, yet it was deserted. It was silent as the grave and just about as cheerful, he thought resentfully. Didn't they know that good old Sam O'Mara was up and doing and badly in need of a drink? Didn't they know that after a binge such as he must have had last night a feller needed a hair of the dog? Well, he would wake one of the lazy beggars up, because he had a vague feeling that there would be no drink at home, that his selfish useless wife wouldn't have thought to provide a feller with what he needed most. Still, dockside pubs are open at the most peculiar hours, and if the first one he came to wasn't open he'd batter on the bleedin' door until it was. Sam lurched on. He was trying to remember just why he had spent the night in a narrow, cold and uncomfortable bed in an ugly dirty house owned by Popeye the sailor, but for the moment at least he could not for the life of him remember.

It was nearly noon before Sam was himself once more. The urge to batter down a pub door had passed, though he still felt pretty groggy and his memory was erratic. He was surprised to find that although warmly enough clad he appeared to be wearing someone else's clothes, for the thick Guernsey and the navy serge trousers were seamen's gear rather than docker's, and the muffler, which was lovely and warm, was not the sort of thing the average working man owned let alone wore. But Sam was not too discontented, for he had money in his pocket, and as soon as the pubs opened he would get himself a couple of doubles and a place by the fire. His memory of recent events had come back to him in dribs and drabs over the past couple of hours, and he now knew why the streets were deserted and why he had spent the night in a doss house. It was Christmas Day, so almost everyone was closeted with their families, but his bitch of a wife had had something called an injunction placed upon him, which meant he could not re-enter his own home.

Sam seethed with fury at the treatment Ellen had handed out, but though he was furious with her, and longed to punish her, he was even more annoyed with their small daughter. Before the kid's birth he and Ellen had muddled along all right. A bit like Punch and Judy in the puppet show on the pier, they had started off by exchanging insults and had then begun trading blows. He was much the stronger and bigger of the two, of course, but Ellen had grown both cunning and capable. She had thumped him on the head with the coal scuttle once – he had not felt himself for days – cracked him across the shins with the poker and threatened him with a pan of boiling fat and sliced potatoes – 'eat 'em and be grateful or I'll empty the whole perishin' lot over your ugly head,' she had said, and he had known she had meant it. But when that miserable whining brat had been born, everything had changed. With the baby in her arms she could not fight back, and even when the child was in its cot she would hiss at him to stop shouting, or reply to a punch in the face by whimpering and getting between him and their little girl. He had found this insulting since he had never hit the child, not even accidentally, and did not intend to, telling himself that he was not such a monster.

But promises, which he fully intended to keep, had not been enough and she had applied for this here injunction and now he was as homeless as any tramp, not even able to exchange a few words with his wife far less go within twenty yards of their house. Nevertheless, he meant to spy on them over the Christmas period, to see if he could find some way, some loophole, which would enable him to obtain some sort of Christmas cheer for himself. He knew that his wife and daughter would be at old Ma Meakin's for pretty well the whole day, coming home very late at night, probably laden with presents both of food and of toys for the child, at a time when the streets were pretty well lit but the jiggers were always black as pitch. He dwelt with anticipatory pleasure on the idea of pouncing out as Ellen and Lana, arms full of gifts, made their way to their back gate.

However, he knew that this was just wishful thinking. There was absolutely no way that Ellen would take their spoilt little daughter round the back after dark. He admitted, grudgingly, that Ellen knew him probably far better than he knew her. She must realise he was homeless save for the doss house, and once they'd discovered who had fouled the floor, and taken the warmest clothing from the pegs, he imagined Mr Popeye would be only too happy to kick him out, make him homeless with a vengeance. What was more, the landlord had probably already called in the scuffers over the missing clothing. Sam groaned; it wasn't bloody well fair. What had he actually done, when it came right down to it? He had slapped his wife around a bit, but didn't everyone? So far as he understood it, that was just marriage, and heaven only knew old Ellen had got her own back one way and another, yet there was she, enjoying a wonderful Christmas Day whilst poor Sam was out in the cold; no grand dinner, no comfortable place by the fire, no hot toddy to drink with the mince pies at which Ellen excelled. His eyes filled with tears of self-pity, but then he remembered that by now the pubs would be open and he still had money. He shoved his hands into his donkey jacket pockets and felt the lovely round half-crown, the pennies and halfpennies, sixpences and shillings, and last of all the crisp beauty of the ten bob note. He would hang on to that note, for until dock work started again after the holiday it might be all that stood between him and the life of a tramp, sleeping on benches with a newspaper his only blanket.

Sam set off in the direction of his favourite watering hole, a pub much frequented by dockers. Crabby Cranshaw was one of his regular drinking partners, and now it occurred to Sam that Crabby might well introduce him to his own doss house, for Crabby, too, had had woman trouble. He had never actually married his Daisy, but had managed to father near on a dozen kids on her. The couple were famous for their ferocious fights and it was no unusual thing for Crabby to find himself kicked out after a particularly drunken argument. When Crabby could not gain access to his own home, he would go first to the pub and then to a doss house which he always swore was near on as good as his home in Snowdrop Street. However, before availing himself of Crabby's counsel, Sam meant to come back after dark and see if there was any way he could gain admittance to his own house after Ellen had taken herself off to bed. He still had his key, and he could help himself to some of the Christmas grub with which the pantry would be laden, snooze in front of the fire, and leave before the first tram came rattling out of the depot.

Sam rubbed his hands gleefully at the thought; yes, if he played his cards right he would have a comfortable billet for the night. Dreamily, he planned the food he would eat, the hot cup of tea he would enjoy before settling down on the creaking old sofa pulled up close to the fire. It would not be the first time by a long chalk that he had spent the night in the kitchen, unable or unwilling to face the struggle of getting his drink-sodden body up the steep and narrow flight of stairs. He would wait, he decided, until his womenfolk had been in bed for at least twenty or thirty minutes. Then he would go down the jigger, ease open the back gate, cross the yard and slip into the kitchen through the back door. He must remember to lie down on the sofa with extreme caution, since the springs had always creaked when they felt his weight. But once settled, with a comfortably full belly and a jug of water to hand in case he grew thirsty after his potations, he would sleep the hours of darkness away. When morning began to grey the sky he would go to the pantry and take as much food as he could carry in the pockets of his donkey jacket. He would sneak out, locking the door behind him, and though Ellen might suspect that he had entered the house clandestinely she would never be certain, and if she was not certain she would think twice before complaining to the scuffers.

Immensely cheered by the thought of the pleasures to come, Sam pushed open the door of the alehouse.

In the warmth and cheer of the pub, Sam found plenty of his old mates who sympathised with his plight, though rather to his disappointment no one offered him a bed. Crabby, however, so nicknamed because he was always taking 'a nip of this and a nip of that', had already decided not to return to his own home that night, due to a row over some missing money. Instead, he had booked himself a place at his regular doss house, and assured Sam that there would be a bed for him if he had half a crown to spare. Sam, fingering the ten shilling note wistfully, said that if his wife really wouldn't let him return to his own house he would be glad to take up Crabby's offer. Until the landlord called time, therefore, the two men drank sparingly, and on being turned out into the cold – for the temperature had not risen above freezing all day – they went along to a Salvation Army hostel where a party for seamen a long way from home was being held. They managed to insinuate themselves into the party by saying that they were brothers married to two sisters, and that the girls had gone into the country to visit relatives. 'But we's workin' the day after Boxin' Day, as soon as dockers is needed,' Crabby, always inventive, had explained. 'So no trips into the bleedin' country for the likes of us. We's okay for a bed, like, it's just we're on the loose daytime.'

The kindly Salvationists had welcomed them, and when they left it was getting late. Crabby, shaking his pal's hand with all the bonhomie of the comfortably drunk, wished Sam luck and then disappeared in the direction of the cheap lodging house.

Sam ambled along, now and then bouncing off a brick wall and cursing as he slid on a patch of ice. When he reached his own road he began to act more cautiously, for here there were no walls or hedges since the front doors of the houses abutted straight on to the pavement. He checked that, so far as he could tell, his house was unoccupied, then went down the jigger and leaned against the wall. He knew the gate would probably be bolted on the inside, but as he had done so often in the past he reached a long arm over it and gently eased the bolt back. Then, like a cat at a mouse hole, he simply waited.

He was beginning to feel cold, despite the drink he had taken, when he heard the sound of approaching feet. Several people, some in small groups, others singly, had passed the end of the jigger, but these footsteps were accompanied by conversation, and he recognised both Lana's high piping and Ellen's comfortable, motherly tones. 'Well, weren't that the nicest party we've ever been to?' Ellen enquired. 'No fightin', no arguin', none of that nasty feeling someone were lookin' for a quarrel. Just a grand dinner, a delicious tea and the best games Granny Meakin could think up.' She gave a gusty sigh of satisfaction. 'And no bloody man to be humoured and avoided,' she concluded. 'Weren't it a grand day, our Lana?'

'Yes, it were lovely. Didn't you think so, Phil?'

In the darkness of the jigger, Sam shrank back against the wall, cursing under his breath. So it wasn't just Ellen and Lana carefully negotiating the frozen pavement, but that bloody little nancy boy, Phil Hodges, and very probably his mother and possibly his father too if Mr Hodges, who was a tram driver, was not on shift. Sam presumed they had been included in old Ma Meakin's invitation for Lana's sake, and cursed again. He wouldn't have minded confronting his wife and Mrs Hodges, but Bill Hodges was a very different cup of tea. During the war he had worked as a stoker aboard a battleship and was a great bull of a man with shoulders as wide as a barn door and fists like Sugar Ray Robinson's. Like many big men he had the reputation of being as gentle as a child, but Sam did not intend to risk an encounter with a fellow twice his own weight, so he waited until the small group had moved on before letting out a sigh of relief. Since she was accompanied by the Hodges, Ellen might easily have decided to come down the jigger and use the back entrance, but she had not done so, and of course when Sam considered he realised why. The Hodges lived on the opposite side of the road, so had Ellen decided to use the jigger she would have been alone with the kid.

Sam waited, ears pricked. He heard his wife murmuring goodbyes, thanking the Hodges both for their company and for the presents they had exchanged, heard her pushing her key into the lock, pulling the door open and ushering Lana inside. More goodbyes were exchanged amidst much goodwill and laughter. Then the front door was closed and locked once more, and even as Sam watched light bloomed in the kitchen. There was scuffling and movement within and Sam guessed his wife was making up the fire and then damping it down so that it would stay in all night. It seemed a long time, for somehow the knowledge that his wife and child were indoors in the warm made the outdoors seem even colder, but at last the light in the kitchen went out and upstairs the light in the little back bedroom, which was Lana's, came on.

Fuming with impatience, Sam stared at the window, saw the curtains pulled across, saw all the lights go out at last and forced himself to wait until he was as sure as anyone could be that the inhabitants of number 21 were fast asleep. Only then did he gently ease open the gate and approach the back door. By now his large stubby fingers were so cold that his first two attempts at getting the key into the lock were foiled by his dropping it on to the back doorstep. He was almost sobbing by the time he managed to get it into the lock, but when he tried to turn it he realised he still had not pushed it in far enough. He gave it another shove and gripped it viciously hard, this time using both hands, for the key was a big old-fashioned one, but even by asserting his full strength he could not get it to turn. It took him three tries and a good deal of sweat before it was borne in upon him that the key simply did not fit the lock.

He stepped back and such was his rage and humiliation that he had actually drawn back his foot, intending to try to kick the door down, when a window above his head shot open and he found himself deluged with a mixture of what he hoped was water and lumps of ice, whilst a voice he knew well said jeeringly: 'I weren't born yesterday, you silly old bugger! The scuffers told me to change the locks 'cos they reckoned you might be fool enough to try to gerrin. You're lucky I emptied the ewer over you and not the jerry. Now bugger off, 'cos there's no way you're going to gerrin and if there's any damage done to my house – *my* house, do you hear me? – then you'll find yourself in a police cell until you've paid for it.'

'If I could gerrin there I'd...' Sam broke off. Rage would get him nowhere except, as she said, into a prison cell. So, though it went against the grain, his tone changed. 'Ellen, my love, it's a mortal cold night and I've nowhere to lay me head...' He was rudely interrupted.

'If you go right now, without giving no more trouble, then I won't report you, 'cos it's Christmas, but if I see your face anywhere near me or mine again I swear you'll regret it,' Ellen said, and to Sam's astonishment her voice was quite calm, almost friendly, but very very definite. Ellen O'Mara had stated a fact and nothing he, her lawful husband, could do would change it. Sam turned away from the kitchen door and slunk across the courtyard and out of the gate, but when he reached the jigger his fury erupted and had to find expression in some act of violence. He still held the useless key in one fist and he turned and flung it with all his force at the bedroom window.

'Don't worry, you ugly cow,' he yelled as the key crashed through the glass. 'If I'd gorrin I'd have rung your bleedin' neck, so be thankful, 'cos next time ... next time...'

But Ellen had closed the window with a final snap and the threats that would once have terrified her were made in vain. Sam slammed the back gate but did not bother to shoot the bolt. His rage had at least warmed him up, but now the knowledge that he must walk all the way to Crabby's doss house chilled his flesh, and brought once more the self-pitying tears to his eyes. He emerged from the jigger, realising it was midnight as the street lamps began to go off one by one, telling himself that he would get his revenge on Ellen and the kid, but not now, not tonight, probably not for many nights to come. He was just about to turn right towards the docks when a hand – a very large hand – seized him by the collar and a voice he did not immediately recognise spoke in his ear.

'Hello 'ello 'ello, what have we here?' The hand did not ease its grip but a large flashlight illumined Sam's far from beautiful features. 'So it's you, Sam O'Mara, makin' that damn awful row. Botherin' your poor wife again, eh? Couldn't you even let her have her Christmas in peace? Well, she'll have a rare quiet Boxing Day, 'cos you'll be in the cells for breaking the terms of your injunction. I just hope Judge Martin is taking the session you'll come up in, 'cos he's a hangin' judge he is. I'm tellin' you, O'Mara, when your wife reports what you've done, your feet won't touch the ground.'

Sam began to whine that he'd done nothing, that he'd merely wanted to call on his wife and child to wish them both a happy Christmas, but Constable Jamieson, clicking the handcuffs round Sam's beefy wrists, gave a disbelieving laugh. 'You're a lying toad, O'Mara, always were, always will be,' he said cheerfully. 'I know you, so you must know me and you must realise that I've been keeping an eye on your wife ever since the court hearing. Who am I, O'Mara?'

Sam looked up – for though the two men were almost of a height Sam was subconsciously trying to make himself seem as small and innocent as possible – into what he could see of the face beneath the high domed helmet. 'Oh, Gawd, Police Constable Jamieson,' he said wearily. 'Wouldn't you know it? Just my luck to walk bang into the one feller I most didn't want to meet.'

Alex Jamieson chuckled. 'If you'll take a bit of advice O'Mara, you won't hang around this area,' he said. 'While you're just about anywhere in Liverpool you'll be tempted to start up old habits, and it won't do. You've got a good wife there and a grand little girl; why not give them and yourself a bit of a break? You've been to sea, haven't you, in the past? Well, I know you have, because you were with the merchant fleet during the war, as I recall.'

As he spoke they were making their way towards the nearest police station, and Sam was reminding himself that at least the cell which awaited him would be warm. He would very likely get a cup of tea, too, and later on a cooked breakfast. And nothing to pay, either, he thought, trying to make the best of things.

'O'Mara, cat got your tongue? I just asked you...'

'Sorry, sorry,' Sam said quickly. 'Yes. You're right, I were with the merchant fleet, but that were a fair while ago; I dunno as I could face going to sea again. I were seasick at the start of every voyage...'

'Better seasick than in the dock on a charge of grievous bodily harm or worse,' the police constable said grimly. 'You're going to have to make a choice, O'Mara; you either forget you have any rights over Ellen and the little 'un and stay clear, or you get as far away from Liverpool as you can. So if I were you I'd tell the judge when the court reopens after the Christmas break that you're applying for a job aboard ship, so's to keep clear of your family. Savvy?' And Sam, thwarted of his longed-for revenge, said wearily that he supposed he would take Constable Jamieson's advice.

By the time Sam had paid his debt to society – he was given three months for breaking the injunction – spring had arrived. Constable Jamieson, who had met Sam the day after he had emerged from Walton prison, was disappointed to find that his incarceration had not been the salutary lesson the court had intended. Perhaps it was because he was heading for the nearest pub and resented the constable's stopping him to have a word, but his whole attitude made it plain that he blamed Ellen and the kid for his imprisonment, and judging by the spiteful gleam in his eye would have taken revenge if only he could have thought of a way of doing so without getting caught.

Naturally enough, the constable had asked Sam whether he had yet tried for work either as a docker or aboard one of the many ships whose home port was on the Mersey, but Sam had growled that he'd scarce had time to turn round since his release and had not yet thought of work; he would collect the dole until a job turned up.

Alex had opened his mouth to tell the man that work was unlikely to land in his lap, but Sam was already moving off and Alex did not attempt to follow him. However, he determined to keep an eye on Ellen and the child, just in case Sam really had not learned his lesson.

As soon as he could he went to the house in Dryden Street, only to find it deserted. He went round to a neighbour, a fat slatternly woman who beamed a welcome at the policeman and ushered him into her dirty kitchen, offering a cup of tea in a stained mug which she had obviously just drained herself. 'I reckon you're wonderin' where the O'Maras ha' gone,' she said as soon as she had closed the back door behind him. 'Her old feller come out of the jug yesterday – he's a bad 'un he is, as I reckon you know – so she's lit off to live with her mum for a bit. Someone telled her Sam were going to sign on a ship, but if the ship's home port were Liverpool he'd still be back here every three weeks or so. Here, come on! Everyone knows scuffers need a cup of char every hour on the hour.' She thrust the dirty, much-used mug towards him and judging by the twinkle in her eye Alex guessed that she knew why he was refusing it.

'But Sam knows where Mrs Meakin lives,' he pointed out, hoping to deflect her mind from the tea. 'That's the first place he'll look; if he's fool enough to try to contact her again, that is.'

The woman chuckled. 'Mrs Meakin's done a swap. They've moved out to Old Swan; one of them tall, wobbly three-storey houses. I'm the only person what knows where they've gone and I swore I'd not tell a soul, 'cept for yourself.'

'Right,' Alex Jamieson said briskly. He grinned at his companion, took a heroic swig of tea from the dirty mug and patted her shoulder. 'Best give me the address, so's I can check that Sam ain't hangin' around there.'

The woman chuckled wheezily and whispered the address, which Alex wrote down in his incidents book. Then he left her to continue on his beat, hoping that Sam would soon grow tired of life on the dole and start looking for a berth.

A week later he had to accompany a heavily pregnant woman to the maternity hospital. She had fallen in the street and started her pains, and having seen her into safe hands he was about to leave when he heard someone call his name. Turning, he saw that it was little Flossy Manners, and retraced his steps, smiling. He liked Flossy, and admired her grit and determination, because despite every sort of difficulty she had stuck to her guns, worked morning, noon and night until she was taken on as a probationer.

'What are you doing here?' she asked, grinning up at him. 'Going to have a baby, Constable Jamieson? If so, I'll put you on my ward, then you can be sure of getting the best possible attention.'

Alex laughed, but shook his head. 'Not today, thanks, you cheeky young varmint,' he said. 'But I've been meaning to have a word with you. You live on Dryden Street, so you'll know Ellen O'Mara – the one who had a baby on the night of the storm five years ago? Her husband beat her up until she got an injunction against him. Well, he got three months inside for breaking it and got out just over a week ago. He's a feller with a big thirst as well as big fists, so I've been keeping an eye. Most of the dock police know him and yesterday one of 'em told me Sam had signed on a coaster, one of them small to middlin' ships which only get back to their home port every six or nine months. All things being equal, I reckon he'll have forgotten his grudge against poor Ellen after a voyage of that length, but it would do no harm for you to keep an eye open and let me know if you see him hanging about.'

Flossy pulled a doubtful face. 'I remember Mrs O'Mara telling me that her old feller got seasick, which was why he quit the sea and started in as a dockie. He can jump ship any time, can't he?'

'Oh aye, in theory,' Alex agreed. 'But the coaster he's on plies mainly up and down North and South America and the West Indies, carrying timber. So if he does jump ship, he'll have the devil's own job to get back to dear old Liverpool. Of course, it's impossible to say for certain, but I'm hoping that Mrs O'Mara's troubles are over.' He looked down at Flossy's smooth fair hair, pulled back from her face in a tight little bun. He liked her a lot, but they were both working shifts and their time off never seemed to coincide, so that what with her exams and his own they rarely met. But she was twinkling up at him and Alex suddenly decided to take the plunge. 'I'm off duty tomorrow, and with a bit of luck this sunshine's here to stay for a few days,' he said. 'Do you like walking? I'm going to catch a bus out to Moreton Shore, take a few sandwiches and spend the day out of doors; care to join me?' He watched as a pink flush crept up her slim white neck and dyed her face a most becoming shade of rose. Then she grinned at him.

'I thought you'd never ask,' she said cheekily. 'As it happens I'm off shift meself tomorrer so I'd be glad to come with you. Tell you what, I'll make a couple of Cornish pasties – big 'uns – and bring some ginger beer. It'll be grand to get out of the hospital and breathe some country air!'

Despite knowing he was acting foolishly, Sam could not resist strolling idly along Dryden Street, though he did not pause outside his old home; that would have been madness indeed. He deeply resented Constable Jamieson's interest but told himself that once he was aboard the *Buds of May* he would do well to forget all about his wife and child.

Nevertheless, the fact that a mere woman had triumphed over him gnawed at Sam like the pain of a bad tooth, and he knew that the only thing which could ease that pain would be paying Ellen back for her cruelty. He told himself that immediate revenge was not possible, but he decided that he would keep his eyes open when he was in Liverpool, and one of these days...

Once aboard his ship, however, he was too busy to dwell on the revenge for which he longed, but in his bunk at night he plotted how he could hurt Ellen without running into trouble himself. He decided his best bet would be through the child, because he guessed that Ellen would always be on the lookout for him whereas Lana would probably have forgotten what he looked like after a few more months; she was only five, after all. He decided that once she was in school he might hang around outside the gates when the children came out. He had no clear idea what he would do but told himself he would not harm the child. He would just take her off somewhere for long enough to terrify his wife; that would have to do, for the present at any rate.

Sam bunched up his pillow and began to look forward to his ship's arrival in the South American port to which it was headed. There would be pretty girls, interesting food and a good deal of drink. Sam smacked his lips; perhaps Ellen had done him a good turn when she made a job on the docks impossible. Liverpool was not the only port in the world, nor was Ellen the only woman. Not that he intended to marry again, not he! But you never knew, he might settle down in some foreign port with a nice little dockside whore and make a home for himself there.

Sam was smiling as he fell asleep.

Chapter Five

'Daddy, why can't I go with you? You're taking Chris and he's only two years older than me. Is it because I'm a girl? If so it's not fair!'

Rhys sighed. The family were in the kitchen having their breakfast and it was the first day of the summer holidays, which meant that Molly would be at home. She had worked, Rhys knew, every hour that God sent at her correspondence course, and had succeeded in obtaining a job as classroom assistant at the local school. She loved the work, particularly as it was a job share, which meant that she and Mrs Gladys Thomas took it in turns, three days on and two days off, on alternate weeks. Mrs Thomas had once been an uncertificated teacher at a school some ten miles from her own village, but now that she was in her fifties she found full-time work too much and was happy to share both the work and the money with the younger woman.

Rhys acknowledged ruefully that Molly was far too busy at Cefn Farm to take on a full-time job. When the time for the gathering of the flock for dipping, washing or shearing came round she was an essential part of the team, and he knew she found the hard physical work of handling the sheep and the fact that she was out of doors a pleasant change from her classroom duties. But now, with a blissful seven weeks of holiday ahead, she had told him that she intended to treat her family to lots of home baking and delicious meals and some exciting outings too. He shook his head chidingly at the ten-year-old Nonny, spooning the last of her porridge into her mouth and gazing at him with pleading eyes.

'Look, Nonny love, Chris, the dogs and myself will be having a long day out, checking the sheep, mending the fences and rounding up any strays. I know you think it's great fun to be out and about and so it is; but tomorrow you'll be off with Rhodri and Chris rounding up the Pritchards' flock. Today your mum could do with a hand, and it's about time you learned to bake.'

'Oh, but Daddy, cooking's easy. Anyone can do it, and besides it's a warm day and once the oven gets going we'll be sweating cobs, me and Mum, and I'll be no use, honest to God I won't, whereas if I'm with you and the dogs...'

Rhys interrupted her without compunction, recognising the hurt Nonny was inflicting, albeit unintentionally, upon her mother. 'Rhiannon, if I've heard you say it once I've heard you say a hundred times that when you grow up you're going to marry a hill farmer. If you can't bake or cook, how are you and your husband to survive? Oh, I know some women buy shop bread and cakes, tins of stewing meat and boiled bacon at enormous prices, but surely you don't intend to copy them? Why, even Chris knows how to do bits and pieces of cooking, but you're so anxious to get out of housework that your mum told me the other day you don't even bother to make your bed properly, but just pull the blankets up and hope no one will notice.'

His daughter's lower lip stuck out, but she made no more objections because she knew that when her father used her full name it meant he was serious. 'All right, Dad; sorry,' she mumbled, and then to Rhys's pleasure she jumped up from her place at the table and ran round and gave her mother a hug. 'I'm sorry I was so horrid, Mum,' she said. 'I know I really ought to learn to cook, it's just that it's the first day of the holidays and I do so love being out of doors.'

Chris collected the empty porridge dishes and carried them over to the sink, then spoke for the first time since the argument had begun. 'Dad didn't take me to round up the sheep when I was ten either, Nonny. In fact this will be my first time, so you've no need to get jealous. You're being treated just as I was, girl or no girl.'

Rhys chuckled. 'And remember, you've promised to go and help the Pritchards tomorrow,' he reminded her. 'If I remember the plan aright, you and Chris are meeting up with Rhodri and getting the sheep down from the heights because you young 'uns make nothing of scrambling up screes which would baffle Mr Pritchard. Rhodri will take good care of you and see you don't go breaking a leg, so you can't grumble over one little day spent helping your mum, can you? Not when you'll have a whole day with Chris and Rhodri.'

Rhys was well aware that his daughter had a crush on their neighbours' handsome son, despite the fact that he was ten years older than she, and laughed when he saw her blush, patting her cheek. 'So no more grumbles, pet. Agreed?'

Chris plunged the dishes into the sink, seized the kettle and poured hot water into the bowl. As soon as the breakfast things were cleared away, Molly made a pack of sandwiches and cake, added two bottles of cold tea, and flung open the back door, letting in the warm farmyard smells as well as the sunshine, then jerked her thumb towards the yard. 'Off with you!' she said gaily. 'We shan't expect to see you again until supper-time. If you aren't back then I'll milk Jessie, and of course Jacob will do any heavy work which Nonny and I can't manage.'

Rhys laughed, lifted his wife off her feet and swirled her round, kissed the tip of her nose and stood her down. 'Take care of yourselves,' Molly said. 'And if you find a sheep in trouble, for the Lord's sake don't go mountaineering, because that's the way accidents happen.'

Chris assured his mother that with the dogs to help them they would have no need to go mountaineering. 'Sheep are just about the silliest animals you can imagine but they hardly ever get stuck in awkward places,' he reminded her. 'Even in the harshest of winters most of them manage to survive.' He grinned at Rhys. 'I remember you telling me once that our flock were half sheep and half goat, because they can scramble up a sheer incline with no more fuss than if it was flat as a billiard table.' He had taken the sandwiches Molly had prepared and now lifted a corner of the greaseproof paper. 'What's in mine, Mum? Not perishin' Spam, I hope.'

'Course not. It's cold mutton,' Nonny put in, and laughed at her brother's crestfallen expression. 'Oh, Chris, you'd believe anything! It's your favourite – cheese and tomato and four of Mum's big pickled onions. See you later!'

As soon as the men had disappeared, Molly began to plan her day, taking care to discuss everything with Nonny, since she could scarcely expect the child to give help where it was most needed unless the need was first explained. So she sat Nonny down at the kitchen table and got out her old recipe book. Together, they discussed what they should bake, what ingredients were needed for each dish and how to divide the work about the house and the farmyard, which was now their responsibility for the day.

Rhys had managed to acquire a farm worker, though he had only done so because Jacob was, if not actually simple, at least extremely slow on the uptake, which meant that no one else was keen to employ him and he was willing to work for a wage that Rhys could afford. Jacob had been with them now for five years, and provided Molly – or Nonny for that matter – told him exactly what to do they could be sure their instructions would be followed to the letter. Molly, collecting her ingredients from the pantry, smiled to herself. Once, Jacob had been sent to the village to fetch the letters from the post office, since Mr Jones was at home nursing a summer cold. He had returned with a lettuce, and when the mistake had been explained to him he had laughed, called himself a fool and returned to the village to collect the mail. On another occasion, Molly had been gathering peas, and had filled her basket before she had picked all the ripe pods hanging from the vine. She had asked Jacob to go into the kitchen and fetch the colander, which he would find hanging on a wall hook with other such utensils, and he had returned with the calendar, saying in a puzzled voice as he handed it to Molly that he did not think she would manage to balance many pods upon its shiny surface. Once again, when Molly had explained, he had laughed at his own stupidity, and to his credit he seldom made the same mistake twice. In fact he was an excellent worker, provided he was told exactly what to do and supervised throughout each task.

Rhys often thought that without Jacob's help he would not now own two good hay meadows and three fields of grain, for though the vegetable garden had been in full production when they had bought the farm the elderly vendors had allowed the meadows and fields to lie barren for years. Although Rhys and Molly had worked like Trojans, Molly had concentrated mainly upon the production of vegetables and fruit and Rhys was initially too busy with the sheep to tackle the extra work of bringing the valley land back into good heart. But when Jacob joined them, the two men had ploughed, harrowed, manured and sown new seed and within two years were rewarded by good crops of both hay and grain. Delighted, Rhys had given Jacob a small rise in his wage and had been rewarded by Jacob's almost dog-like devotion. Knowing himself to be a valued member of the Cefn Farm team, Jacob worked harder than ever and even felt able to make suggestions when appealed to.

Now, when someone rattled on the back door Molly guessed it was Jacob, come to get his instructions for the day, and even as she went towards the door it opened and Jacob's long face appeared round it. 'Mornin', missus; mornin', Nonny,' he said in his slow, flat voice. He eyed the table appreciatively, for Jacob loved his food and was always first to come to the kitchen for his meals, though since he could not tell the time Molly often wondered how he did it. At last he dragged his gaze from the evidence of baking to come and stared hopefully at her, clearly awaiting instructions. Molly told him to feed the pigs and poultry and then return to the kitchen, because by then she would have prepared their elevenses. Jacob nodded enthusiastically but lingered for a moment. 'You going to make them nice little pancakes, missus?' he asked hopefully. 'The ones you spread with butter or honey?'

Molly laughed, then turned to her daughter. 'Well, cariad, would you like to make some Welsh cakes for elevenses? Or would you rather make fruit scones?'

Nonny's fair little face flushed with pleasure; clearly she was beginning to enjoy her involvement in the day's work. 'I'll make the scones first and then do the Welsh cakes, so they'll be lovely and hot and buttery in time for elevenses,' she said eagerly, and waved goodbye to Jacob as he went back outside, smiling happily at the thought of the promised treat. 'Oh, and you promised you'd show me how to make meringues and egg custard, because you said we'd need egg yolks for the custard, and egg whites for the meringues.'

'Yes. Your daddy simply adores meringues, so since the hens are laying so extremely well I thought we'd make some as a surprise. As for egg custard, it would be a crime to waste the yolks. In fact it would be a nice gesture to make a custard especially for Jacob to take home. His mother can't afford to do much fancy baking and last week Jacob told me that they've only got a couple of hens in lay, so I promised him next time we had a broody I'd make sure he got the chicks.'

'Could we make one for Rhodri as well, Mum?' Nonny asked eagerly. 'They do keep hens but Mrs Pritchard was saying only the other day that they're all old and not very productive. I'm sure Rhodri would love an egg custard, especially if you made it in a pastry case so all the Pritchards could have a slice.'

Molly agreed to do this and as the morning wore on she was delighted to see how hard her daughter worked, and how interested the child became in the tasks she was set. She'll be a grand little cook one of these days, Molly told herself, as the two of them began the Herculean task of baking sufficient bread for the week to come. Nonny pummelled gently at first, then with more enthusiasm, leaving the dull work of greasing the loaf tins to her mother whilst she worked happily at her first bread making.

Jacob was not the only one who enjoyed the Welsh cakes, either, Molly thought as the three of them sat round the table to drink their tea and eat the flat little griddle cakes which her daughter had just made. She had decided to have a cold meal at midday but changed her mind when she saw Jacob eagerly eyeing the minced mutton which she meant, presently, to turn into shepherd's pie. The filling was made and cooked; all she had left to do was to boil the potatoes, mash them with some milk, spread them over the top and put the large dish into the oven to brown.

Having eaten his share of the Welsh cakes and drunk his tea, Jacob sloped off to clean down the cowshed, a task he performed every morning, and mother and daughter settled down to continue cooking. There was much hilarity in the kitchen as Molly demonstrated all the methods she knew of separating yolks from whites, including breaking an egg into the palm of her hand. Gently and carefully, she separated her fingers, allowing the white to slip through into the bowl below. Nonny thought it looked easy, but her own first attempt was a disaster, the yolk seeming to have a life of its own. Molly tried to catch the slithering thing whilst Nonny screamed, laughing helplessly, just as the potatoes reached the boil. Molly abandoned the mess on the floor and went over to pull the pan half off the flame. She turned round to tell her daughter that exactly the same thing had happened to her the first time she had tried to separate an egg by hand, and it was then that disaster overtook her. She slid on the broken egg on the floor and grabbed wildly to try to save herself, sending the pan of potatoes and their boiling water all over her legs. The pain was excruciating, and in her effort to escape from the scalding water she somehow managed to twist her leg beneath her, so that Nonny's efforts to help her up were so painful that she could only sob out a protest to be left alone for a moment. 'Fetch Jacob,' she managed between shrieks. 'You can't move me; I'm too heavy. Fetch ... Jacob...'

Nonny stared down at her mother for an appalled moment. What on earth was she to do? Molly lay in a positive lake of steaming water and potatoes with her right leg bent at a most peculiar angle, her face streaked with sweat and lined with pain. But then Nonny pulled herself together and ran for the back door, shouting Jacob's name as she went. He must have been letting Jessie out of the shed, for he did not answer and Nonny fairly flew across the farmyard, screaming his name again. The Pritchards, their nearest neighbours, were five miles off, and though Mrs P was probably in the farmhouse at Cae Hic, Rhodri and his father would be checking the sheep as Rhys and Chris were doing.

But even as she hesitated, Jacob came loping across the farmyard, a worried frown etched on his brow. 'What's the matter, Nonny?' he asked anxiously. 'I heared the missus yellin' and come at once. What's up?'

'Mummy's hurt,' Nonny said briefly. She did not want to start trying to explain to Jacob just what had happened; it would take too long and would only confuse him. Better that he should see with his own eyes, then he could help her to get Molly off the floor and into a chair. The two entered the kitchen at a run and Nonny very nearly followed her mother's example as she slid in a patch of egg and water, but she saved herself by grabbing the table and then bent over Molly. 'Mum? Are you all right? Jacob's here; he can help me to lift you on to the chair, or we might carry you upstairs...'

Molly's eyes shot open. Her face, which had

been as flushed as Nonny's own, was white as a sheet save for a round scarlet patch on each cheek. She had managed to get herself into a sitting position, leaning against a table leg, and now shook her head feebly. 'No, you mustn't move me; I think my leg's broken, and the burns are already forming blisters. Oh, Nonny darling, I'm so sorry, but I think you'd best see if Dr Llewellyn can come and take a look at me. If it wasn't for my leg I'd try to get myself into Minnie the Moocher somehow, but when I was a girl I was a member of the St John's Ambulance Brigade, and they taught us that not moving a patient is terribly important.'

'Right,' Nonny said. She tried to sound decisive and unworried but knew her voice was shaking a little as she turned towards where Jacob had been hovering in the doorway. 'Jacob, would you go into the village and...' She stopped speaking. Jacob had already gone.

Some while later, Nonny stood amidst the scene of chaos which was the farm kitchen, looking helplessly around her. Molly had been taken off to hospital, Jacob had returned to his work, and she was alone in the house. Her mother had been moved with infinite care from where she sat on the floor into the waiting ambulance, which would take her to the big hospital at Bangor, down on the coast. Nonny knew her mother had been brave, had exerted all her willpower to stop herself from screaming out when the men had first had to move her, but she guessed that the little whimpers Molly had given would have been screams of pain had she not wished to save her daughter worry. Jacob was in the farmyard, probably going about the tasks he would normally undertake at this hour, but apart from him Nonny was alone, and would be alone until her father and Chris returned. Sighing, she looked around the kitchen once more. She must get this dreadful mess cleared up before Rhys saw it, because discovering that his wife was in hospital would be quite bad enough without seeing the shambles their kitchen had become.

Nonny was still wearing the big cooking overall which her mother had made out of old meal sacks. It was wet and covered in flour, egg, butter and sugar; it would probably make quite a good pancake, Nonny told herself with grim humour. Sighing, she looked to where the loaves were standing in the hearth to prove. Well, I'd better start being useful and put the loaves into the oven, she decided. I can't do much about the shepherd's pie at the moment, but at least I can bake the bread. She opened the bake oven door and saw a tray of blackened jam tarts and sighed, then got down her mother's oven cloth and fished the charred objects out, thus making room for the loaves. Mustn't slam the door, or the bread will be flat, she reminded herself. And now for the clearing up!

Despite the shock and her worry about her mother, Nonny had the kitchen neat as a new pin by the time her father and brother re-entered it. She thought she had cleared all signs of the disaster, and prepared to tell Rhys exactly what had happened, but her father took one long look around the kitchen before crossing the room and grabbing both her hands. 'What's happened, cariad?' he asked urgently. 'Where's your mother?'

Nonny had had a terrifying and appalling day. She opened her mouth to begin to explain, and instead of words a great wailing sob emerged; she was only ten years old after all, and had had to cope with only Jacob to assist her. Rhys put both his arms round her and gave her a hard hug. 'You poor kid. We met Jacob as we turned into the lane, but you know what he's like. He was in a real state, stuttering and stammering so badly that all I got from him was that there had been an accident involving the baking. Until I walked into the room and saw your poor little white face I imagined burnt loaves or a ruined apple pie...'

The moment her father said the words *burnt loaves* Nonny snatched herself out of his arms and flew to the oven. 'The bread!' she squeaked, wrenching the door open. 'Oh, Daddy, I clean forgot the bread!' Rhys bent and peered into the oven, then picked up the cloth and began to take out the tins whilst Chris, who had been standing back, round-eyed, came forward to shake the loaves on to a cooling rack. Only when this was done did he turn and give his sister a hug.

'I don't know why you're in such a state; even our mum couldn't cook better bread,' he said consolingly. 'Now sit yourself down, little sister, and tell us where Mum is and what's been happening.'

Rhys and Chris listened in complete silence save for a hissing in of breath as Nonny told of the day's happenings, her voice only shaking slightly when she tried to describe the injuries her mother had sustained. As soon as the recital had finished, however, Rhys jumped into action. 'Damp down the fire, Chris, and put the loaves on the window-sill to cool,' he said briskly. 'Which hospital did they take Mum too, Nonny my love?'

'They said she was going to Bangor,' Nonny said. 'They were ever so nice; the ambulance men I mean. Mum told us to fetch Dr Llewellyn, but when Jacob had explained what had happened he got them to send an ambulance straight away. Oh, Daddy, by the time it arrived Mummy was sort of sleepy, and they gave her something before they started to move her which should have made her even sleepier, only I don't think it did because she cried out – just little cries, you know – several times as they took her across the farmyard to the ambulance.'

Chris saw Rhys give a little shiver, but when he spoke his voice was calm and steady. 'She would have been in shock, I expect; very nasty, but they would give her something for it, I'm sure. Now, did Mum take anything with her? A nightdress, slippers, her handbag, that sort of thing?'

Nonny did not even have to think but shook her head immediately. 'No, nothing. There wasn't really time, Daddy, and the kitchen was such a mess with cooking and potatoes and boiling water and stuff all over the place. The ambulance men just wanted to get her where she could be properly looked after, they said. And what would Mummy want with her handbag anyway? She only uses it when you go off for a day out or to market in Wrexham.'

Rhys nodded. 'You're right, of course, but I remember when you were born, love, all the women in hospital had their own things brought from home, slippers and so on. And as soon as Mum begins to feel a bit better she may want to buy some little thing off the trolley – scented soap, or talcum powder, or ... oh, I don't know, some kirby grips to keep the hair off her face, perhaps. So if you'll run upstairs and fetch down Mum's things, Chris can get my old Gladstone bag out of the cupboard under the stairs and we'll pack a few bits and pieces that Mum might need. Oh, and I'll cut one of those nice new loaves and butter the slices, and we'll eat them as we drive along.' He smiled with would-be cheerfulness into the two frightened faces. 'Don't worry, kids, we'll be at the hospital before you know it and seeing for ourselves that Mum will soon be back at Cefn Farm and in charge of us all once more.'

It took a little longer than Rhys had expected; in fact it was a good hour after his return home that the baby Morris set off. As they turned on to the Bangor road, Chris cleared his throat.

'Dad, won't it be awful late by the time we reach the hospital? Will they let us see our mum? Suppose they won't let us bring her home tonight? If Nonny's right and she's broken her leg, she'd be rare uncomfortable squeezed into Minnie the Moocher.'

'I don't think they'll release her tonight,' Rhys said. 'But tomorrow maybe. If necessary I suppose we could hire a bigger car, or perhaps they'll bring her back by ambulance. But whatever they say we must agree with, because they are the experts, after all. The only thing I am certain of is that Mum will be as anxious to get home as we are to have her. And now stop worrying, both of you. The next time I see a lay-by I'll pull in and we can have our little picnic. No point in passing out from hunger; Mum wouldn't want that, you know.'

'But Daddy, who'll do the work of the farm tomorrow if we have to fetch Mum?' Chris asked. 'Jacob's ever so good but he hates responsibility; I've heard his mum say that it goes to his head like a glass of whisky, and makes him do the oddest things.'

Rhys laughed. 'If I have to go to the hospital tomorrow, then you two will be in charge of Jacob; he'll do exactly as you tell him, you know that,' he said reassuringly. 'Ah, here's a lay-by! Get out the sandwiches, Nonny.'

They reached the hospital before the last light had faded from the sky, but though Rhys himself was allowed to go very quietly on to the ward to look at his wife, Nonny and Chris had to wait outside, and when Rhys re-joined them, though he did his best to seem cheerful, Nonny guessed at once that he was worried. 'Mum's been to theatre to have her leg set and plastered and her burns dressed. The doctor told me she had come round after the operation but was in such pain that they gave her morphine. They don't think she'll be awake again until tomorrow so I shall take you home, have a few hours' sleep and then come back here.' He looked from Chris's serious, sensible face to Nonny's white and frightened one. 'Just do your best, and if things don't get done that's simply too bad,' he said. 'I wish you could see Mum, but the hospital rules are strict.

No children on the ward except during visiting hours and that's seven till nine in the evening.'

'But if you're going to come back here tomorrow morning, we shan't be able to visit at all,' Nonny said. 'We don't have a car and we can't drive anyway.'

Chris laughed. 'What about buses, stoopid? Is Miss Rhiannon Roberts too grand to catch a bus? If we get all our work finished by about four o'clock we can take sandwiches and ask the conductor to drop us near the hospital. We needn't get return tickets 'cos Dad will bring us home.'

As they walked back to the car Rhys pointed out the window of Molly's ward, and Chris was struck by another idea. 'You go on to the car, Dad, and wait for us,' he suggested. 'Nonny and me will take a look through the window just so we can see Mum and know she's all right. They can't stop us doing that, can they?'

'No-oo,' Rhys said rather doubtfully. 'Not that you'll see much, but if it'll reassure you...'

'It will,' Chris said at once. He caught hold of his sister's hand. 'I'll lift you up so you can peep inside; just let's hope no one sees us and thinks we're up to mischief.'

Rhys was about to veto the idea, since it had occurred to him that the children might be taken for peeping Toms, but he was too late. They had scampered off, but came back in a remarkably short time, both giggling and red in the face. 'A nurse saw us and nearly gave us a heart attack by popping up and banging on the glass,' Chris said. 'But we explained that our mum was the lady with her leg in the air, and she said to go in through the main entrance and she would be responsible for letting us take a peep at her. Shan't be long, Dad.'

The children disappeared again, leaving Rhys to sit in the car, a prey to a great many worries, for the doctor had made it pretty plain that Molly would not be leaving the ward for several weeks. 'It's not only the compound fracture, and the cracked patella – kneecap to you – but the burns,' he had explained. 'Once the wounds begin to heal the leg will be replastered, but whilst she's on traction your wife cannot leave the hospital no matter how urgently she may be needed at home. Have you no relatives who could take over? No neighbours?'

'I've a very reliable farmworker,' Rhys had said slowly. 'And excellent neighbours, though they are pretty old and live five miles further up the lane. But they have a twenty-year-old son who knows as much about farming as any man living; he'll give us a hand, I'm sure of it. Then there's the Williamses, who live in the village and help out at busy times. He's a retired farmworker and they're always eager to earn a bit of money to augment their pension. I'll call on them first thing tomorrow.'

The doctor had nodded, satisfied. 'You've obviously been giving the matter some thought,' he said approvingly. 'The knowledge that you've got no problems at home will aid your wife's recovery, believe me.' He shook Rhys's hand. 'Good luck, Mr Roberts.'

But now, sitting in the car and waiting for his children to return, Rhys decided that he would have to tell Molly of his dilemma. For even though he was sure everyone would help out for two or three weeks, they would not be able to ignore the work on their own farms for much longer. What should he do? Neither he nor Molly had any family and though Molly had had many friends in Liverpool she had lost touch with most of them; in fact the only person with whom she corresponded regularly was Ellen O'Mara. Despite the fact that they had not met for ten years their friendship had flourished. Rhys knew the two women discussed every aspect of their lives and often talked of a reunion, but so far this had not happened. Molly was always bewailing the many miles which separated Old Swan from Cefn Farm, had planned several times to invite Ellen and Lana to spend a holiday in Snowdonia, but something had always happened to prevent their meeting. If only Ellen were nearer...

With the return of the children, both now rather pale and worried-looking, he bent his mind to reassuring them. 'I was upset too when I saw how pale and still she was, but the doctor said it was largely the result of the anaesthetic, and she would look a good deal better when next we saw her.'

'Good; the nurse said the same,' Chris said. He was in the front passenger seat and turned to give his sister's hand a quick squeeze. 'She asked if we had a relative who would look after us whilst our mum was away and I said Auntie Ellen would.'

'I only wish she could...' Rhys began, but his son swiftly interrupted.

'Dad, I had to say something and say it fast, because the nurse said we could be taken into care if there was no one to look after us. I suppose it might be all right for some children, but it wouldn't do for us, would it? We do an awful lot of jobs on the farm, and you'll have your hands full without us being taken away from you as well.'

Rhys revved the engine viciously. 'Just let anyone try to take you away from me,' he said between his teeth. 'You did very right to mention Auntie Ellen. I'll discuss it with Mum tomorrow, and if she agrees I'll suggest that we try to persuade her and Lana to come to Cefn Farm for a week or two, and if that's not possible we'll get someone from the village to act as a sort of housekeeper whilst Mum's in hospital.'

Nonny had been silent whilst her father and brother discussed their plans, but now she spoke up. 'Daddy, if we have to pay someone how will we do it? The nurse said Mum won't be working for a long time, because when she first gets out of hospital she'll need care and attention. Chris and I can't earn anything...'

For the first time since he had seen his wife lying so still and white in her hospital bed, Rhys gave a laugh of genuine amusement. 'Oh, Nonny, you've done me good! I'm pretty sure we could dip into our savings if necessary, but I hope it won't come to that. The doctor said there are grants ... but anyway, for the time being we'll simply take each day as it comes. Why don't you two try to get some sleep? I'll wake you when we reach the farm.'

Chapter Six

Ellen was ironing when the knock came on the back door. She glanced across the kitchen to where her daughter sat, and saw that Lana had pushed both forefingers into her ears, indicating, as Ellen well knew, that she was doing her holiday task and did not intend to stop in order to open the door, no matter how busy her mother might be. Ellen sighed and headed for the back door. When her mother had died the previous spring she had taken over the house on Bethel Street, paying the rent by working as a school dinner lady, and occasionally acting as shop assistant in the haberdashery which had employed her, before marriage. Ellen considered herself comfortably situated, and frequently told Lana what a lucky girl she was, but Mr Meakin's pension had died with her mother, and there was no longer much left over to provide the little extras that made their lives enjoyable.

Ellen opened the door cautiously. Someone had told her that Sam was in port for the first time in years, and in no pleasant humour. It seemed that he had lost an eye in a dockside brawl some time before and been left with a chip on his shoulder the size of the proverbial beam. But as she peered round the door it was not Sam's face she saw, but a stranger's. A tall, dark-haired man in an open-necked blue shirt and faded trousers, who was giving her a friendly smile and obviously expected to be recognised.

Ellen stared at him; he wasn't the man from the Pru, nor the tally-man, and she didn't think he was one of her neighbours, yet there was something familiar about him, and when he spoke his accent was familiar, too. 'Mrs O'Mara? Or should I say Ellen?' The man smiled, showing very white and even teeth. 'You don't recognise me, do you? I'm Molly Roberts's husband, Rhys, and I've got the kids in the car to prove I really am who I say. We did meet once, but it was more than ten years back...'

Ellen beamed. Now that she looked more closely, she remembered a good-looking young man who had sat awkwardly on her friend's bed at visiting time, twisting his tweed cap round and round and gazing at Molly with such obvious love and delight that she, Ellen, had felt downright envious. Because of her experience with Sam, she had never thought marriage anything but a burden, but seeing the loving light in the young man's eyes she had realised that a good marriage could be a wonderful thing.

'Come in, come in, Rhys!' she said now, pulling her visitor into the kitchen. 'Where did you park the car? I'll send Lana to fetch your kids in, and we'll all have a nice cuppa and a chat. I were about to ask what you'd done wi' Molly, but I suppose someone has to be in charge of the farm. Lana, gerroff your bum and go and fetch your Auntie Molly's children from out the car.' She pointed to where the baby Morris was parked against the kerb, and turned to Rhys. 'Is that it?'

She chuckled. 'Well, it must be, 'cos there ain't another car in the street. Move yourself, Lana, you lazy little beggar.'

Lana, who had removed her fingers from her ears as soon as her mother went to the door, got up and peered doubtfully out into the deepening dusk. She and Nonny had begun to exchange letters, but Ellen saw that she felt shy now and did not want to go to the car alone. Rhys must have realised too, for he held out a hand for her to shake, and told her he'd fetch the kids himself.

'They might imagine you were going to kidnap them,' he said teasingly. 'You stay here with your mum, cariad, while I fetch them in.'

When they were all settled at the kitchen table with cups of tea in front of them, Rhys explained all about the accident. 'I know it seems a lot to ask but we did wonder, Molly and me, if you might come out to the farm for a while,' he finished awkwardly. 'We couldn't afford to pay you much, but there's a grant which would help, and the alternative is allowing Chris and Nonny to be put in a children's home until Molly is allowed out of hospital.' He looked hopefully across the table at Ellen. 'Of course it may be impossible...' he said, and was swiftly interrupted.

'I'd come like a shot and I don't want no money,' Ellen said at once. 'The only snag is me lodger. He works down at the docks in one of the shipping offices; you'll like him when you meet him. He's a little man, kind of quiet, but an ideal lodger. But he's full board. Still, I've a good friend in me neighbour, Mrs Walshall. I reckon she'd feed Mr Taplow for me while I gave a hand at your farm. Not that I'd be much use at milkin' cows or shearin' sheep,' she added hastily. 'Of course, I'd do me best...'

Rhys and his children laughed, whilst Lana gave a tight little smile. 'It's all right, Ellen. I've a farmworker, as I said, and Jacob and myself can cope. It's only the house which would be in your charge, but if that's impossible Molly said you might know someone who'd come out to the farm and act as housekeeper until Molly's back home and not expect to be paid a fortune.'

Ellen shook her head decisively. 'No need, no need whatsoever,' she said. 'Me and my girl would just love to come and help out. Moll and meself have talked about it by letter for years, but somehow we never got round to actually doing anything about it. First I had that full-time job in the jam factory what paid too well to walk away from. I had Mum to look after Lana, you see, so I could work full time. Then my mum was poorly; she had a couple of strokes and as time went on she got confused. I had to be home all the time to keep an eye on her, which I were only too glad to do, because she was grand to me was my mum, nothing was too much trouble, and even when she was ill she looked after Lana as well as I could meself. But now I'm free as air, you might say, 'cos dinner ladies don't work in the school holidays, and once I've got Mrs Walshall to agree to feed Mr Taplow I'll be with you just as soon as I can buy Lana and me a bus ticket.'

Rhys leaned across the table and grasped Ellen's hands. 'You're one of the best. Molly said you'd do anything you could to help,' he said fervently. 'And you won't need bus tickets; I'll call for you in Minnie the Moocher ... that's our name for the car,' he added, seeing the bewilderment on her face. 'She's not very big but there'll be plenty of room for you, Lana and all the luggage you'll want to bring along.' He hesitated for a moment, then asked, 'When can you come? In a week? Two?'

'Day after tomorrer,' Ellen said quickly. 'Now, you've told me how the accident happened – me blood runs cold just to think of it – so tell me how dear Molly is getting on.'

'Day after tomorrow? Are you sure that's not too soon?' Rhys said. 'I don't want to put you out...'

Ellen waved an airy hand. 'To tell you the truth it'll be grand to get out of the city for a bit,' she assured him. 'Oh aye, Lana and meself will be delighted to give a hand, won't we, queen? Now tell me about Molly.'

'Slow but sure,' Rhys said. 'Bad burns take a deal of time to heal and she's still in a lot of pain. Not that she ever complains, but I can tell. And it'll do her a power of good to hear that you've agreed to help out.' He looked rather shyly at the woman seated opposite him. 'Molly would like me to take you to the hospital once you've settled in, so that she can put you in the way of things. So if you really can come the day after tomorrow, I'll tell her we'll visit the day after that. The staff have been very good and have allowed me to see her outside visiting hours, but as far as possible I like to keep on the right side of them. So we'll go in the evening, if that's all right by you.'

'And I suppose you visited her this evening, which is why you arrived here so late,' Ellen said.

'This is a real adventure and it'll be like a holiday for Lana and me, to go into the country and actually stay on a farm. Oh, I know I'll be doing housework, cooking and so on, but I'll enjoy every minute. Won't we, Lana?'

Lana had waited for her mother to consult her before agreeing to go into Snowdonia, far from the streets and friends she knew, but she waited in vain. Ellen did not so much as glance at her daughter when replying to this man's request, and Lana had grown indignant. She told herself that Ellen knew very well that she, Lana, had a great many plans for the long summer holidays, and none of those plans included a trip to Cefn Farm. Lana had never even visited a farm, though her mother and the lodger had taken her into the country several times, where they had walked in woods and meadows, eaten cream teas at country cottages, and sometimes gone as far as the seaside and paddled, Mr Taplow with his trouser legs rolled up and Lana and her mother with their skirts tucked into their knickers.

But now Lana reminded herself that she was a city girl and enjoyed the company of her school friends during the long hot summer days. They had planned to go boating on the lake in Prince's Park, to visit the Walker Art Gallery and the Liverpool Museum, and to queue up at their favourite cinema to enjoy the Saturday rush; they might even buy cheap seats at the theatre for matinee performances. Now, however, none of this would be possible. She would be stuck out in the middle of nowhere with no one to play with but the girl now sitting opposite her at the table, staring with round blue eyes and taking in every detail of the kitchen, of Ellen and of Lana herself. There was the boy too, of course, but in Lana's experience boys did not usually play with girls younger than themselves. This thought actually made her want to giggle, since her best friend was still Phil Hodges, who was twelve. By a lucky chance Mr Hodges had been moved to the tram depot at Old Swan soon after Lana started school, and had chosen to rent a house nearer his work, which was also, again by coincidence, near to that occupied by the Meakins. The thought of Phil's disappointment when she told him she was off to Snowdonia made her angry enough at her mother's calm acceptance of this man's plans to speak up for herself.

She looked squarely across at her mother, and realised with astonishment that Ellen was actually smiling. Lana blinked; was it possible that her mother, who understood her so well, actually thought that she would be delighted with the plan? Would be quite prepared, at the beginning of the long summer holidays, to desert her friends and her neighbourhood and go for heaven knew how long into a strange country? But it was impossible for a child of ten to say such things to her mother; she would have to put her objections much more tactfully. 'But Mum, what'll me pals say when they hear I won't be around?' she asked plaintively. 'Our gang had all sorts of plans, you know we did. And Mrs Hodges said she'd take me and Phil to New Brighton at least once and probably twice. She said a day on the funfair and a day on the beach would make up for not going away this year, 'cos the Hodgeses usually have a week in Rhyl.'

'Well, yes, but your pals will understand that your Auntie Molly and Uncle Rhys need help,' Ellen said reproachfully. 'Besides, Lana, you're going to have two or three weeks of actually living on a farm! I'm tellin' you, queen, most of your pals would give their perishin' eye teeth for such a chance. We've often talked about it; collectin' eggs, feedin' the pigs and the cattle, learnin' to milk a cow and mebbe even ridin' on one of the horses. If you ask me, queen, you're a very lucky girl to have the opportunity. And it ain't as if there'll be no one to play with at Cefn Farm, because you'll have Nonny and Chris and their friends too.' She looked to Rhys for confirmation of what she had said and Lana saw a flush stain his cheeks. He cleared his throat.

'Well, I wouldn't want to give you a false impression, Lana,' he said, smiling at her. 'Cefn Farm is – is a bit remote like. We're several miles from the village, and though there are other hill farms it would take you a couple of hours to reach some of them.' He smiled at her in what was clearly meant to be an encouraging way. 'But as your mum said, you'd have Chris and Nonny, and there's always plenty to do on the farm.'

'Yes, work,' Lana muttered. 'And I don't think I'd be very much help because I wouldn't understand what needed doing.' She had been speaking to Rhys, but now she turned to her mother. 'Mum, if you were to ask Mrs Hodges, or Janet Cobbler's mum, I'm sure they'd have me to stay whilst you were helping Auntie Molly. Couldn't you just ask...'

Ellen sighed. 'Maybe they would and maybe they wouldn't, but I'm not going off and leaving you with either Mrs Hodges or Mrs Jones. They're grand women both of them, but your place is with me and in this instance at any rate my place is with Rhys and Molly.'

Lana was about to start arguing when Chris leaned forward and spoke to her directly. 'You'll like Cefn Farm and you'll have fun there, I promise,' he said earnestly. 'We'll make sure of it, Nonny and me; isn't that so, Non?'

Nonny nodded eagerly. 'Course we will, and if you don't like collecting eggs or feeding pigs or rounding up the sheep with the dogs to do all the work, then you can stay with your mum in the house,' she said, and Lana saw the quick flicker of contempt before Nonny could banish it. 'And it's not only Liverpool people who go to the seaside. When our mum's better, Dad's going to take us down to Caernarfon for the day. We might do that before you leave us, you never know.' She leaned across the table and fixed Lana with a pleading gaze. 'The people at the hospital said that if Dad couldn't find someone to help him cope then we might have to go into a children's home – just until Mum's better, of course. You wouldn't want us to have to go there, would you?'

Lana sighed. She knew she had been behaving badly and felt ashamed, seeing the colour rise in her mother's cheeks and knowing that Rhys and his children must be thinking her thoroughly selfish and spoilt. And after all, they might not have to be at the farm for very long. Rhys had said it would just be until Molly came out of hospital, and in any case they would have to return to Liverpool when the new term started in September. Seven weeks was a long time, but it was pointless arguing. When her mother tightened her lips it usually meant she had made up her mind; better to give in gracefully rather than incur her wrath.

'I expect your farm is lovely and I'll do my best to help in any way I can,' she said. She hesitated, looking from one face to the other. Chris was black-haired, black-eyed and very tanned. In fact, he looked just like Rhys. Nonny on the other hand had a mass of long light brown hair, blue eyes and fair skin with a sprinkle of freckles; no brother and sister could have been more different, except that right now both were looking at her with identical friendly smiles.

'Say you'll come,' Nonny said pleadingly. 'Ever since Mum told me how we were both born at the same time I've wished we could meet. I'm really sorry we've spoiled your plans for the holidays but I'm sure you'll have just as much fun with me and Chris as you would have had with your school friends. We've got a pond with ducks and geese on it and we mean to follow the mountain stream right down to the lake when we have a free day. Our mum tells us that city children are great walkers, so you won't mind walking into the village with us to get the messages from time to time. Then we'll introduce you to our school friends ... oh, say you'll come!'

For the first time since the Robertses had arrived, Lana gave them a genuine smile. 'Of course I'll come,' she said. 'After all, there'll be other holidays when I'll be able to play with me school pals.' She looked at her mother, guessing what her reaction would be, and was rewarded when Ellen jumped up to give her a loving hug.

'You're norra bad kid, just a trifle spoilt,' Ellen said. She turned to Rhys. 'Look, if you and the kids can make do with a doss-down for one night then I can make arrangements tomorrow morning for my neighbour to take care of my lodger and keep an eye on the house. It'll save you two long journeys as well as the petrol money; I ain't never had a car but I've heared folk grumblin' about the price of petrol. There's a couch in the parlour and an easy chair which you and your lad can manage on, and Rhiannon can top to toe it with Lana.'

Lana grinned at Nonny. 'Good thing we're both on the skinny side, and neither of us is very tall,' she said cheerfully. 'Have you had supper?'

Nonny was just saying that they had had a sandwich and a drink of tea but it had been a long while ago when her father interrupted. 'I'll get fish and chips for everyone,' he said, standing up. 'We accept your hospitality with many thanks, Ellen, because if you come back with us tomorrow it won't just be a saving of petrol, but a saving of worry as well. We lit out in such a hurry that I only had time to tell Jacob to milk the cows and feed the stock, so the sooner we're back at Cefn Farm the better I'll be pleased, because heaven knows what else he'll find to do while we're away.'

Chris grinned and spoke directly to Lana. 'He'll have milked the pigs and searched for horse eggs, if I know Jacob,' he said. 'But never mind, we'll be back in time to stop him doing anything really silly.'

Sam and the *Buds of May* had parted company after six months, following a dockside brawl for which Sam had been largely responsible. It had left him blinded in one eye, the result of a jab with the sharp end of a broken bottle, and with an even deeper grudge against women than before, since it was a woman who had both started the fight and wielded the bottle. He had joined other ships, of course, but never since he had boarded the *Buds of May* had he returned to Liverpool; it had seemed pointless whilst the court injunction forbade him to approach his wife, and he knew his own nature well enough to realise that Constable Jamieson had been right: avoiding Liverpool – and his wife and daughter – was his best course. But now circumstances had brought him back to Liverpool for the first time in over five years, since his ship, the *Galliano*, had collided with a half-submerged wreck off the Irish coast and had limped into the Livingstone dock to have the damage repaired.

To his own secret astonishment, Sam had found a sort of affection for the city of his birth rising in his breast. God knew he had seen enough other ports in the years he had been away, but now he realised that none of them compared favourably with his birthplace.

When he had been a docker he had had boon companions who drank with him, yarned with him and occasionally fought with him, and now that he was approaching retirement age he found himself longing for that old way of life. He had even missed hearing Scouse spoken and thought, balefully, that if his wife had been a decent sort of woman he could now be considering settling down. But that bloody woman – what was she called? Oh, yes, he remembered, she was Ellen and the kid was Lana or some such fancy name. Well, if they'd behaved to him as a wife and daughter should, he could have sent Ellen out to work, her being younger than he, whilst he looked forward to a peaceful retirement.

In his mind he could see himself comfortably settled in a cushioned armchair before the parlour fire. He would have a tankard of Guinness on a small table by his side, whilst a good meal – steak, perhaps, and a big pile of chips – would be awaiting his attention upon the kitchen table. Yes, that would be the life! He had worked hard on various ships for wages varying from very poor to moderately good, but had never managed to save a penny. When he had been on the docks there had been a great many perks, which to Sam's way of thinking was a word that applied to anything he might manage to filch. That was what made a dockie's life bearable, in Sam's opinion at least. He had managed to get away with all sorts – fountain pens, wristwatches, the occasional bottle of rum or whisky strapped to his leg with strong rubber bands – but there was little hope of such benefits aboard a coaster laden with timber, or engine parts, or even coal. One had to be content with one's wages and Sam soon drank those away, returning to his ship belligerent and usually penniless. But this time, he told himself, he had been luckier. The crew of the *Galliano* had been paid off, so Sam had money in his pocket. And instead of drinking it away in one enormous binge he intended to make it last until he re-joined his ship – or, of course, until something better came along. Accordingly, he had booked into a seamen's hostel and was now taking a good look at Liverpool to see what changes had taken place during his long absence.

His thoughts continued to wander, however, as he recalled what had made him leave the city and not return. That damned court injunction had happened years ago; surely by now everything would have changed? That miserable bloody scuffer, Constable Jamieson, might still be pounding his beat, since Sam did not reckon the younger man was sergeant material, but he would have better things to think about than Sam O'Mara. If I could just have a word with Ellen, explain I'm a changed man, then she might take me back, tell the authorities that the injunction should no longer apply, and let me start a new life as a retired seaman on a pension, with a nice plump wife to warm my bed and cook my meals and a nice little daughter to run my messages.

If this had been a South American port he would probably have considered selling his nice little daughter to the highest bidder, but Liverpool wasn't like that. The white slave trade was all very well for other continents but Sam didn't want to lose the sight of his other eye if he suggested such a thing to a Liverpudlian.

When he heard the familiar accents all around him, he felt a glow of warmth envelop him. Home! And here he would bleedin' well stay, if he possibly could. He might get work as a docker, or a job in the slaughterhouse where he had once earned good money for a couple of weeks. He went to Paddy's market and bought himself a peaked cap, an almost new navy duffel coat and a pair of serge trousers; then he bought a large box of chocolates to soften Ellen up a bit and a bag of mint humbugs for Lana. He changed in his room at the seamen's hostel, pleased with the appearance of the man who stared back at him from the mirror. With his cap pulled rakishly over his blind eye, and the new clothes giving him an air of affluence, he decided he passed muster. Why should anyone challenge a well-dressed man with money in his pocket setting off to treat his wife to a slap-up dinner? Because he intended to woo Ellen all over again, so that when he told her he was a changed man, and meant to behave as a husband should in future, she would believe him.

Sam sat on the bed, produced a knife, and pared his nails. Then he splashed his face with water. He had not shaved for several weeks and now had a grey and bristly beard, and with one more satisfied glance in the mirror he told himself that his own mother would not have known him had she been alive. For a moment he played with yet another scheme. Suppose he persuaded Ellen that he was a stranger, begged to be allowed to lodge in her house and then, when she had taken him in, told her who he was and claimed his marital rights.

This idea so tickled his sense of humour that he was still grinning when he reached Dryden Street, though he knew in his heart that despite the beard Ellen would recognise him at once. He knocked on the door of number 21 and was startled when a strange woman with several children peering inquisitively around her considerable bulk answered his knock. She looked him up and down, but merely snapped: 'Yes?' in a far from encouraging tone.

Sam stared. 'I've – I've come to see Mrs O'Mara, with news of her husband,' he said. 'Ain't she in? Who's you, if I may make so bold?'

'O'Mara? Never heard of her,' the woman said briefly. She grinned, showing broken and uneven teeth. 'Best try number twenty-four; she knows all the gossip.' Sam began to reply but the woman shut the door so abruptly that he had to jump back or the panel would have flattened his nose.

He stood in Dryden Street, his mind in a whirl. So she had thought to escape him by moving house, but he knew a trick worth two of that! He would go round to her mother's place: he'd bet money that he'd find Ellen and the kid there. Resolutely, he set off.

It took a deal of willpower, but Sam kept off the drink for three whole days while he combed the area for news of his wife. He had tried hanging about the school and had been chagrined to realise that it was the school holidays; no one but cleaning staff would be in the building until the beginning of September. And it was now only the latter end of July. But in any case the school had been a long shot, since he had to admit to himself that he was unlikely to recognise his daughter after so many years. He had been to Mrs Meakin's house first, of course, only to be told that she had moved away four or five years previously. His informant, a small bespectacled man with a rattrap mouth, had stared at him long and suspiciously before informing him that he believed there had been a notice of Mrs Meakin's death in the columns of the *Echo* some twelve months ago. Sam, who had hated his mother-in-law, grinned nastily, then had to hastily reassemble his features into a look of grief as he asked where he might find one of Mrs Meakin's children so that he might express his sorrow for their loss. 'Dunno,' the little man said briefly. 'Good afternoon.' And he had slammed the door as abruptly as had the new tenant of number 21 Dryden Street.

By the fourth day, Sam's thirst was so raging that he decided he would have to have at least a couple of bevvies or do something violent, so he went to a dockers' pub and managed to con several drinks out of men he had once known well. They urged him to remain with them, probably in the hope that he would eventually stand his round, but in this they were disappointed. Sam pleaded poverty, saying that he was saving the rest of his money to buy something nice for his wife and kid. This caused one of the drinkers, a man previously unknown to Sam, to ask him where he lived and what his wife was called.

Sam stared at him, his mind made sluggish by the drink taken after a three-day abstinence. 'Wass it to you?' he asked belligerently. 'I don't know you from Adam! If I telled you me wife's name you might let on to her I've been drinkin'...'

The man began to apologise, to say he meant no harm, when another man, both younger and larger, broke in. 'I don't reckon you've gorra home nor a wife neither wi' a face like the back of a bus and norra penny to bless yourself with,' he said tauntingly. 'I seen you comin' out o' the sailors' hostel earlier. If you've a wife and a home of your own what was you doin' there?'

'Visitin' a pal,' Sam mumbled, and when the docker demanded to know the pal's name Sam glared at him and left the pub, wishing the man had been older and weaker so's he could have lain in wait for him and given him a right pasting. He went straight from the pub to a fish and chip shop, then to another pub, but as dusk thickened he began to suspect that he was being followed, probably by the docker who had been so unpleasant, and though he could see no reason for the man's antagonism he began to worry that he, Sam, might be the one who was beaten up.

By the time he reached the sailors' home once more, however, he had decided that it was just his imagination. He went to bed thinking he might as well forget all about his wife and child. What, after all, was the point? Ellen had survived without him for half a dozen years. In that time she might easily have left Liverpool altogether, might be almost anywhere in Great Britain. She could not marry again, not whilst he was alive, but she could shack up with somebody else if she left Liverpool. Lying in his bed that night he found that he no longer wanted to live out his old age with Ellen and the girl. They had ruined several days of his time ashore by their provocative behaviour in moving house. He realised that for a couple of nights now his most satisfactory dreams had not been of reuniting with his wife and persuading her he was a changed man. No indeed! His most satisfying dreams had been the ones where he found Ellen in some dark little jigger, shone his torch on his own face so that she should know who attacked her, and then smashed his fist into her round, pretty face until blood poured from her broken nose and those nice white teeth of which she was so proud lay scattered on the ground.

Next morning he was still of the same mind and decided he would give up the search, forget Ellen and Lana and spend the day having a bit of a spree before he joined a new ship. There were several coasters berthed in the docks; bigger ships too, though he tended to avoid liners, because they mainly wanted stokers, which was hard and filthy work. He was pretty sure he would be able to find a berth of some sort. Seamen were always quitting one ship and being taken on by another, as Sam well knew, so after a day's debauchery he would leave Liverpool without a regret and head for the high seas once more.

And then, on what should have been his very last day ashore, he had a tremendous piece of luck. He saw a woman climbing into a small and heavily laden car. She had apparently got out in order to buy something from a barrow at the edge of the road, and when she turned to climb back into the vehicle's front passenger seat he saw, with real astonishment, that it was Ellen. He ran towards the car, meaning to demand where she was going and who with, but as he reached out a hand to grab the car's canvas hood, rolled down because of the sunshine, the car jerked forward, and Sam grasped at air, lurched, and landed heavily on his behind. He shouted, of course, demanded that the driver should stop and let him have a word with his wife. But either no one in the car heard or they took no notice, because they left him sitting in the roadway cursing whilst they drove off. Several people had laughed when he had fallen and the barrow boy, who had seen the whole incident, came over to help him to his feet. Sam would have liked to punch him – he was desperate to hit someone – but was forced to mumble thanks instead since the man was both younger and fitter than himself. Rubbing his behind, which had met the road with considerable force, he limped across to the barrow in the man's wake, pointed at random to a pile of oranges and handed over a sixpence. 'That woman ... the one what went off in that car...' he asked breathlessly. 'Do you know her, lad? What were she buyin'? I've got to speak to her before me ship sails.'

The barrow boy shrugged wide shoulders. 'I dunno her name, though she often buys from me,' he said. 'But I do know where she were goin'. It's some farm in them mountains in Wales – what's they called? Oh aye, I know. Snowdonia.'

'Snowdonia!' Sam ground his teeth. 'What's going on? Who were the feller what were drivin' the car?'

The man laughed. 'I dunno. She were just tellin' me her pal what lives on a farm in Wales had a bad fall a couple of days ago and has been took into hospital; she's goin' to give an eye to the feller's kids and keep house whilst his wife's laid up.' He laughed again. 'Eh, lad, but you should ha' seen yourself when the car shot forward and your bum met the tarmac; it were enough to make a perishin' cat laugh.'

Once more, only the size and strength of the barrow boy saved him from a punch on the nose, which was just as well, Sam thought afterwards, since it was at this moment that the man's erratic memory disgorged the most useful piece of information yet.

'Cefn Farm; that's where she said they were bound,' he shouted as Sam turned away. 'But you don't want to follow them there; it's right out in the wild. She telled me it were five or six miles from the nearest village, some Welsh name wi' thirty or forty letters. But if you're real keen to gerrin touch you could always write.'

'Ta,' Sam shouted, actually beginning to smile. 'But I'm off to me ship; we's bound for Jamaica to pick up a load of mahogany. She'll sail on the tide whether I'm aboard or no, so I can't afford to be late. I'll catch up wi' me old woman next time I's ashore.'

Satisfied that the man would probably forget him the instant he was no longer in sight, Sam hurried towards his favourite alehouse. What did Ellen matter anyway? He did not intend to hang around in Liverpool until she saw fit to leave her pal and return home. Tomorrow morning he would sign on with one of the ships taking crews aboard and forget all about his selfish wife.

He had almost reached the pub when a hand fell on his shoulder and a voice he had almost forgotten spoke in his ear. 'Well fancy seeing you after so long, Sam O'Mara! I hope you've not been pesterin' Ellen or the little 'un, because if you go anywhere near either your wife or your daughter you'll be back in Walton jail before you can say knife.'

Sam swung slowly round; yes, his worst fears were realised. It was bloody Constable Jamieson. But Sam reminded himself that on this occasion at least he had done nothing wrong, so he met the policeman's eyes defiantly. 'If you think I meant to come back here when I've kept away for so long, you're mistook,' he said, his voice taking on a truculent whine. 'I don't know where me wife's gone, nor I haven't tried to find out. Me ship's come in for repairs, but I'll be off within a day or so, don't you fret. Liverpool's the last place on earth I want to be.' He looked slyly at the constable. 'Though surely that court injunction can't still be in force, can it? I'll be retirin' in a year or two and mebbe then I'll want to come back home.'

Constable Jamieson shrugged, then delved into his pocket and produced an official-looking brown envelope, which he pushed into Sam's reluctant hand. 'Well, I've done my duty,' he said. 'Good thing you registered at the seamen's hostel, else you might never have got your mail.' He touched the brim of his tall helmet and grinned mockingly at his companion. 'Good day to you, sir.'

Sam was tempted to tear the envelope up without opening it, but instead rammed it into his pocket and hurried to the pub. Once there he fortified himself with several drinks before ripping it open and staring with increasing disbelief at the documents it had contained. The covering letter informed him that he had owed maintenance for his wife and child for the past five years, and could pay off the arrears monthly or alternatively hand over a lump sum so large that Sam nearly fainted. Incredulous, he showed the letter around the pub, telling himself that it must be some sort of joke, that Constable Jamieson must have spotted him earlier, decided to give him a bad scare, and filled in the forms himself. However, other drinkers in the pub, after one look at the documents, assured him that it was no practical joke but the sorry truth. Because he had never been back to Liverpool, never registered at a seamen's hostel in Great Britain, the authorities had been unable to trace him. But now that they knew his details he would be unable to visit any port in the country without a demand for money following his arrival as night follows day.

Sam brooded over this and finally came to the conclusion that there was only one course open to him. He must find Ellen and somehow persuade or scare her into promising to contact the authorities, and say that she had no need of Sam's money. But thinking it over, he knew that what he most wanted to do was to pay her back for the fright he had received upon opening the envelope.

For the rest of the evening, Sam plotted and planned, having decided that he would never have a better opportunity to catch Ellen on the hop than he had now. Thanks to the barrow boy, he knew where she would be living for the next two or three weeks at any rate. And he had sufficient money in his pocket to keep him whilst he put his scheme into action.

He took a deep draught of porter. Yes, it was all bloody Ellen's fault, for it must be she who had alerted the authorities to the fact that she had received no maintenance. Well, if he caught up with her she would receive more than maintenance, he thought vindictively. But it would do no good to batter Ellen for what she had done to him. He would have to work out some plan by which he could get Ellen to renounce her claim to his money. He had realised that finding one woman in the surging crowds of Liverpool was just about impossible; it had been sheer luck that his path and Ellen's had crossed that morning, a piece of luck which might never occur again. By now he had acknowledged that wherever she was living Ellen would never take him back, and that his only reason for following her was to exact revenge for the way he had been treated. He could not remember ever receiving a hard knock of any description without making sure that he got his own back. Sooner or later – sometimes a great deal later – the person who had hurt, insulted or merely jeered at Sam O'Mara would receive their just deserts. If he did not punish Ellen for the contents of that envelope it would niggle at his mind for ever. No, if he was to have any peace he must make Ellen suffer, and suddenly his mind cleared and he realised what he must do.

The injunction forbade him to approach Ellen or their home, but it assumed Ellen remained in Liverpool. Now he knew that she was off to a farm in Snowdonia, many miles from her home. He could come across her there, by accident on purpose so to speak. Sam lurched up to the bar and got himself another drink, then returned to his corner, reflecting savagely that it would have been summary justice if he could have gone into Ellen's house and prigged enough to fill his pockets with cash, but since he had no idea where Ellen was living that was out of the question. He thought hard. If he were still a docker things would be very different; he could move at will about the port and take advantage of any opportunity that came his way. He knew various methods by which a docker could leave the wharves a good deal richer than when he arrived, but he was a seaman and could only legitimately visit the dock in which his ship lay. Rack his brains as he might, he could not bring anything to mind which would suit the present situation.

Finally he decided, much against his will, to take a week's work in the slaughterhouse, hefting carcasses on and off the lorries which would deliver them to butchers' shops as far as twenty miles away. It was gruelling work, for Sam did not have the knack of an experienced handler, but by the end of the week he had not only managed to earn a decent wage, but learned that there was a market for bones and unwanted bits of carcass among the many dog owners in the city. Armed with the money he got through this illicit trade as well as with his week's wages, Sam sloped off to begin the journey into Wales.

Ellen had heard from Molly how very remote Cefn Farm was, how deeply buried in the mountains of Snowdonia, but because she had no experience of country living she was appalled by the great mountains towering above the little farmhouse, and by the silence. There was always the sound of the wind, of course, and the occasional roar of a plane's engine as it passed overhead, but mostly there was silence. Catering for six, too – for Jacob still took most of his meals in the farmhouse – was very different from what she had been used to; rationing had come to an end some years before and Ellen was astonished and not a little dismayed to find that Rhys took it for granted that she would bake her own bread. At first Ellen said nothing, but after a couple of days Rhys drove her down to Bangor to visit Molly and her friend explained the situation. 'Shop bread doesn't keep, particularly at this time of year when the weather's so hot,' Molly had said. 'For some reason, home-baked bread lasts longer. I usually bake once a week, and then I don't just make the bread but cakes, buns, pies and puddings as well.' She had looked at Ellen's appalled face, giggled, and put a comforting hand on her arm. 'Don't look so horrified, Ellen. You see, hill farming is hard work and everyone gets very hungry. I don't believe I've ever seen a fat hill farmer, but they need plenty of good food to keep them going. I've known Rhys to carry a sick sheep across his shoulders for miles, and when you think of the terrain...'

'What's terrain?' Ellen asked doubtfully. 'Oh, Molly, I'll do my best but I wish I knew a bit more. Rhys says you make your own butter; I ain't never heard of anyone doing so, norreven during the war. And he says now the hens is layin' so well I should preserve some o' the eggs in stuff called isinglass. He tried to explain how to do it but when I'm scared me lug'oles don't seem to listen what you might call proper.'

Molly began to laugh, then stopped, a hand flying to her side. 'Don't make me giggle; it hurts my burns,' she said. 'I suppose you might sell the eggs at market but it's a fair old journey to the nearest town and I reckon it would cost more in petrol than you'd get for the eggs. Look, tell you what, next time you visit me bring a pencil and notebook. I'll tell you exactly what to do with the eggs and sort out any other problems you've come across.'

Ellen had agreed to do this but asked hopefully when Molly thought she would be returning home. 'As soon as I blinkin' well can,' Molly assured her friend. 'I'm bored to tears lying here, I don't think much of the food and I worry all the time about Nonny and Chris. Chris fancies himself as a climber – Rhys says he really is good – and wants to join the mountain rescue team as soon as he's old enough, so of course Nonny, who follows him in everything, wants to too. She scrambles up corries and chimneys and rocks so sheer that you and I wouldn't think there was foothold for a fly. She's had some tumbles, of course, though nothing serious, but Chris is just learning to abseil and Nonny wants to learn as well. The chap who's teaching Chris has promised to take her in a couple of years, but he says that as yet her arms don't have the strength to support her body and she's simply got to be sensible and wait.' Molly looked hopefully at her friend. 'You won't let her take any risks, will you, Ellen? Nonny's a real tomboy, always up to mischief. There's a little gang of them – all boys except for Nonny – who spend any spare time they have rock climbing. If you could just explain to her that whilst I'm away Lana is her guest and must be treated with consideration and not subjected to danger, I'm sure she'll listen to you. She's a good girl and always does as I tell her. I know she'll do as you tell her too, but I can't help worrying.'

Ellen, sitting by her friend's bed, patted her hand and then gave a rueful laugh. 'If you're worried that my Lana will want to scramble up chimneys like the sweeps' boys used to do in the olden days, that's one worry you can cast out of your mind,' she said. 'Lana likes pretty clothes and havin' the cleanest hands in the class and playing skip rope or relievio with her pals, to say nothing of trips to the cinema and the theatre. She and your Nonny are exactly the same age, but she's already showin' an interest in boys. In fact sometimes she acts like a little old lady and not like a kid at all. So don't worry that she'll take to the mountains. I can't think of anything unlikelier.'

'That's good,' Molly said absently, and Ellen thought that she had put her friend's fears to rest. She said as much but noticed that there was still a tiny frown between Molly's brows.

'What's up now, queen?' she asked and Molly was opening her mouth to reply when Rhys and the children re-entered the ward. They had been down to the harbour to look at the boats, and then along to the pier to see the huge jellyfish as they floated past, and all four of them were pink-cheeked and smiling. Whatever Molly's worries might have been she did not mention them again, and Ellen was glad that she had not admitted to her friend how much the silence frightened her.

The ward sister had said that as soon as Mrs Roberts's burns healed she would be given a walking plaster and allowed home, so long as Ellen stayed to look after her, and by that time, Ellen was determined, she would be as used to conditions at Cefn Farm as Molly was herself.

When her visitors had departed Molly lay back against her pillows with a frustrated little sigh. She had meant to ask Ellen how the children were getting on with one another, because for the first time for many years she had remembered the possible relationship between Chris and Lana. Molly told herself she did not believe Flossy for one moment, but if the ward maid *was* right, and someone had swapped the two baby girls, then Lana and Chris might be brother and sister. So far as Molly was concerned that was fine. What would not be fine was if Chris and Lana began to grow fond of one another in a more romantic sense; Molly could remember that she herself had had her first boyfriend at the tender age of ten. Chris, however, had never shown much interest in any girl, and teased his sister and her friends to distraction sometimes. Molly permitted herself a small grin. Chris, she concluded, was more likely to make Lana an apple-pie bed and clip her ear if she acted daft than to give her a cuddle.

Reassured, she settled down to sleep.

Chapter Seven

If there was one thing that could be said in Sam's favour, it would be that he was not work shy, so as soon as he got into open country he offered himself as labourer for any work that needed doing. Once or twice, as he journeyed on, he was forced to work for a couple of good meals a day and no pay, but that did not happen often. It was harvest time, when neighbours got together to bring the harvest home, and once he reached mountain country there was plenty of work for a man prepared to take on hard physical tasks such as mending fences, digging ditches and similar work.

To Sam's pleasure, he only had to say that he was searching for an English woman with a little girl of ten or eleven and mention the name of the farm to be given the directions he needed. Thus it was only three weeks after leaving Liverpool that he finally found himself peering through a grove of trees at a low stone house surrounded by farm buildings, and the name *Cefn Farm* written in white paint on a large slab of slate even taller than Sam himself.

Sam tucked himself away in the copse, actually climbing into the branches of a good-sized oak whence he could spy on the inhabitants of Cefn Farm, because for all he knew there might be other farms of the same name or Ellen and the kid might have moved on. Sam had purchased bread, cheese and pickles at the nearest village and now he settled himself comfortably on a broad branch from which he could see the farmyard clearly. Presently he was rewarded by the sight of a woman in a large canvas overall with a bucket swinging from her hand. His last glimpse of Ellen had been as she climbed back into the little car, but he recognised her instantly and felt the old familiar surge of rage and hate. She was doing all right for herself! She had obviously either moved in or married the chap who owned this place, yet she still had the cheek to demand money from Sam, a poor seaman, who at the moment was working as a labourer just to keep body and soul together. Of course the barrow boy had told him she was off to Wales to help a sick friend, but that was the sort of thing she would say. Saint Ellen, he told himself, his face screwed up into an expression of disbelief. That was a likely story! And try though he might he could not imagine how a Liverpool housewife could come to be friends with someone living so far from civilisation. He wondered, rather reluctantly, whether she might be working as some sort of maidservant, but doubted it after he had watched her for a couple of hours. She had the girl with her but he didn't see much of the kid save when Ellen came out and banged a blackened ladle on a big old-fashioned saucepan. This, it seemed, was the call for dinner, for various people came across the yard, entered the building by the back door and shut it behind them.

Sam began to eat his bread and cheese, wishing

he could have some of what the others were having, for though it was a hot day he could have done with something more solid inside him. He imagined he could smell a meat pie just out of the oven and his annoyance with Ellen grew.

Presently, he descended from his tree and made his way to a tumbledown cottage further up the mountain, almost overgrown with bracken; which he had noticed as he approached the farm. He was still not sure what form his revenge should take, but it was clear that it would probably involve the child. He had a pencil and notebook in his pocket, both filched from the small general shop where he had bought the bread and cheese. He meant to write a ransom note of sorts, warning Ellen of all the horrible things which would befall her daughter if she did not write a letter to the authorities saying that she had received the money they thought her husband owed, and now waived her claim to any more. He would need to see the letter, of course, but that was for later. First he must grab the child and scare Ellen witless.

It was a pity in a way that it was necessary to tell her who had kidnapped the girl. He would have preferred to exact his revenge, return the child and make off at once, but that would not stop the demands for money, and since these were the main reasons for the kidnap he would have to admit it was he who had done it. For a moment he feared that Ellen would refuse to write the letter, assuming he would not harm his own child, but then he chided himself for a fool. She knew very well that he had no affection for Lana, had not set eyes on her for half a dozen years and even before that had left her upbringing entirely in his wife's hands. Knowing that he had taken Lana off into this wild country should surely be enough to bring Ellen to her knees. But first he must plan his campaign like a military manoeuvre, and to start with, once he was safely installed in the ruined cottage, he would no longer be Sam O'Mara. He would think of himself as the Watcher, would *be* the Watcher. Sam grinned to himself. Ellen had thought she was rid of him; well, she would soon discover that that was far from the case.

All through that long hot afternoon, Sam – the Watcher – lay in the nest of bracken he had made for himself in the doorway of the ancient cottage, from where he could watch the comings and goings in the farmyard below. He snoozed and plotted and thought about his ransom note with increasing pleasure. How Ellen would weep and wail, how she would go down on her knees and beg him to return her daughter! Then he settled down to wait, for dusk comes late in August, and he told himself that he needed darkness for his plan to succeed.

'Lana O'Mara, how can you possibly stand there and say you're afraid of a sheep?' Chris's voice was scornful. 'I could understand if you were a bit scared of the ram, because he's a grand big fellow and if he once got you on his horns he could likely chuck you into the next valley, but that ewe was bottle-reared by us last year and wouldn't hurt a fly.'

'She butted me in the breadbasket,' Lana said, her voice trembling a little. 'She did, honest to

God she did, Chris. She come up to me, trod on me nice new sandals and butted me.'

'Oh, Lana, she didn't mean any harm,' Nonny said at once, leaping to the defence of the yearling. 'She wants you to play or to give her a bit of something nice to eat, she's not fussy which. But surely you're used to the sheep by now? You actually said you liked the lambs yesterday...'

'Lambs are all right, but they don't trample on me feet,' Lana pointed out. She turned hopeful eyes upon Chris. 'My mum says when we go into the village for her messages, we can buy an ounce or two of aniseed balls or some treacle toffee, whichever we'd rather. Shall we go in today?'

The three children were in the stables, Chris and Nonny energetically grooming Cherry so that Chris might presently harness her to the pony cart, for Rhys had agreed, when asked, that they might drive to the village to fetch the groceries Ellen needed, thus saving them from hefting heavy shopping baskets the four miles back. At Lana's words, Chris heaved a sigh, then nodded. 'Might as well, since we've done all our jobs, haven't we, Nonny? And I'm for treacle toffee 'cos you get more than a couple of ounces of that in one of Mrs Enfys's little brown bags.'

He sent his sister running back to the farmhouse for the list of Ellen's requirements whilst he backed the pony between the shafts and Lana watched.

'Wish I could do that,' she said as he worked, though without much conviction. She had tried to hide her fear of horses from the others but did not think she had succeeded very well. Nonny, mindful of her mother's words, was kind and patient with their visitor, doing her very best to make Lana feel at home, but Chris could not conceal his impatience over Lana's many fears. So it was no surprise to Lana now when he turned a scornful face towards her and answered sharply.

'Wish you could do what? If you want to be a help take hold of Cherry's bridle near the sort of ring thing which holds her bit, whilst I fasten the rest of her harness. She's a placid little thing, never dances about, so your toes should be safe.'

Lana admired Chris and was desperate for his approval, but even so she could not bring herself to actually touch the pony. Knowing nothing of bridles or bits or any other sort of harness she imagined that Cherry, a bay with a black mane and tail, might turn and snap off her fingers before she could get them out of the way. Nonny had told her always to offer food to any creature on the flat of the hand, 'for they wouldn't mean to hurt you but might mistake your fingers for a carrot,' she had explained. Far from reassuring Lana, however, the remark had merely given her something else to worry about. If an animal was so stupid that it could confuse a finger with a carrot then it might easily take a bite out of her cheek, assuming it to be a rosy apple. So poor Lana, even after three weeks of close association with the animals at Cefn Farm, still preferred to remain within doors. The old sheepdog, Feather, who was allowed to come into the kitchen from time to time, mostly ignored Lana, though she did consent to let the visitor stroke her pointed black ears; and when, highly daring, Lana had offered her a piece of bacon rind she had accepted it with such careful gentleness that Lana had actually told her mother that one of these days it would be nice if the O'Maras could have a dog.

But right now Chris was giving an exasperated sigh and Lana decided that the time had come to make a clean breast of her fear. She could not have borne to do so in front of Nonny, because they were the same age and should, in theory, be as brave as one another, but she hoped that with Nonny out of the way she could explain to Chris, even ask him to help her to conquer her timidity. She glanced across the yard to make certain that Nonny was not approaching once more and then sidled closer and put a tentative hand on Cherry's burnished neck. She waited until Chris turned to give her an enquiring look, then spoke out.

'Chris, I'm – I'm not used to animals, you know. It's true there are horses in Liverpool but apart from the one that pulls the milk cart they don't come into our street much. The milkman's horse is called Hepzibah and she's very old. Her teeth are yellow and quite a lot have fallen out, but Mum lets me give her a pat whilst she feeds her sugar or an apple. Mum isn't afraid; she doesn't even mind the green dribbly stuff that runs out of the corners of Hep's mouth when she chews somethin' good. Could you teach me not to be afraid, Chris? I'd try real hard, honest to God I would. I know you think I'm a coward because when I tried to feed the chickens and they flew at me I dropped the perishin' bucket and ran indoors. But, you see, the hens we keep in Liverpool can't fly and they're in a little wire cage anyhow, so – so I weren't expectin' it, that's all.' She looked appealingly at Chris, who was continuing with the work of harnessing the pony without appearing to listen to her.

'Chris?' Lana could hear the slight tremble in her voice and suddenly a tiny spurt of anger gave her courage. Chris was being horrid, she considered. Her old pal Phil would not have dreamed of snubbing her by simply not replying, so why should Chris be so beastly? But Chris had shoved a hand into his pocket and produced a small red apple which he was holding out towards the pony, and only when Cherry had taken it deftly from his palm did he look round at his companion.

'Well, if you'll do exactly as I tell you and try really hard I dare say you might begin to like the animals instead of being afraid of them,' he said. 'Nonny's been trying to help you – she's a good girl is my little sister – but I'm perfectly willing to give you a few lessons if only you won't start squeaking and snatching your hand back, which frankly, Lana, is a enough to get you bitten by the most mild-mannered animal. Can't you understand that? I've seen you offer a sugar lump to Guinness, who is the gentlest creature for all his size, and just as his muzzle gets near your hand and he snuffles to smell what you're offering you go and snatch it back. How would you like it if your mum made you a lovely breakfast and then, when you sat down to start eating, snatched it away?'

Lana giggled. 'I wouldn't like it at all,' she admitted frankly. For the first time, she gave

Chris a broad smile. 'I might even bite me mum's fingers, even if I didn't mistake them for carrots!'

Chris laughed. 'You're not a bad kid, and I dare say if our roles were reversed and I was staying in your house in the city I'd be scared of all sorts: traffic, trams, crowds of people, that sort of thing. So Nonny and myself will take you in hand, only *do* try not to show you're afraid. I don't have a lot of patience, to tell you the truth, and when you flinch if a sheep so much as looks at you ... well, never mind. We'll do our best to sort you out. And now go and find out why Nonny's taking such ages to get the list from Auntie Ellen.'

Chris had no sooner spoken, however, than Nonny came dancing out of the farm kitchen, carrying several empty wicker baskets and the housekeeping purse. 'Auntie Ellen says since we're taking the pony and cart we can bring back our pals so's they can get to know Lana,' she said happily. 'She says we can bring two girls and three boys so that it's even numbers and whilst we're gone she'll prepare a picnic lunch.' By this time Lana and Chris were already in the pony cart, and now Nonny joined them. She turned to Lana. 'You'll like our pals, honest to God you will. Last time they came over we dammed the stream; it was grand work for a hot day and Mum and Dad were really pleased with us. You've never been on the farm for the gathering or the sheep-washing but Dad's talked over and over about improving the pool, and another day's work will make the dam perfect.' Lana muttered something and Chris turned and gave his sister a reproving glance.

'You're an idiot, Nonny; Lana doesn't know

what you're talking about,' he pointed out. He turned back to Lana as he guided the pony out of the farmyard and down the driveway towards the lane. 'There are two or three gatherings every year, when the hill farmers get their sheep into the pens. One is at lambing, another for shearing, and before that the sheep are washed to get rid of maggots and other pests. Some farms have a special dipping bath – we've got one ourselves – but it's nowhere near as good as a proper pool and of course we can wash a fair number of sheep in the river at once, whilst the dipping bath will only hold one at a time.'

'I see,' Lana said slowly. 'But will the sheep come down to the river whilst we're damming it; and what does damming mean, anyway?'

Chris sighed; it was clear that though he had promised to help he found her ignorance truly trying. Nonny on the other hand did not seem to mind how often she repeated something, and now settled down to explain to Lana in carefully chosen words.

'We already have a good pool in the river but it could do with being a bit deeper and a fair bit larger,' she explained. 'The whole business of washing the sheep is quite tricky, you see. You push them in at one side of the pool so that they have to splash across to the other, and when the river's in spate – that means when it's very very full of water – you could lose some of the weaker ones because they would drown before they reached the further bank. So you see it's quite a tricky business choosing the right moment. Once we've built up the wall of the dam, however – you'll see what a dam is when we reach the river – Dad will be able to control the flow of the water, then we can limit the depth of the pool and won't need to lose any sheep.'

Chris grinned triumphantly. 'There you are, a lesson in hill farming and sheep husbandry rolled into one. Isn't Nonny clever?'

'Yes, I gerrit. But what you're offerin' your pals is hard work, norra game at all,' Lana pointed out. 'Will they come if they know you mean 'em to work?'

This time Nonny answered with a snort. 'Huh! Playing around with clay, rocks and water isn't work, it's one of the grandest games in the world,' she said. 'Everyone wears their oldest clothes – the lads will strip down to their underwear, I expect – and when we get back to Cefn Farm your mum will have made a super tea. That's why we're getting the messages early. And I'll guarantee you'll really enjoy it, because everyone does, especially on such a hot day. It's grand to be playing with water and mud when it's so hot, and as soon as the dam is complete and the pool is deep enough everyone will plunge in and slosh around...'

'Won't the sheep mind? I shouldn't think they'll want us in their nice bathing pool,' Lana said doubtfully, and tried not to be offended when both Chris and Nonny burst out laughing. 'You daft girl; the sheep hate being washed and have to be driven down to the river by us and all the dogs, as well as half the neighbourhood,' Chris said derisively. 'Oh, Lana O'Mara, you've got a lot to learn!'

Chapter Eight

Sam had truly intended to make his strike as soon as it grew dusk on the very day he arrived at Cefn Farm, but it had been the first chance he had had to rest and relax since he had started on his search. He had made himself a cosy bed in the dry bracken which half filled the roofed-in part of the ancient cottage, and to his own real surprise he found that he was by no means eager to leave the quiet spot in which he had hidden himself away. He had never been a country boy and had spent his whole working life either at sea or on the docks of Liverpool or other ports around the world. He realised now that he had never known the total peace and quiet which he had just discovered. If he had thought about it he would never have expected to like it, yet he did. He even resented the sounds which occasionally floated up to him as folk called to one another across the farmyard, or started up the engine of the little car, or the very much larger tractor. He began to envy Ellen in a way he had never thought possible. She, he assumed, was being paid to live in what he now considered to be an idyllic spot. When, his revenge complete, he returned to civilisation, he would have to face once more the noise and bustle of the quayside, the cramped and stuffy space in which he hung his hammock and the constant presence of other men; dirty, oily, aggressive men, whose mere presence after the stillness of the mountains would be repugnant to him.

When he woke on the second day, his belly was rumbling and empty and he knew that, if he was going to continue with his kidnapping plan, he would simply have to have food and something to drink. He had woken as the first faint light of dawn greyed the sky, and now he sat up, scratching thoughtfully – for he had not been the only occupant of his bracken bed – and considered what best to do. His observation of Cefn Farm had led him to believe that out here in the sticks folk rarely shut their doors, let alone locked them. And on the previous day he had seen a number of children carrying, into what he now assumed must be some sort of storeroom, a quantity of what looked very like food. There was a window, half open, through which he would be able to see just what the room contained when he got close enough. Sam knew very little about the country but from various things he had heard he imagined that the long low room might be a dairy. Certainly he had seen buckets of milk carried in there the previous day, and so far as he could make out only some of it had come out again to be poured into the large metal churns which stood on the wooden trestle by the farm gate. That would seem to indicate that he was right and the room really was a dairy, so might well be worth a visit.

Sam stood up and brushed dried bracken out of his clothes. He had shed his duffel coat the night before and decided to leave it where it lay. His trousers had deep pockets and he didn't mean to steal so much that Ellen and her fancy man might realise they had been robbed. He just wanted enough grub to last him through the day and possibly enough for him and his victim that night. Having made up his mind, he set off down the hill towards the farmhouse.

A remarkably short time later he was once more ensconced in the ruined cottage, his pockets satisfactorily bulging. He had not needed to force his way in through the window since the dairy also boasted an unlocked door through which he had entered, first removing his boots, knotting their laces and hanging them round his neck. Sneaking in on tiptoe, he had found a long, whitewashed room containing a cold slab upon which were several large pats of butter, a big blue and white striped jug of milk and a bowl so full of eggs that he had no compunction in abstracting half a dozen, since he was sure they would not be missed. There was another door in the dairy which he thought might lead into the house, so he tried it with great caution and was delighted to discover that it was a cupboard containing bottled fruit, jars of jam and three long loaves of home-made bread. The bread was tempting; his mouth watered at the thought of a thick slice of it spread with this wonderful home-made butter and topped off with some of the strawberry jam he saw in a labelled pot. He knew better than to take a cut from the loaf – that really would be noticed – but if he took the whole thing might not Ellen conclude that she had baked one loaf short the previous day? He decided that it was worth giving it a go, and also took a tiny jar of jam, which he supposed must be a make-weight, shuffling the other jars along so that no gap would be apparent. He slipped the loaf into the front of his shirt and pushed the jam into his pocket, using the other pocket for the eggs and the butter. Thus armed with the makings of a very satisfying breakfast he took one last look around him. He knew eggs could be eaten raw though he did not much fancy the idea, but there were pans hanging on the wall; if he took one of them and cracked the eggs into it, or even put them in still wearing their shells, he could make himself a first rate breakfast and there would be enough left over for dinner and tea as well.

Sam chuckled silently to himself as he slid out through the dairy door. He contemplated leaving it a little ajar, so that they might think a passing tramp had helped himself, then changed his mind. What did it matter, after all? Once he'd snatched the kid, Ellen, at any rate, would guess where the food had gone, might even be grateful that he was feeding that spoilt little madam who was her daughter. Sam padded across the farmyard, keeping close to the buildings. He swore beneath his breath when he stood in a cow pat, but nevertheless he did not replace his boots until he was mounting the hill towards the ruined cottage. It was still extremely early. The sun was not even thinking about rising, so he collected a pile of dry bracken and twigs and started a small fire, relieved to see that there was almost no smoke visible. Then he cracked his eggs into the pan and cooked them over the flame, thankful, not for the first time, that he always carried matches. He rolled his own cigarettes but was husbanding his resources, so though he fingered his tobacco pouch wistfully he made no effort to extract it from his pocket. He would have a cigarette when the child was trussed up somewhere and he was waiting for Ellen to cave in and promise she would get the authorities off his back.

He jiggled the pan and watched the albumen gradually grow cloudy and then white as it met the hot butter. Mouth watering, he produced a clasp knife and the loaf and very soon he was devouring his first food of the day: an enormous fried egg sandwich.

As the sun crept up to shine through a narrow gap in the mountains, Sam, peering carefully from his hide-out, saw that down in the farmyard below the day was beginning. Although it was early it was already very warm and Sam watched as the tall fellow with black curly hair, whom he thought of as Ellen's fancy man, came out of the farmhouse and headed for the outbuildings.

Sam had watched with considerable interest the sudden influx of children the previous day and their work on the river, and work it certainly was; hard work, too. They had shifted quite big rocks and dug up quantities of clay with which to fix the rocks in place, all of this with much shouting and laughter. The boys had stripped to their underpants and the girls had tucked their skirts into their knickers and all worked with a will. It had made Sam quite tired to see them using so much energy, and as evening came, and then dusk, he had made his way with the utmost caution down to the river hoping to be able to see at close quarters just exactly what those kids had been doing.

He had once visited a logging company in

Canada, and now recognised the dam for what it was, assuming, however, that the kids had been making themselves a bathing pool, since he had no idea that sheep had to be washed before shearing. Then, having satisfied his curiosity, he had returned to his hide-out.

Now he waited for an outcry from either Ellen or one of the others when they discovered the theft of bread and eggs, but if there was such a discovery there was no sign of it from here. Sam chuckled to himself, visualising the scene inside the dairy: Ellen's puzzlement at the missing loaf and her conclusion that she must have miscounted the day before. He was sure she would not notice the loss of the eggs, though he did wonder about the pats of butter. They had been laid out in two neat rows, so he had taken one pat off each and thought that with luck they would not have been counted and the loss would not be remarked upon. He doubted very much if anyone would miss the jam or the brightly burnished little pan, but if they did, what would it matter? Ellen, he knew, was a somewhat careless housewife; she had been known to throw out two or three of the best teaspoons when she had not noticed them lying in the bottom of the washing-up water, and he had had to give her an absent-minded clack once or twice for running out of bacon or tea. He remembered she had once turned quite nasty when he had suggested she should run down to the corner shop and buy him a bottle of Guinness instead. No doubt she'd be equally careless here.

Sam had finished his breakfast by this time, rounding off the egg sandwich with a large slice of bread and jam. He had taken a long drink of milk from the blue and white jug while he was in the dairy so was not thirsty, and now that the early morning bustle in the farmyard below had settled into silence once more he lay back on his bracken couch, enjoying the warmth of the sun on his face and telling himself that Ellen did not deserve such a wonderful way of life and that, very soon now, she would get what she truly did deserve: worry, misery, and his ransom note.

He gazed up into the brilliant blue of the sky and decided to have five minutes before beginning what to him was a daunting task: writing the ransom note. Overhead a white dove winged its leisurely way across the blue. Sam's lids drooped; his five minutes became ten ... fifteen...

With a smile curling his loose lips, Sam slept.

Ellen carried the full buckets of milk into the dairy and glanced around the room which had become her domain, thinking that she would really miss it when her friend came out of hospital later that day. She had told both Rhys and Molly that she had never baked bread in her life, and this was true, though whenever she had sufficient time at home she baked cakes and pies, knowing they were better value – and tasted better – than the shop-bought ones. Despite her initial fears, however, she had taken to breadmaking like a duck to water. To begin with she had one or two failures, but once she had grown accustomed to the length of time it took for the loaves to prove her baking had, Rhys told her, become every bit as good as Molly's.

So now, as she entered the dairy with her two full buckets of milk, her eyes went straight to the three loaves which she had baked the evening before and had left in the window embrasure to cool. She went across to the cooler and poured in the contents of her buckets. Then she turned to stare at the three loaves, then stared again. There were only two. She remembered perfectly getting the tins out of the oven, each with its burden of perfect bread, shaking the loaves gently from the tins on to a wire tray – there had just been room for the three of them – and carrying it through to the dairy to cool. She had come through what Molly referred to as the still room, and now she wondered whether she had absent-mindedly taken one of the loaves off the wire tray and stood it on the shelf with the jars of jam and bottled fruit. She opened the door to check that no loaf lurked there, and the swiftest of glances showed her that she had done no such thing. No, her memory had not played her false: three loaves of bread she had baked, three loaves of bread she had carried through into the dairy, and three loaves of bread should now be standing in the window embrasure, waiting for her to take one of them back to the kitchen for breakfast.

When Lana entered the dairy a moment later, she found her mother still staring at the loaves of bread, a puzzled frown on her face. She returned Lana's 'Good morning' rather absently, and went on, 'Lana, something very odd has happened. I baked three loaves last night, didn't I?'

Lana, who was laying the breakfast table and had come into the dairy to fetch some butter, shrugged. 'I dunno,' she said vaguely. 'Why d'you ask?'

'Because there are only two loaves on the windowsill now,' her mother said. 'The window wasn't really open – well, just a crack – so I don't think it was an animal. Was it one of you kids?'

For answer her daughter turned and shouted over her shoulder, 'Me mum says someone's took a loaf of bread off of the windowsill in the dairy. Did someone fancy a snack during the night?'

Chris came in and peered curiously at the two remaining loaves. 'If there really is one missing, it'll be a tramp,' he announced. 'They don't take stuff as a rule, 'cos they know that if they come to the door and ask our mum will give them grub and maybe a bottle of cold tea. But if one of them came to the farm late, after we were all in bed, I guess he'd of helped himself. Anything else missing?'

Ellen cast a quick glance round the room, then shook her head. 'I don't think so,' she said. 'Oh well, that's a relief; when I saw two loaves where three should have been I thought I were goin' light in the head. Now, let's get on with breakfast.'

During the meal she told Rhys about the missing loaf, thinking that perhaps he had moved the bread to another spot for some reason, but it was Nonny who provided the most understandable clue. 'The moon was at the full last night, wasn't it?' she remarked, porridge spoon poised. 'The light fell on my face and woke me up so I hopped out of bed and went very quietly to draw the curtains across. I stood there for a moment, looking out, because it was so beautiful, all black and silver; a bit like the cowboy films they show in the village hall every month.'

Rhys raised an eyebrow. 'What's that got to do with the missing loaf?' he enquired. 'Or are you about to tell us that you saw one of the fairy folk sliding down a moonbeam and ending up just under the dairy window?'

'Don't be so horrid, Dad; it's years since I believed in fairies,' Nonny said hotly. 'No, it wasn't anything like that. I thought I saw the shadow of someone heading out of the farmyard; I couldn't see a person, mind, just a shadow. So if Chris's right and it was a tramp I reckon he must have made the shadow I saw.'

'Well, so long as he wasn't after the hens,' Rhys said absently. 'Your mum is so proud of her Rhode Island Reds, and the way her flock is increasing, that I'd hate to admit we'd lost one in her absence.'

Nonny, now eating porridge with gusto, shook her head. 'Don't worry, Dad. When I let them out of their hut this morning every single one came out alive and kicking. Well, all except the broody; she stayed stuck to her eggs and made that sort of growling purr when I went in so I knew she was fine. I put my hand under her to see whether the eggs had started to crack, and she pecked so hard at my fingers that I've got the scars to prove it. I wouldn't have interfered with her, only Mum's coming home today and it would be a lovely surprise if she could see fluffy yellow heads poking out from under the broody's wings.'

Lana and her mother had decided that Molly should be welcomed home by a present from them, and had agonised over what to buy, finally deciding on an embroidered tablecloth for when Molly entertained the members of the local Women's Institute to tea. Now Nonny decided that she too would welcome her mother home with a gift. In the village the previous day she had noticed on the post office counter some boxes of chicks awaiting either delivery or collection, she was not sure which. If she hurried down to the village again today she might be able to buy half a dozen of the dear little things, and present them to her mother as soon as Molly reached the farm once more. She would say nothing about it to Chris, or he would insist on a half share in the gift and she wanted it to be just from herself. However, she did tell Lana, in strictest confidence, about her cunning plan, and the other girl thought it a wonderful idea.

All through the morning Nonny worked at her chores, and when Ellen called that the midday meal was ready she joined the others round the long kitchen table. Jacob was in high fettle, getting as excited over Molly's return as her own family. He had searched the countryside for something to give as a welcome home present, and had ended up with a rabbit, skinned, jointed and ready for the oven, since he said he knew the missus was rare fond of rabbit pie. Old Mr Williams, who had come to the farm almost every day during Molly's absence, had been excited as well. He had cut a grand bunch of Mrs Sinkins pinks from his own garden, and the Pritchards, who had dispatched Rhodri to help Rhys and Jacob in any way he could, had also sent a gift. The previous evening the young man had turned up on the doorstep, grinning shyly. 'My mam's done a big bake and thought you might find a use for this,' he said, putting a parcel down on the kitchen table, and opening it to display an enormous fruit loaf. 'My mam knows Mrs Roberts is rare fond of bara brith, so a welcome home present, it is, from us all.'

He was heartily thanked and invited to share in the supper Ellen was putting on the table, but had regretfully refused. 'Kind of you it is, but I'd best be off home. Tomorrow I've promised to go over to Beddgelert, to help my dad's pal to ear-mark his lambs, so I'll get an early night.'

Now, as they ate their midday meal, Rhys asked who would be accompanying him to the hospital. Everyone wanted to be of the party, but Rhys had to shake his head. 'There wouldn't be room for all of us,' he pointed out. 'Mum's case will go in the boot and she'll sit in the passenger seat on the way home, so there's really only room for Auntie Ellen and one of you kids; which shall it be?'

Chris sighed. 'It can't be me,' he said regretfully. 'Someone's got to look after the farm. And it shouldn't be Nonny because she'll get our dinners and give an eye to the house. Which leaves dear little useless Lana – sorry; sorry, only joking – who'd probably be afraid to stay at the farm anyway once the workers have gone home and there are no grown-ups left.'

Lana stiffened. She had honestly believed that Chris had looked upon her with more favour since the building of the dam, but now it appeared she still had to prove herself, so she said:

'I'll stay and help Nonny with supper and that. I'll help with the chores too. I'm not frightened of the hens any more, so I'll chase them into the hut, count them, and close the pop-hole when they're all safe inside.'

'Are you sure, queen?' Ellen said doubtfully. 'I can tell you mean to be useful and to help Chris and Nonny in any way you can, but I'm sure they'll understand if you'd rather come with me.' She turned to Rhys; 'I've worked as a hospital cleaner in Liverpool, so I know what I'm talking about when I warn you that it takes rather a long time to discharge someone from hospital, especially when they're on crutches – hospital property crutches – and need to return for prescriptions and appointments and so on. Even if we set out in the next half hour I bet it'll be dark before we're back at Cefn Farm again.'

Lana, however, was adamant. Apart from anything else she guessed that Rhys would drive fast on the outward journey, if not on the return, and when the little car swayed and leapt over the poorly maintained mountain roads she always had to fight an urge to throw up. No, she would be better staying with Nonny and Chris and giving what help she could.

Rhys beamed around the table; it was clear he could scarcely hide his excitement and delight at the thought of having Molly home once more. 'Right you are, then,' he said breezily. 'Well, if that's settled we'd best get off or Ellen will be proved right and it'll be midnight before we can seek our beds.'

The children waved the baby Morris off, proud

of the trust that Rhys had placed in them, for there had not been one suggestion that Mr Williams or Jacob should stay beyond their allotted time. As soon as the car had disappeared round the bend into the lane, Chris went to fetch the pigswill and the girls returned to the farmhouse. 'We'll make up Mum's bed with clean sheets and put Mr Williams's flowers beside it,' Nonny said importantly. 'Do you know how to make Welsh cakes? I'll show you; it's ever so easy, and Mum loves them. Then we'll go and see if there's anything we can do to help Chris. Oh, it'll be so wonderful to see Mum at Cefn Farm again!'

From his hide-out well above the farm, Sam watched with lazy interest as the small figures below him came and went. When he saw Ellen and the dark-haired man drive away he went down to the post office in the village and bought a slab of fruit cake, two bottles of beer and four thick slices of ham as well as half a dozen floury white baps, explaining to the girl who served him that he was on a walking holiday in the area. 'Well, the right weather you have chosen for it,' the girl remarked. 'Though my dad, who's a rare weather prophet, says it's too hot; sultry like. He reckons we need a storm to clear the air. And he says we'll get one before very long, too.'

Sam muttered some reply and hurried out of the shop, pulling his cap even further over his low forehead. Then he returned to his hide-out to wait for dusk. Of course it was possible that the odd little car might return any moment, and then he might have to reconsider his kidnap. But he hoped for the best; he had been lucky so far, finding Cefn Farm so easily, managing to steal food without being spotted, and above all discovering the ideal hide-out from which to spy on his erring wife and daughter. Sam was sure, now, that his luck would hold. He had noted that the w.c. was in the little hut right at the end of the long vegetable garden. When bedtime approached, every single one of the inhabitants of the farm visited that hut; that would be the moment for Sam to make his snatch.

Sam took a swig at the Guinness and broke off a piece of the cake, then fingered the cord in his pocket. It was really a good length of binder twine that he had plaited in the form of a rope with a loop on each end. If possible he meant to lure the child up to the ruined cottage, but if she tried to scream or struggle he now had the means to prevent either occurrence. He had found a thick wad of torn-up sheeting which would do very well as a gag, and with the cord round her wrist and his own, like handcuffs, the kid could scarcely run away from him. Satisfied that he had thought of every eventuality, Sam waited.

Ellen had been absolutely right. She and Rhys had arrived at the hospital soon after four, and had not managed to escape until the clock stood at ten past seven. There had been so much to do! The consultant who had treated Molly's burns and the surgeon who had set her leg both had to be contacted, so that they might sign Molly off; then they had gone to the pharmacy with the prescriptions they had been given and had waited ages for ointment and medicines, including painkillers, for though the burns were a great deal better they were still painful. After that, to Rhys's annoyance, they had delivered the meal which Molly had ticked on her menu the previous night, and the ward sister had insisted that she should eat it. 'I doubt your good man has thought of having a meal ready for you when you get home,' she had said. 'Just you eat up this good food, my dear, or it will be wasted, and we don't approve of waste, do we?'

Poor Molly had to bolt a dish of soup, a plateful of shepherd's pie and cabbage, and a small bowl of ice cream before she was allowed to leave the ward, and even then, as Rhys put it, there were other hoops through which they must jump.

But at last they found themselves in the car park, with Molly's little case neatly packed and Rhys in a fever to get them home, though the nurse who accompanied them out to the car, a local girl who obviously knew the area, warned Rhys that he must drive slowly and with care, since though Molly's broken limb was healing well, jiggling over rough country roads might set her back.

Rhys promised to be careful; he would have promised anything to have his Molly home again, and they set off at a pace so sober that had they continued thus it would have been several hours before they reached Cefn Farm. But in fact all too soon weather conditions forced Rhys to drive even more slowly. Rain, which had begun to fall even before they had left the hospital premises, began to simply pelt down, so violently that within moments the windscreen wipers on the little car gave up the struggle, though they continued to swish manfully across the windscreen. 'Good thing I had that meal,' Molly shouted above the thunder of the rain on the canvas hood. 'No chance of getting home by suppertime, unless the rain eases as we get near the valley.'

Ellen, sitting in the back with all Molly's possessions around her, gave a groan. 'Oh, Moll, I made a grand big rabbit pie because Jacob brought one in especially for you, knowing how fond you are of them. I told the kids not to broach it until we got home – I made three mutton pasties, one each for them, so they wouldn't be tempted to – but now it looks as though you'll be eating rabbit pie for breakfast.'

Molly squiggled round in her seat to smile at her friend. 'Ooh, rabbit pie, my favourite,' she said. 'Oh, damn it, the hood's beginning to leak. It doesn't matter if the outside of my suitcase gets wet, so you'd better swap places with it, otherwise you'll be drenched.'

'We'll all be drenched at this rate,' Rhys shouted. 'All we want now is–' He was interrupted by a peal of thunder accompanied by lightning so vivid that he jumped. 'I wish we could get out from under these trees,' he said uneasily. 'But it'll be another four or five miles until we're clear of the forest.'

Molly thought the little car seemed to grit its teeth, hunch its shoulders, pull its canvas hood down over its eyes and slog grimly on. Soon it was necessary to turn on the lights, though they could scarcely penetrate more than a few feet because of the driving rain. 'It's a flippin' cloudburst, ain't it?' Ellen shrieked. 'I wonder what the kids are doing? I hopes as they're norrout in this perishin' downpour. I disremember ever seeing rain like it.'

Rhys turned his head to smile at Ellen, then chuckled. 'That's because it's mountain rain; for some reason the mountains attract the worse of the weather and it always eases off when it reaches the plain. As for the kids, I shouldn't worry about 'em; they've got a lot of sense and even if they weren't indoors when the rain started they'll seek shelter in the outbuildings, so there's no need–' His words were interrupted by a fearful crash of thunder, and even through the trees they could see the brilliance of the lightning as it stabbed and circled around the great peaks.

The storm was so violent that it put Ellen in mind of that other storm, the one that had attacked Liverpool the night that Lana and Nonny had been born. She said as much to Molly, who nodded. 'Yes, I was thinking that myself,' she acknowledged. 'I remember the headlines in the paper the next day: storm of the century, they called it. I should think this one bids fair to rival it, though of course if it dies out before it reaches the big cities no one will even comment.' She laughed. 'Us hill farmers are used to being ignored by the press. When our river suddenly trebles in size and comes crashing down the mountain bringing dead sheep, boulders and even trees with it the local people help each other to cope with the damage, but never expect so much as a word in the newspapers.'

This conversation had been carried on above the howl of the wind and the crashing of thunder, and now Rhys shouted to the girls to keep their eyes peeled since the way ahead was narrow and twisting, and he needed all his concentration and strength to keep Minnie the Moocher on the road. Both women stopped talking and peered ahead and it was Ellen who suddenly shouted at Rhys to stop. 'There's a positive perishin' lake right across the road, and a tree...' she began, but it was too late. The front wheels of the car were submerged, the engine spluttered and died and Rhys jumped out of the car to find himself in two feet of water. Molly would have joined him but he shouted at her to stay where she was, though he was grateful when Ellen pushed forward the driver's seat and came splashing heavily to join him. 'Tell me wharr I must do,' she said breathlessly. 'Forward or back?'

'Can't go forward; it gets deeper, for a start, but the tree is blocking the road anyway,' Rhys shouted. 'It'll be back; I've taken the car out of gear, the handbrake's off and she's pretty light. But what we'll do then, God above knows. As soon as we've got her back on dry land we'll see if the engine will start and if it does we'll drive to the nearest farm. Someone's bound to have a tractor big enough to clear the road at least down into Betwys. Then we can ring the post office just to make sure there's been no trouble at Cefn Farm.'

Molly had wound down her window in order to join in the conversation. She wished she could have given a hand but knew she must not get the plaster wet so stayed where she was. However, the thought of the children brought fresh worries to her mind. 'What if the farm's been struck by lightning?' she quavered. 'Or suppose the river floods really badly and the water reaches the house? Suppose the lightning sets fire to the hay barn? Or the stables! The kids would rush into a burning building to save the horses...'

'Molly Roberts, stop imagining bogeys and prop your leg up on the dashboard, because I'm afraid water may come in through the floor and you know you mustn't get the plaster wet,' Rhys ordered her. 'Right, Ellen? When I give the word, push!'

At about the time the ward nurse was bidding Rhys to drive carefully, Nonny was entering the post office in the village. All the children loved the post office, partly because it sold interesting things such as sherbet dips, slabs of pink and white nougat and brown bags of treacle toffee and also because Mrs Enfys, the postmistress, was a warm and motherly soul who could always be relied upon to be interested in their doings, and to hand over to a child with a large shopping bag some little extra to eat on the way home. Today, however, the small shop was empty, probably because closing time was approaching, and also because of the grey clouds scudding overhead. Long experience had taught Snowdonians to read the weather signs, and if they knew heavy rain or a storm was approaching they left any unessential shopping to another day. So Nonny made straight for the counter, behind which Mrs Enfys was sitting in a creaking basket chair knitting what looked like a very large, very elaborate pink pullover.

'Afternoon, Mrs Enfys,' Nonny said cheerfully. 'Looks like rain, doesn't it? Jacob says there's a storm coming so I just hope it holds off until I get home. Today's the day they let my mother out of hospital. Auntie Ellen has baked a rabbit pie, Chris will give her a bar of chocolate and Auntie Ellen and Lana have bought the most beautiful tablecloth, embroidered all over with sweet peas, carnations and all sorts. So I'm here to spend my pocket money on something I know she'll like.'

Mrs Enfys was a large woman with rosy cheeks and a sweet expression, but whenever possible she remained in her chair, only getting up and searching the shelves when it became absolutely necessary. So now she smiled hopefully at her customer. 'What are you after, cariad?' she enquired. 'Something pretty for Mum? I'm clear out of boxes of chocolates, but...'

'Oh, no, not chocolates,' Nonny said eagerly. 'It's – it's something alive, Mrs Enfys. I saw them when I came yesterday; lots and lots of them, cheeping away in special cardboard boxes. Chicks!' She looked around her as she spoke but could see no sign of the boxes which she had noticed on her previous visit, and Mrs Enfys was shaking her head.

'Oh, cariad, them chicks was all ordered. No one can't go keeping chicks for more'n a few hours on food premises; 'twouldn't be right.' Her round and happy face had fallen, mirroring the disappointment she saw in her customer's. 'Oh, love, I'm that sorry! Tell you what, though; I can order you a box. They come in dozens and there are all sorts, but I reckon your mum would like the Rhode Island Reds 'cos she's got a Rhode Island flock; am I right?'

'Yes, you're right, but I guess it'll be days before the chicks arrive and I wanted to give Mum a present now,' Nonny said regretfully. She glanced hopefully around the shop but could see nothing which would please her mother the way the chicks would have done. She turned to the fat little postmistress. 'What'll I do, Mrs Enfys? I know how much chicks cost so I've brought the right money for a dozen; suppose you wrote a card out saying something like ... money paid for twelve chicks to be delivered as soon as possible. Could you do that?'

Mrs Enfys was beginning to agree when she clearly had another thought. 'I can do it, but I've had an even better idea,' she said excitedly. She fished under the counter and produced a large cardboard box. Opening it, she plunged both hands inside, saying, 'Remember last Easter, cariad? I decorated me window with toy chicks; just bundles of yellow fluff with little wire legs and tiny buttons for eyes. They was realistic-looking, I'll give 'em that. Now what I say is you take a dozen of my Easter chicks, put 'em in a box and give 'em to your mum, saying that she'll have the real ones in a day or two. What do you think, love?'

Nonny was thrilled with the idea. She would explain, of course, that she had wanted to get real chicks and would be doing so in no time, and she could visualise not only her mother's delight but how she would laugh and arrange the chicks in a line across the kitchen table, and tell Nonny that she was the cleverest girl ever.

Thanking Mrs Enfys from the heart, and graciously accepting a sherbet dip as well as a dozen balls of yellow fluff, Nonny had been so busy in the shop, that she had not realised the rain had started, but she very soon did so. She opened the door and stepped into the street, then hesitated in the face of the rain which was beginning to fall now in earnest. She could go back in the shop, but even as she considered doing so she heard Mrs Enfys slowly and ponderously walk across the floor, flip the open sign to closed and turn the mighty key in the lock. She can't have noticed that it was raining so hard, Nonny guessed, and then she shrugged. What was a bit of rain, after all? She might get pretty wet but she had got pretty wet the day before, making the dam. Why should today be any different? So she set off, head down, hands in pockets, telling herself that the rain was bound to stop presently.

Within the first mile, however, far from stopping, the rain had increased in force. The wind got up and she could hear the thunder rolling round the peaks. Telling herself that she did not mind thunder – although she was not too keen on lightning – Nonny kept her eyes on the ground, which was growing steadily more and more saturated, as, indeed, was Nonny herself. Once or twice she considered seeking shelter in one of the little cottages but dismissed the idea. How absolutely awful if her mother reached home only to find her daughter missing! That would never do. It was a pity she only had toy chicks whilst Chris had a real bar of chocolate, but she knew Molly well enough to appreciate that her mother would understand and be as pleased with the toys as with the real thing. The road she was following was a typical country road; a few words of a poem she had recently learned in school came back into Nonny's head. *The rolling English drunkard made the rolling English road.* Nonny giggled to herself. This was a Welsh road, but a Welshman could get just as drunk as an Englishman and from the way this road behaved the original maker of it must have been very drunk indeed. Smiling to herself, soaked to the very skin, her hair plastered to her head, and the sherbet dip no more than a memory, Nonny plodded on.

Sam had descended from his hide-out as soon as the rain began in earnest. He had taken shelter in the cart shed, settling himself quite comfortably in a large cart with red-painted wheels. Had it not been for the rain he would have had a perfect view of the door through which the inhabitants of the farm came and went; as it was he had to peer to see anything at all, and when the thunder rolled and the lightning stabbed he began to wish he had never found Ellen, the child, or Cefn Farm. He did not like thunderstorms, never had, never would. A pal of his had been killed by a lightning strike on board ship, and he had no desire to find himself cut down in the prime of life by a freak of nature.

He had left his small cache of food in the ruined cottage, tucked into his haversack and, he thought, probably safe from the rain since the corner in which it lay was sturdily roofed. He wondered whether he should return to the cottage – he felt exposed and uneasy so near the farmhouse – but he knew that whilst the storm continued he would be unable to see a thing from up there. The little car with the two adults in it had not come back. The two men who seemed to be helping around the place, one very old and the other of indeterminate age, had left the premises shortly after the rain began. Now, he thought, there were just the three kids in the farmhouse. He did wonder whether they would make their way to the w.c. in such fearful weather, especially as it was growing dark, and had almost made up his mind to kidnap the girl the following day instead, when he saw, coming up the lane, a small figure.

Sam climbed laboriously out of the cart and peered, then frowned. How the devil had she done it? He had watched the car leave with the two adults and he had seen the kids dashing from one place to another, presumably doing the chores which the adults had left them. Yet now the girl had somehow managed to spirit herself out of the warm farmhouse and into the storm. Sam grinned to himself. What did it matter how she got there? She was approaching the farmyard at a snail's pace and Sam told himself that she was unlikely to offer any resistance when he suggested that she might come and see an injured dog which he thought might belong to the farm. Sam was no psychologist but he had seen how the children fussed over the filthy sheepdogs and guessed that after his little speech the girl would accompany him at least as far as the ruined cottage. He had played with the idea of catching one of the dogs – perhaps the very old one – and inflicting some minor injury upon it. He thought he might crush its foot, or even break its forepaw, but then he remembered that when one of the straggly creatures had come up to investigate what was happening at the ruined cottage, it had growled as soon as he moved, the hair along its back standing up stiff and straight and its lips parting to show a remarkably fine set of teeth. Clearly, the injured dog must be a figment of his imagination.

Sam checked on his fingers that he had done all that was necessary. He had the cord of binder twine looped at both ends; a running loop at the child's end and a static one at his. He had put all his food and the remaining bottle of beer in the haversack which he had used throughout his journey, and the ransom note, if you could call it that, was tucked safely in his pocket. *Tell them whats hounding me for money as I'm payin' you direct, else you won't see the kid alive again.* Sam gave a satisfied smirk; that should settle Ellen's hash. He could imagine her terror and how speedily she would give in to his demand.

He had not bargained for the storm, however, which made everything twice as difficult. He had imagined that there would be enough light from the setting sun to show him the way to the place where he had planned to hold the girl for twenty-four hours, or longer if necessary. It was a good two miles from Cefn Farm, high up in the hills and well hidden. He knew children got into everything but thought, thankfully, that these children were different. They worked hard, as hard as adults, and though of course they played hard too they spent most of their spare time, as far as he could see, down by the river or in the woods, rarely climbing to the inhospitable heights, for what was there to amuse children in bare rock faces, tumbling mountain streams which would sweep the feet from under you, or treacherous slides of loose shale? So he, looking for a hiding place after he woke from his nap that morning, had found the very thing: a steep cleft, with bushes growing round its mouth, which led into a cave, not large but plenty big enough for two.

The girl was very close now. Leaving the cart shed at a run, Sam crossed the farmyard in a few loping strides and grabbed her shoulder. She gave a startled squawk and tried to free herself from his grip. 'Let go!' she said sharply. 'Are you the man who took our bread? If so...' But Sam hung on.

'Sorry, miss,' he said gruffly. 'I don't know about no bread; I've only been here an hour or so. I've gorra tent pitched on the marshy ground down by the river, but today I come across this dog – it's black and white, some sorta sheepdog, I reckon. It's hurt; can't walk, else I'd have brought it down to that farmhouse.' He jerked a thumb at Cefn Farm and some instinct which he had not known he possessed told him that now was the moment to let go of the girl's shoulder. *She'll run*, a voice in his head warned him. *If you let her go she'll be off home before you can stop her*. But another voice said, *A sick dog'll fetch her*, whilst the first voice insisted, *On your own head be it, Sam O'Mara*.

Sam let her go. 'The dog's in that ruined cottage up there,' he said, pointing. 'I made it a bed of dried bracken, but I reckon it needs more than that.' He was shouting above the roar of the storm. 'Course, it may not be your dog, missie...'

But to his delight the girl was already heading for

the ruined cottage and in minutes they were both inside. 'Where's the dog?' she said, and Sam gestured to the pile of bracken with his haversack humped up amongst it and looking, now he considered it, remarkably like a sick animal. The girl stepped forward. 'Feather? Is that you, Feath–'

She had seen the haversack, knew he lied, and he just had time to grab her arm and slip on the noose before she opened her mouth to scream. But the storm defeated her and before she could fill her lungs for a second attempt Sam had thrust his home-made gag into her mouth and tied it roughly at the back of her head. 'Shurrup and you won't get hurt,' he said roughly. 'This is a sorta – sorta game.'

Even if she had understood the words she made no reply – she could scarcely do so with the wodge of material stuffed into her mouth – but before Sam could stop her she had kicked out so viciously that he was forced to knock her off her feet. She was making gulping noises but he knelt on her stomach and wrenched her boots off, holding them tantalisingly up before all he could see of the pale blur of her face.

'You and me's goin' for a walk; it's a fair old way and the storm's likely to hold us up. You can do it in bare feet if you want to be bleedin' well awkward but I'll put your boots on again if you swear on your mother's life that there won't be no more kickin'.'

He expected an immediate agreement but the girl thought it over for several long minutes before she gave a very small and reluctant nod. Sam was relieved; he had envisaged himself having to carry the brat because without boots she would be unable to scramble over the rocky outcrops once they gained the heights. He knelt down and began to replace her boots. Twice as he was doing up the laces her foot twitched and he jumped back, fearful of a toecap in the teeth, but each time it seemed to have been a subconscious movement; or had it? In the dim light he thought he could see a twinkle in the girl's eyes and oddly enough this reassured him. She would survive.

He pulled the ransom note out of his pocket, and was dismayed to find that it was just about unreadable, a piece of soggy paper, with the pencilled words so faint as to be almost indistinguishable. He decided to leave it anyway; even if it was unlikely to be understood, he knew himself to be a resourceful bloke and would find some way of getting his message across.

He managed to put on his haversack without letting the child get to her feet, but when she did she raised a hand and touched the gag, looking straight at him, not in appeal but with a suggestion. She shook her head slowly from side to side, then touched her own chest, and he knew she was saying without words that if he removed the gag she would not shout. He looked doubtfully at his small captive. He had been gagged once and knew what a horrible experience it was, knew, too, that it could easily go wrong and suffocate the wearer. Until today he would have said that he cared nothing for his daughter, but now he couldn't help admiring her spunk. Chip off the old block, he told himself, unfastening the gag whilst reminding her that it would go into his pocket and should she so much as squeak it would be put in position once more.

If he expected gratitude he was disappointed. The girl merely nodded, then looked down at her wrists. Already she must have been trying to free herself, for the skin of her wrist was chafed and swollen. Good thing, Sam told himself; it meant she was unlikely to drag behind, forcing him to tug continually on their connecting cord. The girl was sitting up now, staring at him, her expression a mixture of puzzlement and annoyance. She did not seem to be in the least bit frightened, which surprised him, but her attitude would probably make the trek to the cave more bearable. Sam buttoned his jacket and bent down, took the girl beneath her arms and pulled her to her feet. 'Come on. We've a fair way to go before we can have a rest,' he said gruffly. 'And don't you go whining or grumbling, else it'll be the worse for you.'

The two of them, the huge man and the small girl, lowered their heads against the driving rain and left the slight shelter of the ruined cottage. The girl – he must remember to call her Lana – made no comment as he turned away from the farm in the valley below and headed up into the mountains. Once or twice he stopped for a moment to stare about him, for the thickening rain made it impossible to see more than a few feet ahead and occasional thunderclaps rendered the night hideous. Sometimes he addressed a remark to his captive, expecting a reply, but none was forthcoming. He had a large wristwatch which he consulted from time to time, and very soon he began to think uneasily that they should have reached the cleft by now. Naturally, he told himself that the awful weather, and the child's slower pace, would affect the length of time it took him to arrive at his hiding place. They had left the ruined cottage not long after eight o'clock; now his watch showed almost ten and still he had seen no sign of the shrubs that hid the entrance to the cave.

Sam stopped for a moment, trying to gather his thoughts. He knew the place was high up amidst the barren rocks and there had been a mountain stream not far distant; he had planned to fill his water bottles at that stream. The trouble, of course, was the bloody rain. The storm was bad enough, the thunder deafening him and the lightning illumining the great peaks which seemed to surround him on every side. But the storm was receding, the thunder grumbling off into the distance, the lightning no more than a pale blur on the horizon. It was the rain and the wind, now, that were his enemies. He said as much to the girl – dammit, he must remember to call her Lana – but once again she made no attempt to reply. He was tempted to give her a clack round the head and tell her to answer when an adult spoke to her, but then he remembered his earlier threat. He had said that if she so much as squeaked he would replace the gag, so now he told himself, rather glumly, that he could scarcely blame her for obeying his instructions to the letter. He supposed, grudgingly, that she wasn't such a bad kid. After all, this expedition was not of her choice, yet she had kept her word. She trudged along in his wake, the cord which bound them no doubt tugging on her wrist as it tugged on his, and of course he realised – as she must – that even if she could summon up the breath to scream there was no one around to hear her.

Sam continued to wander upwards, but when at last they reached the peak and he saw not only that the rain was lessening but also that the clouds were beginning to part, he realised, with a stab of genuine dismay, that he was hopelessly lost. He had no idea where he was, no idea how to regain the valley or the ruined cottage. No idea in fact how to extricate himself and his daughter from the muddle into which he had plunged them.

Despite himself, and knowing that it was useless to rail against fate, Sam felt rage begin to fill his whole mind. If it hadn't been for this bleedin' cocky kid, there would have been no question of his having to pay child maintenance, let alone being hounded for money by Ellen. He had never liked the kid, but he had come closer to so doing over the past few hours because she'd been no trouble and had a deal of spunk. However, she was the only person around on whom he could vent his ill temper, and he was about to start yelling at her when another thought occurred. She'd been in these damn awful mountains for several weeks; in fact for all he knew she might have come here as regular as clockwork, every single holiday since she started school. He was about to ask her to tell him the way back to Cefn Farm when he remembered he had told her not to speak. He cleared his throat uncomfortably; he did not want to lose face but did not think he would have much choice. Shaming to admit he was totally lost, shaming to have to ask a kid of ten or eleven to lead him back to civilisation. Shaming, even, to have to rescind his threat to make her sorry if she made a sound, but all these things would have to be done.

There was a large slab of rock at the summit of the mountain and Sam picked the child up beneath her armpits – she went as stiff as a board the moment she felt his hands on her – and settled her upon the rock, then climbed up and sat beside her. He tried to speak gently but knew it was a poor effort, though he told himself that he was hoarse from breathing hard for so long. 'Lana, I've gorra admit that I'm lost. I were taking you to a grand little cave I found, to wait for 'em to stop houndin' me for money – money what I've not got. You'd like to spend time wi' your ole feller, wouldn't you? Only I can't find the cave, you see. It were the rain and the thunder what put me on the wrong track, but I reckon you know these mountains pretty well. Can you guide us back to Cefn Farm?' Sam peered anxiously into the child's white, exhausted face. 'Can you find the valley, queen?'

The child considered him, her head slightly on one side, but said nothing.

Sam was about to give her a shake when he remembered his prohibition and cursed himself. He had forbidden her to speak and now, out of sheer cussedness, she was going to obey him to the letter. He half raised his hand, then lowered it again. He had not known his daughter at all well when they had shared a house, but in the past few hours he felt he had got to know this older Lana very well indeed. Threats, he was sure, would not move her; blandishments might. 'Look, Lana, I didn't oughter of took it out on you, when it's not you what's been so mean to me,' he said, trying to sound both reasonable and friendly. 'You can talk now... I'll chuck the bleedin' gag away. I wouldn't of used it anyhow, 'cos someone did it to me once and I wouldn't want any kid to go through what I did.'

Sam looked earnestly into the girl's face and saw, in the pale grey light of dawn, that she was looking back at him, the expression on her face a mixture of scorn and amusement. He did not understand why she should look at him thus, but once again he had to admire her pluck. He was three times her size and had five times her strength, yet she was so clearly unafraid that once more he realised threats would be useless, and it appeared that blandishments were not going to work either. Suddenly the sheer misery of the cold and wet in which he found himself made him throw caution to the winds. He grabbed her shoulders and shook her until he heard the teeth rattle in her head. 'Speak, you wicked little bitch!' he screamed, his face not an inch from hers. 'Which way is home? Tell me!'

To his astonishment the child actually grinned. 'Remember Ariadne?' she said. 'So you're lost, are you? Well, that makes two of us.'

When the rain started Chris was in the cowshed milking Jessie. Beside him, old Mr Williams was milking Buttercup under the hopeful gaze of the sheepdogs, who knew that he would direct a squirt of milk straight from the cow's udder into the mouth of any waiting dog, a treat much enjoyed by them all. Presently they both carried their full buckets through into the dairy where Lana, who had still not learned to milk a cow and was unlikely ever to do so, since she could not bear the feel of the long rubbery teats, was waiting for the milk to be emptied into the cooler so that she could sterilise the buckets in the big old sink which she had already filled with boiling water.

She was trying her best to be useful, and when she had finished in the dairy she joined the men in the kitchen, telling Chris that she would start laying the table for the evening meal. Chris grinned at her, for in return he was trying very hard to understand her fear of animals and to help her to conquer that fear. She was all right with the dogs now, she knew, so when he saw the rain begin in earnest he told Jacob and old Mr Williams to set off for home at once, opened the back door to let them out, and whistled for the sheepdogs, who immediately scampered across the yard and crowded into the kitchen. By now the rain was hitting the paving stones of the yard with such force that it looked as though they would soon be an inch under water. Lana would have shut the door, for with the rain it had begun to grow dark, but Chris stopped her.

'Leave it, cariad,' he said. 'Nonny will be back from the village quite soon, no doubt soaked to the skin, and I bet she'll make a mad dash across the yard straight into the kitchen. She's gone to buy something for our mum's present and I don't know why she's so late. Perhaps Mrs Enfys is a bit low on stock, today being Tuesday and the vans delivering on a Wednesday.'

'Okay,' Lana said. She smoothed a hand across Egg's black and white head and well pricked ears. 'When we go back to Liverpool, Mum says she'll mebbe let me have a puppy of my own.'

Chris gave her an admonitory glance. 'Don't you go getting a Border collie,' he advised her. 'They're working dogs, you know, happiest when they're up in the hills rounding up the sheep. If they're miserable and bored they play up: chew chair legs, bark for hours on end, even fight other dogs occasionally. So if you want a puppy you'd best choose a nice little mongrel in need of a home.' He grinned at Lana. 'One with short legs so it won't need too much exercise.'

Lana laughed with him. 'I don't suppose we'll get a dog really,' she admitted. 'Auntie Molly said the city's no place for a dog because if you let it roam free it'll likely get run over and if you shut it up, with only a little yard to play in, it'll go crazy.'

The two talked about dogs as they laid the table. 'I thought Mum would be home by now,' Chris said, going to the window to watch the rain bouncing off the paving stones. 'Good thing the dogs came in before they were drenched; if there's one thing I don't like it's the smell of wet dogs.'

Lana agreed with him, then remembered that she had left her waterproof up in her bedroom and whilst she had no use for it at present she really should bring it downstairs, for the chances were that, as the rain eased, Chris would ask her to go and let the cows out of the shed and drive them to the home pasture. Jacob usually undertook this task, but because of the rain he had gone home early, so the sensible thing would be to fetch the waterproof, hang it on its peg by the back door, and be prepared for a rush out into the downpour. If, upon being asked to move the cows, she had to go upstairs for her mac first, it would be another black mark against her, and with Chris's help she was beginning to do rather well, she considered.

It was the work of a moment to run up the stairs and into the bedroom she shared with Nonny. Once there, she looked rather disparagingly round the room. What a mess she saw before her! Two unmade beds, the clothes they had worn yesterday cast on the floor, the curtains at the window only half pulled back. Tutting beneath her breath, Lana began to put things right. She made the beds up neatly, smoothing the covers and turning down the white sheets. Next she sorted the clothes, hanging up the clean things and bundling the dirty into a pillow case. Then she went over to the window, swished the curtains back as far as they would go, and looked out at the rain-soaked scene before her. It certainly was pretty miserable out there; from where she stood she should have had a clear view of the mountaintops, most of which she could name by now, having been taught by Nonny and Chris. Today, however, the rain clouds were so low that they completely hid the mountains, and the slopes upon which the sheep grazed were largely hidden too, making the scene desolate indeed.

Poor Mum and Uncle Rhys, and Auntie Molly too of course, Lana thought. They're going to have a miserable journey; I bet it will be full dark before Minnie the Moocher comes wheezing and stuttering into the farmyard. And Minnie's hood leaks like anything, so they won't even stay dry. I'll tell Chris I think we ought to have a roaring fire in the kitchen range and the pie ready to reheat as soon as we hear Minnie's engine.

Lana was about to turn away from the window when a movement further up the lane caught her eye. A person or an animal was traversing the deep ruts and muddy hollows, but because the rain was so heavy she could not make out who or what it was. She pressed her nose to the streaming pane and then remembered: it must be Nonny! Doubtless the figure ploughing through the puddles was her poor friend, as wet as though she had been dunked in the river, and keen to get into the warmth and dryness of the farm kitchen.

Lana stepped back from the window, glanced approvingly round the now tidy room, and went over to the rail upon which the two girls hung their clean clothing. Knowing Nonny's tastes she chose a faded cotton shirt, a thick navy blue jersey, a pair of canvas slacks and the appropriate underwear before picking up her own waterproof and balancing it on top of the pile. Then, her arms full, she left the room, descended the wooden stairs into the kitchen and began to arrange Nonny's garments on the clothes horse, drawing it close to the range so that Nonny would have warm things to change into as soon as she had rubbed herself dry.

Chris, cutting the loaf with a large bread knife, stared at Lana's preparations. 'What on earth are you doing, girl?' he asked rather impatiently. 'I've been waiting for you to come and butter this bread.'

'Sorry, it's just that I thought Nonny might like to change out of her wet things as soon as she gets home. I think I saw her coming up the lane when I was in the bedroom,' Lana gabbled. 'I'll help with the bread and butter now.'

The two worked steadily but presently Chris looked across at his companion, a frown marring his brow. 'Did you say you'd seen Nonny coming up the lane? Then where the devil is she?' He bent to peer out of the nearest window. 'It's still raining cats and dogs but I can't imagine that she would shelter in the stable or the cart shed, with the house so near.'

Lana joined him at the window, peering out, able to see very little through the pouring rain. And even as she opened her mouth to admit she might have been mistaken a louder crack of thunder than any they had heard yet split the air, and the accompanying stab of lightning made Lana give a little shriek and step back from the window. Chris was still frowning. 'Are you sure it was Nonny you saw?' he asked dubiously. 'Could you have been mistaken? I wouldn't doubt you, Lana, if Nonny hadn't said this morning that she'd seen a tramp lurking around. Come to that, in August there are usually a number of tents pitched down by Trawsfynydd Lake or on the slopes of Snowdon itself. The only thing is, the holidaymakers don't tend to come this way much, not even the mountaineers; they go for the better-known peaks. So it doesn't seem likely that anyone but Nonny would be heading for Cefn

Farm in weather like this.' He sighed, then swished the curtains closed. 'If she's not home soon we'd better go looking. She's a sensible kid but even a sensible one can slip and break a bone, though in this sort of rain she'd be extra careful.' He turned away from the window to find Lana briskly making jam sandwiches, which she wrapped in greaseproof paper and slid into the big pockets of her waterproof.

'We'll take some grub, just in case she is in trouble,' she said. 'We'll fill your dad's flask with hot tea as well, though I'm sure Nonny will laugh at us when she walks in and finds us dressed and ready to go out in search of her.'

Chris grinned his appreciation, stole one of the sandwiches and began to eat it, speaking rather thickly through his mouthful. 'I'm sure we're being really silly, but better safe than sorry, I always say. We'll give her another ten minutes and then we'll wrap up warm and go in search of her. Agreed?'

Chapter Nine

Nonny had spoken no more than the truth when she had told Sam she did not know where she was, for during the hours of darkness they had penetrated well beyond the Roberts land, and she had no idea where the cave he had spoken of was situated. Had she known she would have taken him to it, since she had the very best of reasons to believe that as soon as it got light rescue would be on its way. Last night the pain in her wrist, the blisters on her heels and the puzzlement and despair in her heart had almost made her want to give up, to cry, to agree to any suggestion he might make provided it would ease the awful aches and pains which beset her. She had been almost grateful when he had replaced her boots, but his big clumsy hands had not managed the laces at all well so that the boots had slipped with every step she took, and very soon large broken blisters had added to the agony of her chafed and bleeding wrist and the bitter cold which seeped, with the icy rain, through every garment she wore until it reached her skin.

At first, Nonny had longed for the dogs to come racing up the mountain in search of her but they did not do so; after all, why should they? They were not hounds, trained to follow a scent, but collies, trained to round up sheep. If I were a sheep I'm sure Feather would find me at once, Nonny told herself, stumbling along in the wake of her hated captor. Every time they stopped, for he too was clearly growing wearier with every step, she had begun to nibble and pick at the cord around her wrist, and though she was making some progress it was very slow and she dared not risk his spotting what she was doing. She already knew him for a vicious and unscrupulous man, but now she was beginning to think that he was also unhinged. Why else would he have kidnapped the daughter of folk who had so little money that they would be unable to raise any ransom, no matter how small? The fact that he seemed to think she was Lana was immaterial, since Ellen was not a rich woman either. When he began to mutter and refer to himself as 'your ole feller' and chuntered on about someone demanding money from him, it only served to convince Nonny more than ever that she was dealing with a madman and must take the greatest care not to annoy him.

Instead, she began to think about his cave. In all their wanderings amongst the high peaks she and Chris had never found a cave and she wondered if this man had done so in truth or if he had just imagined it. Certainly there was nothing even faintly resembling a cave in the countryside which she and Chris had explored. So when she had admitted that she was as lost as he, she had spoken no more than the truth. Even now that the pale grey light of dawn was slowly increasing she could not see one familiar landmark, and realised with a stab of real fear that she and the madman could wander for days, never once coming across somewhere she recognised.

If only she could persuade him to change his mind and go downwards, towards the steep valleys which divided the peaks, then, even if they did not emerge into country she knew, there would be people. She would not dare to ask openly for help, but she was sure she would be able to make folk realise that she was an unwilling prisoner. He would have to untie the twine which bound them to one another too, and though her boots still slipped at every step she was sure she could escape from him, once she knew in which direction safety lay.

In the strengthening light she looked up into his great coarse face and saw that the rage which had boiled up every now and again was fast becoming despair. Even as she watched him, for he was not looking at her but staring bleakly out over the great surrounding peaks, she saw water begin to run down his unshaven cheek. Was it tears? For the first time the light was strong enough for her to see that though one of his eyes was brown and sharp the other was sunk into his head, the eyeball itself as white as though someone had poured milk into the socket. Staring at him, Nonny tried desperately to corral an elusive memory which would not quite let itself come to the forefront of her mind. Someone had once mentioned a man who had been blinded in one eye in a fight, but hard though she tried she could not remember who. Would it enrage him further if she mentioned it, perhaps expressed sympathy? But the truth was she hated him so much that even the thought of speaking to him filled her with disgust; so far as Nonny was concerned he was not a man but a mad bull, and she did not fancy exchanging conversation with such a one.

He had been staring abstractedly ahead of him, but suddenly he heaved a sigh and got to his feet. 'Sun's comin' up; it looks like it'll be a fine day,' he said. 'If we walk in a straight line, followin' the path of the sun, we'll get out of these bloody awful mountains; once we're on the plain I reckon I'll be able to think straight again and decide what's best to do.' He looked down at his companion. 'That's right, ain't it? I left a note in the cottage. When they find it, then they'll know why I took you. They can have you back just as soon as they stop houndin' me for money; have you back and welcome. God knows you're the last thing I want,' he added nastily.

Without waiting for a tug on the binder twine, Nonny slid off the rock and followed closely as he began to descend the far side of the mountain. She was careful to put no strain on the cord between them, since she had almost managed to sever it. It would be pointless to make her bid for freedom up here, miles from any sort of help, but she knew that her nibblings and gnawings at the binder twine had at last weakened it so much that it only needed one sharp jerk and she would be free of him. This, however, was not the moment. If he realised, he might do something truly horrible, for he had started to talk in a low mumble of the things that men did to women, dreadful things which she had never heard mentioned in her life before. She wanted to put her fingers in her ears, to shut out the hateful voice, but that was impossible without revealing that the binder twine was almost worn through. She told herself not to listen, that he was lying, but she could not shut out his words nor the glee with which he repeated them. 'You think when this is over and I've got that bitch to promise not to ask me for more money, then that's an end of it,' he said at last. 'But it ain't, you stupid little cow. Whilst I live I'll make sure I allus know where you are and what you're doing, and one day I'll come for you, see if I don't.'

Nonny made no reply, concentrating on putting as little strain as possible upon the twine, and followed him down the steep and rocky path. Not that it was a path; it was simply the way he imagined would lead to the dreadful scramble up the next peak.

The climb seemed both unnecessary and exhausting to Nonny, and it was on the tip of her tongue to ask him why he had not simply followed the valley when their way was barred by a deep gorge, so deep that when Nonny peered into it she could not make out the bottom. After not speaking for so long, it took a good deal of courage to turn to him and make a suggestion. 'If you were to go down a valley – especially one with a river running through it – it'd be easier walking and it would lead us out of the mountains,' she said. She was proud that her voice scarcely trembled at all and looked up at him defiantly, half expecting a slap or a shake for daring to address him at last. He started to reply, to say that folk lived in the valleys, that up here on the mountain tops he felt safer because he could see for miles, when something, Nonny did not know what, made him clap a great brawny hand to his forehead.

'There's grub in my haversack,' he said. 'A bottle of beer, an' all. Fancy me forgettin,' and I'm that parched.'

Right now, despite her fear and disgust of him, the mere thought of food and drink brought the saliva rushing to Nonny's mouth. The man sat down on a convenient rock a good six feet from the edge of the gorge and began to pull the haversack from his shoulder. If he wondered why his captive sat so still he made no comment, probably assuming that she was as hungry as he and as eager for her share of the bread and ham. He had begun to say, in a wondering tone, that he must be a great fool to have walked all that way without once recalling the food he carried, when a slight sound brought his head up sharply. 'What was that?'

Chris was worried. The ten minutes were up, and if Lana really had seen Nonny coming up the lane, then she must have skirted the farmhouse and gone on up the valley. Had she tried to buy a present for her mother in the village, been unsuccessful, and gone on to the Pritchards' farm? He turned to Lana, who was standing almost shoulder to shoulder with him at the kitchen window, gazing hopefully up the lane. 'Did Nonny give you any idea of what sort of present she was buying for our mum?' he asked. 'It's just occurred to me that if she wanted something alive, a puppy or one of the bantams Mrs Pritchard rears – something like that – then she might have tried in the village, been unsuccessful, and gone on to the Pritchards' place.

She and Mrs Pritchard are good friends; Mrs P says Nonny's like a daughter to her and I know Rhodri treats her a bit like a young sister. So she could have gone there.' He sighed deeply. 'Damn the girl, why did she have to be so bloody secretive? It's not as though we could have told Mum, even if we wanted to, because Nonny is bound to be home well before Minnie the Moocher puts in an appearance. I reckon they've run into some sort of trouble – a tree across the road, or a stream breaking its banks – which is why they aren't back yet.'

He looked indecisively at his companion. She was a good couple of inches shorter than Nonny and nowhere near as sturdy; was it fair to ask her to go with him into the village in such frightful weather? On the other hand was it fair to leave her alone in the farmhouse? He knew she was frightened of lightning, though his constant assurances that thunder was only noise and could not possibly hurt one seemed to have had the desired effect. And suppose he got to the village only to find that his half-guess had been right and Nonny was making her way to Cae Hic, the Pritchards' farmhouse? He felt a surge of envy; he knew his mother admired the bantams and would be far more delighted with a bantam chick than with the most exotic bar of chocolate in the world. But there you were; Nonny was the one with imagination…

'Chris? Why don't we walk up to the Pritchards'? I think Nonny may have been heading there, like you said, but suppose she never reached them? Oh, Chris, if she fell...'

Chris reached up for his own waterproof and Lana's, kicked off his slippers, hooked out his boots, and stepped into them, noting with approval that Lana, following suit, was almost as quick as he. Then he turned to what Molly called her 'scribble board', upon which every member of the family left messages from time to time. *Gone to keep Nonny company. Back soon, C*, he wrote. Then he went over to where Lana waited by the back door. 'You're right,' he told his companion. 'We won't take the dogs because...' He was opening the door as he spoke, and before he could prevent her Feather had slid out into the rain. Cursing, Chris followed her and tried to grab her ruff, already wet, but she eluded him. He gave a frustrated sigh, then turned back to Lana. 'Oh well, one dog isn't too bad. I just didn't fancy taking all of them. Feather's a good old girl; she'll wait by the back door at Cae Hic whilst we fetch Nonny out. I'm sure you're right and she's probably at the Pritchards' simply sheltering from the storm, because the silly girl wasn't wearing waterproofs or her wellies. Come to think of it, we'd best take them with us because she'll be glad of them.' He nipped back into the kitchen, grabbed Nonny's outer clothing and boots and re-joined Lana, who was standing in the yard with a hand on Feather's ruff, looking worried. As they crossed the farmyard and went into the lane she tugged at Chris's sleeve.

'Do you have a torch, Chris? We might need it.'

For answer Chris fished in his pocket and produced a grand big torch which had been a birthday present from his parents. He flashed it at Lana, then stuffed it back into his pocket, just as the girl beside him gave a squeak of dismay. 'Sorry, Chris, I'm afraid Feather's given me the slip,' she said. 'But she'll come back if you call her; she's awful obedient, isn't she?'

Chris agreed that this was so and whistled, whereupon Feather came slinking down the mountainside, wagging a deprecatory tail and licking her lips. But when Lana tried to grab her again she danced just out of reach; and then, to both young people's surprise, Feather, normally the most silent of dogs, began to bark.

Chris was immediately alerted. Feather was a highly intelligent animal; his father always said she was intuitive too, and often obeyed a command he was about to give rather than one he had already voiced. He turned to Lana. 'Something's up,' he said briefly. 'You stay here while I investigate.'

Lana was wearing a yellow waterproof with a matching fisherman's hat, which Chris had thought privately was a right cissy turnout, but now he realised that the girl showed up even in the driving rain and not only when the lightning forked to earth, either. 'You're as good as a torch yourself, so if you stay right here I'll find my way back to you easy as winking,' he shouted over his shoulder, but was not particularly surprised when Lana, shaking her head, began to scramble up the steep path along which Feather led them.

'I'm coming too,' she shouted. 'You might need me.'

Chris chuckled to himself at the mere thought, but did not argue. He knew Feather better than to think she would lead them on a false trail, but what might seem important to a dog might not appear in quite the same light to a human being. However, he accepted Lana's companionship without demur, even taking her hand to help her over the rougher patches, for this was a path which led only to a ruined cottage and in places was completely overgrown with gorse, brambles and the like. Because of the violence of the rain they were almost upon the cottage before they saw it, but there was no doubt that it was Feather's destination for she whipped inside, then turned to make sure they were following. Only then did she begin to quarter the place, nose close to the ground, taking deep and noisy breaths as she did so. Chris shone his torch around the interior of the ruined building. It was only half roofed, though the walls stood firm enough, and Chris was easily able to tell his companion that someone had been camping, or at least spending time, here. There were crumbs of food amidst the dry bracken, in the middle of which was a deep indentation where someone – it was too large to be an animal – had made themselves a cosy nest. A tramp? Possibly, but not, he thought, his sister. She had no need to make herself a hide-out in a ruined cottage or anywhere else for that matter. No, he thought it was probably the person who had stolen the loaf of bread from their dairy the night before. But just in case his sister had come up here for some reason best known to herself, he began to hunt diligently for some sign, and presently the strong beam of his torch lit up a dirty crumpled piece of white paper, upon which he could see that something had been written.

Chris grabbed the paper and smoothed it out with trembling fingers. It was damp and dirty, a good deal of its original message washed away, but he could make out some words. '*I've took the* ... there's a gap here ... *whats half mine anyhow*,' he read aloud. 'Then there's another bit I can't read and after that it says *hounding me for money.*' Chris and Lana stared hard at the paper but neither could make out one further word, and finally Chris propped it up on top of the bracken bed. It might mean something to someone else, but it meant nothing to him, and when he questioned Lana she too shook her head. 'It's no use, and it may have nothing to do with Nonny...' he was beginning when Lana gave an excited squeak and pointed to Feather.

'Take it away from her; she'll kill it, even if she doesn't mean to,' she gabbled. 'Oh, Chris, Nonny must have been here!' Chris had removed from Feather's gentle jaws a pathetic little ball of yellow fluff. He and Lana bent their heads over it, Lana almost in tears over the little creature's fate, but Chris gave a crack of laughter.

'It's not a live chick, stupid, it's just one of those toy ones that Mrs Enfys decorates her window with at Easter,' he assured her. 'But what the devil is it doing up here? I don't understand, but from what you've said...' he looked long and hard at his companion, 'I believe *you* do,' he finished.

'Yes, I think I do,' Lana said slowly. 'I didn't tell you before because Nonny said it was to be a secret, but she meant to buy chicks from the post office for your mum. Only this isn't a real chick, it's just a pretend one. So what on earth was

Nonny doing with it up here?'

Chris was beginning to reply when Feather lost patience. She jumped up, nosed first at the chick and then at Nonny's waterproof, then set off, back into the pouring rain, the rumblings of thunder and the occasional brilliance of the lightning. Chris seized Lana's hand. 'Follow her, and keep an eye out for any sign of Nonny,' he shouted above the screech of the wind. 'I tell you what, Lana, I think Nonny's been kidnapped by someone who thinks all farmers are rich, probably the same fellow who stole the loaf. I can't think of any other possible reason for her being up here. If she'd meant to go to the Pritchards' she'd have stuck to the lane. I think she's been taken.'

'And that note, the one we couldn't read, probably explained it all,' Lana said sadly. The two children continued to follow where Feather led and every few hundred yards they were rewarded by the sight of a soggy little chick, wire legs pathetically extended, bright-eyed little face almost buried in mud, though for the most part, since their way lay upward, it was more often glimpsed in shale or even through the waters of a tumbling mountain stream. Chris counted the chicks as he pushed each one into his pocket.

By the time the first pale grey light of dawn appeared beyond the far mountain peaks both children were exhausted, and Chris had collected ten chicks. He was having to help Lana over the rougher patches of ground and he cheered her up by telling her she was every bit as brave as his sister and by promising her that when they found Nonny he would make sure she knew what a brick her little friend had been. At one point they were so tired that Chris decreed they must rest, otherwise when they did catch up with Nonny and her captor, for by now they were convinced that Nonny had been kidnapped, they would be too tired for a rescue attempt. Lana was only too glad to obey, to sink down upon a large boulder and to sag wearily into Chris's comforting arm, and Feather, too, though still bright-eyed, seemed pleased enough to collapse at their feet, though every now and then she gazed up the stony little track they were following and whined pathetically. She knows we're getting close, and is beginning to be afraid of what we may have to face, Chris thought, smoothing a hand over the dog's soaking wet head. I just wish I could think of some way of rescuing Nonny which wouldn't be dangerous to us all. If only we weren't in such wild country! If only I knew the terrain, come to that. Feather does; she knows we're getting closer ... oh, if only Dad were here!

The sound that had alarmed her captor was not repeated, and despite wanting desperately to have the strength of character to refuse the food Nonny, a sensible child, knew this would be the height of stupidity. She needed all her strength simply to keep up with this horrible man, and when the moment was ripe to escape from him she would need all her strength to do that as well. So she ate her share of the food, drank water from the bottle he had filled from a nearby stream, and when he rose and walked to the edge of the gorge accompanied him closely, one hand in her pocket, the other, its wrist chafed and bleeding, staying near to his so that he should not realise how close the bond was to snapping. Together, almost like friends, they peered over the edge; it was a long, long way down. No one falling from here would hit anything for a very long time, and then they would disappear into the dark depths, the bottom of which could not even be seen. Nonny stepped back, feeling her stomach clench. She was not afraid of heights when she had ropes and crampons and a friend beside her, but this was very different. She was yoked to a madman, who might suddenly assume that they could jump safely from one side of the gorge to the other, a distance, she estimated, of ten or fifteen feet. But she felt a shiver pass through the man's huge frame and glanced up at him. His face was greenish-white and his loose-lipped mouth trembled and suddenly she realised that this might be the end of her ordeal. He was in a blue funk, terrified of heights, terrified of the mountains, terrified of what he had done and of the punishment which awaited him.

She had opened her mouth to speak, meaning to tell him tauntingly that there was no way round the deep cleft in the rocks by which they stood, when, to her very real astonishment, she heard voices. Her captor gasped, then started to shout, words bubbling from his mad lips like water from a mountain stream. The words didn't make much sense; they seemed to be threats of some sort of reprisal jumbled up with promises of future good behaviour, but whilst he was still shouting a black and white sheepdog, ears pricked, tongue lolling, came round the corner of a bluff and Nonny knew it was Feather, and saw that she was closely followed by two figures. One, the taller, Nonny instantly recognised as her brother and knew the other must be Lana. The pair stopped for a moment and Nonny saw how white their faces were and guessed that they realised how dangerous the confrontation might be.

Her captor shouted suddenly that they were only a couple of kids and must promise to guide him down the mountain and back to civilisation or he would throw Nonny – only he called her Lana – into the gorge before which he stood. He grabbed her arm and began to pull her nearer that ominous drop, then let her go, clearly believing the bond between them still held firmly, though Nonny knew that the least little jerk would cause it to part. Then, even as he opened his mouth and began to utter more threats, Nonny pulled away from him and the twine parted and at the same moment Lana broke free from Chris's hand on her shoulder and charged across the intervening ground. The man shouted at her to keep clear, screaming that he would hurl her pal into the depths behind him if she did not retreat, and seeing that his attention was fixed on her friend Nonny gave her captor the hardest push of which she was capable in her weakened state He roared a blasphemy, reached for Nonny's thin little jacket, wavered, tried to right himself then he was lurching backwards towards the edge, still trying to catch hold of Nonny, and such is human nature that for a moment she stretched out a hand to him, offering the only succour she could.

Then Lana reached them and shoved him away from her friend and the two girls fell into each other's arms, their backs to the lip of the gorge, so that they did not see their enemy claw desperately at thin air as he fell, screaming, the sound echoing off the narrowing rocky walls until it ended abruptly, leaving only the howl of the wind and Feather's frightened whine.

For several moments after the man's terrible scream had faded into silence, Chris and the two girls, with Feather beside them, simply sat staring towards the lip of the gorge. Then Nonny, who had not shed a single tear throughout her ordeal, began to cry. She did so almost silently, but Chris heard and pulled her into a rough embrace.

'It's over, it's over,' he crooned. 'I don't know why that horrible man kidnapped you – he left a note in the ruined cottage but the rain had washed most of the words out – though I suppose he wanted money. I guess it was the tramp, the one who stole the loaf of bread, but you foiled him, you clever girl. Dropping the chicks so that we could follow your trail was an act of genius.' He pulled one of the chicks out of his pocket and rubbed it against his sister's tear-wet cheek. Then he put an arm round Lana too, pulling her close. 'We're proud of you, Lana and me, and so will Mum and Dad be, when we tell them about it. And now stop crying, because we got wet enough last night! And as soon as you're ready, we'll make for home.'

Nonny gave a tremulous smile. 'I got the idea of laying a trail of chicks from one of those ancient

Greek stories they made us read in school. It's the one where Ariadne goes into the labyrinth and unreels a ball of thread so she can find her way out again. I'd had the chicks from Mrs...' A hand flew to her mouth. 'Oh, goodness! If you collected the chicks, Chris, then the thread that would lead us home is in your pocket! It took us hours and hours to get here – I only had two chicks left when we reached the gorge – so how will we find our way home?'

Chris was beginning to say that they would simply have to descend into the nearest valley and then search for a farmhouse when Lana interrupted. 'Feather will take us,' she said. And Chris realised that her faith in the old dog was absolute. 'I know Nonny's chicks were a great help, but if it hadn't been for Feather I doubt if we'd have caught up with that horrid man in time to stop him doing something dreadful.'

Nonny nodded vigorously. 'Of course, Feather will take us home as soon as we're ready to leave,' she said. 'But shouldn't we just take a peep into that gorge? I know it's silly, but I keep imagining him crawling up the rock and appearing over the edge to drag me down with him...' She gave a convulsive shudder. 'I know it's silly,' she repeated rather dolefully.

Chris began to say that it was impossible, that no one could crawl up walls of rock which were completely perpendicular, then stopped and got to his feet. 'Impossible or not, I'll just check,' he said, and knew a moment of shame. He knew the mountains, dreamed of becoming a mountaineer one day, yet he had not made sure that the man was beyond help before turning away to comfort his two young companions. He had drawn them some way from the lip of the gorge but now walked to within six feet of it, then lay down on his stomach and squiggled towards the very edge. He looked down, and saw that after perhaps a hundred feet or more the gorge narrowed into a cleft. Chris lay for moments, motionless, just watching. Nothing moved below. He lay there for another two or three minutes, then retreated to where the girls sat, both with an arm round Feather's narrow shoulders, both staring hopefully at him.

'Well?' It was Nonny, her voice only shaking slightly. 'Is he there?'

Chris shrugged. 'It's too deep to see a body, but one thing is certain: no one could possibly survive a fall like that. Later, when we get home, I expect they'll send a team up here with all the right equipment. They'll go down and bring the body up for burial.' He realised that if he didn't do something the girls would simply sit, staring towards the gorge. 'Look, if you're up to it, the pair of you, I think we ought to get going. Just imagine how worried Mum and Dad and Auntie Ellen must be by now. So if you've rested for long enough...'

Both girls rose to their feet with alacrity and Chris realised that they were as eager as he to leave. They had seen a man die – well, if they had not seen him, they had certainly heard his dying scream – and it was only natural that they should want to get away from the place. He turned to Feather who had got to her feet as the girls did. 'Home, old lady,' he said. 'Take us home!'

The Robertses and Ellen did not arrive back at Cefn Farm until midnight, so were not particularly surprised to find the house in darkness, and the dogs slumbering quite happily before the still glowing range. Molly hobbled across to a chair and flung herself into it, stretching her legs out with a sigh of relief, for she had begun to feel cramped and uncomfortable, stuck in the little car for so long. 'Oh, I'd give a hundred pounds for a nice hot cup of tea,' she said yearningly. 'Pull the kettle over the flame, Ellen, there's a dear.'

Ellen grinned and did as she was bidden whilst Rhys made up the fire and then collapsed into the chair opposite his wife's. Suddenly he sat up straight and eyed the dogs, a puzzled frown creasing his brow. 'Where's Feather? Oh, I dare say she went off on a rabbit hunt and got shut out by mistake. Still, it's odd...'

Ellen, who had gone into the pantry for milk, came out again. She looked puzzled. 'Rhys, the kids haven't et the mutton pasties I left for them,' she said. 'They're still in the meat safe.'

Molly got out of her chair and swung over to the scribble board on her crutches. 'Chris's left a message,' she said, and read it aloud. '*Gone to keep Nonny company. Back soon, C.*' She turned round to face the other two. 'That wasn't written ten minutes ago,' she said slowly. 'Something's happened.'

'I'll go and wake Chris, ask him what's up,' Rhys said, heading for the stairs. The two women stared at each other across the firelit kitchen, but had no chance to utter a word before Rhys was thundering down again. He crossed the room in a couple of strides, seized his waterproof from its hook by the door and replaced his smart walking shoes with a pair of black and muddy wellingtons. 'They're still out somewhere; their beds haven't been slept in,' he said briefly. 'Wait here, you two. I'm going to drive up to the Pritchards', see if they're there. Don't worry, I shan't be long.'

It was weeks before Ellen, Molly and Rhys managed to untangle the story as it had happened to the three youngsters, but at least they knew that it had been Sam O'Mara who had kidnapped Nonny, in mistake for Lana. Nonny's description of his one blind milky eye was sufficient to identify him, for though Ellen had not seen him for years she knew that he had lost the sight of his eye in a dockside brawl. At first neither she nor the other two could understand the reason for Sam's weird behaviour, until they learned that the authorities, after years of failed attempts to discover precisely where he was, had managed to track Sam down, and sent him a letter telling him that he owed five years' child maintenance.

Knowing Sam as she did, Ellen realised immediately that his twisted brain would first blame her for the demand and second search for a means of revenging himself upon her. Now, the scribbled note in the ruined cottage made sense. He wanted her to tell the authorities that he had sent the money directly to her. When she did so he would return her daughter unharmed. She shuddered to think what form his rage and hate might have taken had Chris and Lana not caught up with him when they did. The children had played down Sam's fall but both Ellen and Molly knew that it had affected their offspring deeply, knew also that it might be some considerable while before Sam O'Mara no longer haunted their dreams.

All attempts to recover his body, however, were unsuccessful, largely due to the fact that neither Chris nor the two girls could recall any detail at all which might lead the mountaineers to the particular spot where Sam, they assumed, had plunged to his death. Chris explained that when they had been following what they called 'the chick trail', they had been concentrating completely upon the way ahead, and on the way home they had been too exhausted to do anything apart from follow Feather.

Men who knew the mountains like the backs of their hands knew also that there were many clefts deep enough to hide a body from any but the most diligent search. And without some idea of where the youngsters had been taken, they knew that the chances of finding one particular gorge were slight indeed.

Molly would not have blamed Ellen had her friend wanted to shake the dust of Cefn Farm from her feet and return home to Liverpool after such a dreadful experience, but this did not prove to be the case. Ellen said, stoutly, that she felt safer than she had done for many years, knowing that Sam O'Mara was no longer around to plot and plan against her. She would stay with Molly as long as she was needed. She admitted that she missed her home, her relatives, and her many friends in the city. 'If it hadn't been for you, Moll,

I think the peace and quiet here would have driv me mad,' she had said honestly. 'At home, there's always a neighbour popping in either offering to do my messages or suggesting I might do hers. Then our Lana has only got to set foot in the jigger and she'll be dragged off to skip rope or play relievio or gerron a tram headin' for Princes Park or Seaforth Sands. Of course, she loves the hills and the streams and the animals, but I reckon she wouldn't swap lives with your Nonny, happy though she's been here. Why, she's already asked me if we can invite your kids to come and stay with us, perhaps over Christmas, when the shops is at their best.'

Soon after this conversation, Molly had taken Lana aside to find out how the experience had affected her, and whether she could bear to remain at Cefn Farm. Lana assured her that she felt exactly as her mother did: relieved that her father, whom she could scarcely remember, no longer posed a threat, so that she might enjoy the countryside without fear. 'I love the farm and the animals, and Chris's going to teach me all sorts of things,' she told Molly. 'Isn't it odd, Auntie Molly? When I went up into the mountains, following the chick trail, it was as though I got stronger and braver with every mile we went. When we started out I was scared of everything: the dark, the storm, even the sheep. Yet by the time we were coming down again, and I could see Cefn Farm below me in the valley, I felt there was nothing I couldn't do so long as Chris and Nonny were beside me. So if Mum wants us to stay, I'm real happy to do so, honest to God I am, Auntie Molly.'

Molly was vastly relieved in one sense, since she was finding the work of the farm, which she had always taken for granted, more than she could cope with while her leg was still in plaster. Nonny was as helpful as she had always been, but for a long time now Chris had been as useful as any man on the farm, and could not be expected to turn his hand to housework as well.

Happily, therefore, the extended family worked, and by the time the summer holidays were over Molly was able to cope. Ellen said that though she hated the thought of leaving Cefn Farm she was looking forward to seeing her friends and neighbours once more, and she agreed, with enthusiasm, that she and Lana would return to Cefn Farm the following year.

The two women were in the kitchen at the time, doing the weekly bake, and Molly said that perhaps she and Rhys might take a couple of days off near Christmas. She kept to herself the lurking reflection that Lana and Chris were being thrown together in a way of which she could not wholly approve. Although it was only at the back of her mind, she could never quite forget that evening, long ago, when someone might, just might, have switched her baby and Ellen's. That Chris and Lana might one day fall in love was a possibility which she preferred not to contemplate. If it happened, what should she do? Ellen would wonder why she had kept silent all those years, would probably think it was an excuse to stop Molly's darling Chris from marrying a girl with no land of her own, no foothold, so to speak, in the farming community. Yet if she let a marriage between the two go ahead what might the consequences be? Molly knew her bible, knew that a union between siblings was expressly forbidden. Yet here she was, agreeing to Ellen and Lana's spending at least some of their summer holiday every year at Cefn Farm, and suggesting that her own children should visit Liverpool. How devoutly she wished that she had told Rhys what the ward maid, Flossy, had told her! But she had not done so, so it was up to her to do her best to keep the friendship between Chris and Lana as just that: friendship.

So Molly pondered, as she and Ellen cut and peeled, mixed and baked and chatted, as two women will, over their work. And when Ellen said that she realised Molly and Rhys might find it difficult to leave the farm even for a few days, but that Chris and Nonny would be welcome to stay for the whole of the Christmas holidays if they liked, Molly felt she could not refuse on her children's behalf. All she could do was thank Ellen profusely for her offer and explain that, at Christmas, snow sometimes cut the farm off for weeks at a time. 'So we shall have to think carefully, since it would be dreadful if the kids were marooned in Bethel Street for a month,' she said, and pretended to join in Ellen's disbelieving laughter, whilst secretly praying for snow.

Chapter Ten

Nonny and Lana were lying on the grass in Princes Park, looking up at the blue sky above. They were alone, because earlier in the week, at an agreed time, Chris had telephoned to the box in the village to find out how his parents were getting on without him, and Rhys had said that they could do with some help at the dipping, now that they had such a large flock of sheep. Nonny had wanted to go as well, and she knew Lana would have been happy to accompany them, but it would have been rude to abandon Auntie Ellen. She had invited Nonny and Chris to stay for the whole of the summer holidays, and they had only been in Liverpool three days when Chris had been called home.

Fond though she was of her brother, and much as she missed him now that he was away at agricultural college, Nonny had a sneaky feeling that she and Lana would probably enjoy their time together more without him. Fifteen and clothes conscious, they both loved shopping, discussing the latest fashions and visiting cinemas and theatres, things which were not possible in the heart of Snowdonia, whilst Chris was openly scornful of such things. Furthermore, he had not really taken to Lana's friends, and Nonny thought, secretly, that he had been fretting for the farm even before the fateful telephone call. So now she turned her head and addressed her friend. 'Lana?

Is it lunchtime yet?'

Lana laughed and sat up, dusting fragments of grass from her smart navy blue sweater. 'It's much too nice a day to catch a tram back into the city centre, but if you're desperate for a cuppa we'll go to the open-air caff on the other side of the lake.' She then consulted the little wristwatch she wore and announced, 'It's twelve o'clock. After that, shall we take a boat out on the lake?' She got to her feet. 'Can you row, Nonny? You and Chris seem able to do most things, but your river is a bit too fast for a rowboat, I should imagine.'

Nonny followed her friend's example, then shook out her neat pleated skirt. She always brought her best clothes when she paid a visit to the O'Maras, and often went along to Paddy's market to exchange an outgrown garment for a larger one, paying the difference out of her pocket money. At home on the farm she wore slacks and sweaters, or short-sleeved shirts when it was hot, and of course at school there was the uniform, but here in the city she could enjoy wearing pretty clothes, having her hair cut by a professional and using the make-up which she hid from Molly, though she was pretty sure her mother knew all about it.

'I wish I had a watch like yours,' she said. 'Is there such a thing as a cheap wristwatch? If so I'm going to buy myself one and tell Mum and Dad it's what I want for my birthday; then they'll pay me back, of course.'

'Bound to be; you can get anything you want at Paddy's market,' Lana said proudly. She grinned, shooting a sideways look through her lashes at her friend. 'Mum says folk come from all over the world to shop at the Liverpool markets.'

'Well, I want a little wristwatch, if it's not too dear,' Nonny said decidedly. 'And I mean to buy presents for everyone at home; nothing expensive, but just something so they know I've been thinking of them. You're so lucky, Lana, to have a Saturday job. I told Mrs Enfys that girls in Liverpool could get paid work at weekends, but she just said wasn't that strange now, and went on putting treacle toffee into little brown bags for when the kids came out of school.'

'Oh well, you don't have much call for money on the farm,' Lana said airily. 'What would you buy? I don't believe Mrs Enfys sells make-up, even if your mum and dad would let you wear it, and you say they won't until you're seventeen. I suppose you could just save it up for when you come to Bethel Street...'

'That just shows what *you* know,' Nonny said scornfully as they chose a table and seated themselves outside the café. Lana waved to a young woman with a couple of small children seated at another table, then turned to her friend.

'That's Mrs Jamieson; her husband's a scuffer and they're friends of my mum's. Now what were you saying about spending money?'

'Haven't you ever heard of mail order catalogues? They sell all sorts; they've even got a section for tools and that, which a farmer might need. And some of the clothes are really pretty, and quite cheap.' In her turn Nonny looked slyly at her friend through her lashes. 'Only, of course, buying mail order means you can't try them on and you can't browse, and that's the part I like best about shopping.'

Lana chuckled, 'I've noticed,' she said drily. 'That's why your brother won't come out with us. He says you finger things and want to pinch fruit...'

Nonny gave a squeak of horror. 'Pinch fruit? Do you mean steal it? How dare you, Lana O'Mara! Did Chris say that, or was it you? I'm as honest as the day is long.'

Lana giggled again. 'Sorry, sorry, it's just those signs that they've got in St John's market on the peaches. *Please do not squeeze me until I am yours*. What'll we order? A pot of tea of course, but how about a buttered scone? We can share it between us, or have one each if you're really hungry because they're quite big.'

Nonny considered; she knew that Auntie Ellen had packed a picnic lunch which they meant to eat after first taking a boat out on to the lake. If she had a whole scone all to herself she might not be able to do full justice to the picnic, for having got into the habit of making her own bread as well as pies, cakes and puddings whilst at Cefn Farm Ellen had realised there was a good deal to be said for home baking, and the girls' haversack was stuffed with good things. 'Cheaper and better,' her lodger had said upon first tasting one of Ellen's homemade loaves. 'Keep it up, Mrs O'Mara.' And Ellen had been happy to do so. She was fond of Mr Taplow, who told her quite recently that he would be retiring in rather less than twelve months, and hoped that he might continue to live at the small house in Bethel Street. He meant to take a part-time job, he explained, so with his pension and his small wage he would still be able to afford the very reasonable rent she charged.

Nonny considered the scones which she could see a customer eating at another table. They were large, but she was hungry and thought she could do justice both to one of the scones and to Auntie Ellen's carry-out. She had watched as Auntie Ellen made corned beef and tomato sandwiches, spread butter and jam on big, floury baps, sliced cake, selected fruit ... still, she could just do with a scone, a whole one for choice. She said as much to Lana, and then dug her friend in the ribs. 'Your pal over there keeps staring at us,' she said in a low voice. 'I think she wants to talk to you.'

Lana turned in her seat and called across to the older woman. 'How are you, Mrs Jamieson? I see the kids are fine... Hello, Jackie, Paul. What are you up to?'

The woman smiled. 'Mornin,' Lana,' she said pleasantly. 'How's your mum keepin' these days? As for the boys, they're fightin' fit – and unfortunately, fightin's the word. Never did two brothers fall out more often!'

As if it were a signal the elder boy, who Nonny thought must be about seven, jumped on the smaller one, saying jeeringly, 'When we get to the lake I'm goin' to row the perishin' boat, an' – an' I'll throw you overboard if you try to tek the oars.'

'Don't be horrid, Jackie,' Lana said at once, seeing the younger boy's face begin to turn red and his mouth to open in what, she guessed, would be a deafening bawl. 'You know very well you wouldn't throw poor Paul into the water, because if you did the scuffers would come along and carry you off to the deepest dungeon beneath the castle keep!'

'My dad's a scuffer; if anyone tried to t'row me into a dudgeon he'd have his guts for garters so he would!' Jackie boasted, whilst Paul, taking advantage of the fact that his brother's attention was fixed on the two girls, reached across and began to help himself from a large bag of sweeties.

'Mum's fine...' Lana was beginning when she suddenly recollected Nonny's presence, and turned towards her. 'Oh, but I've not introduced you to my friend. Nonny, this is Mrs Jamieson. She lives just round the corner from us and her husband is our local bobby. Me and Mum babysit for them when they want to go out of an evening.' She turned back to the young mother. 'This is Rhiannon Roberts. She comes from Snowdonia; a place called Cefn Farm. We go and stay with Auntie Molly and Uncle Rhys in our summer holidays.'

Mrs Jamieson was beginning to answer when Jackie noticed that his brother had opened the bag of sweeties and was cramming his mouth to bursting point. He gave a shriek of rage and in thirty seconds or less the two were locked in mortal combat, whilst their mother tried to rescue the sweets, many of which had spilled out on to the grass, and threatened her sons with a promise of early bed and smacked bottoms if they did not immediately behave.

Apparently the threat was one which the boys took seriously for they shuffled apart, though Jackie snatched handfuls of grass and sweets before returning to his place at the table. Paul swallowed his mouthful with some difficulty and then approached his brother, both arms held wide. 'Sorry, Jackie; gi's us a kiss,' he said rather sweetly and Nonny guessed that this was the usual way the boys' squabbles ended when she saw them hug each other and scramble back on to their chairs. She picked up the menu, preparing to give her order to the waitress who was just approaching, and was surprised when Mrs Jamieson smiled across at her and suggested that they join forces. Nonny knew very few small children and would much have preferred to eat her scone and drink her tea with only Lana for company, but her friend was nodding, getting to her feet, gesturing the change of plan to the waitress. When they were all settled at the Jamiesons' table, Lana said that she would buy the boys ice creams and Nonny, in honour bound, said that she would share the cost. The boys were given cornets, but were reminded that bad behaviour would now not only call forth early bed and smacked bottoms, but mean confiscation of the ice creams as well. Jackie pulled a face, but Paul, taking his ice cream from the waitress with a polite 'Fanks, missus', settled down to enjoy the treat. Having seen them apparently safely occupied, their mother sat back in her seat with a sigh of pleasure and smiled brightly at the two girls.

'It's been one of them days,' she informed them. 'Sometimes they's good as gold; helpful, even. Other times they's as bad as devils from hell and there's never no accountin' for it. You'd think on such a lovely warm day they'd be happy just to be in the park, but they've set their minds on going on the lake and to be honest I don't reckon I can cope with them alone.' She turned an even more beguiling smile upon her companions. 'Alex gave me a quid so's we could take a rowboat out, but I don't fancy trying to control them in one of them little things. But if you lovely ladies would care to join us...' She left the sentence unfinished, and poor Nonny, who had been looking forward to a row on the lake, looked hopefully at Lana. Surely her pal would realise that the boys could ruin their day? But Lana was smiling and nodding.

'Tell you what, we'll take two boats out; me and Nonny will take Jackie with us and you can take Paul with you. We should be able to stop Jackie from hurling himself – or one of us – overboard, particularly if we promise him another ice cream if he behaves himself.'

This sounded like a good idea to Nonny, but Mrs Jamieson was shaking her head. 'No, not another ice; they'll gobble 'em down and be sick as dogs,' she said. 'A threat to put them ashore if they misbehave oughter work.'

Lana was beginning to agree to this when Jackie butted in. 'I want to row the boat, I want it more than I want an ice cream,' he stated. He turned a round, appealing face made comical by dabs of ice cream towards Lana. 'You'll let me row, won't you, Lana? I promise I won't splash and I'll be good for the whole afternoon. Oh, Lana, say I can row!'

Lana began to say that he might sit on her lap and handle one of the oars when Nonny interrupted. 'I'm rowing, Jackie,' she said sternly. 'I'm a much better oarsman than either you or Lana and I don't want to be dumped in dirty lake water. If you behave really nicely, but don't want an ice cream, what about one of those windmills in the bucket by the door of the café? They have them in all sorts of lovely colours. If you behave we'll come back here after we've handed our boat back and I'll buy you a windmill each.'

The small boy stared at her, eyes rounding. 'A windmill!' Jackie breathed. 'We's always wanted one of them, ain't that so, Pauly boy? Oh, we'll be two bleedin' little saints for a windmill each.'

By the time the three adults and two little boys left the table it was smeared with ice cream, jam and a good many brightly coloured and extremely sticky sweets, and Nonny was wondering why on earth Lana had agreed to take the kids on the lake, though she had to admit that the promise of the windmills had had a magical effect. As they went into the café to pay their bill she took a good look at the bucket. Every time the breeze caught them the whole lot began to twirl, daffodil yellow, scarlet, sky blue and green as grass, and Nonny, just for one moment, almost envied the little boys. She and Chris had never owned such a thing, never even thought of it, but seeing another child rushing round the café area, his windmill whirling above his head, she could see why Jackie and Paul had been so eager to promise good behaviour for such a fascinating toy.

When they reached the lake there was a queue for boats, but after a ten-minute wait they were able to set off. Now that Mrs Jamieson was out of earshot and Jackie apparently absorbed in hanging over the side and smacking the water, Nonny put the question which she had been longing to ask. 'Why on earth did you agree to this?' she hissed. 'If he plays up we'll be in trouble. And suppose they want to stick with us for the rest of the afternoon? I can't think of a way to get rid of them without sounding rude.'

Lana was beginning to reply that she was fond of children when Jackie, still splashing water, spoke. 'You could chuck me overboard,' he said cheerfully. 'Mum wouldn't mind. She likes horrible Paul best, 'cos he's her little yellow-headed darling.'

Both girls hissed in horrified breaths, but Lana leapt into the breach. 'Of course we shan't throw you overboard, chuck,' she said briskly. 'We love you much too much. And as for Mummy liking Paul best, that's just rubbish, you know it is. She has to take great care of him because he's only a baby really, whereas you're almost a grown-up. Now if you'll get your fingers out of the water, kind Nonny will let you have a go with one of the oars.'

As Jackie took his place beside Nonny with a crow of glee and began to plunge the blade somewhat raggedly into the water, Nonny pulled a face at her friend. A few moments later she was informing Jackie, crisply, that though he apparently hadn't noticed, they were going round in circles, and would he kindly let Lana steer them whilst he tugged rather more gently on his oar.

Ashore once more, and only slightly wet, they headed for the café to buy the promised windmills, and as soon as the boys had chosen one each – Jackie's daffodil yellow, Paul's sky blue – they parted, since Paul was growing heavy-eyed and even Jackie was looking weary. Mrs Jamieson thanked both girls for their company and their help, though Lana insisted on accompanying them back to the bus stop. 'See you again!' Jackie screamed, as his mother hustled him aboard the vehicle. 'Thanks for the windmills!'

Paul, on his mother's hip, blew kisses, and nearly decapitated the conductor by waving farewell with his windmill. The girls waved as well, Nonny resignedly and Lana with enthusiasm. Then they turned and made their way back to the part of the park where they had planned to eat their picnic. As they settled themselves on the grass Lana looked curiously at her friend. 'You've gorra face like a smacked bottom,' she observed cheerfully. 'What's up wi' you and kids? They's grand little lads, Jackie and Paul, though like all kids they can be real little hellraisers at times. They were pretty good today, but I still had the feeling, in the boat, that for two pins you really would have liked to chuck Jackie overboard.'

Nonny pulled a face and took another sandwich. 'I don't know how to treat kids, nor how to talk to them even,' she said honestly. 'None of our neighbours have small kids and now that I'm at high school there are none on the bus either, so I'm just not used to them. In a way, they scare me.'

Lana laughed. 'Scare you? For goodness' sake, Nonny, what do you think they can do to you? Eat you?'

Nonny giggled. 'I told you, I don't understand

them at all,' she said. 'But I suppose, if she's a friend of Auntie Ellen's, then you had to join her and the kids and make the best of it. And now let's change the subject. What do you want to do when we've had our picnic?' Nonny would have liked to go round the shops and usually Lana would have felt the same, but today it appeared she had different ideas.

'There's a play area not far from here where lads have a cricket pitch. This afternoon several fellers I know will be playing in a match and I thought we'd go along and watch. I'm quite friendly with one of the blokes; Tim Everett. He said if we were there soon after four o'clock we could join them for tea in the pavilion. We'd have to pretend we were helpers – putting out the sandwiches, pouring the tea and orange squash, things like that – but I'd like you to meet him.' She ducked her head and mumbled something which Nonny did not catch, then stared at her friend and repeated her words rather defiantly. 'Tim and me is going out,' she said. 'I've not said nothing to Mum – she thinks I'm too young – but we're going dancing at the Grafton this evening, and Tim's gorra mate, Rupert Harrison, what says he'll come along to keep you company.'

Nonny had been munching her sandwich but stopped abruptly at her friend's words, feeling as though her stomach had just filled up with ice water. 'Keep *me* company?' she said incredulously. 'But I can't dance, nor I don't want to. You go by yourself, Lana. I'll stay at home with Auntie Ellen.'

Lana stared at her friend, her eyes widening and her cheeks beginning to flush. 'But I *told* you,' she wailed. 'Mum thinks I'm too young to have a boyfriend, too young to go to dances...' she giggled, 'and much too young to snog in the back row of the stalls at the cinema! If you don't come with me she'll guess that something's up and start spying on me. Oh, Nonny, please say you'll come!'

'I can't. I hate meeting new people and I agree with Auntie Ellen, honest to God I do. We're much too young to do all those things and what's more, I don't want to. There's boys at school who've asked me to go walking or to the flicks, but I always say I can't. I'm just not interested.' She became aware that Lana was staring at her as though she had suddenly grown two heads, and the thought made her giggle. 'Look, I reckon I'm just young for my age; that's what my mother says, anyway. I expect I'll get round to liking boys one day, but it hasn't happened yet.' She finished her sandwich, pointed and clicked her fingers. 'Chuck us one of those jammy baps, there's a good girl. I say, you'll have to roll me down the hill to this cricket pitch if I go on eating at my present rate.'

Flossy folded the pushchair and surrendered it to the care of the conductor, then followed the boys, who had rushed straight to the front of the vehicle and were beginning to squabble over who should sit where. Flossy sorted them out with a threat to take away their windmills if they did not sit quietly, then sank into a seat and leaned back, closing her eyes. What a bit of luck it had been, meeting young Lana and the Welsh girl, Rhiannon Roberts, the two girls who had been born at the same time during that terrible thunderstorm. Apart from the mother she had met in the ablutions block, she had never confided her fears to anyone but Alex, but she often wondered whether Rhiannon was anything like Lana to look at. They had been alike as babies, as like as two pins, but then you could say that most newborns resembled each other. She had been seeing Lana for years, of course, and hard though she had tried she had seen no resemblance between Lana and Ellen. As for the father – Sam, wasn't it? – she hadn't set eyes on him for at least ten years, and retained only the haziest impression of what he had looked like.

But now that her wish had been granted and she had seen Rhiannon, she found to her chagrin that she could not bring to mind the face of either Molly Roberts or her husband. She thought they were both dark, but that was about all she could remember, and she wasn't even sure of that. Still, what did it matter? Those two red-faced babies had turned into two lovely girls. They were happy, and totally accepted by their parents. Flossy chuckled to herself. She and Alex had discussed what they had both seen that strange night and Alex, ever practical, had said that for all they knew babies might get swapped every night of the week. After all, the maternity hospital was the biggest in the whole area and mistakes can be easily made.

Now that Flossy was a fully fledged district midwife, she had her own area and did not go into the hospital much. She had laughed at Alex's suggestion that mistakes might be often made; she knew very well that normally this was impossible, babies being labelled almost as they emerged into the world. The only reason that those two little girls had not worn the regulation wristbands was because of the storm and the electrical failure. Anyway, what did it matter? Now that Flossy had children of her own she knew she would never dream of handing one of them over to another woman, even if it could be clinically proved that the child was not hers. You mother a baby and it becomes yours, she told herself. Neither Ellen nor Molly would dream of swapping daughters. She had listened to Alex when he had said she must put the whole matter right out of her mind, partly because he was so much older and more experienced than she, but also because she had not wanted to start what might amount to a witch hunt. And now, having met both girls together, she knew he had been right...

'Ouch! Mammy, Jackie just poked my eye with his bleedin' windmill. Tell him off, tell him off! Make him say he's sorry.'

Paul's indignant yelp brought Flossy's mind back to the present with a vengeance. In sorting out her own two children she forgot the two girls, and presently, harmony restored, the bus reached their stop and Flossy began the tedious task of claiming her pushchair, preventing the boys from leaping on to the pavement before the vehicle had stopped, thanking the conductor for his assistance, and persuading Jackie to carry her picnic bag whilst she erected the pushchair and strapped Paul into it. By the time all these tasks had been accomplished, and the boys were waving to the conductor as though he were their oldest friend,

Flossy remembered only that Lana and Nonny were a kind and friendly young couple, and that it was far more important to shepherd her own little entourage towards home, baths and bed.

The two girls went, as Lana had planned, to the cricket match and Nonny was introduced to both Tim Everett and Rupert Harrison. After their conversation Lana was not surprised when her friend blushed scarlet, and when Tim held out his hand to her, barely touched it with her own. He then introduced her to his friend Rupert, who got a similarly cool reception, and it was plain to Lana that Nonny, who had spent all her life in the wilds of Snowdonia, was terribly shy. There were three other girls, all older than Lana, helping with the cricket tea and with these girls Nonny seemed to have no problem, chatting and laughing as though she had known them all her life. As soon as the boys began to enter the pavilion, however, Nonny froze. She kept ducking into the kitchen, and when she had to carry plates of sandwiches and cakes into the main room she was in such a hurry to escape back to her haven that on one occasion she scattered sandwiches all over the paper tablecloth.

At home once more, Nonny had waited until Ellen was out of hearing before saying shyly that she did not really think her friend was in love with Tim Everett. 'You like my brother, you know you do,' she had said, half laughing, half serious. 'He's about the same age as Tim – getting on for eighteen – so he's a bit old for you, or I suppose you could say you were a bit young for him. But of course you only see Chris a couple of times a year, whereas Tim is always on hand.'

Lana had felt her cheeks grow warm at the mention of Chris, and had promptly punched her friend's shoulder. 'Of course I like Chris; I never had no brother of me own but I reckon that's how I like him, like a brother,' she had said. 'Now you go off and make your phone call and I'll make us cocoa and biscuits; only don't be long, else the biscuits will go cold.'

Nonny had arranged to ring Chris at the box in the village to see how the gathering had gone without her, and now she sniggered, got her coat off its hook and set off. Dusk had not yet fallen but Ellen did not like either of the girls being out alone as evening drew on and called out to Nonny to hurry back.

As soon as the door had closed behind their visitor, she turned to Lana. 'Well? Did you get to the cricket match? And are you going to the Grafton later?' She chuckled. 'I suppose you told her a tissue of lies, but it's in a good cause. Your Auntie Molly's really worried because she thinks Nonny is scared of men.'

Lana gave a derisive snort. 'Of course she's not scared of men; she's just a bit young for her age, and livin' out in the sticks like she does she don't meet many fellers that she's not known from birth, pretty well. She came to the cricket match all right and was pally as anything with all the girls, but she hung back a bit when I introduced her to Tim and Rupert. They're older, see, so perhaps I should have tried wi' fellers nearer her own age.'

'And will she go to the Grafton with you tonight?' Ellen asked sceptically. 'I bet she made an excuse; bet you five bob she won't go.'

'Bet she will,' Lana said at once. 'I've gorra plan...'

So when Nonny came back from her telephone call Lana jumped in at once. 'Look, I've spoken to Mum, and she don't mind us puttin' on our glad rags and goin' to the Grafton so long as we leave at the interval; that's ten o'clock,' she said triumphantly. 'The only thing is, she wants Tim and Rupert to call for us and bring us home, and I'm tellin' you, Rhiannon Roberts, that if you say no I'll cry all night...' she crossed her fingers behind her back, 'because it's the very first time my mum has let me go to the Grafton, and it's only because she trusts you – and the boys of course – to be sensible.' She reached over and gave her friend a warm hug. 'Please say you'll come,' she begged. 'You know I'd do the same for you. And you're right, I do like your brother, only as you say I don't see much of him.'

'And when you do he talks of nothin' but sheep, cattle, poultry and so on,' Nonny said, grinning. 'Oh well, I suppose it won't hurt me to go with you this evening, but I don't mean to dance, so put that in your pipe and smoke it.'

Lana had arranged for the two boys to come round to Bethel Street promptly at seven o'clock, so at half past six they went up to the room they shared and began to choose what they should wear. Lana had several dance dresses, bought with the proceeds of her Saturday job, but Nonny had no such finery, nor, she said defiantly, had she any need of it. At Lana's urging, however, she borrowed a blue taffeta dress, with a dark red rose pinned to the shoulder. She was several inches taller than her friend and was worried in case she was showing too much leg, but Lana, putting on her brand new black taffeta skirt with its many paper nylon underslips, told her briskly not to be such a fusspot. 'You've got a super figure and really good legs,' she told her. 'You'll be the belle of the ball, especially if I tie your curls up on top of your head and let them fall to one side in a Grecian knot.'

'I don't want to be the belle of the ball,' Nonny muttered. 'I'm warning you, no one's ever taught me to dance and I don't mean to start now.' She gave her friend a shove, for Lana was checking her appearance in the only full length mirror the room possessed. 'Let me have a look; if it's too short you can jolly well find me something different to wear.'

But Lana noticed that when her friend saw her reflection, a blush of pleasure warmed her cheeks. With her shining light brown curls piled up on her head and falling in ringlets on either side of her heart-shaped face, and the blue of the dress reflected in the blue of her eyes, Nonny would never lack for partners. Lana herself, with her mass of fair hair falling à la Veronica Lake across one cheek, her large dark eyes and her dimples, was much admired, and for the first time it occurred to her why girls frequently hunted in pairs. If only Nonny would agree, the two of them could make quite a killing at the Grafton tonight.

Promptly at seven o'clock the doorbell rang and the two boys, hair slicked down with Brylcreem, faces shiny with soap and water, and wearing their best dark suits, whistled admiringly as Lana and

Nonny, carrying their coats for it was a warm evening, joined them. Rupert, who was plainly very taken with Nonny, tried to take her hand, but Lana saw regretfully that her friend was having none of it. Instead she clutched at Lana's arm, her eyes widening so much that Lana felt quite sorry for her and told the boys rather brusquely to go on ahead and they would follow.

Later that evening, when the boys had punctiliously delivered them home, Ellen said she could see that Nonny was worn out and packed her off to bed. 'Young Lana here goes out with her pals two or three times a week so she's used to late nights, but you ain't; you're asleep on your feet, gal,' she told her visitor. 'You'll be off for some fun tomorrow if the weather's nice, so Lana can just help me pack a picnic, and then she'll follow you up the wooden stairs to Bedfordshire.'

Lana directed a glare at her mother for letting slip that she had, on previous occasions, let her daughter go out at night, but Nonny seemed to notice nothing amiss; perhaps she was too tired. At any rate she headed for the stairs, and as soon as her bedroom door closed Ellen pushed Lana into a chair, sat down opposite, and said, 'Well?'

Lana sighed. 'I reckon I owe you that five bob after all, Ma,' she said resignedly. 'She came to the dance all right but at first she wouldn't dance at all, not with anyone, and believe me, she had lots of offers. She's real pretty, ain't she, Mum? I knew she'd have plenty of partners and so she would have, but she just shook her head and told everyone: "No, I'm not dancing. I don't know the steps." Of course the fellers all promised to teach her and in the end, just to be polite I reckon, she stood up wi' Rupert but they'd only just started to dance – it was a slow waltz – when she suddenly wrenched herself out of Rupert's arms and gave him such a hard push that he fell over backwards. Then she ran off the dance floor, and out into the street. You can guess what everyone thought, of course ... poor Rupert, you'd have thought he'd have wanted to murder Nonny, but he was very understanding. Anyway, I caught her up, reminded her that we'd both left our best coats in the cloakroom and persuaded her to come back. She was shaking like a leaf, Mum, and giving little shudders, but she's brave, is Nonny. We walked round for a bit whilst she cooled off – she tried to pretend it was the heat of the ballroom which had made her come over fainty-like, but we both knew it wasn't true. You and Auntie Molly were right; she isn't just shy of men, she's downright scared of them.'

Ellen sighed deeply, reached for the loaf and began to slice. 'I thought as much. Now, I've bought some real nice ham off of Mr Thelfall this afternoon, and some ripe tomatoes from the greengrocer next door,' she said. 'I know you want to go to New Brighton, have a bit of a go on the funfair and a paddle in the sea. Pity you couldn't ask them young fellers to accompany you, but I dare say Nonny wouldn't like it.'

Lana chuckled, got to her feet and began to slice tomatoes. 'You're telling me she wouldn't,' she observed. 'I didn't tell you, but before the cricket match we met Mrs Jamieson and her kids. She asked us to share her table in the café and I offered to take one of the boys – the older one – on the lake with us.' She grinned at her mother. 'Now I admit Jackie and Paul are fellers, though very young ones, but Nonny wasn't a bit pleased to be saddled with them. Don't tell me she can't get along with boys of five and seven, because that's just crazy.'

Her mother smiled too, but abstractedly. 'She don't know nothin' about children,' she observed. 'I wonder if this has got anything to do with that other business; you know, when your dad grabbed her and took her off into the mountains. Molly thinks it has, but when she's questioned Nonny the kid just says she's talking through her hat, says she don't mind men at all, and in the next breath adds that she don't mean to marry, nor have a family.' Ellen looked rather shyly at her daughter. 'You see, no one knows except Nonny herself what happened that night. He could have done something she didn't like ... oh, I dunno, there could be a dozen explanations. I suggested to Chris that he might ask Nonny, see if she would open up to him – they're real fond of one another, those two – but he said it wouldn't be no use. Nonny won't talk about that time. The only thing she's ever said, and he always claims she didn't mean it to be heard, was that she had killed a man when she was ten. Apparently, she sort of muttered it when a group of them were talking about the worst things they had done, but when Chris asked her to repeat it she just laughed and said she was talking to herself, and talking a lot of rubbish, what's more.'

'Poor Nonny,' Lana said softly. 'But it wasn't Nonny who killed him, it was me. True, she gave him a push, but I shoved him hard enough to send the air whooshing out of his lungs. That was when he fell backwards...' Abruptly, she buried her face in her hands. 'And horrible though he was, he was my dad,' she muttered.

Ellen jumped up from her chair and rushed round to envelop her daughter in a warm hug. 'He were the wickedest, most violent man in the whole of Liverpool and you done right to rescue your pal before he could chuck her over the edge,' she said hotly. 'I'm telling you, queen, if I'd been there I'd have throttled him with me own hands, and if the scuffers had caught up with him he'd have been in jug for a hundred years. So think on, chuck. You and Nonny between you saved him from something he'd have hated a deal more than a quick, clean death at the bottom of that gorge.'

Lana raised tear-wet eyes from her cupped hands and gave her mother a tremulous smile. 'I know you're right really, and it's daft to blame myself,' she said, her voice trembling. 'It happened a long time ago, and to tell you the truth, Mum, it hardly ever crosses my mind. I used to have nightmares, but they went long since. Chris said that when something really bad has happened, it's best forgotten. He's sensible, is Chris. He said it's a bit like a gnat bite; if you scratch it, it goes on itching for ages and ages. Sometimes it even goes bad on you – septic I mean – which is a real nuisance. But if you leave it alone, never touch it, in a couple of days you can't even see the place on your arm where you were bitten. Chris said the whole kidnap business was like that gnat bite and the quicker we stopped scratching it, the happier we would be.'

'Oh dear, and I've made you think about it all over again,' Ellen said. She gave her daughter another squeeze and pulled a comical face. 'But Auntie Molly is really worried about Nonny. Uncle Rhys says she'll outgrow her dislike of boys, but I don't know. Sometimes these things make more of an impression than you imagine and it takes time to conquer such a deep-rooted fear. Tomorrow, while you're out, I'll drop Auntie Molly a line. When she said she was worried over Nonny's attitude to fellers I suppose I didn't take her seriously enough. Molly's always been a worrier, especially over her kids. But now I understand.'

'Well, she's got something to be worried about, it seems,' Lana said. She stood up, went over to the sink, splashed cold water into her face, then dried it on the roller towel at the back of the door, peering in the mirror to make sure all trace of tears had gone.

'I rather think, queen, that the only people who can persuade Nonny that boys are a part of life which she should be enjoying are you and the chaps you go around with. Find a gentle, studious type, throw him and Nonny together, and Bob's your uncle.'

'I don't see that working,' Lana said at once. The last thing she wanted was to be saddled with someone like Cuthbert Mason, who wore horn-rimmed spectacles but was always walking into things and apologising to lamp posts. He did not play games because his sight was so poor, and seemed to spend most of his time studying. Furthermore, his only friend was Lucas Skidmore and he was just such another, except that instead of straight hair falling in a fringe across his forehead he had thin carroty curls, white eyebrows and a laugh which sounded exactly like the neighing of a horse. Not even for her dear friend Nonny, Lana decided, would she start palling up with that dreadful duo, and in any event she knew Nonny well enough to believe her friend would feel exactly the same. After all, she reasoned, if one was not interested in handsome charming boys why on earth should one like plain and boring ones?

She put the point to her mother, but Ellen only shrugged and said there was no accounting for tastes. 'Look at me, saying "yes" to your dad,' she pointed out. 'I've never hid from you that I were pregnant at the time, so I suppose that's the best excuse I can offer for me mad behaviour. And in them days Sam were ... oh, different. He didn't drink so much for a start, and he were still in uniform.' She sighed reminiscently. 'I were always a sucker for a feller in uniform,' she finished.

The next morning, Nonny apologised fervently for her behaviour. 'I can't explain it, because that Rupert was really nice to me. It was just when he put his arms round me, I felt trapped. All I wanted was to get away, even though I knew I was being a fool. Do tell him I'm sorry next time you see him.'

Lana laughed. 'If he doesn't know you're sorry by now, he'd have to be pretty thick,' she said gaily. 'You spent the entire walk home apologising. And now let's forget it.'

The summer holidays were over, and everything was starting to change, Nonny thought. The baby Morris was a thing of the past, for one thing, for Rhys had bought an ex-army jeep which was a good deal more suitable for such difficult country, and now his daughter's luggage and Ellen and Lana's weekend case were piled in the back, for he had brought the O'Maras back with Nonny to spend a few days at the farm before returning to Liverpool. Ellen was still working when needed, but had time off owing, and Lana had left school and would soon be starting a shorthand and typing course at the local technical college.

Molly and Rhys, after much discussion, had suggested to Nonny that she might like to follow in her friend's footsteps after taking her O level examinations, rather than simply helping on the farm. Ellen had agreed enthusiastically to take Nonny as a non-paying lodger when the time came – she would be sharing Lana's room after all – and this would ease her parents' minds. 'It's not as if you'd be going to strangers,' Molly had said that morning, as she and Rhys sat in the O'Maras' kitchen discussing the idea with Ellen and the girls. 'You already know that several of your pals will have to live in lodgings in order to get decent jobs in the city; with Auntie Ellen eager to take you in, you'll be one of the lucky ones.'

Nonny had known her parents were right, known that she could not stay on the farm. Money was tight – had always been tight – so it was up to her to earn her living. After all, it was what everyone had to do in the long run, and, as she told her parents, she had had a gradual introduction to city life over the years which was now paying off. Once, traffic, crowds of people and even the Scouse accent had worried her, but now she was as at home in Bethel Street as she was at Cefn Farm.

'And I'll be able to come home whenever I can, won't I?' she had asked. 'If I get good grades in all my subjects I could get a really well paid job; I might buy a little car of my own, just a little one, you know, and come home at weekends.' She had beamed at her parents. 'I could have foreign holidays, might even get a job abroad, because my French is really quite good. But I'll always come back to Cefn Farm and Snowdonia, I promise you that.'

But now, bouncing on the back seat of the jeep as it turned into their lane, Nonny waved and waved to Chris, who must have heard the jeep's engine as Rhys had changed gear to crawl up the steep incline which led to the farm. 'Chris, Chris,' she shrieked, watching his face break into a broad grin. She slid the window back and stuck her head out. 'Have you done the milking? If not, I bags I milk Violet.'

The jeep swung into the farmyard and the girls tumbled out. Nonny hurled herself into Chris's arms. 'Oh, I've missed you, big brother! But Mum said you'd be home for the rest of the week, so we'll have lots of time to catch up. How...' But before she could finish the question Lana had pushed her aside, flung both arms round Chris's neck and plonked a kiss on his cheek.

'Gerroff, you!' she shouted gaily to Nonny. 'He's your perishin' brother, not your feller.' She turned to Chris. 'Ain't you the best-looking guy in the whole of Snowdonia?'

Chris's grin broadened, but he detached Lana, turned her round and smacked her smartly on the bottom. 'I don't need you to tell me that,' he said. 'As for the milking, I finished it half an hour ago.' He turned to give Ellen a kiss. 'Hello, Auntie Ellen, nice to see you ... nice to see your baggage too, and I don't mean the suitcases.'

'Yes, she is a bit of a baggage,' Ellen agreed. 'Mad about men, particularly handsome young farmers. And now let's get our luggage inside, so me and Molly can start cookin' a meal.'

Behind the stable door, Rhodri watched Nonny greeting her brother and wished he was not so awkward, so useless with girls; then he made his way out of the farmyard and headed for Cae Hic. When Nonny had left to spend the summer in Liverpool he had told himself over and over that when she got home he would ask her out, perhaps to a cinema in the nearest town, perhaps just for a walk in the hills, but now that he had seen her again, looking so grown up, he doubted he would ever have the courage.

Although he had said nothing to anyone, his mam knew how he felt and had told him to pluck up or he'd lose the girl to some smart young feller in the city. 'Our little Nonny is a country girl through and through, but she's young and heedless and might have her head turned by a feller with money,' she had explained. 'You'll miss her when she goes away, same as I shall, but if you were to tell her how you felt...'

'How can I tell her how I feel when I don't know myself?' Rhodri had said irritably. 'Besides, I'm too old for her. And anyway, I'm too busy to go a-courting, as they used to say.'

His mother had clicked her tongue impatiently. 'Don't be a fool, boy; you're in the prime of life and the gal's fond of you; even if you've not noticed, your da and I have. When she was just a kid she always wanted to be with you...'

Rhodri snorted. 'Of course she did, but she's changed. She's a young woman now. Oh, we're pals, I'll grant you, but nothing more. Nothing more on either side,' he finished firmly, and left the room to the sound of his mother's derisive laughter.

Now, however, he thought how much simpler it must have been in the olden days, when the hero could rescue the girl from the dragon and whisk her off on his white charger without having to explain anything. If there was something he could do for her, he would do it like a shot, but Nonny was self-reliant, ploughed her own furrow, had never as yet asked him for help. But there must be something he could do which would earn her gratitude and make it easier for him to speak.

'Hi, Rhodri!'

Rhodri turned. It was Nonny, panting and pink-faced, still clad in what he thought of as her city clothes, save for the large and muddy wellingtons on her feet. Rhodri slowed to let her catch up with him. 'Hello, Nonny. Did you have a good time in Liverpool?'

Nonny laughed and punched his shoulder playfully. 'Yes, I did, though I must admit I missed the farm. Did you miss me?'

It was an opportunity. Rhodri opened his mouth to tell her that he had indeed missed her most dreadfully, but she was telling him that Molly had sent her to invite him to join them for supper, if he would like to...

The opportunity was gone. And as he regretfully declined, saying that his parents would be expecting him, Rhodri cursed his stupidity. Would he never tell her how he felt?

Molly had watched Lana fling herself at Chris with mounting unease. The girl was pretty as a picture and the exact opposite of Nonny, and Molly had to admit that her son was extraordinarily good-looking. As they went indoors, however, she told herself briskly that Lana was only kidding when she pretended to be interested in Chris; Molly had heard all about Tim and Rupert and various other lads in whom Lana had taken an interest. She grudged Lana none of them, but if the worst should happen and the child started to take a real interest in Chris, then the secret which was always on the edge of Molly's consciousness might have to be told, and God alone knew what would happen then.

But right now everyone was busy, carrying in luggage, exclaiming over the meal – cold ham and salad with plenty of homemade bread and butter – which was set out on the kitchen table, along with the teapot and cups standing ready to be filled upon their arrival. Chris grinned when his mother congratulated him, telling the girls that he had cooked the salad himself, but admitting that he had had a good deal of help with the rest of the chores; Rhodri Pritchard, who could not hear enough about Chris's course, had helped with everything whilst the two young men talked. Chris knew Rhodri would have loved to go to college, knew also that it was not possible. The Pritchards could barely manage Cae Hic even with Rhodri's help; without it, Chris thought, they would surely go under.

It was not long before they were all settled around the kitchen table eating and talking, planning what they should do the next day, and asking Chris what he would be doing when he returned to college the following week. Slightly warily, he admitted that this term they would be learning bookkeeping. 'All about prices and quantities and so on – all the things a farm secretary has to know,' he finished.

Lana, who had been listening intently, turned to her mother. 'Oh, Mum, I'd really love a job as a farm secretary. Are they well paid, I wonder? And do they live in?' She turned away from her mother and back to Chris. 'Nonny was telling me how you mean to enlarge the farm and keep a whole heap more sheep; does that mean you'll need a secretary one of these days? If so, I apply for the job!'

Nonny snorted and stuffed a slice of ham into her mouth, then spoke rather thickly through it. 'Huh! If there's a job going at Cefn Farm, my little friend, it's going to me, not you. Why, you can't even milk a perishin' cow, and as for mucking out the pigsty...'

'Farm secretaries don't muck out pigs, nor milk

cows,' Lana protested. 'They have clean hands and shiny nails and wear smart little office suits. They answer the telephone, order up supplies of animal feed, hay, straw for bedding and overalls for the farm workers. They write down all the prices in one column and how much money the farm got for its wool clip in another, how many eggs were sold at market, how much milk went to the dairy...'

'Oh, pooh; you're just guessing,' Nonny scoffed, but Chris looked at Lana with increased interest.

'She's pretty well right though,' he admitted. 'Well, not about the shiny nails and neat little business suit, but about working on the books. Only most farmers hand that particular job over to their wives.'

Lana squeaked, then fluttered her eyelashes at Chris. 'Right; then I apply for the job as farmer's wife,' she said, then turned to Nonny. 'And that's one job you can't pip me at the post for,' she said triumphantly. 'Pass the bread and butter!'

As soon as the two girls had changed into the old slacks and sweaters they wore on the farm they went outside with Chris and Rhys to do what they could to help with the evening chores. Molly called them all in as soon as it grew dark, lighting the hissing paraffin lamp which hung from a hook in the kitchen ceiling, and sat them down to enjoy a light supper before making their way to bed, for farm hours mean early bed and rising early too. She and Ellen had provided homemade bread and cheese, green tomato chutney and apple tart as well as a large jug of cocoa, and as soon as this simple but delightful repast had been eaten Molly chased the youngsters off to bed, so that she and Ellen might have a comfortable chat. Rhys betook himself to the small room he called his office and settled down to do his books as he did every week, leaving the two women to catch up with one another's news.

Naturally enough what interested Molly most was how her daughter had got along with both Lana's friends and Ellen's, and Ellen had to recount all over again what had happened at the Grafton Ballroom, not leaving out that poor Rupert had ended up on his behind in the middle of the dance floor.

'I asked Lana to find out just what made Nonny react so violently, and she said Nonny had told her that she had felt trapped. She apologised very nicely to Rupert – your daughter has very nice manners, queen – but d'you know, I can understand it. I ain't criticising you nor Rhys in any way, but Cefn Farm is a long way from anywhere, ain't it? She's never had the sort of experience with fellers that other girls take for granted. Didn't you, before you married Rhys I mean?'

Molly thought back. Now that she considered it, she realised that there had always been boys in her life. She had gone to a mixed school; had joined the WAAF which meant that she had worked, and played, with a great many delightful young aircraftmen. No, it would be idle to pretend that she had not had plenty of experience before her marriage. She said as much to Ellen, adding with a smile: 'And I bet you were a devil with the boys when you were young, Ellen O'Mara!'

Ellen, however, shook her head. 'That's where you're wrong, queen,' she said. 'I were scared stiff of men, didn't want no part of all that courtin' business, told me mum I were going to be a spinster and look after her and have a career. And then I had a drop too much and got in the family way, and though I hated the thought of marriage and that ... well, you know the rest.'

Molly saw that her friend was looking at her half shamefaced and hastened to reassure her. 'I knew that you were pregnant when you and Sam got wed, and that you lost the baby,' she said, choosing her words with care. 'But it never occurred to me that you – you hadn't wanted to get married or have boyfriends. Was there – was there any reason for the way you felt? I mean, had you had a bad experience which put you against fellers? Because if so you're probably the one of us most likely to understand Nonny's feelings.'

Molly was thinking hard. If Ellen's dislike of men sprang from a good cause, then there was no reason to link it with Nonny's feelings, but if not, then the ward maid, Flossy, might well have been right. Some mischief-making person really might have swapped Nonny and Lana, which meant of course that she and Ellen had been rearing each other's children. But Molly told herself that whether Nonny was her daughter or no, she loved her exactly the same as she loved Chris. She loved Lana too, but obviously not as much, for they had only met for the first time when Lana was ten – you could scarcely count the meeting in the maternity hospital. So it really should not matter, unless of course Chris and Lana...

But the thought was too horrible to contemplate, and Molly had not failed to notice how swiftly Chris had put Lana in her place when she had tried to flirt with him. Chris regarded both Lana and Nonny as kids and she knew, though he had not told her, that he was taking someone to the flicks and to dances, a girl who was at a college not far from his own. Suddenly she realised that Ellen was looking at her, eyebrows raised, and burst into speech. 'I'm sorry. I'm afraid my mind was miles away. What did you just ask me?' But it appeared that even the easy-going Ellen could take umbrage, for her cheeks had flushed and when she replied it was stiffly.

'Oh, it were nothing much, nothing important anyway. Only I've never telled a living soul...'

The opening of the door behind her cut the words off short as Rhys, pushing a hand through his hair, came into the room. 'Sorry if I'm interrupting, ladies, but I could kill for a cup of tea,' he said plaintively. 'Anyone care to get a brew on the go?'

Rhodri got back to Cae Hic just as his mother put supper on the table. He went straight to the sink to wash his hands, knowing that water would have been brought in, then turned to grin at his parents, already sitting at the table, his father buttering the slices of bread as his mother cut them from the big loaf.

Mr Pritchard returned the grin. 'I'd put money on the fact that you've been pumping Chris about that there course of his,' he commented. 'I wish you could go along with him 'cos I've no doubt these colleges teach all the latest modern methods, but it's not possible. The truth is, Mother and I have never quite managed to put no money aside. We tell ourselves that the old ways is best, but we know it's not true, of course. The Robertses have kept their land in right good heart... Oh, well, there's no use in talking.'

His wife cut a wedge from the large pie which she had just placed upon the table. 'Hill farming's always been hard, and most of the work falls on you, lad, now your da and myself don't have our full strength no more. But we manage. Now tell us how Chris and young Nonny are getting on.' She smiled reminiscently as she dug her spoon into a large tureen of mashed potatoes. 'I'm that fond of little Nonny... I don't mind admitting I missed her sorely whilst she was away in Liverpool with her Auntie Ellen. Did she say she'll pop up to Cae Hic before school starts again?'

Rhodri nodded. 'Aye, she'll come for an hour or two. Wouldn't it be grand now, if she could work at Cae Hic! Chris said his parents were thinking of sending her to secretarial college. Not that hill farmers need secretaries as a rule...'

Mrs Pritchard laughed. 'The poor gal would start at nine o'clock in the morning and finish at a quarter past,' she said. 'Mind you, the Robertses are doing pretty well. What if say three or four of us hill farmers were in business big enough to support a secretary between us?'

Rhodri mumbled some sort of reply and settled down to eat his meal and to think about Nonny. He had known her all her life, had admired her pluck when she had been kidnapped by a feller he had thought was a tramp, and had been amazed when he had suddenly realised that she was no longer a child but a young woman, and a pretty one at that.

Chapter Eleven

Molly loved the spring gathering, when their sheep were collected together in the small stone-walled fields on one side of the rocky mountain stream which crossed their land. Of course, it was impossible to say that they had collected every single beast, because hill ewes were wily creatures who no sooner realised that they were being rounded up than they headed for the woods, the high tops or indeed any other place where they might be overlooked. Nevertheless, Molly thought, with Rhys, Chris and Rhodri on their tail, let alone the dogs, few, if any, would have escaped the round-up.

Once they had got most of the flock together in one of the fields which led down to the water, they would separate the lambs from their mothers – indignant bleatings could be heard for miles – since first year lambs were never shorn. Then the dogs, the family and every neighbour who could be spared would drive the ewes down to the washing pool, which had got wider as the years passed. They would arrange themselves on the stepping stones in order to make sure that each sheep was properly washed, pushing their heads under with crooks or sticks despite the animals' determination to escape this humiliating process.

The Pritchards and the Roberts always arranged their gatherings a few days apart, so that they could help one another, for as the size of their flocks increased, making sure that every fleece was clean and maggot free became more and more difficult. The Pritchards were an old couple, well versed in the ways of hill farming, and had helped Rhys and Molly many a time with advice, the loan of equipment or simply with their presence. Rhodri was now in his mid-twenties, and though he worked as hard as any man could on the farm he had told Rhys privately that when his parents retired he did not see himself being able to manage Cae Hic without employing more workers, and this would be difficult in their present financial circumstances. His parents would need money after their retirement, for they had never paid into a pension scheme, so the farm would have to continue to finance them. Molly had frowned; she knew how Rhodri loved the land, knew he would leave it with the utmost reluctance, and secretly hoped that by the time the Pritchards retired Rhodri would have saved enough money to pay a worker and thus be able to take over the farm. Or he might marry; a farmer's daughter who knew all about sheep, might even bring a dowry of sorts, which might enable Rhodri to keep Cae Hic, for the farm had been owned and run by his family for more than a hundred years.

'Mum! The Pritchards will be here in ten minutes or so; Dad's taken the jeep up to Cae Hic to fetch the old couple, though Rhodri and his dogs won't be along till later. Have you got the kettle on?'

Molly jumped, then put a hand to her heart as

Nonny bounced into the kitchen. 'How you startled me,' she said reproachfully. 'I was just hoping that I'd got enough food for the supper we'll give when the washing's over. I know I did a big bake before we left for Liverpool to pick up Lana and your Auntie Ellen, but I usually put a few dozen spuds in their jackets into the oven and I've not done that this year.'

'Oh, Mum, you always make too much grub, but if you're worried there's plenty of spuds in the clamp still; they can be fetched indoors. I dare say if you ask Auntie Ellen she'll scrub them and do all that's necessary.' Nonny giggled. 'She'll be glad of an excuse not to get involved with the sheep washing. Remember last year?'

Molly smiled at the recollection. The previous Easter Ellen and Lana had come to stay specifically, they said, to help with the gathering. Chris had very naughtily placed Ellen on a stepping stone in midstream, instructing her to push each sheep's head under as it swam past. Ellen, full of enthusiasm, had nodded wisely and taken up her position. She had tied her hair up in a bright red scarf and worn a pale blue sweater and rather smart navy slacks. The very first ewe to come near her had slanted a slotted yellow eye first at Ellen and then at the stick she held, and just as Ellen lunged forward had dodged to one side, so that Ellen's stick had met no resistance and she had plunged head first into the icy water of the mountain stream. Being Ellen, Molly remembered, she had laughed and taken herself back to the farmhouse to change into dry clothes, but though she had worked like a Trojan on getting the supper for the workers ready in good time, she had not again offered to help with the sheep washing. Lana had laughed with the others over her mother's unplanned dip but had made very sure that she herself had kept dry, steering clear of the ewes with their long soaked fleeces. Instead, she had stood well up the bank, directing any stray sheep into the pens which had been prepared for them.

But right now, Molly decided that Nonny was right; Ellen, always longing to help, would much prefer to be given a job inside the farmhouse, although if Rhys said the word she would be out there helping in any way she could. Lana, on the other hand, was still what Molly thought of as an unknown quantity. Sometimes she seemed truly keen to become as helpful around the farm as Nonny; at other times she was careful to avoid any jobs which she considered unfeminine, dirty or hard work. She would collect eggs, feed the poultry, harvest the apples from the small but thriving orchard and help with haymaking or the grain harvest. But she still had not learned to milk, could not groom or tack up a horse, shuddered at the mere mention of coping with a ewe needing help to birth her lamb. Nonny, on the other hand, would always choose farm work over housework. But that will change, Molly told herself. Once Nonny starts at the technical college, if that's where she decides to go, she'll begin to show an interest in clothes, make-up and boys. Then she'll start thinking of one particular boy with more interest ... then he'll ask her out and she'll go happily, then she'll invite him back to the farm...

Molly's mind went back to the conversation she had had with Ellen six months before. Was it possible that shyness with the opposite sex could be passed down from mother to daughter? She thought it doubtful, yet knew that if their situations had been reversed, if it had been she who had not enjoyed the company of boys, then she would have immediately assumed that Nonny's feelings came straight from Molly herself. I'm being downright bloody silly, Molly told herself, just as the kitchen door opened and Ellen came into the room. How often I've wished that dear Flossy had told her story either to both of us or to neither! I wish I could tell Rhys, but that would involve explaining why I didn't tell him at the time. Oh, how I wish there was some magic potion of forgetfulness! The thing is, I do forget most of the time; I only start thinking about it again when something reminds me. And now I've got more important things on my mind.

She turned to smile at her friend. 'Ellen, you're a sight for sore eyes! I was just telling Nonny here – oh, drat the girl, she's gone off – I was just telling her that I'd not prepared potatoes for baking in their jackets as I usually do for a gathering. Rhys needs me because I have to look after Mottle – if a dog is left without a handler they can cause trouble without meaning to do so – so if you can cope with breakfast for anyone who has time to pop in, plus scrubbing the spuds, only you'll have to take a basket and get them out of the potato clamp first, I'd be so grateful.' She smiled sweetly at her old friend. 'Dear Ellen, I wouldn't ask anyone else to miss all the fun of the gathering but I know you won't mind.'

Ellen laughed and went into the pantry, returning with a bag of porridge oats in one hand and a large jug of milk in the other. 'Course I don't mind; I'd rather swim in porridge than in that perishin' mountain stream of yours,' she said cheerfully. 'Do you want Lana to give a hand? I'm ashamed to admit the little monkey's still in bed, but if there's work she can cope with I'll make her get up or she'll get no breakfast.'

Molly was about to reply that this would not be necessary when both women heard feet thundering down the stairs and Lana appeared with her rumpled hair still in its bedtime plait, her sweater askew and her feet bare. 'Sorry I'm late; Nonny woke me but whilst she was washing I must have fallen asleep again,' she panted. She was carrying a pair of worn plimsolls in one hand and now balanced precariously on one leg at a time as she thrust the shoes on to her feet. 'Aha, I see you're still at the porridge stage, so I'm not too late for brekker.'

'If you make some toast whilst I do the porridge then you can choose either to help me in the house or to help guide the sheep into the dip,' Ellen said.

'Chris and Nonny are milking the cows and Jacob is going to feed the stock. But no one's collected the eggs yet, as far as I know; when you've toasted some bread you can do that,' Molly said hopefully. Keep the kid busy, she thought.

Lana pulled a face. 'I'll go and help to carry the milk into the dairy,' she said, but before Molly could reply Ellen laughed and shook her head.

'No you won't, young lady! Those who milk the cows can manage perfectly well without any help. I know you. If your Auntie Molly was making butter you wouldn't be half so keen, 'cos that's real hard work. But just taking the milk and putting it through the cooler is a nice easy job, ain't it? And of course you'd get a chance to give Chris the eye.'

Molly stared at her friend; so Ellen, too, had noticed that Lana was beginning to pay Chris rather too much attention. Not that it mattered, she told herself hastily. Lana had only turned sixteen at Christmas, so she was still not much more than a child and Chris treated her as such. Nevertheless, she was glad when Lana, having first jutted a sulky lip, brightened. 'Well, I'll collect the eggs and feed the poultry,' she said. 'Then I'd best come in and give you a hand, Mum, because if I know Auntie Molly she'll be out there with that gangly young dog of hers, bullyin' the sheep and bossin' the gatherers and never givin' a thought to folks fancyin' a bite come dinner time.'

Dusk was beginning to fall before the last weary ewe emerged, dripping, from the dip. She was old and tired and had produced twin lambs two years previously, but she was a canny creature and had managed to evade the ducking until she was the only sheep left in the walled field. The dogs knew their task was to see her into the water, but whenever they crept close to her she stamped her feet and swung round on them, daring them to come any nearer. In the end Chris jumped over the wall, grabbed her by her neck fleece and stumpy tail and ran her into the deep dip. He ducked her head under and then had to help her up the bank, for the passage of a great many ewes, in scrambling out, had made it treacherous and slippery. At the top, Nonny awaited both her brother and the old ewe, laughing at the state of him, for he was wet to the waist and covered in mud. Then, as the ewe began scrabbling impotently at the slope, she did as Chris had done; leaning forward, she seized the fleece, now heavy with the coloured water, and jerked the ewe bodily on to dry, or comparatively dry, land. She smiled triumphantly as Chris joined her, offering him a hand though knowing it would be scorned. Chris pushed his wet hair out of his eyes and grinned at his sister. 'The day I need help to get out of the dip is the day I'll be drawing my old age pension,' he assured her. He looked around him and Nonny followed his eyes, seeing the yearling lambs circling the crowded pens, checking that their mothers, though they must have smelt very different, were still alive and well.

Chris slid an arm round her waist and began to lead her towards the stepping stones. 'I reckon we've done a good day's work,' he told her. 'I only spotted two sheep which didn't belong to us or the Pritchards; they came from the Evanses' place. Heaven knows how they got all the way over here, but I didn't try to sort them out, so Mr Evans has had two sheep dipped by us for nothing.' He grinned down at his sister. 'I know it's difficult to say for certain, but Dad and I both think we've had our entire flock through our hands today.'

By now they had reached the stepping stones, and tired though she was Nonny refused Chris's offer of help, though she dodged rather wearily across the slippery surfaces and was glad to reach the home side without a ducking. The two made their way into the kitchen to find Rhys, Molly, Ellen and Lana, as well as the Pritchards, Jacob and old Mr Williams, already seated and attacking the piles of food – including a great mound of baked potatoes – that covered the table.

Mr Pritchard looked up as the two entered and grinned toothlessly at them. 'A good day's work we have done,' he said in his sing-song English, for he would not have dreamed of speaking in Welsh whilst the O'Maras were with them. 'Seen our Rhodri, have you? One of the ewes had a tear in her side. She's an old girl but he said he'd stay with her and apply the ointment the vet left, and not to wait for him.' The old man chuckled, addressing Chris. 'Your mum's made enough food for an army, so our boy won't go short.'

However, Molly had scarcely begun to split open the big floury potatoes and cram into each a good helping of her homemade butter when the back door opened and Rhodri entered the room. 'She's fine. She's the one who had twins back in February,' he remarked, sliding into a chair and reaching for a potato. 'A good start to lambing, eh, Rhys?'

Rhys nodded, his face lightening. Hill ewes rarely gave birth to twins, and to have such a birth at the very beginning of lambing must augur well for the season to come.

Nonny, sitting next to Rhodri, jerked at his

sleeve to get his attention. 'You didn't tell me about that. Were they rams or ewes?' she asked eagerly. 'Are they still in the pens, if the mother was so old?'

Rhodri smiled. He looked very like his father must have some thirty years ago, with straight dark hair, a lean, weathered face and a rather serious expression, though when he was amused and smiled, as he was doing now, a long crease appeared beside his mouth, making him look younger than his years. 'They were both ewes,' he said. He grinned round at the assembled company, then turned back to Nonny. 'When supper's over I'll take you up to where I left the mother and her twins, and you can see them for yourself, cariad.'

'Right,' Nonny said. She glanced at Lana who was picking at her food and gazing across at Chris. Nonny guessed that her friend had been trying a mouthful of this and a mouthful of that all afternoon and was now not particularly hungry. She leaned forward so that she could get Lana's attention, for her friend was sitting on the far side of the table, next to Molly. 'Lana? When supper's over Rhodri's going to take me up to see the old ewe's lambs. Want to come?'

Lana hesitated, glanced once more at Chris, then shook her head. 'No, Mum and I are going to do all the clearing up because Auntie Molly and you have had a far tougher day than us.' She smiled across the table at Chris and addressed him directly. 'You'll take me to see the lambs tomorrow, won't you, Chris? And explain about the washing and shearing and dipping and everything? I do want to understand things. It would make me feel a part of the farm, and I'm sure the more I know the more help I shall be when summer comes and Mum and I have our holiday with you. Then I won't just feed the poultry and collect the eggs, I'll jolly well learn to milk, see if I don't.'

Nonny and Chris both laughed and clapped; but Nonny saw a slight frown cross her mother's face. 'Tomorrow's going to be a busy day, Lana,' Molly said slowly, 'because whilst the ewes are penned they have to be examined for disease and so on. Chris will be far too busy to trail around showing you lambs. But I dare say Nonny will take you; then she can keep an eye open for any sign of trouble in the sheep.'

'Oh! But I want to go with Chris,' Lana said frankly. 'When we're together Nonny and I talk about clothes and school and tech, not about the farm.' She turned from Molly to Chris. 'I wouldn't be any trouble to you, would I?'

'Of course not,' Chris said, and Nonny saw him cast a curious glance at their mother. 'But you know there'll be a good deal of scrambling around in rough country, rounding up any stray ewes which need attention. You'll get pretty tired and Mum's right about one thing: I shan't be able to bring you home if you get bored halfway through the morning. Tell you what, Lana, when I come in to do the evening milking you can come out to the cowshed with me and I'll start giving you milking lessons. How's that?'

Lana sighed. 'All right,' she agreed, but Nonny could hear the disappointment in her friend's tone. Lana turned to her. 'What will you be doing whilst your brother's busy with the perishin' sheep?'

Nonny laughed. 'All the usual things,' she said cheerfully. She gestured around the table, at the rapidly emptying plates of food. 'Mum'll need somebody to go into the village and buy supplies; normally I'd ride in on Cherry, but if you want to come in as well and give a hand with the heavy stuff then we'll harness her to the pony cart and take that.' She grinned at her friend's sulky expression. 'Oh, come on, give us a smile! I'll show you how to tack Juniper up and back her between the shafts, then you'll have learned something useful even if it isn't Chris teaching you!'

Lana joined in the laughter which followed Nonny's jibe, though she still felt annoyed that her plan of spending the day with Chris had been thwarted. She could see no reason why she shouldn't accompany him as he worked amongst the sheep and for the first time it occurred to her that Auntie Molly often stepped in to prevent a tête-à-tête with her son. She said nothing now, however, with so many people sitting round the table and enjoying the gathering supper, but when she and Nonny were up in their own room getting ready for bed she asked her friend in a rather plaintive tone whether she knew why Auntie Molly seemed to have turned against her.

Nonny's big blue eyes widened. 'Turned against you?' she said incredulously. 'What on earth are you talking about, Lana O'Mara? My mum loves you like a daughter, you know she does. You must have heard her saying so a hundred times.'

'Oh, she says so, I grant you that,' Lana said rather crossly. 'But didn't you hear her at the supper table just now? I wanted Chris to show me the old ewe's lambs and he said it wouldn't be any trouble, but she started making objections at once.' She sniffed. 'Does she think I'll seduce her one and only into becoming a city boy? Or does she just think I'd make a rotten wife for a farmer?'

Nonny was tugging her thick sweater over her head but for a moment she stopped moving, frozen, apparently, into silence and stillness by her friend's words. Then she threw the garment on to her bed and turned an astonished face towards Lana. 'Not make a good farmer's wife?' she squeaked. 'You and I are exactly the same age, Lana, and the last thing on my mind is getting married.'

Lana felt her cheeks grow hot. 'Oh, how you do leap to conclusions, Nonny. That was just a for instance, as they say. I don't mean to marry anyone for years and years and I'd have to be desperately in love with someone to cut myself off from all the things I like best and take to sheep farming in Snowdonia. It's just that Auntie Molly seems determined to keep Chris and me apart...'

Nonny gave a derisive crow of laughter. 'Keep you apart? My dear Lana, whatever are you thinking of? Mum doesn't have to keep you and Chris apart, because Chris thinks of you as another sister, and not even a useful one. If you're offended because Mum doesn't want you to trail round after Chris when he and Dad and the dogs are working with the sheep, then you're a bigger fool than I thought you were!'

'But she did stop me; she said I was to go with you instead,' Lana mumbled. She felt annoyed with herself. She had had a serious crush on Chris for a couple of years now, thought him the best-looking boy she had ever encountered, and despite what she had told Nonny she truly hoped that one day he would reciprocate her feelings and fall in love with her. In a way, she wanted this outcome from sheer pique. At home in Liverpool she had a great many admirers, lads who offered to take her to the flicks, to dance halls, on coach trips down to the coast. Here at Cefn Farm there were only two unattached males, and nice though he was Lana had never wasted a thought on Rhodri Pritchard. For one thing he was a decade older than she, and for another Welsh was his first language, so though he and Nonny jabbered away happily enough, and he always changed to English as soon as he realised Lana was present, she felt she had never really got to know him.

Chris, on the other hand, was only a couple of years older than herself and she saw no reason why he should not begin to show her the sort of flattering attention which she had come to believe was her due. Now, as she began to undress, not throwing her dirty clothes on the floor as Nonny did – Lana's were not really dirty at all – but hanging them neatly in her half of the wardrobe, she glanced at her reflection in the old cheval glass which Auntie Molly had recently bought at Seth Hughes' auction rooms in Wrexham. She saw a slender girl with a mass of fair hair, big blue eyes set wide apart in an oval face and cheeks just flushing with rose. A pretty girl, and one who would never lack for boyfriends, because in addition to her looks she knew she possessed that enviable quality which years ago had been called 'it'. Now, more frankly, it was sex appeal. She smiled at her reflection, revealing even white teeth and a dimple which peeked roguishly in one cheek. Yes, Chris Roberts would be mad if he didn't fall at least a little in love with her.

Lana was about to turn away from the mirror to continue undressing – she was clad only in vest and knickers – when she was seized from behind and shoved to one side. Nonny, in pink and white striped pyjamas, for she had already shed her clothes and donned her nightwear, dug her painfully in the ribs with a stiffened forefinger.

'Lana O'Mara, you must be the most conceited girl in the whole world,' she said derisively. 'Staring at your reflection and no doubt thinking that there's not a man for miles who doesn't long for your kisses!' She half closed her eyes, tilted up her small chin and affected an American drawl. 'Gee, honey, ain't you the purtiest thing! You're so sweet and gorgeous I could jest gobble you up!' She dropped the mid-Atlantic accent and reverted to her own voice. 'D'you know what Chris would do if he saw you cavorting in front of the mirror like a perishin' film star? He'd laugh like a drain and tell you to stop acting so daft.' Nonny ran her hands across her small breasts, then pointed at her friend's completely flat chest. She giggled. 'I don't know why you wear that horrible pink brassiere, because you've got nothing to put in it. I've got bigger busts than you and I don't wear one.'

'Yours is just fat, not real busts,' Lana said

defensively. 'I'll have bigger busts than you one day, because girls follow their mothers and my mum has huge ones.'

Nonny considered her friend, her head on one side. 'Do you read your stars in the paper each week?' she asked slowly. 'Dad says it's a lot of nonsense and he's probably right, because when you think about it you and I were born at the same time on the same day in the same flipping place, and so we have identical horoscopes, but we couldn't be more different.'

There was a short silence, then Lana stripped off her remaining clothes and pulled on her white cotton nightie. 'What's that got to do with anything?' she enquired, sitting down on her bed and reaching for her cup of cocoa. She yawned exaggeratedly. 'Golly, I'm tired! Do you think your mum will let us lie in tomorrow?'

Nonny climbed into bed and then considered her friend's question. 'You can lie in if you want; you're a guest,' she reminded her friend. 'But I'm a worker, I am. You don't know how many jobs need to be done whilst the ewes are penned so we can get hold of them. The lambs have to be earmarked, you know, and we have to examine the mouth of every sheep, and check them for maggots – not that they're likely to suffer from that if they've been well washed and dipped – see that none of them have foot rot ... oh, it would take all night to tell you half the things we'll be doing over the next few weeks.'

Lana heaved an exaggerated sigh. 'Wake me tomorrow as soon as you've washed, then, and I'll follow you downstairs,' she said resignedly.

'God, me friends in Liverpool don't know the half, do they? They're so envious of me spending time in the mountains most holidays! I do tell them that hill farming's hard work, but I don't think they believe me.'

Nonny finished her cocoa, then scrambled out of bed to blow out the candle on the chest of drawers, for Cefn Farm was still not 'on the electric' as the locals put it. Lana watched dreamily as she crossed the room and pulled back the curtains, then opened the window and hastily shut it again. 'It's still too windy for open windows tonight,' she remarked. 'Ooh, the lino feels like ice on my bare feet.' She leapt back into bed and heaved the blankets up round her shoulders. 'Are you sure you want to be woken? Only I'll be up at first light and that's pretty early at this time of year.'

Lana, cuddling down into her warm nest, was tempted. She knew no one would blame her if she did not get up when Nonny did, but if she lay in Chris would be off up to the hills before she had drunk her first cup of tea, and as always, she would have given everything she possessed to impress Chris favourably She adored him, had hero-worshipped him as a small girl, but now that feeling had crystallised into a far more adult desire to please him, so she reiterated her wish to be woken and then plunged thankfully into sleep.

'Lana?'

In the grey light next day Lana opened sleepy, reluctant eyes and saw Nonny in her underwear, rubbing her wet face dry on her towel. She grinned when she saw that Lana was awake and gestured to the washstand. 'Your turn. I went down and fetched a jug of hot water, so if you'd like to wash in what's left, you're welcome,' she said. 'I'm going to put on an extra sweater and if I were you I'd do the same. Mum's already got the porridge on the go; she tried to get me to bring you up a cup of tea, but I knew you'd only leave it on the side to get cold whilst you washed and dressed.'

Lana, who would have liked a hot cup of tea, muttered beneath her breath but Nonny was busy pulling on the thick grey socks which she always wore inside her wellingtons and did not hear, and presently the two girls, both now dressed, thundered down the stairs and into the kitchen. The room was already bright with lamp- and firelight and Chris, Rhys, Jacob and old Mr Williams were scraping the last of the porridge from their bowls, draining their mugs of tea and getting to their feet. Despite the brightness of the kitchen Lana could see through the low window that the sun had risen and was pouring golden light from behind the distant peaks. It was going to be another fine day.

'Well, well, well, fancy seeing you, Miss O'Mara!' Chris's voice was teasing but, Lana thought, affectionate. 'I do trust my sister didn't drag you screaming and kicking out of bed?'

'No she did not; I asked her to wake me when she'd finished washing, and she did,' Lana said with dignity. 'Ooh, Auntie Molly, that porridge looks delicious.' She looked around the kitchen. 'Where's Mum? Still in bed, I suppose.'

Molly tutted, smiling at her guest. 'You're wrong there, chick; she's gone to the dairy for more milk.' She began to serve the porridge into two dishes. 'Since you two are going to do the work of the yard to release the men to deal with the sheep, you won't need to be out and about all that early. Nevertheless, your stomachs will want lining, so start with porridge and finish up with toast and marmalade; that should see you right till lunchtime.'

As Chris strode towards the sheep pens he was smiling at the thought of Lana coming to grips with her fear of animals. How she could possibly be frightened of sheep was more than he could understand, but she was beginning to get over her fear, fighting it as resolutely as she had said she would. Chris laughed at her and teased her, tried to tell himself that he thought of her as a sister, but in fact he found himself captivated by this new Lana, with her delicate elfin features and her captivating smile. His mother, however, though she had never put it into words, clearly thought that she would never make a suitable wife for a hill farmer. Chris supposed, reluctantly, that she was probably right, but as he began to move amongst the sheep he reminded himself that they were still young. At present, pretty clothes, dancing and film stars were more important, he imagined, than anything else in Lana's life. Oh, he was well aware that she liked him very much, but he supposed that this was a transient feeling, one which only came to the fore when she was at Cefn Farm. Indeed, his own feelings for her were vague as yet.

As he swung open the gate of the first pen and the sheep began to surge around him, he spotted one which was dragging a hind foot and chided himself. This was no time to start wondering about his relationship with Lana; this was a time for keeping one's mind on one's work. Resolutely he pushed through the milling ewes, grabbed the lame one and shouted to Jacob to give him a hand. Work took over; other things could wait. After all, when the school holidays ended, Lana would be going back to Liverpool, a long way from both Cefn Farm and himself. Plenty of time to sort out his feelings; plenty of time.

Nonny approached the Miss Perkins secretarial college in Rodney Street, aware of an uneasy fluttering in her stomach. The school had a first rate reputation and only took pupils with a high educational standard. Molly had been delighted when Nonny had passed all six of her O level exams with good grades and had accompanied her daughter to the college for her first interview, which she had passed with flying colours. The college was run by two sisters, Miss Elizabeth and Miss Matilda. They ran a special course for pupils who had done well at French in school, since Miss Elizabeth spoke French, it was said, like a native, and the other courses were run by Miss Matilda and two employees. Nonny, having spoken both Welsh and English from the time she was two or three, had found the French language relatively easy and had been accepted by Miss Elizabeth for the special class. Now, however, walking slowly along Rodney Street in the college's neat uniform

– navy suit, white blouse and navy Burberry – she began to wish that she had enrolled for a less exalted course. The truth was that over the years she had come to know many of Lana's friends, and even though most of them had gone to the technical college it had never occurred to her that she would know nobody at all in her class. However, she fully appreciated her parents' insistence that she should work as hard as she possibly could and gain every possible certificate and diploma, so that when she applied for work she could command a far higher salary than those pupils who spent their college days just having fun, and at the end of the course barely managed to scrape a pass.

Lana had started her second year at the technical college having spent the first year doing as little work as possible; in fact, achieving only a borderline pass at the end of her first nine months. She had said airily that she did not care, that she was not, and never had been, an academic, but Nonny knew that her own exam results had brought Lana face to face with reality. Then, at the beginning of the new term, Lana had realised that, because of her poor performance, the technical college might easily insist that she repeat her first year again. She had bounced into the classroom, brimming with confidence, and had had to eat humble pie and make a great many promises in order to go up with the rest of her class.

Nonny had gone to the college to meet her at the end of that first day, and on the way home her bravado had suddenly disappeared and she had pulled Nonny into the nearest café, ordered a pot of tea for two and burst into tears. 'I wish I were like you, Nonny,' she had wailed. 'Mum kept saying it were no use cheating at homework – I copied off of Ella, who's real clever – nor pretendin' I understood things when I didn't. She said I'd end up bein' a dinner lady like her, or an office girl, whilst pals who really had worked at tech ordered me about like a skivvy. I tell you, Nonny, if I'd had to resit the first year I'd of shot me perishin' self. As it is I'll be workin' like a slave just to catch up.' She had turned tear-drenched eyes towards her friend. 'Will you help me to get meself back on track?' she quavered. 'And don't tell your mum and dad – or Chris – wharra fool I've made of meself.'

Nonny had promised, though with certain reservations; she knew Lana and feared that, once she was no longer afraid of a resit, she might slip back into her old ways. But I won't let her, Nonny told herself now, slowing her pace to an even more snail-like one as the college loomed closer. I'll keep her up to the mark somehow. It's a pity she's not at Perkins where I can keep an eye on her. The only thing is, I really mustn't let her problems become more important than my own.

She had now reached the college and would have gone up the steps and into the building except that someone grabbed her arm. A small dark-haired, dark-eyed girl of about her own age smiled shyly up at her. 'Excuse me, are you Rhiannon Roberts? I'm Cerys Hughes; your brother said that you and I were both starting at Perkins on the same day so I said I'd try and spot you and say hello...'

'How did you know it was me?' Nonny said,

feeling anxious. Did she have the words 'hill farmer' written right across her forehead? She looked down to check that she was not wearing muddy wellingtons, then looked up at Cerys Hughes questioningly. 'I'm wearing uniform like the rest; so are you for that matter.'

Cerys laughed. 'Your brother said you'd be carrying a red bag – he gave it to you for passing your exams – so I kept my eyes open and so far I've seen navy bags, blue bags, green bags and even a stripy one, but yours is the very first red one I've spied.'

'Well, thank goodness for that,' Nonny said devoutly as the two of them climbed the steps and went through the open doors into the hall. 'But how come you know Chris and not me? You aren't at the agricultural college, are you? No, of course you aren't. You said you were starting here today the same as I am.'

'I don't know your brother at all, not really,' Cerys explained. 'But my brother is at the agricultural college with him – has Chris ever mentioned Tugger Hughes?'

Nonny smiled. 'Yes, of course. I believe I may have met him when Chris got up a party of them to go mountain walking and brought them to Cefn Farm for a drink and a bite on their way back to the bus. I say, what a bit of luck! I was just thinking I didn't know a soul and wondering how on earth I'd get on when you grabbed my sleeve.'

Cerys was beginning to reply that she had felt just the same when a bell rang shrilly and all the girls who had been outside came pouring into the hall, whilst a very stately lady, descending the stairs, clapped her hands sharply, putting an end to all discussion. 'Good morning, young ladies. I hope you enjoyed your summer break and are now ready and eager to start work once more,' she said in a deep, refined voice. 'Miss Beaver will come amongst you presently, taking your names and telling you into which classroom you should go.' She turned to the short plump woman by her side. 'Go ahead, Miss Beaver!'

That night, when the girls returned home, they both had a good deal to talk about. Lana was interested to hear of her friend's meeting with Cerys Hughes, who had told Nonny that she was boarding in a cheap lodging house not too far from Bethel Street. However, it was soon clear that Lana's interest lay mainly in the fact that Cerys's brother was a pal of Chris's. 'Perhaps we could get together sometimes,' Lana suggested. 'You'd like that, wouldn't you, Nonny?'

'Well, but what about work?' Nonny said and immediately felt ashamed, especially when Lana said impatiently: 'Oh, work! I meant in the holidays, of course. Just because we both mean to work very hard doesn't mean to say we can't play hard as well. But of course, if you're going to turn into a really boring person who never has any fun at all...'

Nonny laughed. 'Don't be so daft. Of course I'd like to have fun, lots of it. I was just afraid you might have begun to think you could serve two masters, as my dad says. But of course in the holidays we can do what we like; paint the town red as they say.' She picked up a large sheet of foolscap paper and waved it under her friend's nose. 'See that? It's my homework timetable. It starts today and goes on until the end of term, which is only a few days before Christmas.'

Lana pulled a face. 'You mean you won't be able to come out with me in the evenings...' she was beginning when Ellen, who had been sitting in her favourite basket chair, knitting something pink and fluffy, interrupted.

'Lana O'Mara, do you mean to tell me that you've forgotten how busy you'll be in the run up to Christmas? You've got your Saturday job, remember, and if your second year at college is anything like the first you'll be writing dozens of Christmas cards and buying lots of little presents. I know they do the dip thing at college, but you'll want to buy for Auntie Molly and Uncle Rhys, Nonny and Chris ... and with a big family like ours it takes a good three or four weeks to choose something nice for everyone, so you won't have much time before Christmas for gadding about.'

Ellen was addressing her daughter but it was Nonny who spoke. 'Auntie Ellen, what did you mean when you said that the college would do the dip thing? I don't understand.'

Ellen laughed. 'Everyone buys one present which must cost no more and no less than an agreed sum. Then all the presents are wrapped up and put into a large box, and everybody lines up and takes one present each.' She smiled as she saw comprehension dawn on Nonny's face. 'Everyone gets a gift but no one has to spend more than anyone else; good idea, ain't it?'

Nonny agreed, adding that Molly had taken

part in a similar scheme in the WAAF, and Lana said wistfully: 'Wish we could do that with the cousins! Some of 'em ain't workin', one or two of 'em are mean and the rest don't have no imagination. Last year I were give three boxes of face powder, all the wrong colour, a bottle of nail varnish that I swear I'd give cousin Maggie last year, a bag of cotton wool balls – that's for cleaning make-up off – and a paperback romance what looked like it had already been read.'

Ellen shook a chiding head at her daughter, but could not suppress a smile. 'You shouldn't look a gift horse in the mouth, but I know what you're saying, queen, and it's true that some things do reappear year after year,' she admitted. 'But you're luckier than most; you've gorra well paid Saturday job and they're willing to employ you over the Christmas holidays as well when we're not at Cefn Farm. But it's too soon yet to think about presents, cards and so on. How did your first day go, Nonny?'

Nonny considered before she answered and when she did so it was thoughtfully. 'It was a bit confusing at first but I'm sure I'm going to like it once I grow accustomed,' she said. 'Good thing we're on the phone now, so we can keep in touch. I gave Mum a quick ring on my way home just so that she'd know I was all right, but I had to tell her there was an awful lot to learn. Not lessons, I don't mean, but classrooms, teachers' names, who does what, in fact. There's a big room with desks and a typewriter for each pupil, and they hand round cards with letters and figures on. Then the teacher plays a record of music and we have to type in time to the tune. It's really odd and at first everyone kept giggling, but then the teacher got cross and explained that we must get the rhythm right or we could never become first rate typists. After that nobody dared giggle.'

'Oh, that's old hat; I did musical typing in my first year,' Lana said loftily. 'Everyone does. But what did Auntie Molly say about the farm? How are they managing with neither you nor Chris?'

'Very well, I think,' Nonny said, 'but even if they weren't, Mum wouldn't tell me in case I wanted to go back. It's really important that I do well ... but you know all that. By the way, Cerys says if we can arrange it she and I might both get home for the odd weekend. Her brother has a motorbike and sidecar and he says if I pay some of the petrol he'll take Cerys on the pillion and me in the sidecar.' She beamed at Lana. 'I didn't say anything to Mum, but it would be wonderful to have a weekend at Cefn Farm before the hols start.'

Lana, who had been staring dreamily into the fire, perked up. 'If we squeezed in could we get two in the sidecar?' she asked hopefully. 'Oh, I'd love to have a weekend with Auntie Molly and Uncle Rhys.'

'And Chris,' Nonny murmured wickedly. 'You still fancy my brother, don't you, Lana?'

Lana denied it, with one eye on her mother, but Nonny could tell from her friend's heightened colour that it was still as true as when she had first teased Lana about it. However, she was forced to disillusion her, knowing full well that the sidecar would only hold one. Lana took it well, merely remarking that she supposed she could catch a bus and join Nonny at the farm, but Nonny guessed that the long journey, with several changes, would not be worth doing just for a weekend. 'And anyway, Cerys only suggested it to cheer me up because I was a bit down when we walked home together after class,' she admitted. 'It suddenly seemed so strange to be walking along with the street lamps hiding the stars – you can't see stars from a lamplit street – that I got a bit upset.' She heaved a sigh and turned to Ellen. 'Oh, Auntie Ellen, I know how lucky I am and I cheered up as soon as Cerys suggested the motorbike trip, but it may never come off, after all.'

Ellen smiled her sweet lazy smile and heaved herself to her feet. 'What we need is a nice cuppa,' she said comfortably. 'Then I'll start getting the meal ready; we'll eat when Mr Taplow gets in from work.'

When the girls made their way up to bed that night, Lana chatted away about a boy who had asked if he might walk her home. She had refused, saying she had some shopping to do on the way, but he had not been deterred, it seemed: 'George – that's his name, George Wright – was disappointed, but said he'd try again tomorrow. He's ever so nice looking; you'd like him, Nonny,' she finished.

Nonny made a non-committal mumble. She had no intention of getting mixed up with even the nicest boy; why should she? She had always been single-minded, first over the farm and now over her secretarial course. She had seen how Lana's fascination with the opposite sex and urge to spend her time having fun had affected her friend's marks and she had no intention of falling into the same trap. Besides, if I get married at all, which I don't really want to do, it will be to a farmer; someone like Cerys's brother, she told herself, climbing into bed. Aunt Ellen's house was on the electric, but as Lana clicked the light off a wave of homesickness for the smell given off by a snuffed candle hit Nonny with such force that she could have wept, and presently, when she heard Lana's breathing grow even and knew that her friend slept, she turned her face into her pillow and shed a river of tears.

She had not wanted to leave the valley, her home, her parents and the animals. She had only done so because she had realised that if she did not earn she would soon become a liability, and that her parents wished her to experience the kind of social life enjoyed by Lana. And now the die was cast and it seemed to her that her future stretched ahead of her, a path of duty, barren of all pleasure. To make matters worse, she knew that she could not confide her feelings either to Auntie Ellen or to Lana, her closest friend. To do so would cause hurt, for knowing both Ellen and Lana as she did she feared that it would soon come to her mother's ears that she was not as happy as Molly wanted to believe. But the thought of Molly's distress gave her strength. She would not turn tail and scurry back to Cefn Farm without a single certificate to her name; she would not admit that she was miserable, hated the glow from the street light which had lit up the bedroom when Lana jerked the curtains back. And most of all she would damned well concentrate on the good things in her new life: the lovely shops, the cinemas and theatres, and, perhaps most important of all, the friendship and kindliness of Auntie Ellen and Lana.

Nonny snuggled down and reminded herself firmly that she was no stranger to the house in Bethel Street, nor to the friends and neighbours she had met on previous occasions. But then, of course, she had only been what you might call a holiday visitor. Now she was living here with no prospect of returning home to the farm at the end of a couple of weeks. She lifted her face from the tear-wet pillow and scolded herself. She was not living in Bethel Street for ever; she would be going home to Cefn Farm just as soon as the Christmas holidays arrived. Provided everything went well she would spend all her holidays at home, so why on earth was she being such a baby, shedding tears as though she would never see her parents and her home again? Resolutely she closed her eyes and began an old game which her mother had taught her: things to be glad about, Molly had called it. There was Cerys's friendship, which had already made life much more fun for both of them. There was the fact that Lana had already done a year's secretarial training and so had been able to clear up a couple of problems which had reared their ugly heads when Nonny had begun to tackle the homework she had been given. And best of all there was dear Auntie Ellen who had promised to go with Nonny at the weekend to see if she could find a Saturday job. This thought made Nonny's lips curve into a little smile. Her mother had promised to send her a postal order every couple of weeks so that she would have some money of her own, but how grand it would be to write to her, explaining her generosity would no longer be necessary because she, Nonny, had actually found herself a job! Nonny could imagine how pleased and proud her mother would be, how she would tell neighbours and friends that already her daughter was proving her worth. Nonny slept at last, but even in her dreams the little smile lingered on her face.

Nonny was not the only one who cried on that first night of separation. Molly had told herself over and over that they were doing the right thing, but she had never allowed herself to envisage the time when her darling would no longer consider Cefn Farm her home. Now, however, it seemed that not only Nonny but Chris as well was stretching his wings, preparing to leave the nest. That very day he had rung home, full of excitement, to tell his parents that he was one of only three students who had been offered what he considered a wonderful opportunity. Last term's exam results had been so good and his work at the college's farm so exemplary that he had been offered what the principal had called 'an exchange'. He and two of his classmates were to go for a year to a large farm in Canada, where the most modeen methods were being tested. They would attend a similar college to the one they had left behind two days a week, but the rest of the time they would work on the farm itself, taking part in the trials and being paid a proper wage.

When Rhys had told her what had kept him on

the phone for so long, Molly had seen how his eyes had gleamed with pride and pleasure, and knew that she could not possibly point out how very overstretched they would be without Chris's help during his long holidays from the college. Rhys was saying that he had heard of such things as exchange visits, bursaries and the like, but had never dreamed that his son would be fortunate enough – nay, clever enough – to win one. He had beamed across at Molly, certain that she would share his feelings, never thinking for a moment that her more practical mind saw that for Cefn Farm the loss of Chris for a whole year could be a mortal blow. Nevertheless, she accepted that Chris must seize this opportunity; it would never come again, such things were a once in a lifetime event. So she had agreed with as much enthusiasm as she could muster to Rhys's immediate acceptance of the plan, and waited for bedtime when they were both relaxed in the warmth of their blankets to point out, as gently as she could, that this wonderful piece of luck for Chris posed a problem for the rest of the family. Nonny was a good girl but she did not have a man's strength, and in any event would only be home in the college holidays herself. Rhys had enlarged the flock, keeping all last year's ewe lambs, instead of selling half to market, and actually buying in more stock, and when the next gathering occurred they would need every man they could muster. But Rhys had thought this one out. 'We'll get a live-in farm worker, a young chap who'll be willing to work for a small wage, his keep, and the experience we can give him. He can take Chris's room, and then at holiday times Nonny will simply move back into Cefn Farm and help as much as she can.'

Gradually, Molly began to come round to the idea, particularly since it meant that for a whole year, to all intents and purposes her son and Lana would have half a world between them. However, Chris did not leave for Canada until the spring, so she still had several months to guard her son from an unsuitable, if not dangerous, match. It had already been arranged that Ellen and Lana should join the Robertses for an old-fashioned country Christmas, and this would have to be carefully engineered. Molly smiled to herself. No mistletoe should be allowed to enter the house, any games played must not include 'postman's knock', and sledging expeditions up into the mountains would only be permitted if she and Rhys were present to make sure that no funny business took place; in short no huggles, cuddles or similar signs of affection were to be encouraged between two young people who might – just might – be brother and sister.

But these were thoughts which Molly could not share with anyone; thoughts that were best ignored unless there was some sign from either Lana or Chris that things were about to get serious. This had not happened yet and in her more optimistic moments Molly was sure she was worrying unduly. Chris was going away for a whole year; it seemed unlikely that Lana, the saucy little baggage, would be content to wait for a feller when she could take her pick amongst the throng of boys surrounding her. Molly smiled to herself and cuddled her goose feather pillow. Why, by the time Chris returned to Cefn Farm, Lana might be married, or if not married engaged to be so. Molly smiled, and slept, her worries forgotten.

Chapter Twelve

Molly had just finished feeding the pigs when she heard bicycle tyres crunching over the ridged-up mud on the lane and guessed it must be Jones the post with their mail. Hurriedly she checked that the breeding sows were busily chomping away at the food she had just delivered, then set off across the yard to get back to the kitchen, wash her hands and face and greet Mr Jones.

She crossed to the sink, had a quick wash and was filling the kettle when Mr Jones banged on the door, then shot it open and entered the room. He was grinning. 'Excited are you?' he asked in a fatherly manner. 'Your boy's coming home any day now, ain't he?' He riffled through the letters in his bag, withdrew those addressed to Cefn Farm, handed them to Molly and then slung his bag down on the floor. 'There's a letter from him; going to open it first, Mrs Roberts dear?'

Molly laughed. 'He'll just be reminding me of his arrival time,' she said gaily. 'As you know, his course only lasted a year but he was offered an awfully well paid job to stay on at a dairy farm for a further six months. But that time is now up and nothing would make him put off coming home.' She put the kettle on the stove, then went over to the pantry. 'Tea or coffee, Mr Jones?'

Mr Jones opted for coffee and sat down with a satisfied sigh, taking the shortbread biscuit that

Molly offered. 'How's young Nonny?' he enquired genially. 'A fine girl, that. Good as a man with the stock, she is. Oh aye, she'll make some farmer a grand wife one of these days.'

Molly murmured non-committally, and opened Chris's letter. As she had guessed it was simply a reminder that he would expect to see their smiling faces waiting on the quayside when his ship docked in a week's time. But Mr Jones, having waited courteously whilst she read it, was talking once more. 'You'll have missed the boy sore, that I know from the way me and the missus felt when our Sion took off for Australia,' he said. 'But Rhys has told me how well your lad's done, how he'll be starting a dairy herd himself, as soon as he can get the right stock.' He took another biscuit and popped it into his mouth, then blew the crumbs off his long white moustache. 'A son to be proud of, he is.'

Molly smiled and nodded. She was proud of her son, the new skills he had learned, and equally proud of Nonny, who had come top in most of her examinations and had won the student of the year award, which meant a prize of ten whole pounds and a small cup upon which her name would be engraved. Lana also had passed her exams, doing pretty well all things considered. Nonny had stuck to her guns and kept outings of all sorts to a minimum, but Molly knew that Lana had jumped at every chance that was offered – like a fish to a fly, Chris had said – yet had still managed to get respectable grades. No one else could read her shorthand, not even Nonny, but since Lana read every word unerringly it did not seem to matter much. At any rate she got her one hundred words a minute diploma, as well as a good score in her typing exams, and Molly knew that Ellen was delighted with her daughter and expected her to get work easily, for she was not only good at her job but a pretty, fashionable young woman whom most men would be happy to employ.

Now, Mr Jones took a big gulp of his coffee and smacked his lips. 'Yes, your youngsters have done well. Last time I spoke to Nonny – she come into the post office for some stamps while I was there – she said she'd been offered a secretary's job. I don't know the details, of course, but I reckon it'll keep her in Liverpool for a good while.'

Molly nodded. 'Yes, but you know our Nonny, Mr Jones. She's saving up as hard as she can and as soon as the farm can afford another worker she'll be back. She's never taken to city life and she's still fancy free. She's arranged to come home for her two weeks' annual leave at Christmas because by then Chris will have settled in once more, and I think he and she have plans which they haven't discussed with their father or me.'

Mr Jones tutted. 'The young, the young,' he murmured. 'Think they know everything they does. When Sion come home last he pooh-poohed just about every word I uttered, told his mam I were just an old fogey still livin' in the nineteenth century...' he grinned toothily at Molly, 'which, as I told him, I am – livin' in the nineteenth century I mean.'

Molly laughed with him. She could remember being baffled as a young girl by the fact that the nineteen thirties were referred to as being in the twentieth century. However, before she could admit to her early puzzlement, Mr Jones was poking an inquisitive finger at her two remaining letters. 'One of these is from Nonny; I reckernise the writing. A good gal she is; reckon she writes a good fat letter to her old mum and dad a couple of times a week. Now tell me what's happened to that other one, that girl what's the same age as her ... her mum's Mrs O'Mara but I can't recall the girl's name to mind.'

'Oh, you mean Lana,' Molly said, and felt the familiar little jab of worry. 'She'll be coming here with her mum for Christmas, of course. Ellen and I take it in turns to spend Christmas at each other's houses. Last year we went to Bethel Street but only for two days. Nat was still learning and couldn't be left for long, but he's more experienced now, Rhys says, and he's well up to speed, which is lovely because it means we can leave him with Jacob whilst we both go to meet Chris's ship.'

Mr Jones nodded wisely, then jerked a thumb at Nonny's letter. 'Longing to open that you'll be; carry on while I sort out the letters for the Pritchards,' he said generously, bending to retrieve his bag. Molly smiled to herself. Mr Jones, she knew, was as curious as a cat and must be longing to know whether Nonny's letter contained news of a startling nature. She opened the envelope and scanned the pages; they were few, which was unusual for Nonny, who generally wrote reams. Molly read them at a gallop, so to speak, then turned to smile at the postman.

'Nothing's changed; Ellen will put Rhys and

myself and Chris up for the couple of days we'll be in Liverpool, though the girls will have to sleep on the put-you-up in the parlour so we can have their beds,' she explained. 'Chris will have the lodger's bed; Mr Taplow is going to spend a week with relatives on the Wirral.'

Mr Jones raised an eyebrow. 'Mrs O'Mara thinkin' of remarryin?' he asked hopefully.

Molly choked on a laugh. 'You're a real matchmaker, Mr Jones, but you're way off beam this time,' she assured him. 'Mr Taplow's nearly sixty and when a man's been a bachelor for that long he's not likely to change.'

The postman resettled his bag on his shoulder. 'A pity it is to see a fine woman like Mrs O'Mara without a man,' he said sadly. 'But her first was a wrong 'un I seem to remember, so mebbe it's once bitten, twice shy. Thanks for the coffee and shortbread, Mrs Roberts dear. See you tomorrow, likely.'

Once he had gone whistling off across the farmyard, heading up the lane towards the Pritchards' place, Molly sat down again and pulled her half full cup of coffee towards her, giving another little smile as she did so. He had forgotten to wait and see whether Ellen's letter contained anything of interest. He himself, of course, would have been the last person to admit to curiosity over someone else's mail. He would have said reproachfully, that all he wanted to know was that everything was well – and that is all he'll ever learn from me, Molly told herself, opening the envelope and removing the letter. She began to read.

Dear Molly, I'm fair worried sick about my Lana. She's got this young feller; handsome I grant you, but I'm not keen and nor would you be, Moll. The awful thing is, he reminds me of how Sam used to be years ago. This feller's always boasting, a proper know-all, and I'd take a bet he's a heavy drinker. I've warned her over and over, but there you are. I was just such a fool at her age and God knows my mum warned me often enough, and what notice did I take? Ah well, we all have to make our own mistakes, they say, and I suppose Lana is no different from her poor old mum. So you can imagine, I'll be real glad to get her away from Liverpool and over to Cefn Farm this Christmas. She says if she can spare the time she'll come down to the quayside to meet Chris off his ship, and she won't bring the chap with her because I've told her it's not on. Wish she was still head over heels in love with your Chris, but I dare say he'll have changed a good deal. I'm longing to see you, our Moll, so you can advise me how best to discourage Lana from making a fatal mistake. Love, Ellen.

Molly did not know whether to smile or sigh over the letter. God knew she was keen to have Lana start chasing anyone but Chris. However, she knew it would break Ellen's heart to see her beloved daughter in the thrall of the wrong young man, and she was so fond of Ellen that she hated the thought of her friend's pain. But Lana was young, very pretty, and about to start working as a junior typist for a large insurance company. Ellen had not said how Lana knew the young man, and Molly just hoped that he did not work in the same office. She knew from her own experience that 'out of sight, out of mind' could be true, as was the reverse. Once Lana was in work, meeting lots of people and having very little spare time, she and this undesirable young man would probably drift apart. With luck, he might start carrying on with some other girl, and Molly knew Lana well enough to be certain she would not share. Lana rated herself highly, which in this instance was a good thing.

Molly got to her feet as she heard the men approaching across the yard. She put the letters by her husband's plate so that Rhys could read them while he ate his elevenses, then went over to the stove to make the big jug of coffee the men enjoyed. Next she would begin to prepare the noonday meal, planning all the while how best to welcome Chris home the following week. So much had happened since he left, she reminded herself. Rhys had been as good as his word and employed a young man named Nat for a small wage in return for the experience he would be getting, and though at first Rhys had grumbled that the boy cost them more in food than they paid him in wages he had begun to prove his worth when they had decided to build an extension. He and Jacob and Rhys between them had added two sturdy stone-built rooms to the farmhouse and Molly was looking forward to her son's pleasurable excitement when he realised that he would have a bigger bedroom and, if he wished, his own sitting room too. Nat had already taken over Chris's old room, and Nonny, of course, would remain in the little room under the eaves which she had always occupied.

There were other changes, too. The flock had almost doubled in size and Rhys was looking to buy more land. He had talked with other farmers and had decided not to over-winter his ewes with lowland farmers in future, but to keep them in the hills. Then, when the time came to sell at the big markets, he would only send any ewes which had lost ground over the winter, saving the best for himself and thus ensuring that his flock contained far fewer weaklings than was normally the case.

Another change was the introduction of cattle. Both Rhys and Molly appreciated that their son wanted a dairy herd, but Rhys had been to the Wrexham beast market and had seen two sturdy Welsh blacks, thick-legged, short-necked and solid as a barn door, and coveted them. They were not dairy cattle, but Rhys had bought them anyway; to see, he said, how they would survive on Cefn Farm's mountainous acres.

Now, the men burst into the kitchen and Rhys seized the coffee jug and started to pour the steaming contents into three mugs. He began to reiterate all over again exactly what he wanted Jacob and Nat to do in his absence, and Nat, grinning, reminded his boss that old Mr Williams was coming over with his even older wife to stay at the farm whilst the Robertses were away. 'Mrs Williams is a good cook, so I've heard, and Mr Williams knows all there is to know about hill sheep,' he said cheerfully. 'So stop worrying, guv'nor. You ain't going to be away long enough for us to do much damage.'

Rhys laughed reluctantly. 'You're a grand lad,

Nat, now you've got into our way of things,' he said. 'The thing is, you see...'

Nat finished the sentence for him, having heard it a great many times: '...the thing is, you see, a lot can go wrong in a short space of time when it comes to livestock.'

Everyone laughed, including Rhys. 'You're a grand lad, Nat,' he said again. 'If you've any worries which Mr Williams can't solve nip up to Cae Hic and ask Rhodri Pritchard or his father what you should do. And now let's get on with today's work.'

Molly awoke on the day they were to travel to Liverpool and rolled over to nudge Rhys in the ribs, then thought better of it. Outside, the sun shone from a clear blue sky and the wind stirred the gentle gold of autumn leaves. Normally at this time they would both have been up and doing, but because Molly had decreed that they should pack the previous evening they had not got to bed until after midnight. The Williamses were safely ensconced in what was to be Chris's new room and Molly could tell from the sounds drifting up to their window that Jacob and Nat were working already. It was just lucky that Chris's ship was coming back at a time of year when the sheep were still all over the mountains, it being neither dipping, shearing nor selling, so far as the flock were concerned. In a few weeks frost and snow would make hard work for farmers as they checked on their animals and tried to keep them within the more accessible parts of the farm, but now, in the gold of autumn, Mr Williams, Jacob and Nat should be able to manage pretty well for a couple of days.

Molly got out of bed as quietly as she could and went over to the washstand; it would have to be cold water this morning since she had no intention of going downstairs for hot and finding Mrs Williams already in residence. She began to wash and saw Rhys sit up and rub his eyes, glance at the clock and jump hastily out of bed. 'You should have woke me, woman,' he said reproachfully. 'It's today, isn't it? The day we set out for Liverpool.' He grinned broadly, took hold of Molly by the shoulders and kissed the back of her neck. 'And tomorrow morning, if all goes as planned, we'll be seeing our boy after the longest separation in the world!'

Chris stood at the rail as his ship began the approach to the landing stage. He was filled with a mixture of excitement and apprehension, for he had loved Canada, Canadians and the large farm on which he had worked for the past six months. His boss, a fair-haired drawling man in his early forties, had tried to persuade him to stay, or if not to stay to return after a few months in his native land.

'You could work for me until you'd saved up to buy a li'l place of your own,' he had said, grinning. The grin showed off his gleaming white teeth against the tan of his skin and Chris found himself wondering, not for the first time, how it was that so many Canadians had perfect teeth. But then he was shaking his head and smiling at Rob, for first names were used much more here in the New World than they were in the mountains of Snowdonia, where none of his workers would have dreamed of addressing Rhys by his first name.

'Sorry, Rob, but I've a grand place waiting for me. Maybe it'll never be as big an acreage as you've got here…' he had gestured to the rolling meadows dotted with the black and white dairy herd of which Rob was so proud, 'but I was born and bred in the mountains and I love them. It's tough farming in such country but the rewards make up for the hard work And one of these days, boss, you'll envy me my herd, and tell folk that it was you who taught me all I know about dairy farming.'

Chris knew the offer had been genuine and kindly meant, but even so it worried him. Suppose he found on returning to Wales that Cefn Farm seemed small and insignificant? Suppose, despite his father's hard work, the grass was not rich enough to support dairy cattle? Suppose, in fact, that he began to wish he had accepted Rob's offer? Once he was home it would be difficult indeed to change his mind. He would be letting his father down, something he could not even contemplate at this moment, though he supposed that if he did find dairy farming impossible in Snowdonia his parents, the most loving and sympathetic people he knew, would appreciate that his future was at stake and let him go; sadly, but with understanding.

Chris gave himself a mental shake. Ridiculous to worry yet about what might happen when from everything he had understood from Molly's frequent letters he would find there had been changes at Cefn Farm; changes for the better, of course.

The great ship surged on and now he could see the little dots on the quayside which he knew were people waiting to welcome the travellers. Nonny would be there as well as his parents, and Auntie Ellen, of course. He wondered if Lana might come too; he was very fond of her, regarded her, as Nonny had said, almost as another sister. He strained his eyes, but could not make out individual faces in the crowds on the landing stage.

But thinking about Lana had made him remember Louella May. He had met her at the very start of his time in Canada, for she was the daughter of the farmer upon whose land he had worked. She was a lovely girl, blonde-haired and blue-eyed, with dimpled pink cheeks and red lips. They had become good friends, and when he left her father's farm to take up the place with Rob they had corresponded regularly. Whenever they got the chance they had met up, and Chris had actually suggested that she might like to return with him to England. 'We could call it a holiday,' he had said eagerly. 'What do you think?' Louella May must have known how fond he was of her, must have guessed that this was the nearest he could come to a proposal of marriage until he was once more established on his father's acres, which would one day be his. She had smiled her lovely, brilliant smile, but had not even had to think about it, though he was sure it was with regret that she shook her beautiful golden head.

'I'm a Canadian from the top of my head to the tip of my toes,' she had explained. 'I couldn't live anywhere else; you should understand better than anyone, since you turned down your boss's offer of a permanent place. But one day maybe I'll cross the pond and visit this Cefn Farm you're so proud of.'

He had known, of course, that she was letting him down lightly, so he had replied in a similar vein. 'Trust you to keep your options open, Louella May! And knowing you I'll have half a dozen kids, to say nothing of half a dozen wives, before ever you "cross the pond" as you put it.'

At the time he had been disappointed, even though he had known in his heart what her answer would be. Had she agreed to come to England, if only for a holiday, she would have been committing herself – and him – to a closer relationship, presumably an eventual marriage. And Chris knew he was not yet ready for such a step.

On that thought, the great ship slowed. Sailors were bustling back and forth, the gangway came crashing down and suddenly Chris saw faces, not just the pale blobs he had seen from a distance. He could pick out his father, a head taller than most of the crowd, and guessed that Nonny and his mother would be beside him, though they were obscured by the intervening bodies. Chris bent and picked up his suitcases. He felt extraordinarily light, as though he could have floated down to the shore without so much as setting foot on the gangway. He was home! He had never lived in this great bustling city but had stayed often enough at Auntie Ellen's little house in

Bethel Street to feel a fondness for the place. Snowdonia was where he most wanted to be, but right now he could have hugged Liverpool, knowing it as well as any occasional visitor could, from the twin towers of the Liver Buildings to the hustle and bustle of Paddy's market. As his feet touched solid ground he saw his parents spot him and begin to fight their way towards him. He had meant to be cool and calm, to greet them with restraint, but as his arms went round his mother he felt tears wet on his cheeks.

Rhys grabbed one suitcase and Nonny took the other, whilst his mother hung on to one arm and Ellen clasped the other. They stopped when they reached the main road, exchanged kisses and hugs and exclamations, and Chris, looking round him, was in the middle of saying to Auntie Ellen that he could not see Lana when he spotted her. She came flying along the pavement, pinkcheeked and breathless. Chris held out his arms and Lana flew into them, laughing and apologising for her lateness, gabbling that her boss had refused to let her take a day's holiday and thought she was out hand-delivering an important letter. Chris lifted her off her feet and spun her round, then stood her down and grinned at everyone. 'Well, what a welcome!' he said, half teasing, half serious. 'She's late for the most important day of her life; the girl I'm going to marry!'

Nonny giggled, Rhys gave a snort of laughter, and Chris had begun to say that he was only joking and Lana was not to set her boyfriend on him when Molly gave a little moan and fell in a heap at his feet.

Molly came round to find herself being gently lifted off the pavement, whilst Ellen insisted that they should take her to the nearest café and ply her with strong sweet tea. Molly, horribly ashamed of herself, kept assuring everyone that she was fine, that she had no idea why she had fainted, save that it was probably her excitement over her son's return. Chris looked thoughtful, and took the first opportunity, once they were settled in the café with cups of tea on the table before them, to question her. 'Are you ill, Mum? Is there something you've not told me? You're not – not in the family way?' he asked.

Molly giggled. She still felt ashamed but certainly did not intend to let anyone believe she was pregnant. She looked around the table and suspected from their expressions that the family and Ellen could not imagine why she had passed out, though she thought Lana wore rather a knowing look. She managed to convince them, or so she thought, that it had been the emotion of the reunion which had led to her collapse, and it was only very much later, when they were all back in the house in Bethel Street, that Lana followed her up to the bedroom for a private word. She gave Molly a warm hug, and said: 'I know I ain't clever like Nonny, nor I'm not a farmer's daughter, but was it Chris pretendin' he were goin' to marry me that made you pass out? Chris weren't serious, of course, and marriage is the last thing on my mind – I'm going to have a heap of fun first – but I have sometimes thought you'd not like it if Chris and meself got serious.'

It was an opportunity, a chance to swear Lana to silence and tell all. Molly opened her mouth and looked at Lana's wide blue eyes and suddenly realised she could not possibly do it. It would change Lana's attitude to her own mother ... no, no, no, this was not the moment. Lana hadn't the slightest intention of getting serious with Chris, and Chris had already mentioned a girl with a peculiar name, Lou-something, who had clearly meant a lot to him. Let sleeping dogs lie, Molly told herself firmly. There would be time in plenty to reveal her fears if Chris and Lana ever showed the slightest sign that they were going to get serious.

Molly smiled across the bedroom and saw the pain and anxiety gradually fade from Lana's face as she herself crossed the room and gave the child a warm hug and a little shake. 'Lana, my dearest child, I love you almost as much as I love Nonny,' she said sincerely. 'But I don't honestly believe you'd be happy as a farmer's wife. You love pretty clothes, dancing and parties; the sort of life you live at present, in fact. Besides, you've got a boyfriend, though I know your mum is a bit worried about it. She thinks he's too like your father...'

Lana cut across her. 'Oh, him!' she said airily. 'Mum's right; he's great fun to be with, but he's the sort of feller who'll never settle down, or not with one woman at any rate.'

'So you don't intend to marry him?' Molly asked. 'Well, you should stop teasing poor Ellen, you dreadful girl, because she truly believes you and he are serious and it's not fair to frighten her if there's really nothing to worry about.'

'I've told her and told her...' Lana was beginning, when the bedroom door shot open and Nonny catapulted into the room.

'Mum, Lana, we've just had a telegram! It's from old Mr Pritchard, although I expect Rhodri actually sent it. His mum was taken to hospital yesterday, after you left; they think it's a heart attack. Dad says there's no point in leaving tonight, but we must go first thing tomorrow.' She looked defiantly across the room at her mother. 'I know you'll say I ought to stay here, that my job's important and the money's a great help, but I feel I'd be letting the Pritchards down if I didn't come home with you now.'

'Oh, darling Nonny, surely if you asked your boss for a few days off, he'd agree to it? You've already got two days – or is it three? – and you could offer to have your holiday now instead of at Christmas...'

Nonny looked relieved. 'Maybe you're right; if Mr Lawson can manage without me for three days perhaps a week wouldn't be too much to ask. By then we'll know just how ill Mrs Pritchard is. Oh, Mum, what a thing to happen, and especially when they were going to give an eye to Cefn Farm in your absence!'

'If you're going back to Cefn Farm tomorrow, Mum and I will come with you,' Lana said firmly. 'Mum can take charge of household tasks at the Pritchards' and I'll help Rhodri in any way I can. I'm sure if I tell them at work that Mum and I have been called away because of illness in the family they'll let me take unpaid leave for a week or so.'

Molly was about to reply that it really wasn't necessary when she heard Ellen's tread on the stair. Ellen, arriving in the bedroom breathless but determined, argued that Lana would be a great help, that her job could be done by anyone else in the typing pool and that her help on the farm would not be negligible, and every time she caught Molly's eye she grinned and winked, causing her friend considerable embarrassment. Nonny and Lana might not realise, but Molly knew that Ellen would be only too delighted to get Lana away from her unsuitable boyfriend for a week or so. The fact that the relationship was not serious had clearly not yet penetrated to Ellen.

'Discussion over,' Nonny said briskly, whilst the two older women were still discussing the pros and cons. She seized Lana's hand. 'Come on! We must go straight to our offices and see what can be sorted out. I think relatives in trouble is going to be my excuse, if you have to call it that.'

When the girls had clattered down the stairs, Molly began to explain to her friend that Lana was really serious when she said she had no intention of going steady with anyone, and especially not her current boyfriend. She expected Ellen to be delighted, but instead the other woman pulled a dubious face.

'She'll say anything when she's not with him, but it's a different story when he calls to take her dancing or to the flicks,' she said bitterly. 'What a bloody nuisance that I told her not to bring him round here on Chris's first day home. I'd feel far happier if you could meet him, Molly; you'd know how to deal with him, I'm sure.'

Molly sighed. 'I don't know why you think so; Rhys is the only man I've ever been serious about, so I don't see that my advice could possibly help.'

Molly had come up to the bedroom ostensibly to unpack and arrange the room for the Robertses' temporary occupancy. Now she laid her nightdress out on what she knew to be Nonny's single bed, and then the two women left the room and began to descend the stairs. Molly thought, sadly, that in one way Ellen's pleasure was her pain, for there was Ellen happy to get her daughter out of Liverpool and away from the undesirable young man for as long as possible, and there was she, Molly, reluctant to have Lana back at Cefn Farm and thus very much in Chris's eye. But she comforted herself with the thought that, all things being equal, Lana might take a fancy to Rhodri and never give Chris another thought. Of course he was ten years older than Lana and spoke Welsh as his first language, but that might not prevent him from being attracted by the pretty, lively girl.

By the time she reached the bottom of the stairs and turned into the kitchen Molly had dreamed up a whole scenario in which the bridal couple were smiled upon by Ellen and the elderly Pritchards. If Lana and Rhodri did fall in love, Molly thought, then it would be only natural for Ellen to come and live with them and manage the house, at least until Mrs Pritchard regained her full strength. Oh, it was undoubtedly the answer, both to Ellen's problems and to her own.

Molly followed her friend into the kitchen and glanced up at the clock above the mantelpiece. Rhys had gone down to the telegraph office to send the Pritchards a telegram promising an early return the next day. Since it was almost five o'clock and dusk had already begun to fall, Ellen had gone over to the pantry and was bringing out the makings of the supper she meant to serve, so Molly, sighing, began to lay the table. She had had such plans for the next couple of days, but now they would all come to naught. She had meant to visit the shops; it would have been an opportunity to buy Christmas presents, a chance to look at the new fashions, and she had been resolutely saving her egg money for weeks and weeks. Now all that would go by the board and she would have to look elsewhere. Chris had taken his driving test before he left for Canada, so if he or Rhys could ever spare the time to take Rhodri and his father to visit Mrs Pritchard, assuming she had been taken to the big hospital in Bangor, perhaps she, Molly, could go with them and do her Christmas shopping there...

'What are you dreaming about, Molly gal?' Ellen's voice cut across Molly's thoughts. 'I wonder how long they'll keep the old lady in hospital? I'd like to say I'll stay until she's back on her feet, but I got me lodger to think about. Lana's a good girl, but she's never took to cooking or housework, an' I reckon if I didn't come home with her the place'd be a pigsty by the time I got back and Mr Taplow as thin as a rake, 'cos she'd feed him on bread and butter and tea rather than try her hand at cooking.'

'Oh, Ellen, she wouldn't let you down, not your Lana,' Molly said quickly. 'The truth is, you spoil her rotten. Our Nonny doesn't just pitch in with the farm work and the sheep, you know: she's a good little housewife already. If you'd taught Lana to bake bread and make cakes and pies...'

'Oh, I don't have the patience to keep going over and over the same thing,' Ellen explained. 'Besides, chances are she'll wander off halfway through. She likes an excitin' sort of life does my Lana.'

Molly sighed. 'There's no reply to that,' she said ruefully, 'except what you sow you jolly well reap, Ellen O'Mara. The man your girl marries isn't going to thank you for letting her get away with saying "I don't know how" every time he suggests she does a bit of cooking. Tell you what, why don't you enrol her for evening classes in cookery? They call it domestic science, but it's still cookery. Nonny would go along with her, because she was telling me they learn real fancy stuff – she's got a friend who did that class last year – and I know she'd like to have a go. It would keep them out of mischief two evenings a week for the whole winter.'

Ellen's face had brightened. 'That's a grand idea so it is,' she said excitedly. 'That Harry Wilkinson expects Lana to jump when he says jump, if you know what I mean, but mebbe Lana would tell him no if he come round here wantin' to take her out when she and Nonny were off to this here cookery class.'

Molly opened her mouth to say again that from what Lana had told her she was honestly convinced that Harry Wilkinson had shot his bolt and was no longer a contender for Lana's attention. Then she shut it again. No point in nagging, and anyway, it would do Lana a deal of good to learn to cook and housekeep. She turned her most beguiling smile upon her friend. 'The girls have gone to ask for a week's leave without pay, so why don't we do their packing for them? Then when they get home again we can talk to them about the cookery course. It'll give them something to look forward to when they get back from Cefn Farm.'

Nonny and Lana were successful in their application for a week off, though Nonny, ever honest, felt she had to warn Mr Lawson that she might have to leave for good if things at home proved too difficult. Mr Lawson, a grey-haired, middle-aged man with three daughters of his own, reminded Nonny briskly that he valued her and would be very disappointed to lose her, but admitted that a week, or a fortnight at the most, must be the maximum length of her absence if she were to retain her job. Nonny thought that this was fair enough and commiserated with Lana, who was told bluntly by the head of her typing pool that her place could be filled half a dozen times over. 'Your shorthand's not bad and you type fast, I'll grant you that, but you're too chatty by half,' the older woman had concluded. 'However, the men seem to like you, which is all you worry about, I dare say. But don't you exceed the leave we've given you, or you'll find yourself out of a job, Miss O'Mara.'

Lana had not confided in Nonny what she had replied to this remark, but Nonny guessed that she had said something either saucy or cutting, for all the way home she had talked about other work with the air of one who expects to be job-hunting in the near future. She fancied working at one of the big stores; Lewis's, for example, where sales ladies could also act as mannequins and show off their fabulous and expensive clothing. Shorthand and typing would not of course be involved, but Lana told her friend airily that her qualifications would still be there if she decided at the end of six months that she would prefer office to shop work.

On their return to Bethel Street the girls found that their mothers had done a great deal of work in their absence. Fortunately, perhaps, Molly and Ellen had been so busy talking upon their return to the house that Molly had not unpacked the large case which she and Rhys had shared, so when the telegram had arrived all she had had to do was remove their nightwear and washing things from the case and leave everything else neatly packed away. Ellen had packed her own case and Lana's, made arrangements with a neighbour to look after Mr Taplow if he happened to return before the week was up, and put the evening meal on the table.

The family ate hurriedly and then went straight up to bed, since Rhys meant to start early next morning, as soon as the sky was sufficiently light for him to see his way. As Molly climbed into bed, she thought sadly that this was a very different homecoming from the one she had planned, for she was aware that Chris, having lived for eighteen months in another country, might find Britain strange indeed. But she knew that Mrs Pritchard's illness would affect them all. She remembered her first impression of old Mr Pritchard's tiny little wife. Brown and wrinkled, grey-haired and almost toothless, but with bright dark eyes and a cackle of laughter never far from her lips, she had endeared herself to the Robertses by her unfailing cheerfulness and her eagerness to help in any way she could. Rhys had called her 'the mousewife' at first, but had had to stop doing so when he saw her toting a load a man in his prime would have had difficulty shifting, and it was not long before the whole family came to know her worth.

But now the gallant little woman was ill and in a hospital far from home, and how in heaven's name would her husband and son manage without her? Molly did not believe Mr Pritchard would know how to boil an egg, let alone wash sheets or bake bread. Their farm was not large, but Molly knew how the family had had to strain every nerve to keep their heads above water. She also knew that Rhys helped out whenever he could, as the Pritchards had once helped him, but any suggestion that the family at Cae Hic might employ a labourer to ease the load was greeted with a shake of the head. Pritchards, he was told firmly, had farmed in these mountains for maybe thousands of years and did not intend to risk losing their land by having to pay a worker.

Molly knew that old Mr Pritchard was one of five sons, so in his youth his parents had not needed to employ anyone. But as time went on his brothers had left Cae Hic to make their own way in the world. One of them had gone to Australia, one to New Zealand and another to the flat fields of Norfolk. Only Gwilym, the youngest, had left agriculture altogether, marrying a corn merchant's daughter and taking over her father's business when he retired.

Of course the Robertses had not liked to point out that times had changed, and now it was too late to do so. Both Rhys and Molly knew how terribly hard the Pritchards worked; knew also that without Mrs Pritchard Cae Hic was unlikely to remain in Pritchard hands for another thousand years. Molly knew that Rhys had no idea of their old friend's financial position but suspected that, like most hill farmers', it was hand to mouth, and three people was the absolute minimum needed to run the farm.

Sighing, Molly punched her pillow, telling herself that she simply must go to sleep or she would be no use when they set off at the crack of dawn the next morning. But she knew her dreams would be full of the Pritchards' predicament. If only their place wasn't so remote! It was several miles further into the mountains than Cefn Farm, and Molly remembered that one of the reasons she had wanted to send Nonny to Liverpool was because Cefn Farm, too, was a long way from neighbours and indeed from civilisation. Furthermore, the farmhouse itself was small, for the house in which Mr Pritchard had been born and raised had been old-fashioned and tumbling down and as soon as Rhodri was old enough to give a hand the family had worked like crazy, cannibalising the stone from their old home to build a dwelling which was more like a cottage, or one of the old Welsh longhouses which had once dominated the area. It had a dairy, a couple of small bedrooms and a kitchen-living room which old Mrs Pritchard loved, especially the Aga which her husband had bought second hand when a farm at Beddgelert had been put up for sale. Molly had advised the purchase, and possibly because of every hill farmer's dislike of change they had got the stove for a tiny fraction of its real worth. Molly knew that before its arrival her old friend had baked in a camp oven and had made food as tasty and nourishing as any which Molly herself could produce, but the Aga eased her load considerably.

In addition to all her other tasks old Mrs Pritchard, like Molly herself, had sown and planted a sizeable vegetable garden, which provided them with most of their fresh food. Like the Robertses, Mrs Pritchard also grew fruit: gooseberries, blackcurrants, long pink sticks of rhubarb and raspberry canes. She kept poultry too, and in theory at least the egg money was hers, as was the money for the fatteners in their small pigsty, though Molly suspected that everything Mrs Prichard made was automatically taken by her husband. Despite herself, Molly smiled; if she had kept the money, what would Mrs Pritchard have spent it on? In all these years Molly had never seen her in anything but a long black skirt, a black blouse, and in winter so many black shawls, wraps and scarves that you could scarcely see the older woman's small, seamed face.

It now occurred to Molly, with some alarm, that she had no idea what Mrs Pritchard would look like with her hair loosed from its tight little bun and her body clad in a nightdress. She could not suppress a giggle. In her mind's eye she could see the hospital bed, the sheets starched and white, and there in the middle of it, propped up by pillows, would be Mrs Pritchard in a black nightdress, and a black headscarf pulled defiantly forward to shield her bright, dark eyes.

Still smiling, Molly fell asleep at last.

Chapter Thirteen

As he had promised, Rhys was up and ready to go as soon as a faint grey light appeared in the sky. He had listened to the weather forecast on the wireless, which had given a fine day for the northwest, and hoped to get back to Cefn Farm whilst it was still light. Despite their best efforts, however, it was eight o'clock before the family assembled in the kitchen, where Molly and Ellen, who had been first up, had made a brew of tea and a large saucepan of porridge. Rhys had suggested a sandwich breakfast to be eaten on their way but the women had scoffed at this idea. 'We've packed ab-dabs enough for an army; they'll do for elevenses and us dinners,' Ellen said cheerfully. 'Lucky I got a nice bit of boiling bacon, meaning to have it for our evening meal when we came back from our trip to the shops today. I bought some tomatoes an' all, off of me pal in St John's market, and put 'em in the ab-dabs...' she saw Rhys's puzzled expression and laughed, 'sarnies – sangwiches to you – so's they won't get too dry. But there's nothin' like porridge to line your stomach, I allus say. And we'll take Mr Taplow's big flask full of tea so's to have a hot drink...'

'Did you ask him?' Molly said. 'Well, I don't see how you could have since he's off visiting relatives. What'll he say when he comes back and finds his flask has gone missing?'

Ellen shrugged, but Lana answered for her.

'Oh, Auntie Molly, it's plain you don't know our Mr Taplow! He thinks the sun shines out of our mum; he'll say she were welcome to his flask and anything else she had a mind to borrow. They're good pals, honest to God they are.' She grinned at Molly. 'He's a funny chap but he fair worships my mum. It'd never surprise me...'

'Oh, shurrup!' Ellen said, her cheeks reddening. 'He's just a friend, and I couldn't ask for better.' She turned to her daughter. 'And you've not brushed your hair, you horrid little slut. The minute you've finished your breakfast, get up them stairs and see to it.'

Rhys was an excellent driver, and packed though the jeep was with both people and luggage he made good time. It was a long journey and they made two or three stops – comfort stops Chris called them with a grin as his sister and her friend disappeared into the trees for what Lana had called, with a giggle, 'a private moment'. Chris had offered to share the driving with Rhys but his father had firmly refused. 'You aren't used to driving on the left and the jeep isn't the easiest of vehicles to handle,' he said. 'When we get back home you can take her out in the fields and lanes and get used to her without a lot of traffic. But right now I'd rather take the wheel myself.'

Chris moaned a bit, of course, since he, Molly and the two girls were all squashed up together in the back, for Ellen's ample figure had to be given the front passenger seat. They stopped as Rhys had promised to eat their sandwiches, and were driving into the farmyard by mid-afternoon. Rhys drew up with a squeal of brakes and jumped out to greet Jacob and Nat, who shot out of the farm buildings, mouths already opening to give the news which the family had already heard. Rhys cut across the gaggle of information with which his workers were bombarding him. 'It's all right, we had a telegram last night,' he said briefly. 'I'm going to leave Mrs O'Mara and Lana here – they've kindly offered to get us all an evening meal – whilst the rest of us go on to Cae Hic. I take it Mr Pritchard and Rhodri will be there?'

'You won't find anyone at the Pritchards' apart from old Mr Williams, who's gone up there to keep an eye on things, feed the dogs and the poultry and see that no one walks into the house,' Nat said urgently. 'Rhodri went into the village this morning to ring the hospital to find out if they could bring his mum home yet and there were a telegram for him – well, for his dad really – saying they must get to the hospital as soon as possible because she'd taken a turn for the worse.'

Molly wound down her window and poked her head out of it. 'Is Mr Williams all right, up there by himself, or is his wife with him?' she asked anxiously. 'Oh, I know he's perfectly capable of feeding the stock, but suppose something were to happen? Suppose he were to take a fall, or...'

Nat shrugged. 'Mrs Williams has gone home; she didn't want to stay here on her own and there's no room at Cae Hic. Jacob offered to go with Mr Williams but he wouldn't let him – said it were too far for him to get back to the village each night, though Jacob offered to stay over, even if it meant sleeping on the floor.' He lowered his voice. 'But you know these old Welsh farmers; independence ain't the word ... stiff-necked, mebbe. At any rate they won't accept help if they can possibly avoid it, and to be fair to Mr Williams he's real sensible, and I'm sure he can cope.'

The rest of the family had got out of the car while Nat was speaking, and when Molly followed suit she saw Chris stop, eyes rounding, and realised he had seen the extension. 'Gosh, Mum,' he breathed, 'you've made the farm twice the size, and it's beautifully done. I've always loved our grey stone and the bluey grey slates on the roof and you've matched them exactly.' He clapped his father on the back and Rhys pretended to give at the knees, but his smile spread from ear to ear at his son's obvious pleasure.

'It's good, isn't it? The lads and I worked like dogs to get it completed in time for your return,' he said. 'I mean to grow Virginia creeper up the side just to hide the join, although as you say it's well matched. But just wait until you see the inside! There's a lovely big bedroom, already full of your stuff, and a smart sitting room, so if you don't fancy spending your evenings with the family you can shut yourself away and listen to records, write letters, study the farming magazines if you like, all on your todd.'

Molly saw he was so proud and pleased that he meant to take Chris straight into his new quarters, having clearly temporarily forgotten the reason for their unplanned return, but halfway to the kitchen door he must have recollected himself, for he turned apologetically to his son. 'You go and take a look, Chris, but make it quick.

We're off to Bangor. Or do you think you'd best stay here? I don't suppose we'll be gone long, and really there's no point in you accompanying us. Stay and give Auntie Ellen and Lana a hand with supper. After all, there's a limit to what anyone can do once a body is in hospital.'

Chris agreed reluctantly to stay behind, though he added that he rather thought he would go up to the Pritchards' place and make sure that Mr Williams did not need a hand.

'If you want me to give you a lift before I leave...' Rhys said rather doubtfully, but Chris shook his head.

'No, it's all right, Dad. It's been ages since I got a lung full of good clean mountain air. I'll saddle Wanderer and ride up there; it's been ages since I've ridden a really good mount, too.'

Molly, listening, gave a little laugh. 'Last time Nonny rode Wanderer, she ended on the other side of the hedge! As she said, she had intended the pair of them to clear it, not just herself. So just you remember that Wanderer hasn't been getting enough exercise lately and he's full of beans.'

'I'll remember,' Chris said gravely. He picked up his suitcases and made for the back door, with Ellen, hefting her own bag, just ahead of him. They entered the kitchen to find Nonny already there, bustling about getting cups, milk and the big brown teapot on the table, though when she saw the rest of the party she promptly stopped her work and jerked a thumb at Lana.

'You get the grub started, and brew the tea when the kettle boils,' she commanded. 'Mum's bringing my case in, and Dad's carrying the big one, and as soon as they've taken them upstairs we'll be on our way.'

Lana pulled a disconsolate face. 'Oh, but Nonny, why can't you stay here?' she wailed. 'If you were to help my mum get the supper and unpack and that, I could go with Chris up to the Pritchards'. I'm sure I'd be ever so useful, honest to God I would.'

'Pull the other one,' Nonny said briefly. 'All you want is to be with Chris and he won't welcome you, because there'll be all sorts of work which he can do better by himself without you moithering him.' She turned to her mother. 'Don't you agree, Mum? I say, you've gone quite pale. Sit down for a minute until the tea's brewed.'

Molly sat down obediently and gave her daughter a rather wan smile. 'Sorry, love; I'm afraid today has been a bit much for me,' she said apologetically. 'Mrs Pritchard has been such a good friend to us, so kind and generous, that the thought of her being ill and taken away from her beloved Cae Hic to a cold impersonal hospital down on the coast really upsets me.' She turned to Lana. 'As for you, love, you don't want to be a nuisance to Chris, do you? Not that I think there will be much to do at Cae Hic, not with Mr Williams in charge. Do you know, he's eighty-seven years old and still digs and plants his own vegetable plot, keeps fowl, and sells their eggs at market – well, actually his wife does that – and has a couple of fatteners in a sty at the bottom of the garden. Now, promise me you won't pester Chris, my dear? Apart from anything else, he means to go on Wanderer and you can't ride at all, can you? Not even the little pony Chris and Nonny learned on.'

Lana stuck out her lower lip and it occurred to Nonny, not for the first time, that fond though her mother was of her she seemed to have set her face against Chris and Lana's becoming too friendly. Perhaps it's my imagination though, Nonny thought. Much likelier she simply believes that Lana would make anyone a rotten wife, particularly a farmer. So she waited until her mother and Chris had left the kitchen and then smiled affectionately into her friend's disappointed face. 'Oh, Lana, you look as though you've lost a quid and found a penny,' she said. 'But you know Mum's right, really. You wouldn't mean to, of course, but you'd hold Chris up and he needs to get to the Pritchards' place as soon as possible. I dare say he won't stay long, however, so we'd best start searching the pantry and the meat safe to see what grub we can find for supper.'

Molly was not frightened of hospitals, despite having spent so long in this particular one, or perhaps because of it, for towards the end of her stay she had begun to appreciate the friendly helpfulness of the staff, and the plain but excellent meals which were delivered to her bedside three times a day, so now she went straight to reception and asked which ward her aunt was on, explaining that they had come all the way from Liverpool to see her. She chose to introduce herself as Mrs Pritchard's niece because she knew Rhodri had several cousins, and knew also that as a relative she would be allowed to visit whereas as a friend she might have been turned away.

Armed with the information they required, the three of them made their way quietly through the numbers of staff and patients in the long corridor until they came to one of the single rooms, which had a number and Mrs Pritchard's name on the door. So used had the family become to always addressing the Pritchards as Mr and Mrs that the sight of her Christian name, Mair, was quite a shock and almost caused Molly to walk straight past, except that Rhys caught her arm. 'This is the one,' he whispered. 'Just a gentle tap, my love. I can see her shape under the blankets, and there's Mr Pritchard and Rhodri sitting on the bench with their backs to us, so I think we should go in very quietly.'

They entered the small glassed-in cubicle, and the two men seated by the bedside swung round at the gentle susurration of the opening door. Rhodri got to his feet in one quick flexible movement and his father creaked upright also, a hand pressed to the small of his back, but a big smile chasing, momentarily at least, the fear and worry from his weathered face. Rhys began to whisper that they had come as soon as they could, but Rhodri shushed him, a finger to his lips, then pointed to the door. The Pritchards, Rhys and Molly went obediently out into the corridor, but Nonny indicated by signs that she would remain with the old woman whilst the adults talked.

Outside in the corridor Molly gave old Mr Pritchard an impulsive hug. She had never done such a thing before, never dared to do more than shake his hand, but now she felt the tremble vibrating through his arthritic frame, and felt his cheek wet with tears. She saw that Rhys was holding Rhodri's hand as though the young man were just a small child, and knew instinctively that this was what the Pritchards needed at this difficult moment. Spotting a bench a little further up the corridor she led the three men to it and sat them down. Then, clasping both Mr Pritchard's hands, she asked him if they could help in any way. The old man produced a large and not very clean handkerchief and unashamedly mopped his eyes.

'A stroke she did have,' he muttered, his voice breaking. 'Very ill she do be. The doctor says it's coma, not sleep, yet he says he doubts she'll wake again.' The eyes he turned on Molly were as puzzled as a child's. 'How can that be? I don't understand. If she's not going to wake, she must be asleep, and if she's asleep why shouldn't she wake? Oh, Mrs Roberts, love my Mair I do, miss her we shall, until she do come back.' He turned to his son. 'The boy understands. He tries to explain, but...'

Rhodri put an arm round his father's thin shoulders. 'Coma is really only a word for a very deep sleep, and from such a sleep few do recover,' he said gently. 'Remember, Da, our mam is old, old, old.' He turned to Molly and Rhys. 'This come about because she fell out of the hayloft and that caused her to have what they call a stroke. She were bringing down a bale of hay for the cart-horses ... ah, God, often we've told her, Da and meself, not to climb that ladder, but she'd not heed us. And now this! Poor Mam.'

Molly took old Mr Pritchard's thin hand, calloused from years of hard work, and gently squeezed his fingers. 'We'll do anything we can to help, because no one deserves help more than you,' she said softly. 'When we first came to Cefn Farm all we had was book knowledge, and a deal of that was wrong because it didn't apply to hill farming. We made mistakes which would have cost us dear, only you and Mrs Pritchard were not afraid to tell us what we'd done wrong and what we should do to put the wrong right. Oh, we had kindness from most folk in the mountains when it came to buying and looking after our stock, but you treated us as a good father treats his children and we shall never forget it. Believe me, Mr Pritchard, if we can pay you back in any way we'd be proud to do it.'

Rhys saw the old man's eyes fill up with tears once more at Molly's words, saw him turn his head and wipe them away. He said, bracingly: 'So you mustn't worry about Cae Hic because we'll do whatever you tell us to do. At a time like this you must concentrate on getting your wife well again, and leave the farming to us and to Rhodri.'

The old man nodded tremulously, then turned to his son. 'Good neighbours we do have,' he said in Welsh. 'With such friends as these, we'll pull through, eh, Rhodri?'

Rhodri nodded and smiled. 'And Mam will get well again,' he said, though Molly could hear the treacherous little tremble in his voice which told her that the young man did not believe his own words. He began to get up from his seat on the bench, then looked round anxiously. 'Wasn't Nonny here a moment ago?' he asked, his voice puzzled, 'Could have sworn I saw her, see?'

'You did; we left her watching your mam while you told us what had been happening,' Rhys said quickly. 'She's a good girl, our Nonny.'

Rhodri's grim look vanished and he smiled for the first time since they had taken their seats on the bench. 'A great favourite with my mam she has always been,' he said. 'A grand girl is Nonny. Uncle Dewi always says Nonny's like our mam was as a girl; full of fun yet a hard worker with it.'

Molly saw Rhys smile. 'Aye, your uncle's right,' he said. 'Nonny will be just like Mrs Pritchard one of these days.' He peered through the glass panel in the top of the door, then turned to the others. 'Nonny's smiling! We'd best re-join her.'

Nonny had sat quietly by the bed, but then it had occurred to her to take the old woman's hand. She remembered someone telling her that hearing was the first thing to return to an unconscious person, so it seemed only sensible not just to hold the cold, wrinkled little hand in her own but also to chat. She told Mrs Pritchard how her parents had arrived in Liverpool to meet Chris off the big transatlantic liner and how they had received a telegram saying that she, Mrs Pritchard, had been taken to hospital. She was saying that Mrs Pritchard need not worry about Cae Hic since the Robertses would help Rhodri do everything that was necessary until Mrs Pritchard was herself once more when she felt the slightest pressure of the small, work-roughened hand in her own, and when she leaned over the bed she saw that the old lady's eyes were flickering open, saw she was trying to speak. It was not easy; the whole of the left side of her face was pulled down and her left eye was half closed. When she began to move her mouth, saliva dribbled from the left side of it and ran down her chin, but faintly, very very faintly, a whispered word was forming itself. 'Nonn...'

Nonny leaned closer. 'Yes, it's me, Nonny,' she said reassuringly. 'Shall I fetch dear Mr Pritchard and Rhodri? They've gone outside into the corridor with my mum and dad, but I can fetch them in no time...' But the drawn grey face ignored her words; the old woman was still trying to say something, and it must be something important. Nonny leaned closer. 'Yes, Mrs Pritchard, what is it you want to say?'

'Nonny. Look – look...' It was too hard; the words did not want to come. But whatever she was trying to say was important to her, Nonny knew that, so she spoke quietly but firmly.

'Don't try to hurry, Mrs Pritchard; take your time.' She gave a tiny conspiratorial laugh. 'We've got all day! What am I to look for?'

Mrs Pritchard sighed, then seemed to gather herself for a tremendous effort. 'Look – after – my – boy,' she said in a thin, reedy whisper.

Nonny stared. How on earth was she supposed to look after a man so much older than herself, and remarkable for the hard work and self-sufficiency which had always characterised him? But she knew better than to say such a thing to a woman who, for all she knew, might be dying. Now was no time to quibble, and anyway, she told herself, there were ways in which she could sort of look after Rhodri. She had moved back a little as Mrs Pritchard had finished speaking, but now she bent over the bed and kissed the old woman's seamed forehead. 'Of course I will; we all will, although Rhodri is very capable and much likelier to look after us,' she said. 'But you are going to get better, you know. You'll be looking after him yourself in next to no time.' She glanced towards the door and saw it beginning to open, saw her parents, Mr Pritchard and Rhodri quietly entering the room. 'You can tell them yourself that you're going to get well quite soon now,' she said bracingly, but by the time the others had joined her at the bedside Mrs Pritchard's eyes were closed again and she had let her head fall sideways on the pillow.

Nonny looked up at them. 'I think she's better,' she said in a low excited voice. 'She spoke to me; just a few words, but she knew it was me.' She caught Mr Pritchard's hand. 'Oh, I'm sure the doctor's wrong and she's going to get better!'

'Well, queen, have you made up your mind what you're going to do for Christmas? I suppose if you decide to stay in Bethel Street, I'll be honour bound to stay with you, bein' as how I'm your mum, but I tell you to your head I'd sooner go to Cefn Farm as we planned!'

Nonny had already left for Snowdonia, tucked snugly in the sidecar of Tugger Hughes's motorbike and Ellen and Lana were sitting round the fire roasting chestnuts whilst Mr Taplow was busily brewing a jug of punch. And listening, probably with considerable interest, to the conversation, Lana thought. She glanced across at him, then began to peel the blackened shell off one of the nuts, squeaking at the heat of it.

'Ouch! Oh, Mum, you could leave me here quite safely, you know, while you went off to be with Auntie Molly and the others.' She grinned at Mr Taplow. 'You wouldn't mind being looked after by me, would you, Mr T? I've never cooked a Christmas dinner so it would be good practice.'

Mr Taplow's cheeks reddened and Lana guessed that it was not just the heat of the punch which brought the colour to his cheeks. 'If your mother goes into Snowdonia for Christmas, I – I might be away too,' he said. 'The punch is almost ready. It just needs the juice of that lemon I squeezed earlier to make it perfect.'

Lana stared across the room at their lodger. 'Do you mean to say you're going to stay with that old uncle of yours on the Wirral?' she asked suspiciously. 'I thought he were dead.'

Ellen sighed gustily. 'If he was dead Mr Taplow couldn't very well visit him, could he?' she said impatiently. 'If you must know, young lady, your Auntie Molly's issued an invitation for us to take Mr T along of us. So you see if you decide not to go you'll be spoiling everyone's Christmas.'

'No, no, I'd be just as happy to spend the holiday with you in Bethel Street,' Mr Taplow interrupted, blushing more fierily than ever.

Lana considered. She was very fond of Mr Taplow, would not have minded had he and her mother decided to marry, but she had only been joking when she had pretended she had changed her mind and meant to spend Christmas in Bethel Street. Now, she wondered when her mother would have told her that Mr Taplow would be coming with them to Cefn Farm. She also wondered what had made Auntie Molly invite him. Did she suspect, as Lana sometimes did, that he and Ellen might marry? But somehow Lana had always doubted that her comfortable, fun-loving mother would settle down with plain diffident Mr Taplow. Despite her age – she was fifty-eight – Ellen had a great many admirers, all elderly men, many of whom she had met in the course of her work at the school. She was seldom unaccompanied when she went to the pictures, or to the dances for conventionally minded older people which were held a couple of times a week, choosing partners for both these events with care. And only the other day she had surprised Lana by remarking that Mr Taplow, despite appearances, was an excellent partner, though he specialised in old time dancing rather than the modern sort.

Right now, however, Lana decided that the time had come to admit she was just teasing and had no intention of missing out on Christmas at Cefn Farm. And this year it won't be a sixpenny Christmas because Mum and I have been saving up for weeks to make sure everyone has a good time, and I'm sure Nonny has done the same, she thought.

'Well, madam?' Ellen's voice was distinctly frosty. 'If you're determined to have Christmas at home then I'm telling you straight that your pal Harry Wilkinson will not be welcome in my house, and if push comes to shove he'll not be allowed to take you out anywhere unless he promises to bring you home by ten o'clock.' She shot her daughter a defiant glance. 'You ain't of age so you still have to do what I tell you. I'm just about fed up with your hoity-toity ways, Lana O'Mara, and if you ruin your Christmas by staying in Bethel Street you've only yourself to blame.'

Lana tossed her head. 'If he weren't such a good dancer...' she gave Mr Taplow an indulgent glance, 'and I mean smoochy dances, not the St Bernard's Waltz or the Dashin' White Sergeant ... I'd have give him the elbow weeks back. He's the sorta feller what expects you to pay more attention to him than to the fillum, which is summat I can't stand.' She snorted. 'Thinks he's more attractive and interestin' than Cliff Richard and Albert Finney rolled into one. So now you know why I don't go to the flicks with him.'

'Oh! I thought...'

'You thought the worst, of course,' Lana said, grinning at her mother. 'You thought I was the sort of girl who'd give a feller what he wanted so long as he were handsome and a good dancer. It's too bad of you, Mum, honest to God it is. You brought me up to have some self-respect, yet now...'

Ellen heaved herself out of her basket chair, not without difficulty for she had put on a deal of weight since the far-off day when she had bought it. She put her arms round Lana and kissed her cheek. 'Ain't you horrible to me, queen?' she said reproachfully. 'It ain't what *you* do what worries me, it's what that horrible Harry does. You're an innocent girl, years younger than him...'

'Oh, shurrup, Mum,' Lana said impatiently. 'You've known me all me life, so you should know I were only takin' a rise out of you when I said I might not go to the Robertses' for Christmas. Nothin' would keep me away. I've still got a soft spot for Chris, though of course I wouldn't dream of marrying him. Well, I might if he'd move into the city, but if I had to live at Cefn Farm I'd die of boredom within a month.'

At this point Mr Taplow poured his punch into three mugs and handed them round. Lana sniffed the delicious aroma of lemon, brandy and wine and smiled dazzlingly at her mother's elderly admirer. 'Thanks, Mr Taplow; it smells delicious. And now Mum and I have stopped squabbling, you'd better make your plans for a Christmas in the hills!'

Going to bed that night Ellen pondered on Molly's invitation to Mr Taplow to join them for Christmas. She just hoped that her old friend had not got hold of the wrong idea. She liked Bob Taplow, of course she did, but not ... well, not in the sort of way which Molly might have imagined. He was her favourite companion for old time dancing and the cinema, but she felt none of the palpitating eagerness for his caresses which she remembered from her early days with Sam. Not that she had had any experience of Mr Taplow's caresses; far from it! He was both shy and respectful, had never even kissed her cheek, and probably never would.

He was the ideal lodger, she told herself now. Not only did he hand over his rent each week, he also included a little present: chocolates, flowers, a pretty ornament for her china cabinet, a book she had said she would like to read. The chestnuts and the punch had been the little extras this week and as he gave them to her he had said, with the shyest smile, that he hoped his gift would put them all in the mood for Christmas, being as the holiday was so close.

Ellen sat down at her dressing table and began to brush out her thick mass of greying hair before braiding it into its night-time plait. Most of her other men friends took it for granted that she would allow them to kiss her goodnight after they had taken her dancing or to the cinema, and Ellen thought that this was fair enough; they had spent money on her, after all. Perhaps she liked Mr Taplow so much simply because he was different. Perhaps it was because she knew him better, through living in the same house, than she knew her other admirers. Now, looking at her reflection in the mirror – sparkling brown eyes, rosy cheeks and the great mass of her hair as she wielded the brush – she told herself that despite her years she was still an attractive woman.

When Molly had issued the invitation, suggesting that Mr Taplow might like to join them for Christmas, she had been delighted. Although, like her daughter, she could not even imagine living so far from civilisation and the things she loved, she still thought there was no better place for a holiday. And Mr Taplow had astonished her when she passed on the invitation by the revelation that he had spent a good deal of his youth on his uncle's farm just outside Great Sutton on the Wirral. Indeed, after his father's death, when he was ten years old, his mother had taken over the job of housekeeper on the farm and he, young Bob Taplow, had looked after the poultry, milked the cows, fed the pigs and of course assisted at both haymaking and corn harvest. 'Mind, there'll be nothing like that to prove my worth over Christmas,' he had admitted. 'And I dare say they wouldn't want me interfering anyway. But if they should need a hand you could say I'm not inexperienced in country ways.'

Ellen had reported these facts to Molly and been assured that her friend would now be doubly delighted to welcome the extra guest for the festive season. Rhys had offered to come and collect them but Ellen had told him that this was unnecessary. They would get public transport as far as Betwys-y-Coed, if Rhys would pick them up there in the old jeep and take them the rest of the way. They would, of course, be burdened with baskets, bags and a great many packages, but Ellen and Lana would not have dreamed of arriving at Cefn Farm without all their Christmas presents wrapped and ready and a great many items of food to help spread the expense of the great day itself. Molly would cook a couple of chickens which had been fattened to bursting point, but Ellen would bring sweets, chocolates, jars of mincemeat, and a big bag of oranges as well as such luxuries as Brazil nuts, a packet of Woodbines for Rhys and a bag of fudge for Chris, as she knew he had a sweet tooth. Mr Taplow had already bought four bottles of wine which he said he knew to be a good vintage and Ellen, who was not fond of alcohol, had crammed into the luggage a bottle of egg nog with which she intended to make herself the drink she called 'snowballs'.

Another two days would elapse, however, before they set out on the long trek to Cefn Farm and Ellen was checking over in her mind whether she had got presents for everyone. This particular present buying had not been as easy as usual because it included the Pritchards. She had met them often and liked them very much, but the fact that their first language was Welsh made conversation a little difficult. Mr Pritchard spoke some English, Rhodri was equally at home in both languages, but although Mrs Pritchard might have understood a few words Ellen had never heard her speak in any but her own tongue. Ellen had taken Nonny's advice and bought pipe tobacco for Mr P and chocolates for his wife.

Furthermore, Ellen knew, Mrs P was only going to be at home because the doctor at the hospital, as Welsh as Mrs P herself, had told Molly that if they kept the old lady on the ward over the festive season he thought it might prove fatal. 'She'll die just to spite us so she will,' he had informed the horrified Molly. 'She's not going to get any better than she is now, not if she has all the physiotherapy in the world. I do believe she might even get a trifle of movement in her left side if she was at home. The reason we've not discharged her earlier is because there's no woman at Cae Hic to look after her, and from what her son tells me he and his father have all they can do to keep up with the farming. It's very kind of you to say you'll have her with you, or go up daily to the Pritchards' place;

her husband was telling me they'd spent Christmas together for the past fifty or so years, and it means a lot to them. But are you sure you can cope? They're strong chapel, so the minister will visit them on the day itself ... oh, I'll leave it to your discretion, Mrs Roberts. If you're sure you can manage I'll release her to you and young Mr Pritchard on the day before Christmas Eve.'

So now, checking over the presents she had bought, in her mind, Ellen thought of the lovely shawl which a kindly neighbour had knitted to go with the chocolates for Mrs Pritchard, the pipe tobacco for Mr Pritchard and the box of coloured handkerchiefs for Rhodri. It was easy buying gifts for Nonny; Ellen simply doubled up on whatever she bought for Lana, and of course she and Molly, being so close, knew each other's tastes. The earrings which she had admired and bought would look delightful against her friend's rich chestnut hair.

Satisfied that she had done all she could to prepare for her stay, Ellen finished off her plait with a rubber band and stood up. She was already wearing her long cotton nightdress and now took off her dressing gown, telling herself that she must not forget to pack it, knowing that however hard Molly and Rhys tried their bedrooms would be a good deal colder than those in Bethel Street. Not that she ever felt cold at Cefn Farm once she got into her bed, because not only did it have a wonderful feather mattress into which one sank, but a heap of beautiful woollen blankets surmounted by a patchwork quilt which had belonged to Molly's grandmother kept the occupant of the bed as warm as toast.

Now Ellen climbed into her own bed, shrugged the blankets up over her shoulders and allowed her mind to dwell pleasantly on the days to come. It would be great fun introducing Mr Taplow – she must remember to call him Bob – to the many delights of Cefn Farm. Ellen's feet wriggled further down and found the hot water bottle she had placed there earlier. Good, it was still deliciously warm. She was just marvelling over the fact that Mr Taplow had said he could milk a cow when her thoughts became dreams and she slept at last.

When Dafydd had told her that she was going home, old Mair Pritchard shed tears of joy. She wanted to tell her dear Davie, as she had always called him, that she was delighted, would get well now, but she still could not make her treacherous tongue say what it ought. When Davie asked her if she had enjoyed the roast lamb, mashed potatoes and gravy which had been served by the hospital staff, she had wanted to say that the lamb was mutton, the gravy watery and the potatoes lumpy, but when she opened her mouth the words came out all wrong, causing her to weep with frustration. She had hated the ward, though she understood that the staff were only doing their duty when they made her sit up and washed her with offensive thoroughness, but she had known all along that she would not get better until she was in her own home. And now, because it was Christmas, she was to be allowed the wish that she was still unable to put into words; like everyone else, she was desperate to get home for Christmas.

She had lost track of time, but guessed it must be only a couple of days before the great day itself, when a conference was held about her bed. She listened eagerly but the talk was in English, too fast and difficult for her to follow. Doctors nodded, wrote on the chart which hung on the foot rail, smiled and seemed full of the Christmas spirit. She had gathered at last that she was to go home, and her dearest Davie confirmed it. He told her in slow, gentle Welsh that the discussion had been over the method of getting her there, but this was now decided; she was to be taken the very next day in an ambulance. She would not go to Cae Hic at first, but to Cefn Farm, and though this was a trifle disappointing it was still a good deal better than being in hospital. When a nurse came to her bedside, telling her that her son had just delivered a Gladstone bag with her clothes in it, she gave the young woman a lopsided smile of delight and actually spoke. 'Goood, good,' she crooned, and after some thought added, 'appy; 'appy!'

The nurse smiled, 'Like all of us you are, Mrs Pritchard dear,' she said. 'Everyone wants to be home for Christmas.'

There was a hard frost on departure day, and despite being bundled up in a multitude of garments, blankets and shawls old Mair Pritchard saw her breath form a mist before her face as she was wheeled out to the waiting ambulance and tenderly placed on the long bed inside it. Rhodri was in front with the driver so that he could give directions, whilst Molly sat close to the old woman, holding her hand and chatting away reassuringly to her as the driver wended his way through the traffic, heading for the mountains.

If the journey had seemed long in the jeep, it seemed a good deal longer in the ambulance. Unable to see out, Molly began to feel queasy, but Mrs Pritchard, knowing she was heading for home, seemed to grow stronger with every mile that passed, and when the vehicle drew up alongside the back door at Cefn Farm she actually gave a little crow of laughter, seized Molly's hand and declared: 'Home. I home!'

'Well, very nearly,' Molly assured her. 'Remember we told you in hospital that you would be with us for two or three days.' She chuckled as Rhodri and the ambulance driver threw open the van doors and began to transfer the old woman from the bed to a stretcher, whilst she ran ahead to open the back door. Bright light streamed out, and good cooking smells, and as Mrs Pritchard was deposited in a basket chair near the glowing fire she gave a sigh of deep content. This might not be her own home, that would be for tomorrow, but it was the next best thing, and she knew herself to be amongst friends. She saw her son thanking the driver, pressing something into his hand and ushering him out to his vehicle. Then he returned to the kitchen, shutting the door on the cold and dark and beaming with real pleasure as Molly gave her visitor the kiss of welcome whilst Nonny made tea in the big brown pot, poured some into a feeding cup and held the spout to Mair's eager lips.

Molly crouched beside the old woman, telling

her that they would have a full house this Christmas, that Ellen and her daughter would be with them and would be bringing a friend, their lodger, Mr Taplow. Mair nodded and smiled, not even trying to take in all that they were telling her. Soon Rhys and her dear Davie would be here; soon, therefore, it stood to reason that she would be taken to Cae Hic and get well again.

Chapter Fourteen

Christmas Eve came at last. Ellen, Lana and Bob Taplow had journeyed by train and bus and then by jeep to arrive at Cefn Farm before dusk had fallen. When they walked into the kitchen, however, laden with bags, packages and cases, it was to find their hostess arguing with the elderly man they knew was Mr Pritchard. The three of them blew into the kitchen with Rhys and Nonny, who had accompanied her father in the jeep, to find Molly clearly distressed and Mr Pritchard apologetic but firm; his dear Mair wanted to wake up in her own home on Christmas morning, and he saw no reason to deny her such a simple wish. He was promising Molly that he would wrap his wife in blankets, cover her with a waterproof in case it began to rain or snow, pop her into the farm cart with his old horse, Nell, between the shafts and take her at a gentle pace the five miles from Cefn Farm to Cae Hic. Rhys, who had left the farm earlier to fetch their guests, was astonished, for there had been no question of Mrs Pritchard's leaving the comfort of Cefn Farm when he had departed. They had made up a bed in the parlour, the room was as warm as toast with a fire blazing on the hearth, Molly had moved the wireless set from its usual place in the kitchen so that the old woman might have it beside her bed, and everything had seemed arranged so that the invalid might join in all the Christmas festivities.

Molly was tearful, reminding Mr Pritchard that she had promised the doctor she would keep his wife with her until the district nurse could make other arrangements, but though Mr Pritchard nodded his head and patted her hand, it soon became clear to everyone, including Nonny, that nothing would do for the old lady but to return to the home she had known all her married life.

'But weren't you warm and comfortable last night, Mrs Pritchard dear?' Molly said in her somewhat stilted Welsh. 'I know you couldn't face a big meal, but you had chicken broth, and bread and butter, and tea.' She smiled hesitantly at Mr Pritchard. 'I'm sure you're a very good cook, Dafydd, but the Aga might be out; certainly the farmhouse won't be warm and comfortable. Do think again before you move your wife.'

Nonny, knowing herself to be a great favourite with Mrs Pritchard, dropped the bags she was carrying and went across to kneel by the older woman. 'Mum's right, Mrs P,' she said gently. 'Cae Hic will be cold and you really aren't fit enough for a five-mile journey in the farm cart. Please think again! You know we promised to take care of you, and how can we do that if five miles separate us?'

Mr Pritchard cleared his throat. 'Cae Hic is not cold; made up the fire before I left this morning I did,' he announced. He looked appealingly from Molly to Rhys. 'If you could let me have some of that chicken broth and a loaf of your good bread then we'll manage very well. It's not as though Mair means to stay for the great day itself; I'll bring her back for her dinner tomorrow, though I doubt she'll eat much. But she's a fancy to wake up in her own home on the day of Christ's birth, and deny her I cannot. Can you understand? So good you have been to us...'

Rhodri broke in, and Nonny saw from the slight flush on his high cheekbones that he was embarrassed, though he clearly meant to stand by his parents. 'I know you promised the doctor that you'd look after Mam, and so you shall,' he assured Molly, then turned to Rhys. 'You'll lend me the jeep to run us home, won't you? And I promise you I'll get up at the crack of dawn and bring her back here before you've had a chance to miss her. It's – it's the only thing she's asked of us and to deny her would be hard...'

'Would be impossible,' Rhys said with a wry smile. 'Very well, but I don't mean to let you drive off with only your father to hold her steady over that rough track. You can drive and your father can sit one side of Mrs P and I'll sit the other, to steady her over the bumps.'

'I'll come too,' Nonny said firmly. She turned to her mother. 'You don't mind, do you, Mum? I think we all ought to have that lovely meal you've prepared before we set out. And there's no need for Dad to come along; heaven knows there's enough for him to do here! I'll look after Mrs P, and if Rhodri and his father can make me up a bed of some description, I'll sleep in the kitchen.' She turned to the Pritchards, who were watching her intently. 'If any of you need me all you have to do is give a yell and I'll come running. And if Mrs P agrees, we'll be back here in time for breakfast to wish each other a merry Christmas.'

Rhys looked relieved and agreed that if Nonny wouldn't mind she would be far more useful when they arrived at Cae Hic than he could possibly be. 'I'm no nurse,' he said apologetically. 'And I'm no cook, either, though I guess anyone can heat up a pan of chicken broth, and make a plateful of porridge. But if you're sure, Nonny my dear...'

Molly was murmuring doubtfully that she supposed it would be the best solution when the back door opened and Chris came in, shivering and beginning to take off his coat.

'It's freezing cold; real brass monkey weather...' he was beginning and then, Nonny guessed, he must have sensed something in the atmosphere, for he stared round at the assembled company, eyebrows rising. 'What's up? Don't say the dogs have run off with the turkey!'

Nonny laughed. 'Not exactly; but Mr P wants to run off with Mrs P, so that they can both wake up in their own home on Christmas morning,' she explained. 'Dad's agreed that Rhodri can drive them back to Cae Hic in the jeep, Mr P has assured us that the place is warm and I'm going along to do any nursing necessary.' She smiled warmly at the old woman. 'Not that there's likely to be any,' she ended.

Chris nodded his comprehension. 'Right. Then will you set out at once? Only you'll want to get back here before dark.'

'No, you don't understand,' Rhodri put in. 'Nonny will stay the night at Cae Hic and I'll drive the whole party back to Cefn Farm first thing in the morning, hopefully in time to share your breakfast.' He grinned at the younger man. 'Obviously, the best place for Mam is in your parlour with the whole family on hand if help is needed, but we've talked that all out and come to the conclusion that it's more important for Mam to have what she wants, and that is a night in her own home.'

'Fair enough,' Chris said. 'If you can't persuade her to stay then you've little choice.' He suddenly seemed to become aware of their three guests, still standing rather awkwardly in front of the range. 'I say, I'm awfully sorry, Auntie Ellen, Lana, Mr Taplow. I'm afraid I forgot my manners. Grand to see you all, and especially Mr Taplow, at Cefn Farm.'

'Call me Bob,' Mr Taplow said. He gave Chris a rueful grin. 'I'm afraid we arrived at just the wrong moment, but things seem to have got sorted out now.' He turned back to Molly, who was pouring tea into several mugs. 'I do trust that tea is meant for us, but before we enjoy your hospitality, Mrs Roberts, I think we should carry our luggage up to our rooms.'

Immediately all was bustle as Chris and Nonny showed their visitors where they were to sleep and then helped them with their luggage. Lana, knowing that she always shared Nonny's room, danced up the stairs chattering gaily until they were out of earshot of the kitchen, when she turned to her friend, an anxious look on her face. 'Is it really all right to take that poor old woman all the way up the valley in your dad's old jeep?' she said. 'It isn't as though it were a proper made up road, it's really only a track. She'll get bounced about something dreadful, no matter how carefully that Rhodri of yours tries to drive.'

Nonny, lugging Ellen's suitcase, pulled a rueful face. 'Of course it's not all right, it's madness,' she said rather breathlessly as Lana flung open the bedroom door and dumped her bags down in front of the washstand. 'The trouble is, Mrs P never asked for anything all the while she was in hospital, except to go home. Apparently, when they told her at the hospital that she was coming home, she took them literally. She knew she was stopping off at Cefn Farm, because we were careful to tell her that, but she truly believed it was just to be...' she giggled, 'a one night stand, so to speak. Then, she thought, she'd go to Cae Hic. Somehow she's managed to convince herself that once she's there her speech will return and the left side of her body will start to obey her when she gives it instructions. I talked to the doctor who specialises in stroke patients and he said quite often the patient knows exactly what they want to say but when they begin to speak the words either come out wrong or won't come out at all. And it seems the same can be said of movement. Mrs P's brain says reach out with your right and left hands and take the bowl of soup, and she truly believes that this is happening, whereas in reality it is only her right hand which receives the message from her brain and acts upon it.'

'Gosh, Nonny, ain't you clever?' Lana breathed. 'And what do you think about her going back to Cae Hic, then? Do you think she really will improve once she's there? If so, then everyone's done the right thing.'

Nonny shrugged and was beginning to reply when Ellen came into the room, her arms full of gaily wrapped parcels, which she dumped on the bed. 'Don't you look at none of them packets, 'cos they're all for tomorrer,' she said breathlessly. 'Can I stick 'em in your chest of drawers? Your mum says you won't mind. I won't unpack until after the meal, which Molly is getting on the table right now.' She sniffed ecstatically, chin in the air, nostrils flaring, looking so like one of the Bisto Kids that Nonny had to hide a smile. 'God, I'm so hungry I could eat a perishin' horse! Come on down, the pair of you, so's I can get my teeth into that rabbit pie.'

'Are we all set then? Are you sure you're warm enough, Mrs Pritchard dear?' Molly smiled as the old woman, in a positive cocoon of blankets in the back of the jeep, her husband by her side, nodded and tried to say something, but as usual the words got tangled up and emerged meaningless. 'I've packed a hamper with stuff you might need, though Rhodri swears he'll have you back at Cefn Farm in time for breakfast.' Molly turned to Rhodri, sitting behind the wheel. 'The wind's getting up. Oh, dear, I hope to goodness we're doing the right thing. Mind you and Nonny get your mum straight into bed as soon as you reach Cae Hic. She's got a stone hot water bottle at her feet and the rubber sort roundabout waist level...'

Rhodri had slid his window back and grinned at Molly through the aperture. He had come out earlier and started the engine, not wanting to have to crank it with the starting handle whilst his passengers were aboard. Now he revved up and began to close his window. 'You do worry too much, Mrs Roberts,' he said reproachfully. 'You've done everything and more for our mam; now you must let Da and me make our contribution to her happy Christmas.'

Molly laughed. 'I only hope we're not doing your mam a bad turn,' she said guiltily, 'but it's what she wants and perhaps that can't be bad. Remember, Rhodri, if you need anything, anything at all, you have only to get into the jeep and come down to Cefn Farm.'

Nonny, sitting on the far side of Mrs Pritchard, leaned across and gave her mother a reassuring smile.

'I'll take care of them all,' she said gaily. 'And Christmas breakfast is one of my favourite meals, so you can be sure I'll get everyone up in good time. We'll pack dear Mrs P in all her blankets and scarves and shawls and shovel her into the jeep and come bowling home in time to carry you up a nice hot cup of tea.' She turned to her companions. 'We'll do that, won't we? That way, no one's Christmas will be spoilt.'

Mrs Pritchard nodded vigorously, though it was impossible to know whether she had understood all that Nonny said, but Mr Pritchard smiled his comprehension. 'Aye, that's right,' he said, and then, as the car began to move forward, he settled back in his seat and put an arm round his wife's thin, well-muffled shoulders. 'Off we go, my dear love,' he said. 'Your boy will drive slowly and steer clear of the ruts and we'll be home before you know it.'

Molly crossed the farmyard, heading for the kitchen, trying to banish her fears for the invalid. To be sure the two farms were only five miles apart and the jeep, though elderly, was usually reliable, but Molly hated to think that something might go wrong. But Nonny and Rhodri were sensible; capable too. I'm a fool to worry, Molly told herself. After all, if something does happen they can return here and no bones broken. She entered the kitchen on the thought and smiled at Ellen and Lana, who were doing the washing up with much clattering of plates and dishes. Her friend raised her brows. 'They got off all right?' she asked, then tutted, screwing her normally happy, sweet-tempered face into an expression of disapproval. 'I don't agree with her going, mind. It's mortal cold out there, not the sort of weather to take an old woman half a mile, let alone five. But of course it weren't in your power to refuse. The pity of it was that she and her husband had got hold of the wrong end of the stick. They thought home meant Cae Hic. Oh well, I suppose it were a natural enough mistake. I remember you telling me that the old feller had told the doctor he and his wife had always woke up together on Christmas morning. Well, they would have been together at Cefn Farm...'

Lana threw her tea towel down on the draining board, picked up a pile of clean plates and began to replace them on the dresser. 'Do stop carping on and on, Mum,' she said impatiently. 'You've just said Auntie Molly had no choice but to let them go, so why keep on about it? What's done is done, and I'm sure Nonny and that Rhodri man are quite capable of getting the old people back to Cae Hic.' She laughed. 'If you ask me, Rhodri would have carried his mam ten miles, let alone five, on his bleedin' back rather than disappoint her. Now, is there anything else what needs doing to get ready for tomorrow?'

Molly smiled at her young guest, glad of the opportunity to change the subject. 'Yes indeed; there are some sticks of sprouts under the pantry shelf, and some mushrooms too,' she said. 'If you bring them out, Lana, together with the potatoes you'll find next to the sprouts, we can start preparing the vegetables.' She cocked her head, hearing footsteps approaching the back door. 'Ah, here comes Rhys. Last thing at night he just checks round the poultry house and the outbuildings to make sure there's no foxes or other predators on the prowl.'

Rhys entered the kitchen with Bob Taplow close on his heels. They brought a gust of icy air in with them and both headed for the glowing fire, Rhys shutting the kitchen door with a bang behind him before he crossed the room. He grinned at the three women. 'Well, are you still fretting because our house party has shrunk?' he enquired genially. He chucked Molly under the chin. 'I know you, Molly Roberts. You're a born worrier, you are, and you'll spend the night imagining all sorts of horrors, but remember, the Pritchards are by no means alone. Rhodri and Nonny will make sure fires are made up, kettles are boiling and beds aired before anyone gets into them.' He rubbed his hands together, then smote Bob Taplow across the back so hard that the older man reeled. 'And I've found myself a grand worker in your lodger, Mrs O'Mara! He's just milked Jessie and despite her efforts managed to stop her from kicking the bucket over.'

Mr Taplow smiled and looked pleased. 'I guess it's like what they say about riding a bicycle; once learned, never forgotten,' he said. 'Ah, I see you've got the kettle on...'

Rhys peered into the teapot. 'A cup of tea is all very well, but this is Christmas Eve and merits something stronger, I believe,' he said. He turned to their guest. 'Ellen tells me you brew up a remarkably good hot punch; tell me what you need and we'll have the ingredients on the kitchen table in no time.'

Bob Taplow agreed and actually went to his room and fetched two lemons which he had brought in the hope, he said, that he might be invited to brew his punch, and presently Chris came in, having checked that all seemed well with the sheep, to find his parents and their guests laughing and joking over an enormous bowl of steaming punch. He had had to go halfway up the mountain to check on the ewes whose lambs would be born in the spring, and took the mug of punch which Lana handed to him with real gratitude. 'The sky is clouding over, which means it won't be quite so cold tomorrow,' he remarked, taking the proffered mug. 'Are those mince pies I see before me? Chuck us a couple, Auntie Ellen.'

Molly had intended to have an early night, and hoped that her guests would follow suit, but because of the punch, the preparation of the vegetables for the next day and a game of Pelmanism which caused much hilarity, and went on for longer than one would have believed possible, it was eleven o'clock before Chris and Lana collected up the playing cards and said that they would do a last round of the yard and outbuildings before they came to bed.

'It's not necessary for you to go out into this cold, Lana my love,' Molly said quickly. 'I'm boiling the kettle for hot bottles and cocoa, so why don't you join the queue?' Lana shot Molly an odd sort of look and once again Molly wondered whether Lana suspected that she was not loved. It was not true, of course; Molly loved the child, she was just afraid that given the slightest encouragement Lana and Chris might ... but she was being ridiculous! Circling the freezing farmyard on Christmas Eve was scarcely the sort of inducement to lovemaking which Molly was imagining. So she watched the two young people changing slippers for boots, struggling into their coats and enveloping themselves in scarves, woolly hats and gloves. There was much hilarity as they did so, but when Chris pushed open the back door and gestured to his companion to go out, all laughter ceased. Snow whirled past the doorway, driven almost horizontally by the wind, which had scarcely disturbed the branches earlier in the evening. Molly gasped and snatched at her son's arm. 'How long has this been going on?' she asked wildly. 'Oh, Chris, suppose the jeep got caught in this storm? Suppose...'

Chris had wound his scarf round his mouth, but he pulled it down to answer her. 'Don't be daft! They'd have been home and probably fast asleep in bed before this little lot started. I heard the wind getting up earlier, but it wasn't more than an hour ago at the most.' He turned to Lana. 'Perhaps you'd better stay indoors...' he began, but Lana just laughed and plunged into the snowy farmyard.

'You start on the left and I'll start on the right,' she shouted. 'Your dad closed the hen house earlier, so the poultry should be all right. In fact, it's the foxes that I feel sorry for.'

Back in the kitchen, Molly filled hot water bottles and made mugs of warming cocoa. Rhys had assured her that the depth of snow in the farmyard proved without doubt that the snow could not have started to fall before ten o'clock at the earliest, which meant that the Pritchards and Nonny would have been safely tucked up in Cae Hic long since. Armed with this knowledge, Molly made her preparations for her guests' comfort, but she was glad when the back door burst open and Chris and Lana, snow-covered, came back into the room.

'All serene out there,' Chris said, beginning to brush snow off his outer garments whilst Lana pulled off her borrowed wellingtons and beat the snow off her coat before hanging it on its hook behind the door. Chris crossed the room and gave his mother a hug. 'And now you can just stop worrying,' he instructed her. 'You've had a hard day and tomorrow, knowing you, you'll be working from dawn to dusk, so you *must* get a decent night's sleep.'

Ellen, fetching biscuits out of the pantry,

seconded this remark. 'We've done the veggies and I've made the stuffing. Lana is going to do the bread sauce and Nonny will scrape the carrots,' she reminded her friend. 'What time do you want us up tomorrow, Moll? Only let's have a bit of a lie-in, eh? It's not as though we were kids, dying to get at our stockings!'

'Well, it isn't really light at this time of year until around eight, and if I know our Nonny she'll have hustled and bustled them into the jeep by then,' Molly said. 'If the blizzard goes on blowing, of course, it may well change things. But for once in my life...' she smiled affectionately at Rhys, 'I'll try to do as my husband tells me, and stop worrying.'

'Good,' Rhys said, but Molly saw that he was looking guilty. She raised her brows at him, wanting an explanation. 'Well, Chris and I will probably get up pretty early, if the blizzard has stopped, that is, to check on the sheep... If any of them are in trouble...'

Molly sighed, handed out bedroom candles and stood on tiptoe to turn out the hissing pressure lamp. 'Who's talking about being a worrier now?' she asked, smiling fondly at Rhys, stretched out in his favourite chair in front of the range. 'But I think the wind's dropping; perhaps we can both stop fretting for a few hours.'

She and Ellen went upstairs together and followed Lana into Nonny's room to collect the presents from the chest of drawers. In time-honoured tradition, Molly would put them beneath the tree in the parlour before anyone else came downstairs in the morning, ready to be handed out after the family had eaten Christmas dinner and listened to the Queen's speech. She was just about to leave the room, her arms full of interesting packages, when Lana spoke up. 'What's that one, Auntie Molly?' she asked. 'The one in plain brown paper?'

Molly had opened her mouth to say that it was nothing to do with her when she gave a squeal of dismay. 'Oh, how awful,' she said, her voice trembling. 'It's Mrs Pritchard's medication. They handed it to me in this brown paper bag, with a list of instructions. I forgot all about it, and put my parcels on top, then asked you to bring them up here when you had a moment, Ellen. Oh, my God! Mrs Pritchard was supposed to have a dose before she went to bed and another after her first meal of the day. Oh, whatever shall I do?'

The small party arrived at Cae Hic after a relatively smooth journey, for Rhodri, knowing how frail his mother was, had driven with the greatest care. The weather remained extremely cold, and by the time they entered Cae Hic's farmyard flakes of snow had begun to drift lazily down from the lowering sky. Nonny was anxious lest the sight of the flakes might upset the invalid, but Mrs Pritchard's face remained calm, except when a remark was addressed directly to her, whereupon the right side of her mouth would twitch into a little smile. When the car stopped as close to the house as Rhodri could get it, Nonny abandoned her post beside the old woman and ran to the kitchen door. She knew it would be unlocked, did not think the old couple had even got a key, though she also knew that they shot a large bolt across before they went to bed each night, particularly when there were gypsies in the vicinity. Now, she entered the kitchen and saw by the glow from the damped-down fire that there was a lamp standing on the table, hopefully full of oil and ready for lighting, as well as several candles and a tall container of spills. She lit one at the fire and carried it over to the lamp, and then the half-dozen candles in their old-fashioned holders which were grouped on the Welsh dresser. Then she checked that there was no obstacle which might impede old Mrs Pritchard's progress to bed, for she had promised her parents that she would see the old lady tucked up before doing anything else.

Sometimes, Nonny told herself, it was a good thing to have a small compact house, or cottage rather, for Cae Hic was one-storey, because it meant no stairs. As you entered the big kitchen the main bedroom was on the left and Rhodri's little slip of a room was on the right. You had to walk through it to reach the dairy, and that was the extent of the house. Nonny decided on impulse that she would advise Rhodri and Mr Pritchard to put the old lady into one of the creaking wicker armchairs to have a rest after the drive. Molly had sent a flask of hot chicken broth in the hamper of goodies she had prepared, and Nonny thought that she would get Mr Pritchard to give his wife some of it in the feeding cup the hospital had sent home with her whilst she made the bedroom as comfortable as possible. There was a paraffin stove in there which she would light to take off the worst of the chill, and when she had done that she would renew the hot water bottles which her mother had packed around the invalid and put them in the bed. By the time the broth was drunk – it would be a slow business because Dafydd Pritchard was shaky, nervous of doing something wrong for his poor dear wife – everything would be ready for settling the old lady down for the night. After that she would go out with Rhodri to see that all was well on the farm. Rhodri had only joined them at Cefn Farm after he had done all the chores at Cae Hic, of course, but she knew he would want to check everything one more time before seeking his own bed.

Nonny was still making up the fire, riddling the ash and putting on fresh fuel, when the back door was flung open and Rhodri appeared with his mother in his arms, looking as though she weighed no more than a feather.

'Put her in the armchair whilst her room warms up. I've got the kettle on and I'll refill her hot water bottles so we can get her into a warm bed,' Nonny said instructively. She grinned at Rhodri. 'You've always said I was bossy; well now you know that bossiness can come in useful at times. As soon as we've settled your parents we'll check the stock. Where's Spot? He'll round up any sheep which managed to escape you earlier.'

Rhodri grinned too. 'Ah well, being bossed by a girl as pretty as you is a downright pleasure; good as a Christmas present,' he said.

Nonny stared at him. 'Was that a compliment,' she asked suspiciously, 'or were you just fooling around?'

'Of course,' Rhodri said soothingly, and it was not until afterwards that Nonny realised he had not answered her question at all.

Having settled the old woman in one of the fireside chairs, with Mr Pritchard encouraging her to drink the broth from the spout of the borrowed feeding cup, Nonny and Rhodri began to gather together a couple of pillows and a number of blankets. Nonny opened her mouth to ask about sheets and pillowcases, then closed it again. She remembered her mother telling her that bedlinen was an unaffordable luxury so far as a good few small hill farmers were concerned. 'And anyway, getting straight between the blankets is a lot warmer, if not quite as hygienic,' Molly had told the young Nonny when her daughter had returned from spending a happy day ostensibly helping Mrs Pritchard to do her weekly bake and make the beds but probably, Molly had thought, proving more of a liability than an asset.

So now Nonny made no comment on the lack of sheets but helped Rhodri to pull two chairs together, add a stool and spread two sheepskins in place of a mattress, and then smiled at her host when Rhodri asked whether the homemade little bed would do her. 'And it is little, indeed,' he said rather ruefully. 'A good thing it is that you aren't a strapping wench because if you were your legs would be hanging out at one end and your head at the other.'

Nonny giggled. 'What you're trying to say is I'm an undersized weakling,' she said cheerfully. 'Now, I know I said we'd arrive back at our place before breakfast, but I think we should be practical, and that means checking the fuel in the Aga and building up the fire and damping it down so that when you return here after breakfast to do your chores tomorrow the kitchen at least will be warm.'

'Right,' Rhodri said briskly. 'A good thing it is that we've really only the one room; Mam and Da thought a parlour was swanky, seeing as how there's only the three of us.' He cast a contented glance round the big, old-fashioned kitchen, still earth-floored, the walls whitewashed, the Aga casting out a most welcome warmth to supplement the heat from the fire. Rhodri indicated the glowing flames. 'I reckon you'll be snug as a bug even if you are sleeping in a kitchen instead of a bedroom, and taking your morning *paned* in an earthenware mug instead of a nice china cup.' He cocked an eyebrow at her. 'Don't tell me you'll miss the parlour; if we had one it would only be two fires to light instead of one.'

Nonny saw that he was grinning, also saw something she had never suspected before: Rhodri was not exactly ashamed of the way he and his parents lived, but in some strange way he was wishing things were different, that the Pritchards had the same sort of lifestyle as the Robertses.

So, bearing this in mind, she, too, glanced around the big kitchen. 'I shan't regret anything,' she said firmly. 'I'll sleep like a log once I get into bed, but don't you think we'd best drink our cocoa and have a couple of biscuits before just checking the stock? It was a cold drive and I reckon we could all do with a hot drink.'

Rhodri nodded and went over to the stove where the kettle was hopping its lid. He made four cups of cocoa, then produced a bottle of something from a cupboard by the sink and proceeded to pour a tot of what was obviously alcohol – brandy, Nonny thought, wrinkling her nose with distaste – into the first two cups. He was about to do the same to the remaining two when Nonny shot out a hand and stopped him. 'No thanks; cocoa will be enough for me,' she said firmly. 'And as for your mother, she's on some pretty strong medication and mustn't drink spirits.'

'Right you are. But I wasn't trying to get you drunk, you know, just to warm you up,' Rhodri said rather reproachfully. 'As for Mam, as you can see I've not even made her a full drink. She's supposed to take her medication before she goes to sleep. I'm not sure whether it's nasty, which most medicines seem to be, or quite nice, but if it's nasty she'll appreciate a mouthful of cocoa to take the taste away. I'll make certain that the mug she gets only contains cocoa, however, Miss Prim.'

As Nonny had suspected, it took some while for Mrs Pritchard to finish the broth, so she heartily agreed with Rhodri when he went through to the bedroom and stood the mug of cocoa down on the bedside table, telling his father not to let his mam drink it until after her medication. 'It's not a full mug – less than a quarter, in fact – but enough to take the taste away if the medicine's nasty. And whilst she finishes the broth and you get her medication down her Nonny and I will take Spot and check that the beasts are all safely settled down for the night. You do know the medicine when you see it, Da? I believe she has a different sort mornings and evenings.'

His father grunted assent. 'Go you off, the pair

of you,' he said gruffly. 'Take the big electric torch by the back door and don't let Spot scare the sheep.'

Rhodri laughed at the idea that their aged and experienced sheepdog could scare anything, then he and Nonny muffled themselves once more in their outer clothing. Rhodri checked that the fire had been damped down, then pushed open the back door and came to an abrupt halt. He turned to stare at his companion, eyes narrowing as they both stepped into the farmyard and into the whirling snow. 'When did this start?' he asked through the woollen scarf muffling his mouth. 'Good thing the beasts are all in; the horses prefer to be out, but because I suspected that the weather might change for the worse I brought them in with the cows. It'll make it easier to check them; easier to keep foxes and badgers from pestering them too.'

Nonny opened her mouth to point out that to the best of her knowledge badgers were solitary creatures, not interested in farm stock so far as she knew, but got out no more than a few words before snow filled her mouth. Instead she punched her companion in the biceps and laughed at his pretended yelp of pain. 'Have you closed the poultry house yet?' she asked. 'It's one thing to keep the beasts in their stalls but I should think the hens will have gone stir crazy if you shut them up whilst it was still light. It sometimes seems to me that hens get as much of their grub pecking away between the cobbles as they do out of the meal bucket.'

'Ah, it's clear to see that you come from a big

farm and meself from a small one,' Rhodri pointed out. 'On market days and such, if we can persuade Mam to leave the farm and come into Wrexham or Ruthin with us, then we close the poultry in before we leave, which is quite early in the morning. We scatter corn all over the floor and even in the nesting boxes, and searching it out and squabbling for possession of every grain keeps the hens happy until we're able to release them into the yard in safety.' Rhodri chuckled. 'I've heard you say often and often that if you decide to marry one day it will be to a farmer; most of us hill farmers are in a small way, so unless you drop lucky you'll have a lot of learning to do. My mam knows how to make a ha'penny do the work of a penny and sixpence do the work of a shilling...'

'So do I!' Nonny said indignantly, having to raise her voice against the increasing shriek of the wind. 'So do Mum and Dad, because even if they're finding things a bit easier now, when they first came to Cefn Farm it was a hand to mouth existence. In fact, Mum was only saying the other day that if it wasn't for the kitchen garden and the home-grown vegetables and fruit we wouldn't be having the sort of Christmas she's got planned.' She laughed as they dodged into the cowshed, warm and sweet with the scent of the cows' breath and their milk. 'She used to say the Christmas after I was born was a sixpenny Christmas because none of the presents she and Dad bought cost more than that, but of course I was only a matter of days old, so I didn't care one way or the other. Well, children don't count the cost of what they're given, do they? I can remember Chris and myself getting as much fun out of the cardboard box Mum had brought the groceries home in as we would have if it had contained the pedal car that we both wanted.'

'Did you ever get a pedal car?' Rhodri asked, curiously. 'I never did, but I had a bicycle when I was quite young. When the Yanks went home, anyway. Apparently they abandoned heaps of bicycles – couldn't very well take them home to the States – and an uncle of mine who had worked at one of the USAF airfields asked if he could have one of the smaller ones for his nephew. I'll grant the Yanks this much: they were generous to a fault, so I got my rusty old bicycle and they gave my uncle a whole quid to get it put right. Of course we put it right ourselves, me and Da, and the quid went into the kitty, so's if I got a puncture or needed new batteries for my lights they were paid for, so to speak.'

In the dim torchlight, Nonny grinned at her companion. 'How do you think me and Chris got our bicycles? I suppose you thought they came straight from the cycle shop?' she said derisively. 'They didn't. Chris was thirteen when the Post Office issued new bikes for their staff in what they described as "difficult rural areas". That's why his has got that huge basket on the front. And I got mine at about the same age when Auntie Ellen saw an advert in the *Echo* for a lady's bicycle going cheap. Ten bob it cost, and it's taken me all over the place with only a couple of punctures when I expected too much of it.'

Rhodri laughed and took her hand in a light clasp. 'And I was brought up in a dog kennel, given nothing but tea leaves to eat and rainwater to drink,' he said teasingly, and Nonny saw the flash of his teeth as he grinned at her. 'Come on, let's bolt for the back door. The snow's not easing off at all. I think we'll have a full blown blizzard by morning.'

They had returned to the kitchen, filled their hot water bottles and drunk their cocoa before Mr Pritchard emerged from the bedroom, looking anxious. 'Can't find Mam's medicine, though I think I've looked through every bag and basket we brought back with us,' he said worriedly. 'She says not to fret, missing it once won't hurt, but the doctor said she must have it twice a day.' He turned to his son, his forehead wrinkling in perplexity. 'What'll we do if the hospital didn't put it into our luggage? That worried I am, Rhodri my son!'

Nonny cut in before Rhodri had had a chance to answer. 'Don't worry, Mr Pritchard. My mother checked over every single thing she was given by the hospital and packed it away in a Gladstone bag. I'm very much afraid, though, that it may have been left behind at Cefn Farm. Still, that's no problem: Rhodri can get into the jeep and drive down to fetch the stuff, or I could saddle up one of the horses and ride down for it. But do tell me – how did you know that your wife said one missed dose of her medication didn't matter?'

The worried frown had been smoothed from Mr Pritchard's face as Nonny talked, and now he gave her his goblin grin. 'Understand most of what she says I do,' he explained. 'Married fifty years, we've been; words we don't need when a glance can say it all.'

Nonny was delighted with his reply, showing as it did the depth of the old couple's love for each other, but nevertheless she shook a reproving head. 'Mrs P is wrong, though, Mr P. The hospital thinks the medication is important and the doctors there know more than we shall ever do. As I said, either Rhodri or myself will bring it back in time for her to take the necessary dose before she sleeps. Now you start getting yourself ready for bed, and by the time you're between the sh – blankets, I mean, we'll be mixing up the medication and feeding it to your good lady.'

Mr Pritchard laughed at this description of his wife, but was clearly greatly relieved, and apart from renewing the cups of cocoa which the old couple had already drunk, he said nothing more. In the firelight's glow, Nonny raised her brows at her companion. 'Well, which is it to be? The snow's going to drift, you know, so it might be better and easier if we took to the horses. An animal can go round a drift or even take to the fields, but the jeep has to stick to the track, which may already be impassable. Mind you, I don't believe it is, because the storm hadn't long started when we went round the outbuildings.' Nonny saw that Rhodri was shaking his head, and raised her brows. 'What's up? Don't you agree that one of us should go down to Cefn Farm? I know we haven't searched your parents' baggage ourselves but your da was so anxious that your mam should have her medicine that I'm sure he's gone through it with a fine-tooth comb.'

'It's not that,' Rhodri said. 'What worries me is

that your mother may already have discovered she still has the medicine and be sending poor Rhys up with it. If he takes Wanderer they'll undoubtedly choose to come by the fields, but which fields? We could easily miss one another if I took the jeep, and if I took one of the horses and chose the same route as your father we could still miss each other with the blizzard and the dark and everything.'

Nonny sank into a chair and put her head in her hands, but when Rhodri put a comforting arm round her shoulders she pushed him away. 'Don't! I'm trying to think,' she said crossly. 'If it's only been snowing for an hour, you'll still be able to see the ruts and puddles of the lane. But later it will be really treacherous, and you're right: whichever way we choose we can't be certain of meeting Dad. Look, the only really important thing is to get Mrs P's medication. My parents will have exactly the same dilemma that we've got, but knowing my dad he'll have thought of the obvious solution; he'll think you'll take the jeep in order to get there more quickly so it's likely he'll take our tractor. It's the nearest thing to "new" that we've got on, the farm,' she added with a chuckle. 'All the other big machinery is shared, as you know very well. So shall we bank on their having realised the medication is still at Cefn Farm and Dad's hurrying up here aboard the tractor to hand it over? In which case we simply sit and wait, knowing that Dad will arrive with it just as soon as he can.'

The two young people stared at one another across the kitchen table. Then Rhodri shrugged. 'Tell you what, we'll wait for half an hour and if no one has turned up in that time, I'll drive the jeep down to your place. But I'm sure...'

Even as he spoke they heard the guttural roar of a tractor as it came slowly up the steep and rocky track. Nonny was so delighted that she hurled herself into Rhodri's arms. 'The cavalry have arrived,' she squeaked.

Rhys had not enjoyed the drive up the rugged mountain track between Cefn Farm and Cae Hic. He had been asleep in front of the range when Molly had shaken him awake to explain what had happened, and though he completely agreed with her that the medicine must be taken straight to the Pritchards' he had said it in a sort of daze, and could not help hoping that the Pritchards would realise the medicine was missing. If they did so he was sure Rhodri would jump into the jeep and come charging down the track, but when he voiced this thought to Molly, though she patted his arm consolingly, she also shook her head. 'He might think you or Chris were already on your way,' she explained. 'Because of the snow – it's still blowing a blizzard – he might think you will saddle Wanderer and go over the fields. If so you might miss each other. Which do you think you ought to do, my love? If you decide on Wanderer, I'll go and tack him up.' She peered doubtfully through the kitchen window. 'Only for my own part I think the tractor is the best bet.'

Rhys nodded reluctantly. If he took the tractor he could be there and back in half the time, and soon tucked up in his cosy bed. And one did not have to tack up a tractor but merely climb aboard, start the engine and set off. He said as much to Molly, who nodded.

'Shall I wake Chris? He could go instead of you.'

Rhys laughed. He was beginning to wake up properly, and knew that if Chris took the tractor he and Molly would simply worry themselves sick in case he had an accident. Besides, Chris had been so tired that he had gone straight to bed as soon as he and Lana had checked the stock. So Rhys gave Molly a kiss and patted her cheek. 'Don't be daft, cariad. Now where's this medication?' He had already donned his thickest coat and was winding a big muffler round his neck, jamming his cap down on his head and stepping into his boots.

'It's here, in this brown paper bag,' Molly said, flourishing it. 'I'll tuck it well down into your pocket, where it will be safe from the wind and snow.' She looked up at him, her eyes bright with love. 'You will drive carefully, won't you, my darling? Tell you what, why don't you spend the night at the Pritchards' and come home when they do tomorrow?'

Rhys pinched her chin. 'Well, for one thing it would mean sleeping on the kitchen floor, which I can't say appeals to me much, and for another the journey home, being all downhill, will be a piece of cake. I doubt it will take me more than half an hour at the most. Now stop fretting and have a nice hot cup of cocoa ready for me when I get back, because I don't intend to linger. Oh, and I'll have some of that gingerbread you made the other day.'

As he said the last words he was pushing open the kitchen door, and heard Molly gasp behind him as the gale tried to slam it in his face whilst snow swirled in. Rhys felt the flakes splatter his cheeks and in a way was glad of it, since it woke him up completely. He let the door crash to behind him, fought his way across to the cart shed where the tractor stood, and presently set off into the storm.

It was going to be a rough ride, there was no doubt about that. The faltering beam of the tractor's headlight scarcely penetrated the whirling flakes, but Rhys knew the track well, so he changed into a low gear and crawled on. In fact he was surprised when he suddenly realised that the faint light he could see ahead was coming from Cae Hic, for so total had been his concentration that he had not realised the journey was almost over. He drew up alongside the door and it shot open before he was even down from his seat, to reveal his daughter's beaming face. 'Get inside, Dad!' she shrieked. 'We've got the kettle on.'

Rhys crossed to the door in a couple of strides, entered the kitchen and slammed the door behind him. Then he grinned at Nonny, holding out her hand for the medication, and at Rhodri, pouring hot water into a large mug. 'If that's for me, thanks but no thanks,' he said breezily. 'I can't stop; it's hell out there and the sooner I'm back in my own bed the better.'

Rhodri began to apologise, saying it was their carelessness in not checking which had led to their leaving the medicine behind, but Rhys shook his head.

'No, Rhodri, it was most certainly not your fault,' he said firmly. 'Molly got it mixed up with her Christmas presents, and by the time she discovered it the storm was well under way. But all's well that ends well; the instructions are in the bag, so the sooner you get a dose into your mam the better.' He turned and gave his daughter a pat on the cheek. 'I'll see you both in the morning for breakfast. Don't be late; it's bacon, kidneys, and scrambled egg. You wouldn't want to miss that.'

'Very true,' Nonny agreed. She looked hard at her father. 'Dad, you're soaked. I'm sure Mr Pritchard would lend you a dry cap and muffler, though the rest of his things would be much too small...'

Rhys grinned. 'No point, love. I'd be wet through again in five minutes. Now you get yourself off to bed so you're ready to come down in the jeep tomorrow morning.' He hesitated, looking from Nonny to Rhodri. 'But if this storm keeps up you're not to attempt the journey to Cefn Farm, not with the old lady I mean. She truly mustn't go out with the gale blowing the way it is, and by then the snow will be drifting; it's already started in places. I promise you that if it's still as bad as this...' he indicated the snow which they could see racing past the window, 'then Mum will pack a basket with your Christmas dinners in it and either Chris or myself will bring it up in the tractor. Understood?' Rhodri glanced at Nonny, and Rhys suddenly realised that Rhodri would not mind at all if he had to spend Christmas marooned at Cae Hic provided that Nonny was with him. Rhys blinked. It had never occurred to him that the other man might be keen on his daughter. He had always thought the ten years' difference in age was too great for either party to consider the other as a possible partner, but now... He looked from Rhodri's serious face to Nonny's gay and smiling one. Was it really possible...? He and Molly had always hoped that Nonny would marry into the farming community. Well, was not Rhodri a farmer? But now they were assuring him that they would not take the old lady out into the storm, said they would be quite content to remain at Cae Hic until the weather changed, so he nodded to them, pulled his muffler up over his lower face, climbed aboard the tractor and set off once more.

Half way down the hill he realised that his worst fears were coming true: the snow was drifting quickly. There was a long ridge ahead of him; difficult to judge the depth but he guessed it would be three or four feet, but the tractor, he knew, could take a drift of that size in its stride. He ploughed through it, but a little further on he was suddenly aware that his headlight was not just going dim but flickering, and a couple of minutes later it died.

Rhys groaned, then told himself that it made little difference; all the headlight had done was light up the whirling flakes. In fact it was easier to see now that its treacherous light was extinguished. He pressed on, even more eager now to get home, for weariness and the strain of peering through the snow was beginning to catch up with him. At one point he began to wonder whether he had actually driven off the track, and jerked his head round to look behind him. He realised he could see his own tyre tracks coming from Cae Hic but not the tracks approaching it. Puzzled, and more than a little worried, he slowed his speed and scanned the ground behind him, and when he turned to face front once more he realised with horror that he had climbed the bank without realising it and the engine was shrieking as one of the big wheels spun with nothing to grip. Rhys fought to bring the tractor back on the track, saw the whirling snow blotted out as the vehicle tilted sideways, felt pain and terror engulf him, and knew no more.

Chapter Fifteen

For the first half hour, Molly busied herself with all those little jobs which a housewife can always find, and for the second half hour she spent a good deal of time peering through the window at the fast whirling flakes, but after a whole hour had passed she began to worry seriously. Something had gone wrong, she knew it in her bones. She played with the idea that the Pritchards might have asked Rhys to stay the night, hoping that the storm would be over by morning. Then she wondered if the medication had come too late and the old lady was so ill that Rhodri had bundled her into the jeep and driven her off to the village where Dr Llewellyn could be roused at need. When Rhys had been gone for an hour and a half, Molly could bear the suspense no longer. She went through to Chris's lovely new room and shook him awake, which took some doing, for like the rest of them Chris had had a long and tiring day and had fallen into a deep and dreamless sleep. Molly awakened him at last, however, chiefly by saying, 'Chris, I'm so frightened. I need you.' That had penetrated the mists of sleep all right. Chris shot upright in his bed, eyes dilating. Molly had brought the lamp in with her and by its light Chris stared wildly round the room.

'Mam? Is someone ill?'

'Yes ... no... I'm not sure,' Molly gabbled. 'But Chris, darling, Dad went off over an hour and a half ago to take Mrs Pritchard's medication – oh, you don't know, do you? It got left behind by mistake; it was all my fault. Anyway, Dad took it and went off in the tractor ages ago. He should have been back by now. Oh, Chris, I'm beginning to believe he must have had an accident. The tractor may have broken down ... oh, I wish I hadn't persuaded him not to take Wanderer. What should we do?'

Chris was already struggling out of bed. 'I'll dress, and go on foot. If the tractor broke down and Dad's walking he's bound to take a good deal longer than you'd expect,' he said consolingly. 'Don't worry any more, Mum; that'll be it. I know the tractor's fairly new, but engines are unreliable things. Is the storm bad, then? I can hear how the wind's got up since I came to bed.'

'It's frightful,' Molly said with a shudder. 'Do you think you'll be quicker on Wanderer, Chris, or on foot?'

Chris shrugged, and added the thick Guernsey Molly handed him to the clothing he had already put on. 'I'll take a look at the conditions and make up my mind when I see how bad it is,' he said.

The two of them made their way through to the kitchen, and Molly seized the kettle and made another cup of cocoa. 'Drink that; it'll warm you up,' she said. 'I think I ought to go with you.'

Chris was about to reply when they both heard someone descending the stairs, and Lana's face appeared round the door. 'What's going on?' she asked. 'I can hear Mam snoring through the wall. I tried and tried to go to sleep, but what with Mum's snoring and the storm it's been just about impossible.' She looked curiously at Chris. 'You're dressed! But you went to bed even before the rest of us did, because you were so tired.' She looked wildly around the room. 'It's not morning, is it? Oh crumbs, don't say I've been awake the whole perishin' night!'

Molly opened her mouth to reply, but Chris was ahead of her.

'Dad went off on the tractor to the Pritchards' to take some medicine which got left behind by mistake,' he said. He grinned reassuringly at the two women. 'I'm afraid I was fast asleep or I'd have gone in place of my dad, and now Mum's worried because...'

Lana's eyes, which had been half closed, opened to their fullest extent and she glanced up at the clock over the mantelpiece, which read just past one. 'I should think she would be worried; it must be a couple of hours since we found the medicine amongst your Christmas presents, Auntie Molly,' she said. 'But of course if the tractor has broken down and Uncle Rhys is having to walk, it could be ages before he gets home.'

Chris nodded. 'That's what I've been telling Mum,' he said. 'So I'm going to take a flask of hot cocoa and a snow shovel and make my way up the lane until I either find Dad and the broken down tractor, or reach Cae Hic. I know it isn't likely, but if the tractor broke down anywhere near the Pritchards' place Dad may well have gone back and taken shelter there.'

'I don't think he would,' Molly said doubtfully. 'He knows what a worrier I am, and he knew I'd wait up for him.' Her tone suddenly sharpened, 'Lana, where are you going?'

Lana was heading for the stairs, but turned back to smile at the older woman. 'I'm going to get dressed, Auntie Molly,' she said cheerfully. 'You'll wait for me, won't you, Chris? I shan't be two ticks.'

'Oh, but I don't really think...' Molly began, but she was speaking to empty air; Lana was already out of hearing. Sighing, Molly turned to her son, who was employing himself by making the flask of cocoa he had mentioned earlier. 'You don't really want Lana with you, do you, Chris?' she asked hopefully. 'She'll hold you up ... you'll be quicker without her...'

Molly stopped speaking, aware suddenly of Chris's intent gaze. 'What makes you say that, Mum?' he asked. 'Sometimes I wonder if you know something about Lana which the rest of us don't. It's not that you dislike her ... oh, I don't know...'

Molly put her hands to her hot cheeks. 'I'm very fond of Lana, it's just that I don't think that she'd make a very good wife for a hill farmer,' she began rather feebly, only to be swiftly interrupted.

'For God's sake, Mum, who's thinking of marriage?' Chris said crossly. 'I'm certainly not, and neither is Lana. She's a good time girl if ever I met one, but great fun to be with and I think a good friend in time of trouble. As for not being a suitable wife for a hill farmer, how can you say such a thing? Are you trying to tell me you knew all about sheep when you married Dad? You've often told us you were a city girl, but you learned all right. Why shouldn't Lana? I know you imagine that you might come with me and be more use than Lana, but you're wrong, you know. She's young and strong; cheerful too. You know very well that if you came with me I'd have to slacken my pace, but Lana will keep up. She may not be as useful as Nonny would be but it's a close run thing.'

Molly felt abashed by her son's words. 'You're right, of course,' she said quietly. 'I wouldn't be much use. If Lana really wants to go...'

She stopped speaking as Lana came crashing down the stairs and burst into the kitchen, beaming at mother and son. Molly reflected that the girl must be wearing every garment she had brought with her. Chris stoppered the flask and turned to grin at Lana. 'You're round as a balloon in all those clothes, but you're very sensible because we'll be bitterly cold before we've gone half a mile,' he observed. He was in his stockinged feet, but went over to pull his boots on, then donned his waterproof, helped Lana into hers and turned to smile reassuringly at his mother. 'I don't suppose we'll be long, but just remember, there are two of us. In the unlikely event of my breaking a leg then I've got Lana to run home and fetch help,' he said breezily. 'We'll go via the big barn and persuade Eggy to join us. I don't know what use he'll be but I'd like to have him with us, just in case. See you later, and don't worry if it takes us longer than you expect, because if the tractor has broken down we'll want to do our utmost to mend it.'

He tugged the door open on the words, gave Molly a pat on the head and a cheerful grin, then took Lana's arm as the pair stepped out into the swirling snow. 'See you!' he shouted over his shoulder, kicking the door shut behind him, leaving Molly a prey to her own thoughts. What an idiot she had been, to try to stop Lana accompanying Chris! Whatever was it that she feared? The two youngsters had always behaved like brother and sister, joking and laughing, pushing and shoving, mocking and insulting. The fact that they were now young adults did not seem to have changed their attitude to one another in any way. The trouble is, Molly told herself, I've got into the habit of trying to keep them apart and it's a silly habit and one I ought to break. And really it's most awfully good of Lana to go out in this fearful weather. Oh dear, I pray that the tractor has broken down and that Rhys and the children will soon be home!

It was tough going as Chris had anticipated, and he reflected that though his mother seemed to have doubts about Lana's strength she was keeping up without hanging on to his arm, though he did offer to give her a hand as the track steepened. As they slogged along she chatted of her work and her friends in the city, asked intelligent questions about Canada and was the first to see, ahead of them, the bulk of a large object almost blocking the lane. She grabbed Chris's arm, for he had had his head lowered against the gale, and bawled into his ear at the top of her lungs. 'What's that, Chris? It looks as though your guess was right and the tractor has broken down. I can't see Uncle Rhys, so perhaps he's gone back to Cae Hic – or maybe he's gone across the fields and is back at Cefn Farm already...'

But Chris, peering ahead now, suddenly broke into a shambling run, which was the only gait possible in snow so thick. 'The tractor's on its side; almost upside down,' he shouted, his voice sharp with fear. 'Hurry, Lana, hurry!'

They arrived beside the tractor at the same moment, and despite the dark and the snow, which was driving almost horizontally, it was immediately obvious to Chris what had happened. Something must have gone wrong with the steering so that the tractor had veered up the steep bank, which would have been invisible in the deep snow, and overturned. His heart, which had begun to pound as soon as he saw the dark shape of the tractor against the snow, redoubled its rate as they drew level with the vehicle and he saw his father. From the waist down Rhys was pinned beneath the tractor, and the snow around him was bright with blood.

Chris dropped to his knees and began the fruitless task of trying to heave at the vehicle, but it was impossible to budge it and he turned a desperate face to his companion. 'I can't tell if he's alive or dead, but we've got to get the tractor off him,' he said breathlessly. 'Go to the village Lana, go as fast as you can and bring help. Don't go to Cefn Farm – our mothers couldn't do a thing. Get hold of all the able-bodied men and tell them to bring planks, wheelbarrows, snow shovels, anything that might help.' He had rooted out a strong and sturdy branch from the bank and now he began to push it under the tractor wheel. 'I'm going to drive this branch in alongside Dad to see if I can take some of the weight off him.' He turned to glare at his companion. 'Why the devil haven't you done as I said? Get to the village! Fetch help, damn you!'

But Lana, who had seemed so sensible, such a good companion, was kneeling in the snow a couple of feet from Rhys's body and retching miserably. At Chris's words, however, she pulled herself together and spoke in a wavering voice, scarcely above a whisper.

'Oh, Chris, all that blood! Blood makes me sick, the sight and the smell of it! Oh, poor Uncle Rhys...'

Chris interrupted, his voice rising. 'Fetch help!' he shouted into her white and frightened face. 'If you don't go now and he dies, his death will be on your head. Bugger off, Lana.'

Lana began to whimper. 'Wouldn't it be better if you went, Chris? You can speak Welsh...'

Chris turned on her again. 'Have you got the strength to thrust this branch under the tractor wheel? Of course you haven't. And you're sick at the sight of blood,' he said contemptuously. 'Get going.'

Lana gave a strangled sob, but turned back the way they had come. 'I'm sorry, Chris, it was just the shock...' she began, but Chris was too busy to heed her and presently he was aware that she had gone and he was alone with his father in the still falling snow.

Working desperately, Chris managed to get the branch under the tractor wheel and began to ease another larger branch alongside it. He was aware that he had been hard on Lana – pretty, delicate Lana – but told himself that he had been forced to frighten her into obeying his command. She would have been no use here, but if she reached the village in time and brought back help she would have atoned for her reluctance to leave the scene. He knew he must have hurt and worried her but felt no compunction, telling himself that Nonny would not have argued. But then his father groaned and Chris fell on his knees and began to scoop out snow from around the captive legs. He prayed Lana would hurry but knew in his heart she would do everything possible, not just for his sake, but for his father's.

Digging like a dog, Chris was grateful that the snow was fresh enough to be easily penetrated, yet he had to proceed with great care. He told himself that the moment the tractor moved he must stop digging for fear that its weight might shift to an even more dangerous position. He laboured on.

Lana sobbed as she ran, slogging through the soft snow, her misery twofold, for she had grown to love her friend's quiet, dependable father, and was ashamed that she had not immediately obeyed Chris's instructions, but had argued; argued when the fate of Rhys Roberts hung in the balance. How could she have done such a thing? And by arguing, she told herself miserably, she had probably lost

Chris's regard, worse, his affection, for she had begun to think recently that he was becoming fond of her. Lana was not aware of precisely when her own feelings of admiration and friendship had turned into something stronger, but now, drily sobbing with misery and exhaustion, she told herself that Chris would never regard her in future as anything but a silly girl, too wrapped up in her own feelings to give the help which he had so desperately needed from her. If she had forfeited any chance of his love, it was her own fault.

Lana reached the first cottage on the outskirts of the village. The wind was still whipping the snow into her face and there were no lights in the windows, but she did not hesitate. She ploughed her way up the path and battered on the door, shouting at the top of her voice that help was needed; that Rhys Roberts's tractor had turned turtle, pinning him beneath it, that he was on the track between Cefn Farm and Cae Hic. Then, without waiting to see whether her shriek had been understood, she ran back into the road and headed for the next cottage.

The men from the village came, fighting their way through the blizzard, arriving at the scene of the accident looking like animated snowmen. They realised at once, as Chris had done, that actually moving the tractor might easily cause more damage to the man pinned beneath it unless they took their time and acted with extreme care. The men had brought spades and shovels, planks of wood and a gate, taken off its hinges, to carry Rhys to an ambulance, for Lana had dialled 999 from the telephone box in the village and the voice the other end had promised that the rescue vehicle would set out straight away. Dr Llewellyn turned out too, brisk and efficient as always, despite his years. He listened to Rhys's laboured breathing and announced that they must keep him warm at all costs, for though the icy conditions had probably helped to stop the bleeding what he needed now was warmth.

It was two in the morning – Christmas morning – before Chris watched his father being loaded into the ambulance, and by the time it trundled off towards the hospital everyone was exhausted. Chris invited the workers to return to Cefn Farm, his voice flat with despair, for he had seen his father's horribly mangled legs and thought it would only be a matter of time before his mother had to face up to the worst news of all. No one accepted his invitation, but they all sent their good wishes to Molly and told Chris that they would pray for Rhys when they attended morning service later that day.

Chris and Lana peeled off from the rest and returned to Cefn Farm. Ellen was there, pale-faced and hollow-eyed, to tell Chris and Lana that the ambulance had picked Molly up and taken her to the hospital with her husband. 'She said he was her reason for living, and she was his,' she told them, with tears in her eyes. 'They'll take him to the hospital in Bangor; perhaps when he's stronger he'll go to some specialist place... I don't know, I suppose it's too early to say.' She put an arm around her daughter's shoulders and gave her a squeeze. 'You've done all you can, you two.

Now you must get to bed, because you'll want to see your father tomorrow, Chris, and the hospital won't want you turning up and passing out from lack of sleep.'

'Right,' Chris said wearily, beginning to strip off his soaking outer clothing and kicking off his boots. He was turning to head for his bedroom, knowing that Auntie Ellen was talking good sense, when Lana spoke.

Her voice was husky with unshed tears, but she caught Chris's arm and ignored him when he tried to shake her off. 'Please don't go on being cross with me, Chris,' she begged. 'I can't help being sick at the sight of ... so will you forgive me?'

Chris carefully detached her detaining fingers from his arm and spoke stiffly. 'You did your best, I'm sure, so there's nothing to forgive,' he said. 'Do as your mum says and get some rest.' He turned back suddenly. 'Oh, Auntie Ellen, I've just realised: no one's told the Pritchards what has happened, so they'll be down here as soon as it's light expecting...' his voice broke, 'expecting a jolly Christmas breakfast.'

Ellen smiled reassuringly at him. 'And that's just what they'll get,' she said cheerfully. 'Of course they'll have to hear what's happened, but we still have to eat, you know. We'll visit the hospital around lunchtime, I reckon, but I do believe I ought to cook the turkey. What do you think?'

Chris was about to reply waspishly that the turkey could go to the devil for all he cared when he remembered that these two women were his guests and deserved more consideration than he had given them so far. He turned back and gave mother and daughter a rather watery smile. 'Put it in the dairy, on the cold slab. Perhaps tomorrow, when everyone comes in for their dinner, we can eat it then,' he said. 'You look pretty tired yourself, Auntie Ellen.' His grin became livelier. 'Get up them stairs and leave a note on the table for Nonny and the Pritchards. I'm sure they'll understand and leave us to sleep for a few hours.'

'Righty-ho, you're the boss,' Ellen said obediently, heading for the stairs. 'Shall I wake you when breakfast is cooked?'

'No need; as soon as the jeep comes into the yard I'll wake,' Chris said. He went into his room, closed the door and fell on the bed fully dressed. I'll just close my eyes for five minutes, he told himself, and was asleep on the thought.

Ellen saw Lana into bed and watched her fall asleep as soon as her head touched the pillow. Only then did Ellen steal softly out of the room and return to the kitchen. She sat down at the table and pillowed her head on her arms. She would stay here so that she might be awake to cook breakfast as soon as the party from Cae Hic returned, she told herself. She was older than Lana and had had a far less traumatic night. She did not want the Pritchards and Nonny to find only an empty kitchen with the fire smouldering dully and not so much as a plate of porridge on the table.

Yes, she would stay awake.

Ellen slept.

Mr Taplow woke. He had retired to bed as soon as they had finished playing games the night before, but had had a restless night because of the storm which had battered the farmhouse. However, the wind had eased in the small hours, and though he imagined that the snow was probably still falling it did so silently. He reached out to the bedside table, picked up his old-fashioned gunmetal watch and peered at its face. Good gracious, it was half past eight, high time he got up to help with the preparation of breakfast.

Mr Taplow was a man who lived by routine, and saw no reason why today should be any exception. He got out of his bed and pulled back the covers to air, went over to the washstand – he had to break the ice on the water in the jug – and had a cold but exhilarating wash. He rubbed himself dry on the rough towel and began to dress, checking his watch again because it seemed so very quiet in the house below. From what he remembered of his own childhood, farmhouses and farmyards were noisy places. Dogs barked, cockerels crowed, farm workers shouted to one another and clanked buckets full of milk or poultry meal or pig food. Then there were farmers themselves and their wives and children. He remembered his aunt's stentorian voice as she shouted for her family to come in for meals; surely the farm kitchen below him was too quiet?

Fully dressed at last, he slipped on his shoes and went across to the window, pulling back the curtains a trifle. The snow had stopped and frail sunshine gilded the snow-laden trees and the roofs of the outbuildings. Mr Taplow smiled to himself; so the snow was the reason for the quiet! It muffled sound, of course, and there was little point in letting out the poultry for it looked to be six to eight inches deep; far too deep for a hen to enjoy rootling around the yard.

If they had been at home in Bethel Street, Mr Taplow would not have hesitated to go down to the kitchen to start the breakfast if Ellen was still not up, even perhaps to make her a cup of tea and carry it upstairs, knocking politely on her door and making sure that she was respectable before he entered her room. But here everything was different, because he was a guest. If he went downstairs early, would it be considered impolite? But after a further five minutes of indecision he decided that it was too cold to hang about up here when he knew there would be a grand fire in the range. He swished the curtains right back – still no sign of life in the yard – then went over and made his bed, plumping up the pillows and smoothing the counterpane. After that he headed for the stairs.

He reached the kitchen and went in to find Ellen asleep with her head on her arms and the fire guttering low. The curtains were still drawn across the windows and the lamp was still lit, though by now it was broad day. Mr Taplow hesitated. He was pretty sure that everyone had gone to bed not long after him; why, then, had Ellen chosen to sleep on the kitchen table? It seemed very strange, but no doubt his landlady would wake presently and explain what had happened. Mr Taplow crossed the kitchen and pulled back the red and white gingham curtains to let in the winter sunshine, and as he did so Ellen stirred and yawned, stretching her arms out in front of her and blinking like a rosy-cheeked child disturbed from deep slumber. For a moment she looked wildly about her as though she, too, was surprised to find herself sleeping in the kitchen instead of her warm bed, and Mr Taplow found himself fighting an urge to give her a Christmas kiss on her warm pink cheek. Would it be permissible? There were bunches of holly in the parlour, he had noticed the previous evening; unfortunately there did not seem to be any mistletoe.

But Ellen was getting to her feet, hurrying over to the range and distractedly beginning to pour on fresh fuel from the tall hod which stood on the hearth. Then she turned to her lodger. 'Oh, Mr Taplow – Bob, I mean – we've had the most awful night, but I'm so sorry I fell asleep. I really meant to greet you with a grand breakfast, even though the news is dreadful. I wonder if Lana is awake yet? She was with Chris when he found him, so I suppose she's trying to sleep it off...'

Mr Taplow took Ellen by her shoulders, sat her down and picked up the kettle. It was empty, and he filled it from the pump at the sink, then stood it on the range. 'I haven't got the faintest idea what you're talking about,' he said frankly. 'Perhaps you'd better start at the beginning and keep going until you reach the moment when you woke up. I take it something happened after we all went up to bed...'

Whilst Ellen told her lodger the story from the moment they had realised Mrs Pritchard had left her medication behind to the moment he had pulled back the curtains, she had been working on getting the breakfast things together, and by the time she had finished her story and Bob had exclaimed with horror she had put several slices of Molly's home-cured bacon into the big black pan and a most satisfactory and delicious smell had begun to fill the kitchen. Mr Taplow's mouth watered, and when he said as much to Ellen she gave him her twinkling smile and said that the smell of bacon was the best wake-up she had ever known, far more effective than the loudest alarm.

'But it might be a kindness to take Chris and your daughter a jug of hot water to wash in,' Mr Taplow suggested. 'They seem to have had a terrible time and would probably appreciate a warm wash, whereas I myself, having spent the whole night in a gloriously warm and comfortable bed, found the cold water invigorating.'

Ellen agreed and presently they were joined by two heavy-eyed young people, both in dressing gowns and slippers and both eyeing the food Ellen was cooking with undisguised greed. After all, as Ellen told them, everyone must eat and it would be a crying shame to let bacon, kidneys and scrambled egg go begging, to say nothing of a great deal of golden brown buttered toast and a good many mugs of hot coffee.

'But shouldn't we have waited for the Pritchards before we ate?' Bob Taplow asked suddenly, with a forkful of bacon halfway to his mouth. 'I thought that was the arrangement.'

Chris laughed. When he had entered the kitchen he had looked grey with fatigue and worry, but the warmth of the room and the good food had brightened his eyes and brought a flush to his cheeks. 'If my mum and dad were here they would insist that there was nothing like a good meal to line the stomach and prepare one for whatever the day ahead had to offer,' he said. 'I woke worried sick about my father and I'm worried about him still, but rushing off to the hospital with only a cup of tea inside me wouldn't help anyone. So eat up, Mr Tap – oh, I'm sorry, eat up, Bob, and when the others get here we'll decide what to do.'

Lana leaned across the table and patted their lodger's hand. 'Oh, poor Mr Taplow; Auntie Molly invited you for a wonderful Christmas break and this has to happen,' she said remorsefully. 'When the others arrive we'll have to decide who's going to the hospital and who's staying here, because the jeep can only really carry four people ... well, five if three of them are quite skinny. And of course there's farm work waiting to be done.' She turned to Chris. 'The cows have got to be milked, and the stock fed...'

'That's right,' Chris said. 'And someone will have to tell Nonny and the Pritchards what's happened. It'll be the most dreadful shock.'

Even as he spoke they all heard the sound of the jeep's engine as the vehicle turned into the farmyard and stopped directly outside the door, which almost immediately shot open to admit Nonny, her face sheet white and her eyes enormous, with Rhodri and Mr Pritchard close behind her, Rhodri with an arm round his father's frail shoulders.

'What's happened?' Nonny said, her voice trembling. 'We passed the tractor; it was upside down and there was what looked like – oh, God, it was Dad, wasn't it?'

Chris jumped up and crossed the kitchen in a couple of strides to take his sister in his arms. Then he ushered the little party into the warm kitchen and saw them settled in chairs before he answered.

'Yes, it was Dad. The tractor climbed the bank, which I don't suppose Dad could see in the snow, and it turned over on top of him. It – it pinned him to the ground, but Lana managed to get the men from the village to come up – Dr Llewellyn too – and we got him out. He's in hospital in Bangor. Mum's with him; we're going down there once we've done the work on the yard.' He broke off, eyebrows rising, and addressed the old man sitting at the table and staring dully before him. 'But where's your wife, Mr P?'

Mr Pritchard glanced helplessly around the table, as though he expected to see her sitting in one of the kitchen chairs, but he did not speak, so his son answered for him.

'My mam died this morning, about an hour before we left,' he said quietly.

Chapter Sixteen

Molly and Ellen between them had planned how this Christmas was meant to be down to the very last slice of plum pudding and mince pie. It should have been a wonderful Christmas, the very first one when she and Rhys had been able to buy really good Christmas presents for everyone, especially for Chris, Nonny, Lana and Ellen. But instead of being a wonderful day it had turned into a nightmare. Mr Pritchard scarcely spoke, seeming just to want to return to Cae Hic, and once there he huddled by the Aga and refused to do anything. He would not even make up the fire when it burned low or riddle the ash, and when his son tried to talk to him about farming matters he just stared as though he could not understand a word.

For several days Rhys's life hung in the balance, but at last he was considered well enough to be taken to a hospital in Liverpool where the surgeons had hopes of saving his legs. It was too far for Molly to travel daily since she could not drive the jeep, so she stayed with Ellen and the girls a mere couple of miles from the hospital in which her husband was incarcerated. Nonny had given in her notice to Mr Lawson and to everyone's surprise, including Ellen's, Lana, too, had quit her job. She said that even if Chris and Nonny thought they could manage without her, she knew better.

She might not be able to do half the things that Nonny took for granted, but she could do ordinary housework, keep the place clean and see that food was on the table three times a day. Nonny expressed her gratitude in every way she could think of, because she knew that Lana had been looking forward to the dances and parties she would normally have enjoyed upon the O'Maras' return to the city, but Chris, taciturn for once, said little. Nonny, who had always thought that her brother and friend were good pals, put Chris's sudden change of attitude down to his worry over Rhys, but when she suggested this to Lana her friend shook her head. 'He can't forgive me for throwin' up when I saw your dad's blood all over the snow,' she said bluntly. 'And then he wanted me to fetch the chaps from the village...'

'But you did!' Nonny exclaimed. 'I know you did! He told us so.'

'Yes, but I didn't want to go at first. The men mostly seem to speak Welsh and I was afraid they wouldn't understand. I said I'd stay with Uncle Rhys and Chris could go into the village. He hasn't forgiven me, not yet. But he will when he sees I mean to be like you, Nonny. I'll learn to milk and help a lamb to get born. I already know how to tack up a horse, from watching you and Chris, though I've never done it myself...'

'It's awfully good of you, but you shouldn't have given up your job, Lana. It will be grand to have your help for a couple of weeks when we all go back to the farm, maybe even a month, but after that you'll want to come back to Bethel Street, you know you will.'

'Shan't,' Lana said with a cheeky grin. 'It's my life, and I'll do what I want to with it. I'm going to train to be a hill farmer's wife.' She sobered, suddenly. 'You think I can't do it, but I'll surprise you yet.'

The two girls were in the hospital waiting room, which was deserted save for themselves. The doctor in charge of Rhys's case had impressed upon them that it was important his patient should not grow anxious or excited, which meant he was allowed only two visitors at a time. When Molly and Ellen left the ward, therefore, Nonny and Lana took their place, sometimes only for ten minutes, and then they all returned to Bethel Street. Now, Molly and Ellen entered the waiting room, both looking fagged to death. Molly gave a huge yawn. 'He's sleepy, and not inclined to talk or, I suspect, to listen,' she announced. 'I've passed on all the messages from Chris about how he and Rhodri, old Mr Williams, Nat and Jacob are managing, but though he nodded and even smiled I doubt if he took much in. You'd better not stay very long, so we'll wait for you in here.'

'Right,' Nonny said quietly. 'Have you told him about Auntie Ellen helping out at weekends? And that kind Mr Taplow doing the same? People are so good; neighbours from as far away as Beddgelert have promised to help when the ewes start lambing. But Auntie Ellen and Mr Taplow spend half their lives travelling between Bethel Street and Cefn Farm, which isn't fair on them; don't you agree, Mum?'

Molly smiled. 'I agree, but right now I'll accept help from anyone,' she admitted. 'We'll just have to see how we go. Rhodri and Chris get their heads together every now and then and parcel out the work, but of course whilst Mr Pritchard is so poorly...'

Ellen broke in, her face flushing. 'He can't still be in shock, can he?' she said rather impatiently. 'It's four whole weeks since Christmas Day; surely he realises the load he's putting on his son? He could at least get them both a meal and make up the fire when it begins to burn low. I think he should be told to pull himself together.'

Molly patted her friend's arm. 'I don't think he can; pull himself together, I mean,' she said quietly. 'I think he's simply given up and is waiting to die. He and his wife went to school together, have known each other all their lives ... but it's no use talking. We'll just have to wait and see.'

Nonny nodded. 'You're right, Mum. Rhodri says the same, and he should know.'

'Well, I guess you know best,' Ellen said, sinking into a chair. 'Hurry up, you two. I'm dying for a cup of tea and my bed.'

After her mother's words Nonny expected her father to be almost asleep, and so he was, but he still managed to give the girls a small and weary smile. 'How's it going?' he whispered. 'When your mum left just now, Nonny, I suddenly remembered I'd not asked after the Pritchards. I pulled myself up on my elbow, and was about to call Molly back when I felt a jab of pain in my right foot.' He grinned palely at them, 'I was so surprised I forgot to call out, but you must tell Mum because I've had no feeling in either leg until now.'

'Oh, Dad, that's wonderful,' Nonny breathed. 'I'll tell Mum as soon I see her; she and Auntie Ellen are in the waiting room, so we can all go home together. Oh, this must be the beginning of you getting better, I'm sure of it.' She bent over Rhys and kissed his forehead, then backed away from the bed, her expressive blue eyes full of tears, but she said nothing until they had left the ward and her father behind them. 'Isn't it awful to be glad about pain?' she said as they turned towards the waiting room. 'Oh, Lana if only this really is the beginning of Dad getting better, how wonderful that would be!'

When they reached the waiting room they shared their news with Molly and Ellen and Nonny was delighted when she saw the breathless pleasure on her mother's face. 'I know your father and he'll suffer any amount of pain if only he can walk again one of these days,' Molly said. 'Even if he can only oversee the work done by others that would satisfy him, for a while at least.' She gave her daughter an impulsive hug, then pointed to the coats and scarves which the two girls had abandoned when they entered the warm hospital. 'Get yourself dressed in your cold weather gear and we'll all get home to Bethel Street as soon as possible. You girls will be making an early start in the morning to go back to the farm so that Chris can come and see his father. It's good to see how Rhys's eyes light up when they fall on him. He's interested in every detail Chris can give him and keeps impressing upon us that we can employ a couple more men if necessary and pay them out of our savings. Though people have been so good that we've not needed to do so as yet.'

Warmly dressed, the four women set off for the tram stop. It was bitterly cold and there was snow on the wind, but Nonny knew it would be even colder in Snowdonia, knew that Chris and Rhodri would be anxiously checking on the ewes, for sometimes despite the farmers' best efforts a ewe would lamb early, putting herself and her offspring at risk. Nonny longed to be back at the farm, yet in a way she dreaded it. If only Chris had been able to remain with her she would have been quite confident, would have enjoyed the challenge in fact, but her arrival meant that Chris would climb into the jeep and drive off to Liverpool, not returning until the next day. They would then spend a couple of days together whilst Molly, Ellen and Mr Taplow held the fort in Bethel Street, and then Nonny and Lana would return once more by public transport back to Bethel Street.

If only the fact that Rhys had felt pain in his foot meant something! It was all very well saying that time would tell, but time was not on their side. Once lambing started, farmers who had given their help generously would have problems of their own to face. Before then, Nonny told herself, we've got to get sorted out. There's poor Rhodri, his father a burden now instead of a help, doing his best by working twenty-four hours a day and eking out his savings by employing a fairly useless lad to see to the cows and hens, keep Cae Hic warm and cook the food with which kindly neighbours supplied him. At least the lad's presence ensured that Mr Pritchard did not freeze, and he would have been fed as well had he eaten what was presented to him. Nonny had known the old man too long to think that he realised what a burden he was to his son, and she understood that there was nothing anyone could do until Dafydd Pritchard recovered from the death of his wife.

The tram rumbled up beside them and they climbed aboard, Nonny's mind still fixed on the problems which would face her next day, whilst Lana chatted about boys, clothes and dances.

Once back in the house Nonny was thankful to climb into bed, remembering to wind her alarm, for she and Lana had to set off before it was light the next morning in order to reach the farm by mid-afternoon. Drowsily, Nonny went over in her mind the things she had to do before she abandoned civilisation and returned to the wilds, though even the thought made her chuckle. It was how Auntie Ellen had thought of the farm in the early days, before she had visited them so often that she had grown accustomed to the conditions there. Downstairs, in the kitchen, were two large haversacks packed with food: Auntie Ellen's contribution to the next few days, because Nonny and Lana would be too busy seeing to the flock and the other animals to start baking. In addition there were clean clothes for Chris and some for themselves, though most of theirs she and Lana would wear on their backs.

What else? What else? Nonny's tired mind said. She was bound to forget something, to remember it only as she and Lana climbed aboard the train which would take them on the first leg of their journey. Nonny sighed deeply, heard Lana begin to give little purring snores, and slid into slumber.

It was early April and Rhys was beginning to grow impatient, both with the hospital and with his own inability to force his legs to walk, when the surgeon asked for an interview with Rhys and Molly.

He took them along to Sister's room, sat them down, and spoke to them seriously. 'Mr and Mrs Roberts, what I'm about to say will come as a shock to you, but once you have thought it over I trust it will not be an unpleasant one.' He was a tall lean man with sandy hair, a pair of tiny-gold-rimmed glasses and an understanding smile, and now he pushed his spectacles further down his nose so that he could look at Molly and Rhys over the top of them. 'Don't worry, I'm not going to tell you that you'll never walk again; that, Mr Roberts, is in the lap of the gods. What I am going to tell you, however, is that unless you take my advice you almost certainly will see little improvement. In fact you may deteriorate quite sharply.'

Rhys opened his mouth to speak at the same moment as Molly, but Mr Callahan hushed them peremptorily. 'Let me finish, if you please. The fact is that despite every effort we have made you are already struggling against osteoarthritis, and if you were to return to Snowdonia where the winters are so harsh and the summers usually so wet I'm telling you now that your condition will worsen. But if you and your wife make up your minds to live in a more congenial climate, then I have every hope, if not of a complete recovery, at least of an easing of the pain. I truly think that though you may always have to employ crutches you will walk again. But not, I fear, if you remain at Cefn Farm.'

Rhys stared at him, his face gradually paling. 'But how could we possibly buy another farm? And all I know is hill farming anyway,' he pointed out. 'You aren't suggesting I should become a clerk of some description, I trust? Because I simply couldn't do it. No one would employ me, would they, Molly?' He turned appealingly to his wife. 'Since I left the Royal Air Force after the war I've always farmed, and I always will. What other option is open to me?'

Mr Callahan smiled and patted Rhys's shoulder. 'I have a brother who practises in Sydney – Australia, you know. I telephone him once a month and write often, but lately we have been in almost constant touch, with your problem, Mr Roberts, very much in mind, and I can assure you that if you go to Australia there will be employment for both of you on what they call a sheep station. You would be well paid to manage the place, and Mrs Roberts would be paid to cook and clean and so on for the station hands. Apparently the farm in question is owned by an old lady who does not want to sell it and does not intend to see it fall into disrepair. It has been in her family for many years, but she is the last surviving O'Rorke and can no longer cope. She has had managers but they have not been satisfactory so she mentioned the matter to my brother and asked him if he knew of a suitable couple who might take over. But as far as I am concerned, the climate is what matters most. It is hot during the summer, warm during the winter and very very dry, save for perhaps a month of rain around July and August. It is the very thing for you, I promise you, if only you can bring yourself to leave your beloved Snowdonia, at least for long enough to give it a try. I believe you would be almost pain free from the moment of landing in New South Wales; isn't that an inducement to follow my advice?'

Molly heaved a sigh; every time she thought of the winters they had endured at Cefn Farm she had wondered how Rhys would cope, for she had noticed, when she pushed him out for a little walk in his wheelchair, how even the relative coolness of the air outside the hospital had made him shiver and demand more blankets and another pair of socks. She and Chris had discussed trying to sell up at Cefn Farm in order to move down to the west country but they had dismissed the idea as not being practical. Property in the west country was more expensive and acreages far smaller than in the Welsh mountains. She looked from Rhys to the surgeon.

'I've been thinking about it too,' she admitted, carefully avoiding her husband's eyes. 'I think I realised that Rhys would not be able to manage our acres, many of which are difficult to access for a healthy man with uninjured legs. But we must have time, Mr Callahan. Will it be all right if we go home as planned in a couple of weeks and discuss it with our family? You see, this way we shan't have to sell up because from what you've said we would be paid in Australia and would not have to touch our savings. That would mean that our children could still keep Cefn Farm, though it would be very hard for them without their father and myself to advise them and help with the work. Will Mrs O'Rorke mind if we neither accept nor reject her offer for two or three weeks?'

Mr Callahan gripped Rhys's shoulder once more. 'She knows very well that an important decision such as the one you would need to make will take time,' he said. He smiled at Molly. 'Perhaps it's hardest of all for you, Mrs Roberts, to leave your home and your children ... everything you know and love, in fact. But it's not as though you'll simply be a wife, waiting for your husband to come in each evening. You will have an important job, staff to do as you tell them and a very good salary. And of course all the excitement of a new country, new friends and so on.'

'We'll have to think about it,' Molly said again. 'We will have a family conference as soon as Rhys and I return home. We should be able to give you a decision say in three weeks.'

Mr Callahan nodded and handed Rhys a sheaf of papers. 'There are photographs of the sheep station – they call them stations not farms in the outback – and a great deal of information regarding accommodation, conditions, the jackaroos – that's their term for farm workers – and so on. Read it whenever you've got a moment, and remember, you are not being offered a one way ticket. If you hate it, and your health does not improve, then you can come home.' He held out a hand first to Rhys and then to Molly. 'Good luck! It takes a great deal of courage to change your lifestyle, but I have faith in your ability to do so.'

It was May, and Rhys's first day at home since the accident, and the whole family – and that included Ellen, Lana, Mr Taplow and Rhodri Pritchard – almost filled Cefn Farm's kitchen. Every face wore a beaming smile, though Rhys could not help noticing that Rhodri looked pale and strained, for it had only been a short while since the lad had come into the kitchen after a hard day's work to find his father apparently asleep, huddled up in his chair, pulled close to the fire. Rhodri had crossed the room and said cheerfully: 'Goodness, Dad, asleep already? It's not yet five o'clock.'

He had put a hand on his father's shoulder, about to say he would make some porridge, for the old man had been subsisting on what Rhodri thought of as slops – tapioca pudding, semolina and porridge – ever since his wife's death. But when his hand descended the old man had fallen sideways and Rhodri, his heart in his mouth, had bent down and scooped him up in his arms, murmuring that he should not fall asleep so near an unguarded fire, but knowing, even as he said the words, that he was speaking to empty air; Dafydd Pritchard was no more.

Rhodri had carried his father through to the bedroom the old man had once shared with his Mair, laid him on the bed, and begun to do all that had to be done. Then he had gone down to Cefn Farm to break the bad news.

But now in the kitchen all was rejoicing, for not only was Rhys home at last but spring had well and truly arrived. The trees were in bud and on the banks and verges snowdrops and celandines had given place to primroses and violets, and the last time Nonny and Lana had gone to the hospital they had taken in a great bunch of primroses, Rhys's favourite flowers. He was still in a wheelchair but assured them that he could manage short distances on crutches, but the surgeon's words were still very much on his mind and the look that he cast around the kitchen was wistful as well as loving, for in his heart he knew Mr Callahan was right. Even the cool May breeze had set his bones to aching and he knew – or believed – that a winter in this place might well be the death of him. He was happy enough to be sitting by his own fireside with his family and friends around him, and he had assured Molly, who was fussing over him like a hen with one chick, that he felt fine, but he had decided that he would not break the news of the Australian offer until he had heard how the youngsters had managed without him. Already, however, his back ached and his legs and feet felt as though someone had lit the fire under them. Unaccustomed exercise had even affected his shoulders and neck, but nothing could take away the sheer happiness of being at home, even though he doubted he would be here for long. But when Ellen pressed a cup of tea into his hands the truth must have become apparent; he could not hold it and the cup rattled and tipped so badly in its saucer that he was quite content to let Molly take it hastily from his grasp and tilt the tea into the feeding cup which he had hoped never to have to use again.

Molly saw his reluctance and, brushing the hair

off his damp forehead, said in a low tone, 'You old idiot; you know what the doctor said ... this won't happen in a warmer climate. I know you've longed for this day, dreamed of it, but as soon as you've drunk this tea Chris is going to help you to bed. Don't you have a good son? He's given up his lovely ground floor bedroom so you won't have to climb the stairs, and he's going to lend his strong arm to get you through there on your crutches...'

'I don't understand it; I'm weak as a kitten,' Rhys mumbled. 'Yesterday I walked all round the hospital on my crutches; today it was all I could do to cross the kitchen.'

'Oh, Dad, you're expecting too much,' Nonny said reproachfully. 'When you wake up tomorrow, after a good night's sleep, you'll be a great deal better. You've had an awfully hard day today, remember. I never realised getting out of hospital was such a complicated business! All those people you had to see, all the medicine you had to collect, forms to sign to say you were only borrowing the crutches ... and then there was the journey. I know Chris drove as carefully as he could, but the melting snow has made the roads treacherous and I expect you kept wanting to jam your foot on the brake...'

'I did,' Rhys admitted, giving the ghost of a chuckle. He turned to his wife. 'Nonny's right, cariad; I've been expecting too much. If Chris doesn't mind helping me to bed, then that's where I'll go just as soon as I've finished this grand cup of tea. And don't bother to bring me any of the delicious supper which I can smell coming from the oven, because I'm afraid I shall be fast asleep the moment I get between the sheets.'

Molly bent over and kissed him, and he whispered in her ear, 'This has made me realise more than anything else could have done how right Mr Callahan was about Australia. We'll tell them in a day or two, when I'm a bit more settled. Can you wait that long?'

'Of course I can, my love,' Molly said softly. 'But I think the children will completely understand and tell us to seize the opportunity with both hands. Now drink your tea and be off to bed. We can talk more when I join you ... if you aren't asleep by then, that is!'

Two evenings after Rhys's arrival home, the family gathered in the kitchen once more so that Chris and Rhodri might report to Rhys and Molly how they had managed in their absence.

It soon became apparent that they had managed very well indeed. True, they had employed Nat on a full-time basis, but the lambing had been successful, with almost no losses from either the depredations of foxes or the failure of the occasional ewe to suckle her offspring.

Rhys glanced around the table, knowing that what he was about to say would probably destroy or at least alter all the plans the young people had made. But it was no use putting off the evil hour. The sooner the problem was sorted out the better for everyone.

Haltingly at first, but then with more confidence, Rhys outlined what the surgeon had told him: that he would be very ill advised to face even one more harsh winter in Snowdonia. From the silence which followed this remark, and from the lack of surprise on the faces surrounding him, Rhys imagined that everyone had already guessed as much, so now he pointed at Chris.

'You've always known that Cefn Farm would be yours one day, when I drop off my perch,' he said cheerfully. 'I might easily have stuck my spoon in the wall when the tractor rolled on me. So you see, though it is coming earlier than any of us expected, you must decide whether you can manage Cefn Farm without us and how each of you feels regarding the responsibility and so on.' He smiled across the room at Rhodri, standing behind Nonny's chair, with one hand on her shoulder. 'You have problems of your own, Rhodri, as well I know. For many years we relied on your father and mother to point out our mistakes, and tell us how to remedy them. Since then, of course, Chris and Nonny have turned to me for the same sort of advice, but that won't be possible when Molly and I are in Australia. But you'll still be here, Rhodri – or at least I hope you will – and you are very much more experienced than my children could possibly be. Would you be willing to help them as your father helped Molly and me?'

Rhys was looking at Rhodri as he spoke and saw the young man's hand tighten on Nonny's shoulder, saw his daughter look up into Rhodri's serious face and give him a tiny smile. Why on earth don't those two make a match of it Rhys found himself thinking; there's a light in Rhodri's eyes which speaks volumes. But it's not my affair, of course. The young man nodded. 'Help I will whenever help is needed,' he said briefly. 'Go on, Rhys.'

'In a month or two you'll tackle the shearing and the dipping. Then you'll know what the wool clip will be worth this year. Not that that will be your main source of income; it's the sale of the yearling lambs which will tell you how large or small your profit.' He looked around the circle of faces, until his eyes fixed on Chris. 'Can you cope without me and your mother, once Rhodri has gone back to Cae Hic?'

Chris grinned at his father, his eyes sparkling. 'I think you'd better hear about our plans, Dad, before we go any further,' he said. 'We had already realised that even if you did come back to Cefn Farm it would have to be in an advisory capacity, perhaps for many years. We knew Mum would do her best, knew also that you would need nursing, so we had a conference of our own – me, Rhodri, Nonny and Lana – and we've decided that our best bet is to combine the two farms, which means the two flocks and the two acreages as well. We had planned to keep the yearling lambs this year to increase the size of the flock again, and Rhodri meant to do the same, but after a lot of discussion and argument we decided it wasn't practical yet. We need the money and at present we don't need the extra work. But with Rhodri, Nonny, Lana and myself, to say nothing of Jacob and Nat, we should be able to manage pretty well.'

'And I'll come over with Mr Taplow at weekends,' Ellen said eagerly. 'Anything you want bought which isn't available in the village, Bob and

I can get for you and bring over when we come.' She turned to Molly with a half-ashamed smile. 'You may think I'm not much use, dear Molly, but I can cook, clean and generally make and mend, whilst Bob can do most things around the farmyard. And we wouldn't dream of asking for money because we'd enjoy it, honest to God we would.'

Molly found herself feeling suddenly of little account, a sensation she did not like at all. Fortunately, however, she realised that this was plain old-fashioned jealousy and swallowed the ungrateful retort which had hovered on her lips.

'It's very good of you and Mr Taplow, Ellen,' she said rather stiffly. 'But surely Lana should return to Liverpool? She could soon get another good job, and continue with her social life.' She turned to Lana. 'Don't think I'm ungrateful, dear, but I can't see you exchanging your gay life for a muddy farmyard, animals which scare you and the odd trip into the village in the pony cart.'

She would have said more, but Chris broke in, 'No, Mum, you've got it all wrong. It's been five months since Dad's accident and Lana has thrown herself into the breach like a good 'un. She can milk, tack up the horses, help the ewes to give birth, and do just about everything our Nonny does, besides all the housework.' He had been sitting next to Lana and now he leaned over and pinched her cheek. 'She's a real little treasure, Mum, don't you think different. In fact, she and I have talked about getting hitched one of these days.'

Molly stared. She had dreaded this moment, but

she had known when Mr Callahan had talked of Australia that she would have to tell all before she left. She cleared her throat and began to speak, addressing Ellen because she suddenly realised she could not bear to see the look of heartbreak on Chris's and Lana's faces.

'We've always laughed together, haven't we, Ellen, over the fact that our babies were born pretty well at the same moment at the height of a thunderstorm, when all the lights had fused and the hospital was in a state of flux. Well, something happened that night which I never told a soul, but I have to tell you now.'

A rich tide of crimson invaded Ellen's face, and she gave a guilty giggle and pressed her hands to her hot cheeks.

'Oh, Molly, I know what you're going to say,' she said. 'I'm afraid I took advantage of the power cut to sneak out of the ward and go along to the nursery. You see, I'd hardly held my baby for two minutes before that. The nurse had snatched her out of my arms and the porter had taken me off to the ward. I felt cheated, as though my little Lana was more theirs than mine, so when everything was quiet – it was still dark, but the lightning lit up the whole hospital every few minutes – I put on those horrible hospital slippers and shuffled along to the nursery. There were only two brand new babies still wrapped in their little hospital gowns; all the rest were very smart in clothes that their mothers had brought.'

'Not the gypsy baby,' Molly said in a hollow voice. 'Wasn't she still in a hospital gown?'

'Well, yes,' Ellen admitted. 'And she wasn't a

girl she was a boy.' She stared reproachfully across at her friend. 'I know you know what I done, and I know I done wrong, but let me finish. I was standin' by the cot holdin' my dear little girl when I heard the baby in the next cot start to whimper. It were Nonny, of course, though I didn't know that at the time I couldn't bear that she should cry – frightened of the storm, no doubt – so I huddled Lana up in her blanket and picked up little Nonny. I kissed her neck and rocked her in my arms until she slept again, and then I replaced her in her cot and snuck out of the nursery.' She grinned at Molly. 'That was it, weren't it? But how did you know?' Before Molly had a chance to reply that she had not known Ellen gave a gasp. 'I know!' she exclaimed. 'Your baby's bootee fell off and when I put it back I had to tie the ribbon 'cos it had come undone. I's cack-handed, always have been, so I couldn't make a proper bow. I suppose you guessed someone had been meddlin' and knew it must be me, 'cos ours were the only two babies in the cots near the door where the nurse must have put them for ease.' She looked guiltily across at her friend. 'I know I shouldn't have touched someone else's baby ... do you forgive me? I reckon it's the reason I love Nonny so much.'

'Of course I forgive you,' Molly said, her voice small. 'Oh, Ellen, you don't know how you've relieved my mind! Do you remember Flossy, the ward maid? She told me the next day that she had seen someone in the nursery picking up two of the babies and in my heart I've always wondered whether there had been a muddle ... but I couldn't imagine why anyone would do such a thing, so really it was just a mystery. And now you've solved it; what an idiot I was to worry!'

Molly had been sitting beside Rhys in one of the fireside chairs, but now she jumped to her feet and bent down to give Lana a warm hug. 'My darling girl, I'm absolutely delighted that you are going to be a proper part of our family,' she said warmly. 'I do hope you and Chris will get married before we leave for Australia!'

As soon as he could, Chris sought Lana out. She was in the cowshed, and the moment Chris appeared she dropped her shovel and flew into his arms, planting an exuberant kiss on his cheek. 'You were right and I was wrong,' she said jubilantly. 'I've always thought Auntie Molly didn't like me and would fight tooth and claw to stop us marrying, but you said it would be okay and how right you were. Oh, Chris, I'm so happy!'

Chris returned the hug and dropped a kiss on the top of her head before replying. 'And can you guess, my pretty little pea goose, just why my dear mama has so blatantly tried to keep us apart?'

Lana's eyes rounded. 'Then I *was* right,' she breathed, 'but I still don't understand. Are you saying it had something to do with the business of the babies? If so, I still don't get it.'

Christ tutted. 'All these years Mum has worried that you and Nonny might have been swapped in the cradle, like in an old-fashioned drama,' he explained. 'She was afraid we might be brother and sister!'

Lana stared. 'But how could anyone think that?' she asked. 'Apart from the colour of your hair and eyes, you and Nonny are exactly alike. Surely Auntie Molly couldn't fail to see it?'

Chris considered this, then shrugged. 'It's a mystery to me, but I do believe that was what she thought,' he said. 'And now that your mother has burst the bubble and owned up we can get married with everyone's approval. Oh, Lana, I'd want to marry you even if you couldn't milk a sheep or shear a cow.'

Laughing, the two of them began to wield the shovels once more.

The day after the family conference, there was a good deal of planning to be managed. The idea was that Nonny would work with Rhodri at Cae Hic and Lana and Chris would manage Cefn Farm. Chris pointed out, rather tartly, that since Lana was going to marry him no one would be surprised when she moved into the farmhouse. Nonny and Rhodri, however, were a very different proposition, since Nonny told everyone who asked that she did not intend to marry anyone. Chris, shrugging, said that in that case she would have to stay in her old bedroom whilst he and Lana would sleep in the extension.

'And you'll just have to cycle up to Cae Hic each day,' Chris told his sister. 'I think you're mad, but I suppose it's your business.'

'Yes it is,' Nonny said huffily. 'And anyway, when the weather's bad I'll ride Wanderer, because a bicycle would be a nuisance not a help. And now let's forget it; we've made our plan, and

I'm sure it will work.'

But once Lana got Chris to herself, she brought up the subject once more. 'I know it's got something to do with what my horrible father did or said to her on the night of the chick trail, but there's nothing we can do about it until she realises for herself that she's being daft.'

She and Chris were in the big barn, checking the ewes, and now Chris raised his brows. 'But the chick trail was years ago,' he objected. 'Surely she can't be afraid that horrible old man survived the fall into the gorge? Why, even if he were still alive, which is next to impossible, and meant her harm, he would have acted by now.'

Lana nodded. 'You're right, of course, but fear isn't logical. Sometimes I think she'll never get over it, which is a sad shame, but sometimes I think something will happen which will bring her to her senses. However, it's no use nagging her. We'll just have to wait.'

Rhodri and Nonny were in the big barn seeing to a couple of lambs whose mothers had refused to suckle them. It was one of Nonny's favourite jobs to feed the new lambs from a baby's bottle, and now she sat on one bale of hay whilst Rhodri sat on another, both with a lamb between their knees tugging away enthusiastically at the red rubber teat attached to its bottle, and both smiling contentedly as the little creatures sucked, eyes half closed in ecstasy, tails wagging feverishly to show their enjoyment of the meal. It was warm in the barn and Rhodri was relishing this rare chance to be alone with Nonny. Though he said very little, he sat slightly sideways so that he could watch her profile, delighting in the way that her small, straight nose wrinkled when a lamb tugged extra hard at a teat, and her mouth curved into the enchanting smile he had grown to love. Not that loving her got him anywhere. He was a quiet man, not given to flowery speeches, but sometimes he was sure that Nonny loved him back. Knowing little of women, however, he could not imagine why, if she loved him as he loved her, she would not agree to become his wife.

Ellen, entering upon this idyllic scene with two mugs of tea, smiled indulgently. 'Any of 'em twins?' she enquired, handing one mug to Nonny and the other to Rhodri. 'I remember Rhys used to say hill sheep had their work cut out to feed themselves and one lamb, let alone two. Then he'd take the weaker of the lambs and bring it up in the farmhouse until it were strong enough to make its own way in life. Will these lambs come into the kitchen?'

Nonny shook her head. 'No, because they're none of them twins. These are the ewes' first lambs and the mothers just aren't sure how they should be treated. We try to persuade each ewe to accept her lamb, and of course if she won't we have to take over, but we're quite hopeful, aren't we, Rhodri, that the mothers of these two will let them suckle. That's why there's only a small amount of milk in the bottles. As you can see, the ewes are already beginning to take an interest in what their lambs are doing.'

Ellen settled herself comfortably on a bale of hay and took over Nonny's lamb so that the younger woman could drink her tea. 'Me and Bob Taplow have decided that he'll take some holiday, being as how your mum and dad will be off to Australia by the end of the month. He's took time off next week, so you needn't think you'll see the last of us tomorrow.'

Nonny and Rhodri stared. 'But won't his firm mind?' Nonny asked at last. 'I should have thought they'd veto the suggestion at once.'

'Apparently they're quite pleased, because they're training someone else to take his place and doing it gradually like this will help everyone,' Ellen said.

Nonny drained her mug of tea and stood it down on the hay bale next to her, then stared very hard at the older woman. 'Auntie Ellen, why don't you and Mr Taplow marry? He's so nice, and such a help that I'm astonished you could refuse him. Wouldn't you like to be married? I know your life with Sam was hell, but Mr Taplow is completely different. He'd put your happiness above his own, and he's not a drinker...'

Ellen interrupted, her eyes rounding with surprise and indignation. 'Marry Mr Taplow? And how might I do that, pray? I'm not a widow, you know; I'm still married to that pig. It isn't as though I could divorce him, or say he was dead, because I can't do either. Yes, he disappeared that awful night, but the fact that he's never reappeared in this part of the country doesn't mean to say he's not alive and kicking somewhere else, wicked old bugger that he is.'

Rhodri opened his mouth to point out that he was sure the man was dead, could not possibly have survived that fall, or the subsequent terrible cold which had kept the mountains unscalable for many weeks, but before he could say anything Nonny leaned forward eagerly and spoke directly to Ellen. 'Oh, Auntie Ellen!' she exclaimed. 'I know just how you feel, because I feel the same. He – he said terrible things to me; he said he'd find me wherever I hid and whatever name I might go by. I knew he was mad, and bad too, I knew I should take no notice, but I can't forget. If I knew he was dead ... but in my heart he's alive and just waiting, as he waited in the cart shed that dreadful night.'

Ellen put the lamb she was holding down and heaved a sigh. 'I've allus thought it was something that evil bastard said to you what put you off the fellers,' she said. She turned to Rhodri, who had moved away from them and was trying to persuade his ewe to let her lamb suckle, but he turned his head on hearing his name.

'Sorry, Ellen; didn't hear you. What was that you said?'

Ellen opened her mouth to reply but Nonny shushed her. 'Leave it, Auntie Ellen,' she hissed. 'It's best not talked about, else the nightmares will start again.' She looked around, and gave an exclamation of delight. 'Oh, look, my lamb's starting to suckle, and so is yours, Rhodri! We'd best go back to the kitchen for our own meal and leave these mums and their babies to get on with it.'

Later, as they finished their meal, Rhodri glanced rather diffidently round the circle of faces, then cleared his throat and spoke. 'If Mr Taplow is really going to stay on for a few days, then I think I'd better seize this opportunity to take a little holiday. My da's relatives are all old, or dead, but my mam had a niece – good pals we were as kids – who I'd like to catch up with, explain what's happened to her Aunt Mair.' He turned to Chris. 'You can manage without me for a few days, maybe a week? I'll be back before the next gathering, that's for sure.' He was watching Nonny as he spoke and saw a frown gather, but she made no comment when Chris said it would be fine with him, but what about Nonny?

'You'll be the person most affected,' he said, turning to her. 'Can you cope without Rhodri for a few days?'

'Of course – a couple of weeks if necessary,' Nonny said coldly, but her eyes were anxious. She turned to Rhodri. 'Who is this niece, anyway? And why haven't you mentioned her before?'

Rhodri looked uncomfortable. 'Never saw no need,' he mumbled, staring fixedly at his feet. Then he looked up and smiled at her. 'Older than you she is, see? But a grand girl nevertheless. You'd like her; her family rear sheep.'

Nonny raised her eyes to heaven. 'Of course, if she rears sheep I'd be bound to like her,' she muttered. 'I suppose you think I'm nosy, but I'm not. I'm simply interested, that's all.'

'Good,' Rhodri said decidedly. 'Well, I reckon I'll be back within the week, or mebbe ten days.'

When Chris and Rhodri met later that day the grin they exchanged spoke of knowledge shared. 'She'll miss you something dreadful, you know,' Chris informed his friend, and no name was necessary for they both knew who he meant. 'You'll take Eggy as well as your old Spot?'

Rhodri considered, then shook his head. 'No; if I were really going off to see my cousin then I'd not need one dog, let alone two. But I'll take Spot, for company like.'

Chris nodded. 'And you'll take care? And if you have no joy and decide it's useless, you'll never have to tell anyone your real reason for going.'

'That's right,' Rhodri said laconically, but in his heart he knew he had several reasons other than the obvious one for his 'little holiday'. He thought it might help his cause for Nonny to manage without him, realise that she relied on him, not just for the work of the farm but for other, more personal things. And he had noticed that the mention of a cousin had not pleased her, had worried her, in fact. So he set off hopefully, telling himself that he could do no harm by chancing his luck for once. Too traditional I am, he thought, too hidebound. Let's see where a bit of originality gets me.

Chapter Seventeen

As it was a Friday, Nonny and Lana were taking the pony cart down to the railway station to meet Auntie Ellen and Mr Taplow. Lana was actually driving the pony cart and looking forward to boasting to her mother, Nonny knew, about her ability to manage Cherry and still do all the housework she and Nonny had managed to get through that day.

Neither Chris nor Rhodri was with them; Rhodri had not yet returned from his 'little holiday' and Chris was driving the jeep all the way to Liverpool to bring his parents home for the weekend too, since their departure date for Australia was now only a matter of weeks away. Rhys had had to go back to the hospital to have physiotherapy and electric treatment on his damaged legs, but he and Molly liked to spend what time they could at the farm. Naturally, Chris had offered to bring Auntie Ellen and Mr Taplow back with them, but they had insisted on travelling by train so that Rhys might be as comfortable as possible on the journey. And though Rhys and Molly were looking forward to the new life that was opening before them, they still had natural regrets about leaving the old, so it was with mixed feelings, Nonny knew, that they examined what the youngsters were doing in their absence. Improvements and modernisation were all very well, but Rhys and Molly clung to the old ways. If they had had their way they would still have been making butter in the dairy with the old wooden churn, and shearing the sheep one at a time with hand clippers, she told herself, whilst Chris and Rhodri employed men who, with the use of electric clippers, could shear the combined flock in a day, often without so much as nicking any part of the beast they sheared.

But now, sitting at her ease in the pony cart whilst Lana took the reins, Nonny felt she could relax for a change. She realised she would miss her parents horribly when they left, but was sure that Rhys and Molly were doing the right thing. She knew all too well the terrible cold which winter brought to the mountains. When you were young and fit you could take it in your stride, but when you were her father's age and already crippled with arthritis, it would be madness to turn down the chance of a home – and a job – in a climate which would help rather than hinder your recovery. As the pony trotted along the winding lanes and the slightly wider roads which led to the station she drank in the delicacy of the wild roses, the pink and gold of the honeysuckle and the wonderful scent from the creamy meadowsweet. Usually she was driving so kept her concentration on the road but now, as a passenger, she could look around her and appreciate the beauty of the summer countryside.

Presently her thoughts wandered. Two whole weeks had passed and she was missing Rhodri horribly. Not that she intended to let anyone else guess her feelings, telling herself that he was her best friend as well as her fellow worker and it was natural that she should miss him.

There was this cousin, as well. Why had he never mentioned her? He must have known that she would be interested in a girl who, like herself, worked on a hill farm, rearing sheep. But now that she thought about it, she realised that when they were together it was usually she who chatted, telling Rhodri every little detail of her day. In fact, she confided in Rhodri even more than in Chris, being very aware that Chris's confidante was Lana now. Naturally, when they were married he would confide in his sister less and less, but it didn't matter; Rhodri was always there...

'Hey, dreamy! Are you listening to me? I said I thought we ought to have a grand party the weekend before your parents get aboard that ship for Australia. Of course I know one of the busiest times with the sheep is coming up, what with washing, shearing and dipping, but after that things go quiet for a week or so; we could have the party then.'

Nonny smiled to herself. 'Chris always said you were a party girl at heart,' she said accusingly. 'Now you've decided that if you can't get to parties in Liverpool you'll bring them to us in Snowdonia.' She dodged a swipe from her friend and slid along the seat to be out of range. 'All right, all right, a party's a grand idea. When Mum and Dad go back to Liverpool we'll start planning the party and sending out invitations. It'll be more fun if it's a surprise, don't you think?'

Lana agreed that this was so, and began to list the names of the many farmers and villagers she knew had helped the family, not only since Rhys's accident, but from the moment they had started hill farming.

Presently, however, Nonny stopped her. 'There won't be room for half that number in our kitchen,' she pointed out, 'and yet there isn't one person we could leave off the list. I suppose we could have the party in relays...'

Lana interrupted her. 'That would ruin the whole point of the thing,' she said reproachfully. 'No, no, the sensible thing to do would be to hold the party in the big barn. Since Auntie Molly and Uncle Rhys have to spend so much time in Liverpool it will be an easy matter to prepare it without their knowing. You've heard of barn dances, haven't you? Apparently they started in America. Folks sit on hay bales and clear the middle of the floor for dancing, and they have long trestle tables against the walls where they lay out the food and drink...'

Nonny beamed. 'You're a wonderful girl, Lana O'Mara, but I don't believe we should have dancing, because of Dad's legs. But suppose we put on entertainment, though? Heaps of folk either play an instrument or sing; we could get up quite a little concert party. Rhodri will know who does what...'

'And that reminds me,' Lana cut in. 'When do you think Rhodri will be back from seeing this cousin of his? Didn't he tell you?'

They had reached the station by this time, and Nonny was beginning to reply indignantly that Rhodri was welcome to visit anyone he pleased without asking her permission when the train drew up alongside the platform with a clatter and a roar, and Ellen and Mr Taplow appeared, both smiling broadly. They exclaimed with surprise and pleasure as they climbed into the trap, and were soon being let into the secret of the party.

Ellen listened to their plans with interest but then made a suggestion of her own. 'Wharrabout combinin' it with your weddin' – yours and Chris's?' she said. 'I know you said you wanted a quiet weddin' but there's nothin' to stop you using the party as a sort of super reception.' She chuckled, and poked her daughter in the back. 'Think of the presents; they'd be piled up that high they'd reach the barn roof.'

Lana, carefully steering the pony and trap out of the line of vehicles and turning it to face towards home, laughed. 'You are awful, Mum; we agreed on a civil ceremony so that folk wouldn't have to shell out,' she reminded her mother. 'Still, if we gave a big party it would be different. Nonny and I were just saying that it should be a surprise, but of course we'll ask Chris as soon as Uncle Rhys and Auntie Molly are safely out of the way, see what he thinks.'

'And we ought to ask Rhodri if he'd like to contribute...' Nonny began, only to be shouted down by Lana.

'No, no, no! Oh, you may say that because the two farms have combined the party is as much Rhodri's business as ours, but I'm sure he'd disagree. You and I, Nonny, have still got some savings and we won't spend our money on silly things like wedding cakes and bridal bouquets. We'll spend it on ingredients and that, and get lots of neighbours to do a bake for us, saying that that would be the best sort of present we could ask for. I'm sure we can put on a marvellous party without involving Rhodri in any expense. He hasn't had much chance to save since his parents died, and I happen to know for a fact that he's already bought our wedding present – it's a whistling kettle – so I wouldn't want him to have to splash out any more money on us.'

'Right,' Ellen said, and turned to Mr Taplow. 'What do you think, Bob? Could we combine me daughter's nuptials with a party for Molly and Rhys, without folk thinking badly of us?'

Mr Taplow was all for the idea, and the rest of the journey was spent in planning the party. Indeed, when they arrived back at Cefn Farm and saw the jeep parked outside they had hard work not to continue the discussion, but Lana enjoined them to silence, saying that it would ruin the surprise if they gave the plan away by even one word.

Later, they settled down to their evening meal, talking animatedly of the treatment Rhys was receiving, and of the plans Molly was making to start packing their cabin trunk with the things they had decided to take with them. In fact it was not until halfway through the meal that Rhys suddenly cocked his head and said: 'Where's Rhodri? He usually comes down to Cefn Farm for the main meal of the day. He's not still working, surely?'

'He's gone to visit relatives,' Nonny said briefly. 'But he'll be back any day now.'

'I'll collect the dirty dishes,' Molly said, getting to her feet, 'whilst you girls bring out the pudding – assuming you've made one, that is!' She had walked across to the sink with the used crockery and cutlery, Nonny was serving a vast apple pie and Lana was handing round bowls whilst Chris offered a jug of custard when the back door shot open, and Rhodri entered the room. He was in his shirt sleeves, his jacket tied round his waist by its arms, and his face was split by the most enormous grin. Nonny, unable to stop herself, dropped her serving spoon and flew across the kitchen, but stopped just short of him, feeling a hot blush burn up in her cheeks.

'Oh, Rhodri, you've been ages,' she said. She tried to take his hands, but he shook his head and gently disengaged himself, then reached round to the haversack on his back, pulled it off across his shoulders and undid the straps. Then, from its depths, he pulled out a black eye patch and a frayed length of binder twine. He flung both on the table and looked challengingly at Nonny for a moment before adding a third object. A small, yellow, toy chick, filthy, faded and almost unrecognisable, which caused Nonny to clap a hand to her mouth to stifle a scream.

'Clenched in his hand it were,' Rhodri said, indicating the pathetic little bundle of yellow fluff. 'The eye patch were in his pocket and the twine...' he swallowed convulsively, 'were still round his wrist. I'll lead the mountain rescue team up there tomorrow, though why good men should risk their lives to bring back the body of a scoundrel is more than I can say.' He had scarcely glanced at Nonny, but, now he turned on her a look of such tender compassion that Molly, watching him, could have wept.

'Nonny? Do you know what these bits mean?' he said in Welsh. 'He's gone for ever and need never trouble your dreams again.'

There were exclamations from everyone sitting around the table and Ellen jumped to her feet and went round to give Rhodri a hug. 'Nonny ain't the only one what needed proof that the old bugger has gone for good,' she said exuberantly. She turned to Bob Taplow, a broad smile spreading across her face. 'I'm a widow, certain sure! Remember what you asked me a couple of years ago, Bob? Well, if you was to ask me that same question now, you'd get a very different answer!'

'Glad I am,' Rhodri said absently, but his eyes never left Nonny's face, and when he saw the tears trembling on her long lashes he put out a gentle hand and stroked her cheek. 'Well, cariad? Is this proof enough for you?' he asked in Welsh. 'He's dead and gone, your nightmare fantasy, and will never trouble you again.' And then Rhodri, who was so shy, so reluctant to show emotion, gathered Nonny into his arms, and, in front of everyone, kissed her mouth.

The publishers hope that this book has given you enjoyable reading. Large Print Books are especially designed to be as easy to see and hold as possible. If you wish a complete list of our books please ask at your local library or write directly to:

Magna Large Print Books
Magna House, Long Preston,
Skipton, North Yorkshire.
BD23 4ND

This Large Print Book for the partially sighted, who cannot read normal print, is published under the auspices of

THE ULVERSCROFT FOUNDATION